Esau

BOOKS BY MEIR SHALEV

The Blue Mountain
Esau

Esau

A Novel

Meir Shalev

TRANSLATED FROM THE HEBREW
BY BARBARA HARSHAV

Originally published in Israel in 1991 by Domino Press Limited.

FIRST EDITION

Designed by George J. McKeon

Library of Congress Cataloging-in-Publication Data
Shalev, Meir.
    ['Eśay. English]
    Esau : a novel / Meir Shalev ; translated from the Hebrew by Barbara Harshav.
      p. cm.
    ISBN 0-06-019040-X
    I. Harshav, Barbara, 1940– . II. Title
PJ5054.S384E813   1994
  892.4'36—dc20   94–32910

    97 98 ❖ / HC 10 9 8 7 6 5 4 3 2

Esau

Duke Anton
and the Servant Girl Zoga

(An Imaginary Story About People Who Never Were)

D uke Wilhelm of the House of Gessler was killed in a hunting accident at the age of five. A goose soared off, wings beating, a rifle
thundered in the thicket, the child fell to the ground, twitched,
and screamed. His shouts glided over the meadow, got tangled up in the
reeds, banged against the poplar trunks. But the dogs could only retrieve
foxes and birds, and by the time they reached the little body of the Duke it
had fallen silent. The culprit, a coarse cowherd who had snuck onto the
hunting preserve to poach a pheasant, took his life that very night in the
throes of distress, leaving a young widow, an incoherent letter of regret, and
an insoluble riddle: How can a man commit suicide by shooting two bullets
into the back of his own neck?

Wilhelm was one of a pair of twins. He was a sturdy red-haired child,
and by the age of four he was shooting woodcocks startled out of their nests
and sending falcons and bloodhounds over the fields. A few days before he
was killed, he was given his first rifle, a real Mannlicher although scaled
down, the handiwork of the best gunsmith of Europe, Elijah Nathan of
Monastir.

Now the dead child reigned over his two living parents. The bereaved
mother paid an enormous sum for Gianini's *Pietà* and hung it in her dead
son's room. For hours she lay huddled in his little bed, staring at the glow
emanating from Christ's body and drawing strength from the mighty figure
of His Mother, known to art scholars as the *Madonna Robusta* because

Gianini's Virgin is a big broad-shouldered woman with the small sharp nipples of a boy and long muscular arms. The father bolted up the Gessler hunting lodge, sealed its doors with wax, and took refuge in the two occupations known for their benign influence on a man's soul—research and collecting. He compiled maxims, accumulated miniatures and micrographs, and studied the phenomenon of stigmata in Catholic women. He is known today as the first person to describe Louise Lateau, the French seamstress whose palms bled every Friday.

Wilhelm's twin, Duke Anton, would come to his mother, beg her to get out of his dead brother's bed, bring her pieces of Lübeck marzipan, the candy she loved; but she heeded neither his pleas nor his lures. Only at midnight would she get up and go to the castle bakery, where she would weep and eat loaves of bread fresh from the oven; and on rainy days, she would go outside and soak her hair in the downpour. Within a few months, her son's death had turned her into a red-eyed, runny-nosed, overweight woman. She hired Ernst Weber, the well-known painter of children's portraits, and for weeks she described the dead boy's face to him. Weber drew hundreds of children who were all indeed dead, but none was hers. At last a solution was found: the French photographer Marcel de Vine was brought; he photographed the mother's face as she talked about her son, retouched whatever he had to, and obtained a marvelously faithful likeness.

Years passed. Father and mother enclosed themselves in their private fortresses of grief, and Duke Anton, once a delightful boy, turned into a spoiled and impatient lad. All his life, he felt as if his dead brother were holding on to his heel. He himself had no penchant for hunting but devoted his time instead to women, self-indulgence, and carriages. In those days, equality and fraternity—the "French maladies," as the Duke's father put it—had already begun to lose their first charm, but Duke Anton understood those concepts in his own fashion and bestowed love on girls of all stations, with no discrimination, on *grandes dames* and low dames alike; and they all looked alike in his bed. He took to offering himself to women in the hackneyed French style: "Voulez-vous coucher avec moi?"—but he uttered the words with disingenuous impudence and panting articulation, all the while pressing his thin thighs close to his interlocutor lest she doubt the firmness of his intentions.

As a suitor, the Duke was generous and entertaining; he claimed and proved that egotists are the best lovers, and made a name for himself as a master of sensuality, voluptuousness, and debauchery. At night he slept in a bed full of little sable dolls, whose caress can't be matched even by the most pleasurable and knowing touch; and every morning, after his old nanny finished powdering his skin in sensitive places and dressing him, two young men bearing mirrors entered the room and very slowly turned him around so he could examine the full glory of his reflection from all sides. Breakfast was served "two and one half hours after sunrise, on the dot," and an astronomer drew up a special schedule of sunrises, a table even Swabian chefs could understand, for the proper management of the kitchen.

The Duke ate from plates whose rims were adorned with the words "Honi soit qui mal y pense" in gold letters, and he was so finicky about the freshness of his food that a special dining hall was built for him with a pool of running water for eels, a small, gleaming pen where calves and piglets spent their last night, and an oven of Jutland bricks, heated with peat, for baking the best rolls in the world.

However, Duke Anton's most famous and best-documented fastidious-ness was not in the domain of eating but was expressed rather in the deli-cate and prolonged closing of his eyelids when he passed water, as if his handsome face were unwilling to be involved in the occupations of the nether parts of his body. Because of this habit of his, a few drops always remained on the marble tiles in the privy and when he was a child, his nanny was ordered to hold his member and aim it when he applied himself to his minor calls of nature. When the Duke insisted on continuing this practice, even on attaining adulthood, his *bizarrerie* was bruited about and became one of the most popular and pleasurable services of the elite whorehouses of Europe. In Poland it was dubbed "We've Got a Little Fun-nel"; in Spain, "The Blind Bull"; in France, "A Shot in the Dark"; and in Viennese establishments it was called "The Duke and the Nanny." All these are documented and recorded facts, and anyone who doubts can find them in Caldwell and Marten's *Life Styles in European Palaces of the Nineteenth Century*, even though it is unwise to put blind faith in historical chronicles, particularly the writings of those two.

In their second volume, Caldwell and Marten claim that as far as self-indul-gence was concerned, the only person who surpassed Duke Anton was Car-dinal Beaudoin of Avignon. Indeed, Duke Anton regarded the Cardinal as a role model, memorized his writings, and strove to emulate him. Inciden-tally, this Beaudoin of Avignon was also a distinguished traveler and scholar. He left some illustrated studies such as *Hellenistic Mosaics in the Lands of the Levant,* and maintained that the well-known fact that the eyes of the figures will follow you if you walk around a mosaic is merely the result of a

3

correctable condition of cross-eyedness. At the age of fifty, the Cardinal accompanied Napoleon's armies to the East, and was lucky enough to discover in the Holy Land a very desirable find, the foreskin of the Infant Jesus. A few years later, he set out on another journey to find Jesus' baby teeth, and vanished.

Needless to say, because of Jesus' Ascension to Heaven, his foreskin and baby teeth are the only remnants of his corporeal body. The greatest skeptics, even those who denied the Holy Trinity itself, knew that the Savior's foreskin wouldn't rot and that the gleam of his baby teeth would not be dimmed. Many searched for them, and many, like Beaudoin, lived to repent their quest. The most famous example is Baldwin IV, the Crusader king who didn't feel pain, but was afflicted with leprosy the moment he saw the foreskin. That case has been published in the famous book of memoirs of his tutor, William of Tyre, and there is no need to describe it again here. Lesser-known victims, like the German traveler Klaus of Cologne and the Danish clairvoyant Pia Schutzmann, came to Jerusalem in search of them, were immediately assaulted by yearnings for solitude, and shut themselves off from the world, the former in the grotto beneath Teropion, the latter in the Convent of Dominus Flevit.

Yet there were also believers who weren't harmed at all and who managed to find such a plethora of foreskins that the Lutheran minister August Grimholz, in his book *Franciscan Deceits*, said that, if all the mendacious foreskins of the Messiah were sewn together, you could erect an enormous tabernacle of them to lodge all the foolish Crusaders who ascended to Jerusalem. But this Grimholz was known as a Doubting Thomas and a drunkard, and suffice it to state that he supported the identification of Golgotha according to Gordon, and went so far as to cast doubt on the "Garter of Our Lady," brought from the Holy Land by Michele di Prato, even though it emanated the distinctive odor of a virgin.

The joke of fate is that all this has sunk into the abyss of oblivion by now, and that the name of Cardinal Beaudoin is known today for some trivial research he did in his reckless youth at the Catholic school of Toulon, in which he concluded that the best, most fitting and pleasant wiping of the behind was done with a fledgling goose. "First with the beak and then with the down," explained the young novice priest to his joyful companions, and this bon mot—"Premièrement, le bec, ensuite, la plume"—became the motto in circles that could afford such pleasures. Duke Anton, who was born years after the Cardinal's disappearance, added it to his collection of principles and commandments, and ordered his steward to breed a small flock of geese to supply him with the goslings required for his major calls of nature.

The Duke also had scientific inclinations. In addition to fashionable experiments in the invention of a flying machine heavier than air, which everyone was busy at in those days, and the perfection of the steam-powered bicycle, a blazing and slow vehicle that emitted smoke and shrieks, the Duke devoted some of his youthful years to research in genetics and astronomy. He tried to refine a homozygotic strain of white ravens and observed the stars from a special bedroom whose transparent ceiling was a gigantic polished lens. It magnified the stars at night and was covered with a black cloth in the day because it heated the room unbearably and had singed two Italian girls who overslept there one morning.

Here we may note that in that very year the Duke entered the holy covenant of betrothal, and that his fiancée was the Austrian princess Rudolfina, a bovine blond, possessor of a prodigious chest and wallet forced upon him by his father's advisers. The physical and intellectual dimensions of the Princess were in inverse proportion to one another, and she was known especially for her dreadful mouth odor, the sort that cannot be diminished even by myrtle root ash. Her muslin collars and the broad silk slopes of her breasts were perpetually littered with the carcasses of mosquitoes and butterflies who chanced, poor wretches, into the malignant jet stream of her breath.

A few months before the date set for his wedding, Duke Anton announced to his parents that he wished to set out for the East. The Duke was not afflicted, God forbid, with that tendency of the upper classes, especially the English, who have plenty of leisure time and overflowing pockets, to fall under the spell of the Orient and its folk. No! All the Duke wanted was to amass a small treasury of experiences and memories to ease the suffering and boredom awaiting him on the far side of the wedding.

"For what is married life," he quoted to his father the saying of the Catalán poet Juan Jimenez, "if not the dire, desolate, and dusty road leading us to death." The Duke's mother, who looked like a giant sponge by then from so much mourning, rain, and bread, burst into tears; but his father, the collector of maxims, could not repress a smile and granted him both the necessary permission and funds for the journey. He set only one condition—when Duke Anton entered Jerusalem, he was to address to her walls the last words of Henry V: "Should God grant me a venerable old age, I shall conquer you!" And he was also to walk with eyes closed along the Via Dolorosa and envision in his mind's eye the last steps of the Lord, in the tradition of the Templars, for the Gessler men were members of that order.

The Duke memorized the very latest travel books, by Clemens and Melville, and their ancient predecessors, the books of the Traveler of Bordeaux and the Pilgrim of Hanover, and assembled an entourage of advisers, statesmen, goslings, bodyguards, and scientists. He ordered his light, fast two-wheeled cart and his white Lippizaner horse readied. And he took his Jewish physician, Dr. Reuven Yakir Preciaducho, and his maidservant, Zoga, a devoted, gigantic Albanian whose vocal cords had been cut in her childhood by the Janissaries. She was mute, but strong enough to carry him to bed in her arms on nights when he was inordinately defiled and ravished; and after the death of his nanny, she also undertook the aiming of his member at the toilet. The woman was handsome, fair, with thick eyebrows, and she had two uvulae in her throat. When the Duke was bedeviled by a foul humor, he would ask Zoga to open her mouth wide: one peep at the two uvulae was enough to make him burst into childish laughter. But her most important feature was her blood type, which matched the Duke's. Anton had low blood pressure, and his sexual agitations drained most of his blood into his loins, causing him migraines and weakness and even profound swoons, whereupon Dr. Reuven Yakir Preciaducho would decant Zoga's strong blood into his veins and revive him.

A photographer and a writer also went along to document the journey, and every other day they sent reams of paper and photographic plates to the Duke's parents, who were amazed at the discrepancies between the pictures and the words. Indeed, except for their agreement that the journey began at the railroad station in Vienna and ended in great misfortune in Jerusalem, you might have thought these were two different expeditions.

In Istanbul, Sultan Abd-el-Aziz entertained the Duke, gave him letters of introduction to the Pashas and heads of the Millets, and bestowed on him a vast traveling tent replete with silk hangings and carpets, bronze platters and damascene cabinets, a secret hideaway for copulation with a triptych mirror to reflect love from ever new angles, an alabaster washbasin, and a Circassian concubine specializing in European tastes. The Duke gave the Sultan his father's regards and his gift: a portable gallows, fruit of the ingenuity of German engineers, unparalleled for easing and simplifying the work of government in remote districts. The gallows, which looked from the outside like an innocent box on wheels, concealed a few folding instruments of torture and killing, operated by a team of two technicians and a mule. It could travel on mountain paths and be pushed through narrow village lanes to reach any nest of insurrection. That very day, the Sultan set off for the nearby barracks to try out his new gift on his prisoners there, and the Duke's entourage boarded the *Miramar* and sailed straight for the land of Egypt.

In the Duke's father's collection of maxims, Alexandria is described as "an ancient whore of men and generations." Duke Anton was indeed greeted by her warm, wet breezes and an honor guard of sweating drummers and horses. He visited the scorched remains of her great library, mourned her lost wisdom, toured her racing stables, famed for their splendid Arabians and jockeys, descendants of the fabled horsemen of Siena. In the evening, attended by his two tutors, the Prussian and the Swiss, he conversed with a pair of twin boys devoted to pederasty and love of small livestock. They reminisced about filth, winked delightfully, and offered to put on a "show" which, they claimed, the Prince of Wales and Austrian Crown Prince Rudolf had enjoyed very much.

In the evening, the Duke was taken to the governor's palace, where he observed the performance of a belly dancer with a bitter and tempting odor of sandalwood wafting from her navel. Then he was plied with coffee and sticky cakes heavy as lead and tasting like goat vomit blended with honey. To clear his mind, he went walking with his guards on the promenade, nodding and smiling wanly at the local traders, all in white suits and red tarbooshes, and all holding ivory flyswatters.

At night, his hosts took him to the famed establishment of Madam Antonius. "The only whorehouse in the world that sells annual subscriptions," his adviser whispered to him. Here Anton thoroughly authenticated all the gossip and rumors about the anatomical endowments of Abyssinian girls, and when he was invited to bend his ear to the vagina of one of them, an unwitting smile spread over his face, for the tides of distant seas rose from the conch of her flesh, and a marvelous fizz of waves, and even, it seemed, the siren songs of the drowned and the lament of the mermaids, and Zoga, the unhappy Albanian servant, nearly died that night of envy and loss of blood.

"Sated and happy, the Duke boarded the *Miramar* and sailed from the Land of the Pharaohs to the Holy Land," the writer of the expedition informed the Duke's parents, and described the shallow waves of the deltas and shores of the marshes, the soft and mighty dugongs wallowing in the warm water, the yellow sands of Philistia, the black rocks of Jaffa. But the photograph shows a pale, weak lad supine on his bed. The Alexandrian delicacies were still rumbling in the Duke's guts, and dozens of goslings were tossed from the *Miramar* to expire in the salt water, repelling even the seagulls, the most stinking and predatory of all birds.

In the port of Jaffa, another governor awaited him, his beard smelling of fish and gunpowder. The Duke asked to see the staircase where the prophet Jonah descended, and a crew rowed him as close as possible to the Rock of Andromeda. Lunch was served at the Catholic church, where he was also shown a pitcher containing a turgid white liquid they claimed was "Mary's milk." Whereupon a thin pain began trickling through Anton's body, like the pain Persian women feel when their husbands are lying; but the Duke described it to Dr. Reuven Yakir Preciaducho as "a hot hourglass in my stomach"; and then he said, "No! Like a crooked needle"; and then he groaned and said, "Like love, but in my liver." And though every pain held a warning and a prophecy, he did not take the hint, but got into his light two-wheeled cart and set off for Jerusalem.

Four huge Rottweilers ran alongside his chariot, their noses sniffing in every direction, his moneybags tied to their thick necks. Ahead and behind traveled six carts of advisers and crates. Orchestras and Turkish army patrols and a motley throng of children, flies, solicitors, jackasses, and beggars raised dust and a ruckus around him. At sunset, they overtook an enormous caravan of Russian pilgrims, and the amazed Duke saw that the men walked at the head and the rear, and in the middle was a gigantic wooden cart harnessed with ropes to hundreds of women and bearing a mighty bell that weighed at least seven tons. The women were stooped over, groaning with the effort, while the men sprinkled water and tears on them, and shouted encouragement and support. At the head of the group strode a tall, sturdy peasant with a big beard, the face of a poet, and massive hands. The Duke instructed his advisers to ask him the meaning of the women and the bell, but the pilgrim stared at them with terrifying Pravoslav eyes and refused to speak; and the Duke went on his way like a deer chased to his killers, not knowing his fate.

In the evening, they stopped in a small, dusty town. Like the entire country, it boasted only remnants of the past. The ancient olive groves turned silver in the full moon, displaying their "trees planted back in the days of Vespasian," as recorded in the writer's daily report. Marble capitals and hewn stones, skeletons of majestic buildings, burgeoned in the mire of the lanes, and the photographer joked that he couldn't photograph them because they wouldn't keep still. Here too a reception was held, and afterward the new Turkish governor invited the Duke to view Anatolian wrestling, which was adored by his soldiers. Bald, muscled men in leather breeches smeared their bodies with olive oil and began grappling with one another. A smell of blood, mud, and semen rose in the air. The Duke vomited and was taken to see the town's underground reservoirs, and then, with what was left of his strength, was rushed up the church spire. From here, the governor told him, Napoleon had fired on an unlucky muezzin who had climbed up to the nearby minaret before dawn and jarred the Emperor's sleep with his chants. The governor hinted to Anton that it was both possible and a common practice to take some passerby up to the minaret so that honored guests could test their aim against the sniping of the Great Eagle. But to the sorrow of his host, the Duke was content to sleep in Napoleon's bed, along with the fleas who hadn't had a thing to eat since that historic night. In the morning, Zoga helped him hit the hole where Napoleon had also passed water, and this time the Duke felt the sharp pain of glass slivers teeming in his lower abdomen. He groaned, leaned back, and rested his neck on the servant woman's broad shoulder. Then he went to dine at the Anglican school for girls, observed them at their embroidery, and recorded in his notebook: "All the students look alike, as if they had suckled from the same wet nurse, and all their eyebrows run together"; and despite the incessant pain in his belly, he continued on his way.

On the horizon, the dim wall of the mountains of Samaria and Judea began to turn blue, emerging through the dust that never settles. Duke Anton passed the foothills of the mound of the ancient city of Gezer, descended into "the valley of robbers where Joshua Ben-Nun made the moon stand still," and, as is customary, cast a bramble branch into "the well full of the venomous spittle of Satan where nothing floats." The caravan passed a stinking *khan*, climbed up a narrow vale between exposed, bare mountains, went down and up and down again, and stopped to rest. Here, at a bend in a stream, in a small village called Kolonia, the Duke ate huge yellow grapes whose end-of-summer sweetness scalded his throat, tossed coins to children and drank cold spring water smelling of sage. He withdrew behind a velvet hanging very urgently with two goslings, and when he finished, the caravan ascended a steep, tortuous slope paved with stones. The armies of Titus had climbed up that very slope, his adviser informed him, and the Wandering Jew had climbed down it as he set off on his trek. Anton had left two more low crests behind him when Jerusalem appeared, lurking beyond the mountain.

Fortified by its Turkish wall, which brought a smile to the face of the Duke's artillery adviser, winking with a thousand loopholes and illuminated by the sunset, the old city appraised her new victim. She shot him with her tried-and-true ammunition: darts of gilded turrets, nets of sky, and the deceitful light of dusk that looked like it could be swallowed. The Duke's knees buckled. All at once, as if on cue, the winy air was sliced by the knife wings of swallows, the flash of the patrol's trumpets, and the smell of the sweat of praying men. The Duke had read in Melville's book of that blend of "Jerusalem evening breezes, stinking and perfumed by excrement and incense," and yet his heart throbbed. "Should God grant me a venerable old age, I shall conquer you!" He remembered the words but was beginning to doubt them himself.

Now the city served up the standard evening supplement: lengthening shadows of towers, emptying *souks*, gold domes growing dim, and a few other poetic sights well known to all her admirers. The Duke felt the shudders promised by the Holy Scriptures and tourist guides whispering at the base of his back in a delightful tremor. In his journal, he recorded that Jerusalem is "the only city in the world that has body odor." This comment, incidentally, is somewhat reminiscent of the journal entry of the anti-Semitic tourist Victor Burke, who wrote thirty years later that the stones of the Western Wall "have bad breath."

The Mutasaref of Jerusalem, who joined the Duke at Antimos's Orchard, walked beside him on little feet, stopped him at a corner of the wall, informed him that this was where David slew Goliath, and announced that in honor of his coming he had given the Christian churches and monasteries permission to ring their bells, something they had been forbidden to do for three hundred years. The Duke was asked to raise his hand, and all at once the bells pealed, their echo borne on the hills. The ancient clappers, most of which had never struck and by now were freighted with long-standing desire and accumulated anger, hit the passionate metal bodies, and a mighty cloud of rust and faith rose and covered the eye of the city. The event went unobserved by the chroniclers but is mentioned in several musical studies, as by the musicologist Gustav Sterner, who cited it in his *Big Book of Bells:* "The bell, and not the drum, is the real instrument of catharsis."

Duke Anton was filled with religious piety, and that made him easy prey. A strong quake wobbled his knees, and a dull, warm sword twisted in his guts. He wept, he swooned, he was transfused immediately with Zoga's refreshing blood, and he revived. His servants erected his magnificent silk tent among the quince trees of Kharm-a-Sheikh, a garden that no longer exists but in those days stretched from the Tower of the Storks to the famous old pine whose seeds were brought to Jerusalem by the Crusaders.

That night, in the Duke's camp, no one slept. The writer filled dozens of pages with the splendor and glory of the city, the photographer screamed that her light would burn his plates, the astronomer drew up tables of her sunrises, and the general spotted his sheets dreaming of her surrender. She, who had smashed the brains of kings to crumbs of deceit and folly, brought a rabid foam to the lips of priests, and confused the minds of prophets with her tall tales—she crushed the wretched Duke in just a few hours. He sat next to the pine, failing to grasp that even the mighty tree, older than all the denizens of the city, had not yet gotten used to her lies, that had the tree been graced with feet, it would had fled from her long ago.

The next day, the Duke went off to the Via Dolorosa and, as commanded by his forefathers, the Templars, walked from the Pretorium to the Church of the Holy Sepulcher with his eyes shut, surrounded by guards and visions that kept him from bumping into the stone walls. At the Fourth Station, he put his hands on the traces of the Virgin's footsteps in the Mosaic of the Sandals, and was afflicted with the expected contortions. At the Sixth Station, he also wept; and at the Station of Saint Veronica, the priests insisted on taking out the white silk handkerchief and wiping the tears, the sweat, and the blood from his face too. Throughout the journey, the Duke never opened his eyes, so no one knows what he saw; but when he returned to his tent, he sent his photographer to photograph the path he had just walked. "Take a step and a picture, a step and a picture," he ordered. He himself went off to the Tomb of the Four Princesses on the slope of Mount Scopus, where he was shown a mess of vertebrae and ribs, teeth and femurs, like pieces of a frightening erector set. It was impossible to tell who was Pharaoh's daughter, who was Na'amah the Ammonite, who was Jael, princess of Tadmor, and who Louisa, the Crusader saint. "The dead," his adviser whispered to him as they left the cave, "are the strongest guild in all of Jerusalem."

Meanwhile, the photographer arrived at the Via Dolorosa. Bowed down under the weight of his enormous camera, whose wooden legs straddled his back, escorted by two Turkish soldiers and seven donkeys carrying the heavy photographic plates in their saddlebags, he took a step and took a picture. At first everything went fine, but when he came to the final Station, inside the Church of the Holy Sepulcher, the Greek Patriarch dispatched his coiled-haired priests who beat him within an inch of his life. The next day, when the Greek Patriarch learned the identity of the beaten man, he was most embarrassed. He rushed to the camp, bowed and rustled in his robes, and invited the Duke to his summer abode. The two of them got into the cart and drove to the top of a hill west of the city, to a small monastery named for Saint Simon. They sat next to a little green bell tower surrounded by cypresses and pines; a woman shrouded in black served a delicacy of melon slices with lemon, sugar, and mint, and the view was sharp and splendid.

On their return, jolly as a little boy, the Patriarch said that hidden beneath the Church of the Holy Sepulcher was a mosaic of Aphrodite, a Hadrianic remnant of her temple, "and because of that, the floor there is hot, even in winter." He winked suddenly, and then joked about the annual fraud of the descending of the Holy Fire and asked if he might take the reins and drive the chariot. "Men keep on playing," he apologized, "even if they're church leaders."

Night fell. New pains capered in Anton's body. At camp, he was awaited by a pesky choir of sages, rabbis, and leaders of all the Jewish communities, who didn't know where he came from and therefore stood outside his tent singing the national anthems of all the countries of Europe, one after another. Then they shoved a young Jew forward, and he proffered a nacre box containing fifteen wheat seeds. The Duke, who was weary and in pain and a stranger to the refinements of Eastern hospitality, had no idea that the fifteen seeds were a micrographic treasure on which the fifteen Jewish Blessings of Dawn had been written with a brush made of one hair. His eyes red and swollen, he smiled, muttered his thanks, and swallowed the seeds which had taken half a year of minutely precise work. A shock wave traversed the Jew's face, and a kindred wave rattled the Duke's guts. He dismissed his guests, and when he saw that the official portable latrine was surrounded by advisers and guards, he looked for another place to relieve himself.

He got away from the rabbis, both Ashkenazi and Sephardi, who were wrangling about which would walk on his right and which on his left; crouching, he crossed the dirt road going down to the Kidron River, knelt hastily, and crapped in the shadow at the base of the mighty rock of the wall. Now that he felt lighter, he realized he had forgotten to bring a gosling, quickly pried a stone from the dust, and wiped his behind with it like a lowly ass drover. Relieved, he stood up and walked until he came to the entrance of Bab-a-Zahara, and in a flash, as if the city had sucked him in, he was drawn into her stone intestines, sank, and disappeared.

A little while later, his servants noticed his absence, and a great fear descended on them. The Mutasaref was awakened and grew hysterical at once. Lying between his perfumed sheets in terror and grief, he began plucking the hair from the head of the lad lying beside him. Everyone recalled the terrible case of the disappearance of the Russian Consul's twenty-year-old daughter, who was found dead a week later in some Palestine Exploration Fund dig, stripped of her golden clothes, her naked body swaddled the way the Bedouins across the Jordan swaddle their infants. But the Duke, who knew nothing of that, was wandering alone in the dark lanes, sighing with relief, happily poking the metal tip of his walking stick into the cracks between the cobblestones. He went through the Arch of Lazarus, passed the double doorway of the Monastery of White Orphan Girls, crinkled his nostrils at the reek of blood from the slaughterhouse of Sheikh Abou Rabah, and came to a small square, well known to tourists for its reddish cobblestones, a memento of Saint Pelagia. Here the Seljuk horsemen sheared the Saint's hair, and her blood spilled out of the amputated locks and soaked the pores of the stone.

Silence and darkness reigned. Overhead, a lusty laugh sounded now and then. The summer heat radiated from the stones of the city even after sunset, and people dined on the flat roofs. Watermelon rinds were hurled down from time to time and smashed on the pavement. Duke Anton groped for one of them and smelled its fragrance. Driven by some incomprehensible impulse, he sank his teeth into the remnants of redness and saliva stuck to the gnawed rind, and chewed with pleasure. Two Franciscan friars emerged from the darkness, and one of them tossed him a coin, for by now the dust of the city covered his clothes, dimming their splendor, and in his contemptible hunger he looked like a beggar. Later on, a door opened wide and the screams of a tormented girl were heard. The Duke trembled, almost fell, but recovered and went on walking.

Suddenly he felt several figures closing in on him from behind. First he thought they were robbers and tightened his grip on his stick, which was a gift from the father of his fiancée, Rudolfina, and had a steel knob and tip and a Basque rapier concealed inside it. Three bodies entirely veiled in long cloths seemed to be gliding over the ground without sound and without feet. They caught up with the Duke, two on his right and one on his left, laid soft hands on him, either to caress him or to grab him, and kept saying over and over, "Hadidu . . . Hadidu . . . " It was only by their soft voices that the Duke could tell they were young women, for their faces and curves were invisible.

"Hadidu . . . Hadidu . . . ," they repeated, and the Duke, who didn't understand what they wanted, smiled and wondered what to reply. He was embarrassed, as a man from the West may be when caught among the wretches of the East, disgusted by them body and soul, but afraid to offend their only possession—their honor. He was about to shake them off and cross the street, but before he knew it the three girls had spread out their arms and enclosed him in a circle of clasped hands.

"Hadidu, hadidu," they laughed.

"Hadidu," said the Duke heavily, and felt weakness spreading through his muscles, pain falling away from his flesh, and the wonderful pressure stirring in his member, which had already raised its head in curiosity, as if it understood the opportunity even before its owner. Now the girls began dancing around him, and the Duke, relaxing and smiling, began unwittingly to circle with them. Their pace accelerated, their scarves slipped off, the green and brown bangles on their necks rang like bells. Sweet bubbles burst in his flesh as he stumbled and was dragged into their sucking whirlpool. He wanted to walk on and break through the ring of arms that encircled him, but one of the maidens doffed her cloak with an imperceptible movement, stood there in loose, filthy cotton pants, face veiled, and shapely tattooed breasts exposed, and began dancing in front of him, tinkling tiny bells on her arms and retreating with a steady, lugubrious, and knowing slink. Not the seductive ass twitching that can be resisted with experience and closed eyes, but the female gesture no man can fail to heed, the gesture of entreaty, a plea for help. The Duke followed, her two companions escorting him like guards. Suddenly, filled with suspicion, he stopped, but one of the girls rushed in front of him, smiled, and came close to him, her arms stretched taut behind so that her breasts pricked his chest, with a thrust so soft he lost his balance altogether. They giggled, leaned over him, picked him up and brushed the dust off him, and kept on chattering in their foreign tongue, in an unpunctuated torrent that sounded like encouragement and apologies; and that sweet, irritating word, "Hadidu . . . Hadidu," was ever on their lips. Immediately they imprisoned him once again in the circle of their arms, and when he stood up and tried to walk on his own they let him, but kept him surrounded in their ring of bells, spinning endlessly.

Suddenly the circle stood still and the trio pressed close to him, making him so weak he had to lean on them, since his strength was gone by then. Their high, laughing voices, the spicy air that blew on him from their lips, the incomprehensible words, their filthy fingers putting little sweets redolent of faded roses and rotten almonds in his wide-open mouth that wanted salvation and air.

"Voulez-vous mourir avec moi?" he whispered, as if the words too had been put in his mouth. "Do you want to die with me?"

They reached the end of the lane, where an awful roar was heard, a roar that can be made only by the mute women of the Balkans, and the mighty shape of Zoga loomed up between the walls, coming to the rescue of her master. One of the girls tripped her with a nimble foot, and as the big woman slid and struck her head on the stone wall, all three girls moved a paving stone aside. One light puff into the hollow of the Duke's neck and he fell into the ancient cave beneath the street, into the adroit arms waiting for him in its depths, arms that slowly enveloped him and laid him down and covered the opening above.

The next morning, when Duke Anton returned to his tent, his servants hardly recognized him. His ruby ring had vanished, his hair was disheveled, his face wore a raffish and insolent expression. Tattooed script sparkled on his nose, and on his forehead was a crest of jasmine flowers that elicited an appreciative smile from the Turkish soldiers guarding the camp. They understood at once that the Nawarites had captured him in one of the lanes, led him to their hashish dens in the ancient stone quarry beneath the Church of the Fish, emptied his wallet, besotted him with Mariani wine, and spent the whole night there with him. The dancers of Nawar, the Turks explained to the Duke's tutors, bestowed the diadem of jasmine on those who succeeded in surprising their bodies with an unfamiliar trick, and only four men had won it before the Duke: two Janissaries, a cattle drover from the Sudan, and a French cardinal. The entire entourage surrounded the dazed Duke while the wretched Zoga, a big bruise on her forehead, knelt in front of him, weeping and kissing his dirty, wounded feet, and pulled thorns and stone slivers from his skin and the hairs of his groin. Then she carried him to the tent and stripped off all his clothes. Upon examining him, Dr. Reuven Yakir Preciaducho discovered two more tattoos, on the Duke's foreskin and buttocks, and ordered him returned to Europe at once.

That very day, the tent's silk hangings were folded and pressed into big cedar chests, the thalers and francs went back into the moneybags on the dogs' necks, the gold forks and spoons were locked in iron boxes, the silver and crystal goblets were packed in layers of wool, and the remaining goslings were released at the wall. The Duke was put in an ambulance carriage with sealed windows and taken at a gallop to the port of Jaffa, whence he sailed in a gunboat that had been patrolling the shores of the Holy Land from the moment he set out on his journey. All the way he slept a great deal, and when he woke he ate with a tremendous appetite, smiled all around, and spoke not a word. He didn't even ask about his beloved Lippizaner or his light cart.

The writer described the Duke on the return journey as "deep in contemplation," but in the picture the photographer sent, Anton looks as if he's sleeping with his eyes wide open, a vulgar smile all over his face. Dressed in a nun's habit, he was smuggled into the excellent hospital of Liège. For two weeks, the finest specialists toiled over him: surgeons peeled the disgrace of that night from his buttocks and nose, poets and priests plucked the grief of Jerusalem from the crevices of his soul, and physicians purified his intestines of filth with enemas of ash and laurel.

As for the Duke's tattooed foreskin, however, a great concern arose. None of the doctors was willing to assume such a heavy responsibility for the happiness of his fiancée and the continuation of the dynasty. Finally, they called in an old Jewish ritual circumciser from Alsace, and despite Zoga's agitation, anti-Semitic curses, and screams of pain, he successfully circumcised the Duke and was wise enough to take off with the foreskin in his pocket. Three days later the steward of the palace treasures appeared, presented the skin of the Duke's nose, and showed that what looked like ornamental tattooing was in fact amazing micrography: a dozen verses from Chapter 25 of the Book of Genesis, written in Hebrew. Everyone immediately began searching for the foreskin, but by then the Jewish ritual circumciser had sold it to an anonymous collector of curiosities and fled to America.

A month passed. With scarred nose, peeled buttocks, and mournful member, Duke Anton married the girl he abhorred, the Austrian princess Rudolfina. Everyone was amazed that the groom didn't so much as look at any of the women at the ceremony, but they assumed he was still weak from the journey and the operations. No one understood that Jerusalem, borne everywhere in the blood of those she contaminates, had not relinquished her prey. Not until three months later, when his circumcision had fully healed, did the Duke turn his eyes to women again. But now his taste was changed. He no longer pressed his loins to his female interlocutors, nor did he say, "Voulez-vous coucher avec moi?" In a deep voice and a tone of awful urgency, he asked, "Voulez-vous mourir avec moi?" And his eyes were so remote and terrifying that the women knew he wasn't looking at them but at his memories, and they were speechless with awe.

In the end a girl of seventeen, his second niece on his mother's side, did yield to him. This was the young Swedish Baroness Hedwig Vrebohm, owner of the famous copper mines in the city of Falun. She was a tall, precocious girl who didn't know her own beauty and from infancy had adhered to the principle "One time only." This practice of hers naturally impoverished her parents and exhausted her tutors, for she would never eat the same food twice, wear the same garment twice, or go where she had already been. "Life ought to be a one-way continuum of isolated phenomena," she said. The Duke had first encountered her when she was about three years old, and now he met her again at a banquet in his father-in-law's palace. At the end of the banquet, when the butler served the men cognac and the women almond liqueur, the young Baroness refused the goblet, saying, "I've drunk this beverage before."

The Duke invited her out to the balcony, and there he asked her his question, in those words none of the specialists had managed to purge from his flesh. His heart beat like a bell, for he knew she would agree.

"Yes, chéri," said the one-time-only Baroness. "I'm willing to die with you, but only once." Then she looked into the dark garden and remarked matter-of-factly that she had never been to bed with a man.

The next day the Duke took her to the Gessler hunting lodge. Zoga went with them, weeping all the way, those bitter tears soothsayers weep when their prophecies come true. When they arrived, she burst the sealed doors with her big shoulders, aired the silence and mourning from the rooms, made the bed, and quietly went outside. Anton lay with his love one time only, and then their four hands lifted the blood-soaked sheet and spread it out to the light, and together they read and deciphered the future written in its designs.

The Duke took out the pistols he had brought. "Shall we shoot one another or each one himself?" he asked.

"Each one himself, chéri," said the Baroness. "I trust you." Then she laughed and said, "But only once."

The Duke cocked both hammers and gave the Baroness a pistol. They twined their arms as Swedish soldiers do when they drink a toast, and aimed at their temples. The pistols roared together, and a grimace of hope rose on Zoga's face, for she heard only one shot. Screaming, she heaved her mighty body against the door, rushed inside, and discovered the two corpses.

The chroniclers agree that the words "I trust you, but only once" and the laugh that accompanied them were the last utterances of the Baroness Hedwig Vrebohm, even though none of them was there at the time of the suicide. As for Duke Anton's last words, there are two versions, both apparently false because equally plausible. *The Book of Death* by Joseph Enright (Oxford University Press) states that they were "Yes, my dear, only once"; but *Famous Last Words* by Frederick Altenberg states that they were "You won't feel any pain, I hope."

There is a third version. It maintains that the Duke didn't say anything, for the moment he opened the box of pistols and saw the green felt padding, he understood that he had never loved anyone but Zoga, the two uvulae in her throat, her blood flowing in his veins, her hands that could carry him and aim him. He had never slept with her, and now he wanted her for the first time, but the loading and cocking had a momentum no one could stop, certainly not he who executed them. The Duke saw himself loading and cocking and twining his arm in the arm of the Baroness and smiling and pressing, and he knew that the brain spraying was his brain and his blood was the blood of his beloved.

Chapter 1

On July 12, 1927, close to three in the morning, the splendid, sporty light carriage of the Greek Patriarch suddenly sallied forth from Jaffa Gate. Minus the familiar team—the Patriarch, his Arab coachman, and his Lippizaner horse. Two small children sat in the driver's seat holding the reins, and harnessed between the wooden shafts was a tall, fair woman, broad-shouldered and handsome.

A few hours earlier, when darkness descended on Jerusalem, no one had imagined what surprises she kept furled in her wings. Like all other nights, this night too opened with the traditional local sunset, mighty in splendor and impression. Afterward the city hurried to gird herself in her well-known darkness, pretending to be settling deep in dreams. From the chalky wrinkles of her body wafted smells of urine and ashes, rotting Dabuki grapes, and the scum of cisterns. Behind them gathered other embellishments of the night: prophecies from out of sleep, mad sighs conjuring up the End of Days, the hungry howls of cats and orphans, wishes and expectations.

Everything was waiting.

In the entrance of the *Kishlah* prison, the British guard was pacing back and forth, up to the end of his watch. The dwarf baker of the Armenian Quarter was praying for his dough to rise. The little notes in the Wailing Wall were waiting for the angel with the silken bag, the parched cisterns for downpours, the alms boxes for driblets of money.

Time, "the Great Teacher," moved slowly.

Antique merchants were waiting for suckers, the gray rocks for the stonemasons' chisels, the abandoned wives of the Great War for return and redemption. At the Dome of the Rock the Mauritanian Guards were circling, roaring, practicing strangleholds, and waiting for the heretic who would dare ascend the mountain and defile it with the slobber of his dog's breath.

The dead, "the bulk of the residents of the Holy City," were waiting too. They stretched out the bones of their hands for the charity of skin and flesh. They turned the empty sockets of their eyes to the End of Days, that imaginary horizon, where earth and time meet.

In the hidden cave, the king stretched on his couch, grated and rattled his ribs. A light, foul wind blew in the caverns of dust, strummed the strings of the lyre hanging at his head, hovered over the remnants of red hair stuck to his skull, played on the blade of his sword and the smooth surface of his shield. But the child who will proffer the flask of reviving water to his jaws, the innocent, awestruck child who will place a small palm in his rotting hand and lead him out of his grave to his waiting people—he tarried too, and didn't come.

And in the east, beyond the Mount of Olives and the Pillars of Azazel, a new day was waiting to be born. July 12, 1927, was all spit and polish in honor of its participation in the sublime annals of the city. Jerusalem, whose joints and people had lost their suppleness, whose flesh grew malignant stones, whose nights were tormented by memories of glory and pain— Jerusalem waited for the great leap, the liberating rise, the fluttering wings of the City of God.

Chapter 2

Suddenly, with no restraint or reverence, that light chariot burst forth from Jaffa Gate, its sides glittering with silver crosses, a black canvas taut over its ribs, its two silent wheels well oiled, that beautiful and mighty woman harnessed between its polished shafts. Her two little sons, one a redhead built like his mother, one delicate and dark, sat in the driver's seat holding the reins with their four hands. Both of them were endowed with the gaping, wondering look of the nearsighted, and despite the differences in their appearance, you could tell they were twins.

Inside the cart lay their father, apprentice baker Abraham Levy, bound with ropes and gagged, angry and anguished. He had never been late to work in the bakery. Ever since he turned ten and was sent out to help support his family, he had always come early, stirred the yeast, lit the fire, and sifted the flour even before the boss arrived. Now, he thought irately, all of them were waiting for him: the boss is furious, the yeast is waiting, the oven is cold and worried—and he, Abraham Levy, is brought like a lamb to a burnt offering in the perfumed carriage of the priests.

Short of height and lean of flesh, covered with empty flour sacks and a lather of impotent wrath, Abraham cursed the day he brought his wife from the Galilee to Jerusalem. Her ways—the manners of an amorous mare, said the neighbor women—had already sapped his strength, ground down his patience, and given him a bad name in the courtyards of the Jewish Quarter and all over Jerusalem. His own community pitied him for wedding the *chapachula*, the slovenly one, the Ashkenazis slandered him for marrying into a family of converts, and his name was a proverb and a byword even among the fickle young Moslems who drank forbidden raki in the cafés of Mustafa Rabbia and Abbuna Marco.

"Alta alta ez la luna," sang the mischief-makers whenever they saw Abraham Levy pass by in the street; they twirled red fezzes on one erect finger, mocking him in his own language. "Oh-so-high is the moon," they hinted at his short stature and the white skin of his wife, whose beauty ruffled the calm of their flesh, appeared to them in their dreams, and stained their sheets with pale spots of disgrace.

Bulisa Levy, Abraham's grumbling mother, didn't sleep a wink either. "My daughter-in-law, you buy cheese from her or you get blows from her," she sighed. "When I see white ravens, Abraham, only then will I be at ease from the woman you brought home." True, her own ancestors were just poor cloth dyers, but they had been brought to the city in the days of Caliph al-Walid. "Valero? Elyashar? Who were they anyway?" She puffed up her fat cheeks. "We're fifteen generations in Jerusalem, and they came here only a hundred years ago."

"Somos Abrabanel," people mocked her behind her back, but Bulisa Levy turned and left with a swing of mighty buttocks. Over the years she had tended and fostered the family honor delivered into her hands for safekeeping, until that *cabailla*, that insolent mare, came and smashed it to wretched slivers. And as if it weren't bad enough to have a daughter-in-law of such coarseness, stupidity, and giant limbs, she also declined to fill and light the nargila for her mother-in-law, as a good daughter-in-law should, she smacked the neighbors' son, a scholar who got fresh with her at the courtyard gate, she vomited on the floor when she was asked to cook meat for the family, and ate nothing herself but ricotta cheese, raw vegetables, and sweet rice pudding with milk and cinnamon.

"*Princessa de sutlatch*, with her rice pudding, for her all year long is Shevuot," the female relatives and the women of the courtyard grumbled at the well. "She drinks milk all day long, even when she's not sick."

When the convert woman passed through the stone alleys, accompanied by the faithful and violent goose she had brought with her from the Galilee, making her way through the maze of proprieties and the thicket of virtues, she felt the interrogating eyes assessing her frame and limbs and digging holes in her skin: gazes of wonder, of lust, of curiosity, of hostility. Passersby flattened themselves against the walls as she walked, some with a wet and evil smile, some with held and yearning breath, some with a hissed curse. And she, a grimace of embarrassment trembling at the corners of her mouth, bent and hunched her broad shoulders, as if she were trying to shrink her body.

Her gray eyes annoyed the women because of the enormous space between them, a sign of the perfect regularity of her menses and the health of her lungs and teeth. The men were bothered by her thick, fair eyebrows. Everyone knew that such eyebrows betokened abundant golden pubic hair, which hadn't been seen in the city since the days of the Crusaders, but only the Armenian photographer Pagur Dadurian had proof.

Dadurian was the apprentice of the Armenian photographer Esau, a well-known monk, who left behind the famous series of daguerrotypes of Mount Zion. Unlike his distinguished teacher, Dadurian understood that photography also had commercial value. He set up the Dadurian Studio in the Anglican Archway, photographed couples on the eve of their wedding, retouched the moles on the faces of cadis and rabbis, and sold postcards to Pravoslav pilgrims smitten with holiness and English tourists addicted to the East. He hired a group of Bedouin models and photographed them for a series of postcards called *Types du Jerusalemme*. Sometimes he dressed them up as Moslem religious sages, sometimes as immigrant Jewish ritual slaughters from Hadramawt, and sometimes as wandering Nawarite fortune-tellers. With the right makeup, they could also manage to portray Saint James and his sisters the virgins, and Moses and the daughters of Jethro.

But one day Dadurian journeyed to Budapest and brought back an enormous, late-model camera and a series of bawdy pictures that proved that the camera "could see under clothes." The rumor took wing, and whenever Dadurian went out with his licentious new camera, women fled screaming to their houses and closed the iron shutters in the naïve belief that those would defend them from the power of the lens.

"Just say yes or no!" pleaded the men who assembled at the Dadurian Studio, and some even offered him money. But Dadurian pretended to have a secret, left his tormented interrogators to stew in the turmoil of conjecture, and said he wouldn't show anyone his pictures of the "yellow Jewess."

Chapter 3

It was three o'clock in the morning. The woman pulled the carriage to the city wall and looked around warily. Her eyes lingered on a few fellahin who had come to the city early and were waiting for the markets to open. They had already unloaded their wooden *saharas* full of tomatoes and grapes, hobbled their donkeys' front legs, and put sacks for food and dung on muzzles and backsides. Now, huddled in their cloaks, they crouched in the ditch near Jaffa Gate, smoked, and brewed coffee on a small bonfire of twigs.

Three hours earlier, she had snuck into the yard of the Patriarchate. Through the windows she could see the eighteen members of the Holy Synod sitting in their midnight convocation, sipping cognac, loosening their sashes and the coils of their hair, and gossiping about the contemptible copulation customs of Coptic monks. Under cover of their gales of laughter she had dragged the carriage off and now she was filled with terror and impatience. She knew that in the morning the Greek Patriarch would rush to the High Commissioner, raise his pampered voice in a shout, flap his robes, and make the High Commissioner send the whole British police force on her trail.

The donkeys tossed their heads, brayed, and pawed the ground in incomprehensible fear. When the fellahin got up to calm them, they spied the carriage and the woman between its shafts. Terror gripped them. In those days, evil nocturnal spirits swarmed in the streets of Jerusalem and in the imaginations of her inhabitants. On summer nights they rose from the

Beit Hisda pool, from the caverns of Al-Wad, and from the cellars of the Red Turret to breathe fresh air and play tricks. They made rabbis and nuns slip on the smooth steps, stole food from wire boxes hanging in kitchen windows, penetrated the parched wombs of barren women, and ran riot in the dreams of sleeping children.

Wanting to get the fellahin out of her way, the woman stamped her foot angrily, dropped the carriage shafts, stretched her long neck, and unleashed a terrifying wolf's howl. A deep, awful roar answered her. Mighty stones were flung from the top of the wall, cries of fear from sheep, people, roosters, and dogs rose all around. Flocks of bats and doves emerged from the clefts of the city, from her cracked towers and crumbling caves.

"El-a'emura el-beda," shrieked the fellahin. "The white devil!" They hurled their tin mugs and flew off like scared finches.

"Go into inside," the woman ordered her little twins. For a moment even she was terrified, because she too thought it was her wailing that had loosed the chains of the earth. But she immediately reconsidered, her eyes froze in rage and determination, and a furrow was plowed in the space between her brows. The redhaired boy panicked, scurried into the carriage, and disappeared under the cloth canopy with his fettered father. His brother opened his black eyes wide and stayed in the driver's seat.

The young mother fastened the harness to her shoulders, picked up the wooden shafts, and gripped them with redoubled force. She took a deep breath and broke into a run. With long, light strides she sprinted past crumbling walls; in a downpour of stones and shouts she leaped over pits that opened before her feet; she tore through the shrouds of smell that enveloped the city—vapors rising from burning bakeries, from broken spice jars, from the overflowing fetidness of the sewer, from the puddles of coffee left by the early worshipers. She, who drank only milk and hated the Jerusalem custom of beginning the day with a mug of coffee, now rejoiced at the destruction of her enemies. "Drink, drink the cafeiko, sloppy cha-pachula," Bulisa Levy would tell her every morning, and with her bony gums she would chew the softened biskochos she dipped in the mug. "Drink, alocada, may you finally get some sense with the help of the Holy-One-Master-of-the-Universe."

For only ten seconds did Jerusalem quake. The dull thunder had stopped now, but the stones went on rolling as if life had stirred in them. The annals of the city were shuffled like cards. The stones of the altar were confused with the stones of the city wall, stones of catapults with pieces of mosaic and benches of bath houses. A headstone turned into a cornerstone, pillars into gravel, a ceiling into a floor. On the Mount of Olives, the tomb-stones bounced like dice, exchanging corpses with a sound of crushing and blasting.

At the same time, the Patriarch's stolen carriage climbed westward and passed the Russian Compound, where the pilgrims were already kneeling and thanking God for His revelation. The woman made her way among the terrified inhabitants of Nahalat-Shiv'a and Even-Israel, who were huddled in the street; passed the sundial of Mahane-Yehuda; gave the low houses of the Abu Basal neighborhood a wide berth; and stopped for a moment between the two gatekeepers that stood at the western entrance to Jerusalem in those days: the madhouse on the left and the old age home on the right. From here, the city dwindled, evaporated, its last houses melting and blending into the boulders of the wasteland.

She turned her head around to the city and spat angrily. Then she smiled to herself with satisfaction, tucked up the hem of her dress, stuck it in the cloth belt at her waist, and continued her light tramping. In mute confidence, her bare feet moved in the dark like the strong white wings of the barn-owl that dwelt in the graveyard *de los Karaim*, the one they used to scare us children with. Through the tiny rents in the cloth canopy of the carriage, I heard the madmen's screams of envy and encouragement, saw them clutching the bars of their windows as they accompanied our flight with yearning eyes. I saw the spot of Jerusalem grow distant, saw my twin brother Jacob laughing and holding Mother's reins, saw the long wings of her thighs that never stopped moving. I smelled the flowing sweat, I heard the tumult of the pink lungs, the blowing of the mighty heart puffing its blood into the peerless body. I imagined the strong ligaments of the knees, the supple pads of the heels, the muscles breathing under the skin of her calves—my mother, the convert Sarah Levy, the white devil, the yellow Jew-ess, Sarah Levy née Nazaroff.

Chapter 4

I was born in Jerusalem in 1923, the first of two twins. My father, Abraham Levy, was an apprentice baker and some time later acquired his own bakery. A short man he was, with a mild voice, who, by dint of his occupation, could hide from the company of human beings. My mother loved him with a boundless and unreasoning love that began the first time they met, and ended, I hope, before her final days.

About that chapter in my father's life, the chapter before our birth, I know only a few details. I generally tend to overlook the fact that people are endowed with life and a history before they intersect or touch my life. Why? Maybe because I grew up with a twin brother, or maybe because of excessive reading of books. Perhaps I had better not tell you, my dear, but I feel it mainly about the women I love. Like comets, they come out of chaos, and like comets, they dissolve into it.

To prove his existence before our birth, Father used to show us two old photographs and tell us a lot of stories. The photographs I didn't believe since Dadurian Studio conferred on its customers costumes of other nations, vistas of other lands, and even faces of other people. I didn't believe the stories either, for they were constantly changing, but since I'm not a stickler for truth myself, I know how to refine out the dross. I assume, my dear, you can do the same with my words.

At any rate, on that night, my father left Jerusalem for the third and last time. The first time was to serve in the Turkish army, and the second—to take Sarah our mother for his wife. "Once for war and once for love," he would say. The third time he refused to define.

Of his father, the sage "Hahan Levy," he told wonderful things. "Ashkenazi rabbis would ask his advice. From the *Sarahya*, the seat of the Turkish government, they sent him holiday gifts. From the *waqf*, the Moslem authorities came to him for arbitration." But between the words was an image of a wretched presser of tarbooshes, his house steeped in poverty and disease, five of his eight children dead before they reached the age of six. When he was ten years old, our father Abraham was sent to the bakery of Isaac Ergas to help support his family. "He's got a good boss," Bulisa Levy would say, "good and pathetic." And Ergas the baker did show him kindness and never treated him harshly like other bosses. "Soft and good like the Armenian dough," Abraham said of his master. Forty-one years old Ergas the baker was at that time, bald, skinny, a virgin, and people thought he would remain a bachelor forever. In his childhood, he had been beaten cruelly by the stick of the "rubbi," a religious teacher of small children, and ever since then he had stammered. The old *bulisas* of the Jewish Quarter said that not only his eyes but all his limbs dripped tears into the dough and that was what gave his *Frenzila* bread and his *pitikas* the airy saltiness they were famous for.

"In his dough, yeast works on pain," they explained.

And indeed, black tufts of the hair of affliction thrust up out of Ergas the baker's ears, drooped like gloomy ferns on his lobes, and proved to everyone that internal pressures were torturing his flesh. His workers whispered that he molded himself female images of dough, put black mounds of poppy seeds on the lower belly and Hebron raisins on the breasts, and observed their white flesh as it moved and rose and swelled. Abraham was witness to the great scandal that occurred one Friday when the women came to the bakery carrying covered pots of *hamin*. Ergas the baker shot the pots into the depths of the oven one after another—until he raised the hem of one of the dresses with the long shaft of the baker's shovel. The shrieks summoned the woman's brothers to the bakery, who beat Ergas with sledgehammers and cobbler's boot trees until he passed out from pain and amazement, and it was only plasters of rubia flowers and myrtle leaves that brought him around. He lay in his bed murmuring, "By mistake . . . mistake," and soiling his sheets with blood and tears.

That Saturday evening, the sages assembled and instructed Saporta the matchmaker to drop everything and quickly find a wife to calm the flesh of the baker and the temper of the community.

Saporta smiled blissfully. Ergas the baker was hardly a tempting prospect, but the matchmaker regarded him as a professional challenge as well as a chance to solve the problem of "*Las Yagas*," girls smitten by fate who had not yet found husbands.

"*Tenjereh y tapon*—every pot has its lid," he always claimed.

The matchmaker gave the sign, and a terrifying procession of candidates—hunchbacks, lunatics, barren women sent back to their fathers' homes, women who were hard of hearing and slow of comprehending, deflowered virgins, women with suppurating wombs, yeast infections, and musty underarms—erupted from the cellars of Jerusalem and crawled to the bakery like a centipede of misery. Even though he knew in his heart of hearts that he couldn't be choosy, Isaac Ergas fled to his oven, sweating there until the workers came to light the fire.

In the end an orphan was found for him, "a cow *con* defect," a lame maiden with marvelous black eyes, a harelip, and the skin of an apple, so smooth and fragrant it earned her the nickname "Mansanika."

"She will make you a good wife," Saporta the matchmaker told him.

"But her legs . . . " Ergas tried to protest.

"Legs? What about her legs?" asked the matchmaker.

"She limps," whispered the baker.

"And what are you? A dancer?" asked the matchmaker. "Legs don't matter!" He bent over to the baker's ear and put the palms of his hands together. "Like oysters in the sea, Señor Ergas." He slowly spread his palms. "The oyster isn't important, but you open it . . . Like this . . . and there you have a pearl waiting for you."

Ergas was embarrassed. The matchmaker put an arm around his shoulder.

"You tell me, what is the most important thing for a man, the most important!"

"Love," answered Ergas timidly.

"*Amor ez solo una palabra!*" snorted the matchmaker with the contempt of a connoisseur. "Love is only a word. Favour is deceitful and beauty is vain, and even fear of the Lord shall not be praised. The most important thing for a man is gratitude. A woman who is grateful to her husband will do everything for him. She will cook and wash and raise the little ones, may there be many. She will charm you with the taste of Adam's fig tree, she will warm you in winter like Abishag and cool you in summer like Abigail, she will stay you with the flagons of Shulamith and will give you pleasures even Bathsheba didn't grant David, things a man is afraid to ask even in his heart."

Ergas the baker imagined the taste of Eve's ripe figs and all those Shunammite and Carmelite joys even King David, the psalmist of Israel, didn't savor, and his whole body rippled.

"A grateful woman and a nonchalant man," Saporta said dreamily. "That's the best match."

"Nonchalant," Ergas repeated, considering, impressed.

"For the woman," quoted Saporta, "her weapons are with her. And remember one more thing. In private intimate matters, the woman can lie, but never the man. Don't ever forget that."

But in private intimate matters, when Ergas the baker lay with the grateful Mansanika, kissed her eyelids lovingly, and stroked her apple-smooth skin, his nonchalance dissolved as if it had never existed. For the first time he knew true bliss, which is like pain and time and love: everybody talks about it, but nobody can describe it in words.

Here Father would break off the story, skimp on the details, and skip straight to the bitter end. Nevertheless, it was clear that at the height of private intimate matters, as Ergas the baker was longing to be buried in Mansanika's ripe fig and transported on the Rivers of Eden of her womb, he suddenly felt something like a small, warm hand emerge from her hidden depths, grab his crown, and press with a strange heartiness, like a handshake.

A horrible fear shriveled the baker's heart. Such surprises had never featured in the modest repertoire of his fantasies. He immediately recognized the hand of the *Brosha de los Novios*, the she-demon of bridegrooms. Terrified of the magnitude of his dread and pleasure, he leaped from his bed with an anguished cry and fled from the room to the alley. Fear gripped his muscles so hard that it took seven butchers and porters to catch him and drag him back to his house.

From that night on, the erections of Ergas the baker never flagged, and his face stayed pale as whitewash, for all his blood was hoarded by his embarrassing, painful, and eternal stiffness. Through the years, until he was killed in the pogroms of 1929, he suffered from torments of the body and distress of the soul, from curious and compassionate eyes, from mocking fingers pointing at him. "Woman is more bitter than death," he warned Abraham. He never approached Mansanika again, and everybody knew he didn't touch her, not even with the tip of his little finger.

Chapter 5

A braham had a good friend named Elijah Nathan, son of the distinguished micrographer Bekhor Nathan, who was famous for his ability to write the blessing of Jacob on a thumbnail and the Book of Ruth on a single dove egg.

During World War I, Abraham Levy and Elijah Nathan wanted to evade being drafted into the Turkish army. Once every few days, search parties hunting for deserters descended on the Jewish Quarter led by Aaron Tedesco, the Mutasaref's permanent denouncer, a Jew who could sniff the sweat of frightened people even if they plunged up to their necks in cisterns or hid behind stone walls. Abraham and Elijah huddled in the cellar of the *Kortijo de dos puertas*, but Aaron Tedesco twitched his nose at the cobblestones, indicating that they should be taken up, and the two were caught. The very next day, Abraham was sent to Damascus and from there to Mesopotamia, a name that stirred my childhood imagination, though it was merely the name my father gave to what is now called Iraq.

In Mesopotamia, Abraham was a *Huzmachi*, an officers' orderly. He polished boots, made beds, oiled saddles, laundered and ironed his masters' uniforms. Elijah Nathan stayed in Jerusalem. He was a member of a family from Monastir in Macedonia, and like all the other Monastirials, he too was fair of hair and eye, eager since his youth to learn languages, mathematics, and astronomy, and to plumb the mysteries of infinity, a subject that naturally occupied the Monastirials because they were compulsive observers of the celestial bodies and the depths of the heavens. Now Elijah amazed the Turkish officer with his scientific education and his command of languages, and was thus left to spend the war in Jerusalem, in the Kolarasi Building opposite Nablus Gate, as a translator and decoder in the headquarters of the German general Kress von Kressenstein.

A few years after the war, Elijah married Duduch, Father's sister. Marriage made him a jealous and crazy man, and indirectly also caused his death, and Father never stopped missing him, adoring him, and telling stories about him. He believed that the Monastirials "weren't born in this world but descended from the stars," and following the same logic, he claimed that their astronomical observations were simply homesickness. From the little I know of you, my dear, I imagine you would call that "retrospective contemplation."

When the war ended, Abraham stood up, took his water bag, a bunch of dried dates, and a small piece of *kishek*, and set out on his return to the Land of Israel. He dreaded the harsh hand of the retreating soldiers, who had lost any semblance of human beings, and because of his fear, he decided to return to the Land of Israel on foot. *Kishek*, incidentally, is a hard, dry Arabic cheese preserved like a stone for many years, and an easy temptation to metaphor, for when you moisten it, it comes back to life, exudes a rich odor, and recovers its good taste.

My brother Jacob didn't believe that Father crossed the desert on foot. "Just look at him," he would say when we were growing up. "He can barely find his way to the toilet. I guarantee you, even the Turkish army didn't take good-for-nothings like him."

But Turkish army words spilled from Father's mouth time and again. He shouted *"yavash, yavash,"* when we mixed the yeast too fast, and *"Caravanaia"* to call us to the dinner table. When we forgot to close the doors of the *gareh*, the rising chamber, and the dough got hard, he said, *"Galata,"* and sometimes he asked Mother to make him the soldier's mess—a loathsome dish of lima beans, lentils, kidney beans, and raisins that stunk up the whole house and, for some reason, gave him an attack of nostalgia.

"Fear can make you as brave as King Solomon's Eagle," Father insisted on the veracity of his trek through the desert. He had one story of heroism in his past, and he damn well wasn't going to let anyone take it away from him. "By day I hid and by night I walked. I walked and I sang," he kept telling my skeptical brother, me, and himself. In the Turkish army he met conscripts from the Herzeliya Gymnasium of Tel Aviv, and from them he learned songs that weren't known in the courtyards of Jerusalem. His voice was high and pleasant, his eyes were wide open, the wrinkles were taut on his neck. He sang:

In the fields of Bethlehem
On the road to Efrat

A tombstone stands
On an ancient grave.
And when midnight comes
From the land of the dark
A beauty will arise
And abandon her grave.
Eastward to the Jordan
She marches in silence.

The desert stones tore his shoes, his mouth filled with dust, and he almost broke his legs in the jerboa holes. He saw the tracks of bustards, desert birds who run so fast that all you can see of them are little pillars of haze rising up from their invisible feet. He saw the bulging eyes of the viper peeping out of the sand, and the stony droppings of the wild ass, that donkey of the desert, who doesn't drink and doesn't urinate "and breathes with his asshole," Father explained, "so as not to dry up the spit in his mouth."

One morning, when he lay down to sleep in the shade of a rock, he saw a big, soft surge of brass hovering over him; the nymph butterflies in their great westward migration. These butterflies flew as fast as a man walks, and the sight of them encouraged Abraham to jump up and go with them, his face gilded with the deep gold of their wings. Before dawn he grew tired of walking and lay down on the desert ground but got up when he could no longer bear the cold, hopped and waved his arms. On every side, the cracking sound of rocks was heard. All day long they absorbed the heat of the sun, and now they were splitting in the searing cold of the night.

At night the desert wolves would pass close by him, lean and sinewy, never weary, eating and sleeping, playing and giving birth on the run, their steps flowing and silent. Even they didn't notice him, for by now his scent had become the scent of dust, and when he lay down to rest on the ground, he disappeared from view. Wrapped in a cloak, camouflaged and clinging to the sand like one of the stones, he lay on his back and gazed at the firmament. In those days the sky was dotted with myriad stars that looked to him like coriander seeds with impenetrable shells and a cold hidden gleam burning beyond them. He watched them, drew lines from one star to another, created pictures and astrological signs not known even to the Babylonian astronomers who had watched the same skies and the same stars thousands of years before him.

Sometimes he heard the faraway weeping of desert jackals and the tinkling of distant caravans, but the noises seemed very close and frightening, for he didn't yet know that the desert is like the sea, carrying sound across enormous expanses. Only when he returned to Jerusalem and told Elijah Nathan about the noises he had heard in the desert did his friend explain to him that because of the slowness of sound waves he had in fact heard the weeping of the lyres of the Babylonian exiles, the tread of the armies of Tadmor and Persia, and the rumble of the shields of Alexander the Great's phalangists marching to their death in the East. It was an aural Fata Morgana, "a mirage of the ears," Elijah told him excitedly, an echo of illusions only a happy few were lucky enough to hear.

Afterward all the nymph butterflies expired and Abraham continued on his way. One day he was terrified to hear shrill screams of dread, "like a thousand Bulgarian virgins shrieking," and when he climbed a crest, he saw Bedouins rounding up a herd of deer on the other side. The splendid animals were pursued with torches, yells, and drumming, and were corralled between two walls of stone and earth a few kilometers long. At first the walls were simply low dirt ramparts set far apart and didn't look suspicious; then they grew higher and closer, and by the time the deer understood the trap, they had no way out, for the walls came together at a big pit. Abraham saw them trying to leap over the walls, falling and breaking their thin backs in the pit, dying of outrage and burst veins, spitting blood from their delicate mouths. The Bedouins swooped down on the deer, pulled back their necks, clamped their heads between their knees, and slaughtered them with one swing of a curved knife before their souls could take flight and leave their flesh defiled for eating.

After ten weeks, Abraham came to the bed of a big river and followed it south for four days, feeding on fish caught in the warm autumn cisterns and on the purple fruit of the jujubes that grew there in abundance. From that river he reached the Yarmuk, and from there the Jordan, which was narrow and shallow in that season. He passed over the Jordan on foot and immediately fell to the ground. Thus, in a few dozen words, I think to myself, my father crossed the great desert. From him I learned that the word is the quickest vehicle, that no obstacle can hinder it, that it is faster not only than wind and light but also than truth.

From there he went to Tiberias. "Good people from the Abulafia family" took him into their home, gave him food and drink, salved the wounds on his feet, burned his tattered clothing, replaced it, and sent him on his way. He climbed the crest of a mountain range and saw a spacious plain sloping gradually from the east and the north, with a wall of steep mountains laced by ravines to the south. A rivulet traversed the earth, black dots of cattle grazed in the mown fields, prickly plums grew here and there, and the yellow stubble of summer's end encircled black islands of basalt. Ravens hopped in fields that were already plowed, wagtails flew merrily, rising and falling in the air, flocks of storks glided south.

Abraham reached the plain at an hour of grace: that hour when sunbeams penetrate the gaps between the clouds and illuminate pieces of the world, as if they wanted to turn the human heart to the really important details. In one of those lighted squares he saw the houses of a village and turned his steps toward it, hoping to find food and shelter for the night. His feet hastened down the gentle slope, and his heart rejoiced. After days in the desert, the soil of the plain and the approaching houses of the village looked like a promise. He leaped over clods, circumvented a Bedouin encampment in a big crescent, went down across the riverbed, and made his way among the reeds on the banks.

Suddenly his skin prickled. He looked around and saw a young woman lying in a field, wearing a coarse, filthy dress, asleep in the scanty shade of a plum tree. Very quietly he approached, looked at her, and was filled with amazement and yearning. Tall and fair she was, her shoulders broad, her chest moving with her deep, slow breaths. A wave of yellow hair shaded her forehead and brushed her thick straw-colored eyebrows, whose like he had seen before only over the weary, reddened eyes of Russian pilgrim women in Jerusalem. She was sleeping with her limbs spread loosely, a sign of confidence and childishness, but Abraham didn't know how to read the signs in female bodies. Accustomed to the dark, pliant presence of the little women of Jerusalem, he found himself all excited by the foreign colors of the sleeping woman, by the health of her fair body and the length of her thighs outlined under her dress. He didn't yet envision the future, and at that sweet decisive moment no love can do without, "the moment when sense dies like a butterfly in winter," he came a little closer until his shadow fell on her face, and said in a soft, parched voice, since his throat and palate were dry with longing and wonder, "Good day to you."

The reclining woman jumped like a doe out of the thicket of her sleep and disappeared in a wink. Surprised, Abraham looked around until he discovered her yellow head peeping out from behind a basalt rock, her eyes, open now, their blue turned gray and alien, frightened and menacing at the same time.

"I'm a friend, I'm a Jew," he called out in embarrassment. "Don't be afraid."

She stood up and straightened her threadbare dress. Abraham looked at her and smiled.

"Hello," he called out again, but the woman didn't answer him or come to him. They stood like that a while, examining one another, until rain began falling and a tense expression arose on her face.

"*Di katchkes, di katchkes,*" she cried in panic. "Mother and Father is going kill me."

The voice that came from the big body astonished Abraham. It wasn't the voice of a woman but the voice of a little girl. The daughter of Titans. Again he looked around, and only then did he notice the geese grazing in the field, like white spots through the curtains of rain. He began chasing them, and saw the girl running barefoot in front of him, her steps light and long like the steps of a wolf, her breath the breath of a wild ass, quiet and deep, her whole body expressing a harmony and beauty and strength that dazzled him with fear and lust. Together they outflanked and encircled the geese, and led them to the village in the pouring rain.

Abraham looked at her downcast face and her clenched mouth. "What's your name, little girl?" he asked.

"Sarah."

"How old are you?"

"Twelve."

"*Dami la mano, Sarika,*" he said with sudden daring, for now he knew she wouldn't understand his words. "Give me your hand."

The girl gazed at him and his hand stretched out to her. No one had ever called her "Sarika," or any other endearing name. The name Sarah was promised her even before she was conceived or born, when her whole family converted to Judaism, and her parents took it seriously and didn't dare exchange it for a nickname. Now she smiled timidly at Abraham, and her hand trembled in his. Years later, my brother Jacob and I heard that little girl speaking out of the body of our mother, wondering in deep groans of torment and kneading, loud and slow, why and wherefore she had fallen in love with the thin foreign man who suddenly appeared in the field, held a slim hand out to her, married her, begot her children, and embittered her life.

The clouds split in a thundering rip, and the downpour turned into a terrible deluge. Sarah's dress clung to her body, her hair grew wet and heavy, hot and glittering like a placenta. The gray basalt rocks turned black and gleamed. Vapor rose from them in a shimmer when the drops of the first rain of the season touched the flame of lava congealed in their flesh. Years later, when she described that moment to us, she compared the rustling of the stones to the whisper of the fiery hot loaves of bread when they're taken out of the oven and sprinkled with the glaze that makes them flash.

Her family lived at the edge of the village, in a poor black basalt house. She opened the wooden gate of the courtyard, drove the geese into their pen, went into the house, and didn't invite Abraham to follow. As he was trying to make up his mind whether to leave or wait, a big bearded man came out of the house and beckoned him in.

A Syrian sheepdog, large and ravenous, sniffed him suspiciously, detected the desert smells hoarded in the pores of his skin, and reverently backed off. A short woman was setting the table. At the back of the room three mighty lads were playing with river pebbles they tossed nimbly from hand to hand. Sarah stood by the wall undoing the sheaves of her wet hair. She wrung them out the way laundresses wring sheets, and water flowed from them by the bucket.

Ever since I came home to take care of him and release Jacob from the yoke, my father has often repeated the description of that picture, the little girl engraved in his heart, who was to be his wife and our mother: her handsome head bent, drops on her eyebrows and nose and lashes, her strong hands wringing streams from her plaits. Even though he spoke derisively, the rain evaporated from her warm hair, and a strong wet smell rose from her head like a thick mist.

Many years later, at his wife Leah's closed door, his face shriveled and pale, his right hand with its little finger lopped off hidden in his pocket, my brother Jacob told me that every man bears in his heart one picture of his wife, "a picture with your eyes closed," he called it, a picture seared in memory like a brand. "For the rest of his life he puts her in that picture. Puts and compares, puts and curses, puts and weeps."

But Father, who, despite all his efforts, couldn't match Jacob's suffering and disasters, keeps telling us what he has always told us: "That's how I fell into the trap"—infuriating us with the sweetness of his violent eloquence.

"Over there in America, you forgot what it is to live with him," says Jacob. "Well, now you'll remember."

Chapter 6

My grandfather Dyedushka Mikhail was a rich Pravoslav farmer in his day. He had apple orchards, two wells with wooden water wheels, a well-tended forest of poplars, ten span of oxen, and hundreds of geese. You've surely read of such places in books.

In Astrakhan, the district where he was born, near the shores of the Caspian Sea, Mikhail Nazaroff was known as *Otyetz Kolokolov*, Father of the Bells, for he regularly contributed money to cast church bells. In 1898, three events occurred, among which there would be no connection at all, if not for your questions, my dear. Duke Anton of the House of Gessler set sail for Alexandria, my father was born in Jerusalem, and Mikhail Nazaroff came to the Holy Land at the head of four hundred and fifty pilgrims dragging a gigantic brass bell to the Church of Mary Magdalene.

The bell was cast in Odessa and set on a mighty wagon specially built for it. The men pulled it to the port, and the *Santa Anna* set sail for Jaffa, where the women were harnessed to the wagon. From that moment on they all fell silent, for so they had sworn to do until the bell was hung in its place. Long after, you could tell who had participated in that journey by the way they walked: with strenuous, ponderous steps, as if they were striving against a strong wind. Thus Dyedushka Mikhail returned to his village and his house. He brought with him a small but heavy collection of stones—from Golgotha, Mount Tabor, the Sea of Galilee, and the grotto in Bethlehem, and he even got hold of a sliver of the rocks that had held up the Cross. Then he took out the gifts he had brought his family: dried flowers from Jerusalem between two olive wood covers, a tin lamp whose wick was lit from the Holy Fire of the Holy Sepulcher, embroidered fabrics, two abandoned goslings he found near Bab a-Zahara, white shrouds baptized in the Jordan and dried out by now, though that smell rose from them again as soon as they were moistened.

Once home, he hurried to his village bells, and a terrifying thing happened to him. As he pulled the ropes and the clappers began thundering, he was assailed by terrible pains in the joints of his arms. At first he thought that dragging the big bell had injured his sinews, or that he had contracted some Oriental disease or one of the malignant depressions Jerusalem infected her pilgrims with. But when the pains recurred the next day, and went on into the day after that, and began ringing and resounding through his body until they knocked him to the ground weeping and shouting, he understood it was a sign from heaven and knew what he had to do. He took to his couch (Mother always said "couch" instead of "bed"), closed his eyes, and dreamed he had to convert to Judaism.

For a whole month the village deacon argued with Mikhail Nazaroff but couldn't shake his will. Our grandfather remained firm in his decision. He harnessed three horses to his carriage, went to the city, and brought back a *mohel* and a *"rabbin"* who circumcised all the men of the family according to the covenant of our Father Abraham. The men were bound with ropes to the big table in the barn, and pitchers of vodka were poured down their throats to dull the pain of the circumcision, but awful shouts of torment burst from the barn, struck the fences, and rolled over the fields. The doves and sheepdogs were terrified and fled the courtyard. Only Dyedushka Mikhail refused to be tied down, and asked to be circumcised standing on his feet, and with a flinty rock at that. He girded his loins, leaned his back on the barn beam, put a wooden wedge between his teeth, and ground it to crumbs when the *mohel* cut off his foreskin.

Mother wasn't born yet, but she heard the story so many times that she felt her father's pain. In her account, she closed her eyes, peeped into that barn, saw his fingers turn white and his face scrunch up like a newborn baby's, and after he came to and smiled his first Jewish smile, it no longer had its old familiar lines.

A year after his conversion, Mikhail Nazaroff sold his house and fields, loaded his pregnant wife, his two sons, his plows, his furniture, and his sacks of seed into three covered wagons, clucked his tongue at the big oxen and the flock of geese born from the pair of goslings he had brought from Jerusalem, and ascended to Israel with all his belongings. Mother was born on the way to the Land of Israel.

Dyedushka Mikhail bought himself a plot of land in the plain, cleared it of stones, burned off the curse of rebellious weeds and the iniquity of prickly pears, plowed and sowed, and every morning he prayed and blessed his Creator, who had made him a Jew and brought him to the land of

"Avram, Isaak, and Yakov," to dress it and keep it. "Everything good, everything good," he kept smiling at Baron Rothschild's agents, who questioned him about his situation and presented him as an example to the Jewish settlers who were constantly complaining and demanding and were furious at the new neighbors who never asked for help.

The Hebrew spoken by the converts was meager and heavy, and Grandfather's prayer book was written half in Russian and half in Hebrew. "I read in the Russian," he grumbled at those who mocked him, "but the Holy-One-Blessed-Be-He looks over my shoulder and reads in the Hebrew." Out of shame, Sarah refused to go to the village school, and for the same reason her parents and brothers grew taciturn and didn't talk much even among themselves. My brother Jacob, who worked at their farm as a young man and was close to them and loved by them and knew them better than I did, though I look more like them, told me that this characteristic persisted even among their children. Mother herself couldn't read or write to the day she died, and her language was meager and flawed, which gave Father both pleasure and shame.

The convert gravely recited the blessing over food, squinted at Abraham to see what impression the prayer made on him, and then explained to him that they didn't eat meat, only vegetables, beans, eggs, and mainly dairy products. "*Moloko, moloko,*" he repeated, and Abraham, though he didn't understand the meaning of the word, heard and nodded. Now that he had a roof over his head again, now that an oven was warming his bones and wolves weren't circling him on stealthy paws and massacred deer weren't screaming in his ears, he took heart and looked at his hosts with a slight, concealed derision. "Your mother the *goya* and her father the *goy* and her *goyish* brothers, Russkies all of 'em, were so scared of the slaughtering laws they decided to give up meat altogether." He put on airs for me and Jacob years later, and even turned our bar-mitzvah into a day of anger and quarrels.

When he told Mikhail Nazaroff he was heading home to Jerusalem, the old convert was moved. He himself was afraid to return to the Holy City, for she knew him from the pilgrimage he had made in the days of his blindness, and the bell was there too, a resounding memento of sin and transgression. He regarded Abraham as a man with a halo hovering over his head, and Abraham, filled with pride, bit into an egg rolled in hot ashes with a strange and wonderful taste of smoke clinging to it, and enjoyed the vegetables the converts grew in their yard. Sarah brought to the table a steaming pot of groats in milk, spiced with tart green leaves, and he dared to glance at her very briefly, but long enough to embarrass her and make her blush until she buried her face in her plate; and when the meal was over she got up and disappeared. Abraham was left with the sons and the parents, all of them silent; they hunted stray bread crumbs on the table with big slow fingers, and looked at him with ten admiring and weary blue eyes. At last the father indicated that they had to go to sleep and led him to the small barn in the yard.

The barn, like the house, was built of warm black basalt stones. A few sacks of rye lay to one side, an Arab plow leaned against the wall, torn yokes hung on hooks. A balding horse groaned and complained near him, as if grumbling to himself about the tedious tradition of his forefathers that obliged him to sleep standing up. Two skinny Arab cows stared at the visitor, and the geese were so smelly and suspicious they almost suffocated him. Abraham, who was finicky and even in the most difficult times kept in his pocket the *ridoma de colonia*, his vial of perfume, sprinkled a little around him with the priestly gesture he still makes today. By the way, we got to see that vial many times, for Father treasured it like the apple of his eye, and over the years, as he became even more fastidious, he started sprinkling it on embarrassed guests after a brief and emphatic sniff, for the older he got, the more critical and arrogant he grew.

He stripped down to his long Turkish underwear, folded his coat and placed it on a stone so he could put his head on it, lay down on the edge of the worn blanket he was given, and spread the rest of it over his body. For a long time he looked at the dripping ceiling and imagined he couldn't fall asleep. He had a strange characteristic: from the day he was born he slept with his eyes wide open. "He deams bad deams," Mother would explain gravely in a tone of admiration and empathy. When he came back from the bakery after his nightly toil, Jacob and I used to sneak into their room to test whether our father was sleeping or only playing dead. We'd climb into his bed, make faces at him, stick our tongues out over his wide-open eyes, and even try to close his lids with our fingers until he'd wake up and smack us: "I'm alive, jackasses! Seed of *Azno!*" But we didn't stop that game of ours, since Father, like all people and birds of the night, was tired and withdrawn in daylight, and didn't play with us much.

When he was little, his parents were frightened by his sleeping with wide-open eyes. They swathed his head in an infant's turban crowned with amulets and a sprout of rue, and took him to Bulisa Zimbul, the eye healer. She diagnosed at once that "the baby steals dreams of Samaritans," and heaped on his eyes an oozing, stinking handful of mud from the bottom of Elijah's Well, the deepest well of the Temple Mount. This filthy remedy immediately caused a dreadful inflammation of the cornea and almost cost father his eyesight. The skeptics were about to call in Dr. Burton, the English physician, but in a last-ditch effort, Bulisa Zimbul smeared Abraham's corroded eyelashes with a blue argentite stone. It made him look like a tiny whore, but it did cure the inflammation.

Bulisa Zimbul's fame soared to new heights when it was known that she had even succeeded in curing a disease she herself had caused, but Abraham went on sleeping with his eyes wide open. Bulisa Levy was terrified, did not set foot in the women's *mikve* of Hamam-el-eyn, and thus withdrew from conjugal relations with her husband. "The child sees," she said, and turned her back to him, her thighs clenched in fear. "When I see white ravens or when he closes his eyes," she announced after her husband demanded to know when she would be kind enough to fulfill her wifely obligations. Then the blind sage Bekhor Bajaio was called in from Hebron to establish domestic peace. Bajaio came riding on his guide donkey; from his saddlebag, he took a tailor's measuring tape, a gleaming set of compasses, and candles that had already been lit. A whole night he sat next to the child, and once an hour he groped over Abraham's wide-open eyes with his feathery fingers and discovered that they didn't follow what was going on in front of them. At last he soothed the parents and decreed that Abraham did not see but was sleeping "*dormir de zadikim*, the sleep of the just, of those who wait the coming of the Messiah." Tempers calmed, and nine months later his sister Duduch was born.

When the geese settled down from the piquancy of the cologne, and Abraham fell asleep, the big fair girl came to get firewood from the barn, and for a moment she stood over him, a pinioned goose in her arms, her long legs rising on both sides of his shoulders, her dress spreading like a firmament above his face, her wet head in the sky.

Abraham lay for a long time, frozen, weak, and trembling. He stirred before dawn when a wonderful aroma, yearned for and forgotten, wafted to his nose, the aroma of wheat bread baking close by. He got up, wrapped himself in the blanket, and peeped outside. The rain had stopped, the sky was clear and deep, and the aroma was coming from a small shed at the end of the yard. Barefoot, hesitant, he approached and looked through the fence. Sarah and her mother were standing there baking bread in a clay oven. They were whispering to one another, and Abraham understood that in his honor they had taken out the wheat flour, kept for special occasions.

Abraham, who hadn't tasted fresh wheat bread even once throughout all the years of the war, who had eaten only hard rye *galatas* that broke his teeth and his heart, inhaled the aroma of bread and knew the war was over, that he had come back home, that love was rising on the horizon of his life. He withdrew into the barn, fell to the floor, and burst into tears.

Chapter 7

Knowing my father as I do, I can confidently say that he devoted most of his journey from the valley to Jerusalem rehearsing his hardships in the war and the desert so he could use them to impress everybody he knew. But when he got to Jerusalem, he understood that his glory did not lie on that path. Here he encountered suffering greater than his own. The signs of starvation, illness, and death had not yet been erased from the city. Tales of horror and affliction were still told. Terrible hunger had reigned in the city during the war. The distended bodies of infants were tossed out of houses. Moslem women lay in wait for the Mutasaref's carriage and stole the oat bag off his horse's head, and when the whip was brandished over them, they tore off their veils to show him ravaged faces and cheekbones threatening to pierce their skin.

His father had died of hunger, pure and simple, and his older brother, Ezekiel, who had escaped from the Turkish army headhunters, was wounded in his flight; no one knew what had happened to him. Ezekiel was a nimble and manly porter of wine barrels and flour sacks, "good-hearted as a dove in the cracks of the Wailing Wall and strong as the elephant who carried the Queen of Sheba." Even after so many years, Father's naïve similes still amuse me and infuriate Jacob. When Tedesco and the platoon of Turkish soldiers came to take him, Ezekiel broke the denouncer's nose, beat the soldiers off, and ran away. The bullet caught up with him near Hamam-el-eyn, and he "escaped from those who wanted his life with the slug stuck in his leg," leaving behind traces of blood and footprints that began at Zion Gate and ended among the seashells on the beach at Jaffa. Bulisa Levy and Duduch, the younger sister, were left alone and sank into abject poverty.

"Will we go to those people?" Bulisa Levy wondered when they told her that the Elyashar family had managed to bring a few sacks of wheat from the other side of the Jordan. But by the time hunger persuaded her and she went, "those people" didn't have a single grain left. She and her daughter fed on the grass of the field and fought with jackals, other people, and dogs for the right to rummage through piles of garbage. They stole bitter sesame rape from goat pens and searched for half-digested grains of barley in crumbled horse and donkey droppings. They had no coal for heating, no shoes, no medicine—none at all—and if not for the help of the Swedish and American missionaries who lived at Herod's Gate, they would have succumbed to disease and starvation. Many maidens sold their bodies, and "the whole city heard them, because they were so thin, the poor things—their bones rattled on the beds like *toyakas de Purim.*"

The day after he returned, when all the tears of joy had dried and all the neighbors had seen him, Abraham went to look for his friend Elijah Nathan and found him sitting at his regular table in the Beit Ne'eman library studying the subtleties of tense in the English language. The two embraced and burst into tears. Father told him his experiences in the army and the desert, and Elijah smiled pleasantly and said, "Let it alone, Abraham, let it alone. The main thing is it's all over." He himself, as I said, served in Jerusalem, and contributed his bit to the alliance between the Kaiser and the Sultan by translating artillery manuals from German to Turkish and eggplant recipes from Turkish to German. Father even remembered that Eggplant Imam Bayaldey was translated into German as *Der Immamm ist in Ohnmacht gefallen,* and he laughed when he told the story.

Every morning Elijah had peeped out of his window to see that the other possibilities were worse. In the courtyard of Kolarasi, recruits and deserters lay around in fetters, waiting to be sent to the battlefield. Their wives and children sobbed behind the fence, while he, lucky Elijah Nathan, stayed behind in Jerusalem.

It was only the sunrise that troubled him. The Monastirials, people of cogitation and observation, used to assign scientific missions to their young men, and ever since his bar mitzvah, Elijah had risen early every day and climbed Mount Scopus to record the exact time of the sunrise. He had been attacked by a mania to record all the times of the sunrise for forty-nine years, and to devote his declining years to deciphering their correlations and secrets. Even now, despite the military laws, he would take off to the mountain at sunrise and hurry back after recording his data.

One morning, when Elijah was sneaking back into headquarters, as luck would have it, he encountered in the corridor the German general Falkenheim, whose five senses had been confused during the night by two

Daughters of Nawar. The general, who had a strange bouquet of jasmine flowers sticking out of his head and was in a foul mood as a result of his empty testicles and wallet, swung his hand, gave Elijah an awful slap in the face, and sent him to be court-martialled for desertion. His Turkish commander, who was very fond of him, reported to the general that the accused had been executed, and without telling a soul, he locked my uncle in one of his subterranean storehouses in the enormous building, along with material to translate. The next day that Turkish officer was sent to battle in Gaza, where he was killed, and my uncle Elijah remained imprisoned and isolated in the depths of the building along with dozens of cases of canned food, thousands of documents, and a dismantled wooden model of the Temple signed by the missionary Konrad Schick. Behind it Elijah found a big, strange wooden cabinet with wheels and shafts. At first he thought that Konrad Schick had also made a replica of the Ark of the Covenant, but he quickly discovered folding arms inside the cabinet, and further investigation revealed three nooses as well as a terrifying wooden spit and a rusted guillotine. This was the portable Turkish gallows of the Jerusalem district. Elijah was filled with dread, but later, when he grew accustomed to the presence of the monstrous device and the cold and boredom increased, he carefully read the attached instructions and translated them for fun into all the languages he knew. Then he broke into the next room, where he discovered hundreds of beautiful stuffed water fowl, swamp cats frozen in mid-pounce, glassy-eyed vultures, a balding tiger, and jars of preserved reptiles. It was the collection of the Lutheran minister Ernst Grimholz, who, like most nature lovers in those days, harbored a lust for murder and taxidermy that couldn't be concealed even by scientific research. Thus Elijah turned from a worthless expert in eggplant cookery, field maneuvers, and parabolic trajectories, into a useless connoisseur of the fauna of the Land of Israel.

In 1917 winter came early, and my uncle spent the last months of the war in isolation and cold. He didn't suffer from the darkness because he had the night vision of an owl—a faculty developed in all the Monastirials by continual stargazing. He tried to warm up by jumping, quick translation, and futile kicks at the heavy door, and maintained his composure by marking the passing days on the wall. His despair increased. There were days when he was weary of his life. From time to time he screamed piteously, hoping someone would hear him. But the walls were very thick and Elijah understood that even if passersby did hear his cries for help, they would think them merely an echo of the ancient cries of some tortured person who had died here, for even he was hearing them now.

At Hanukah he had been in the cellar a whole year. Snow was falling on Jerusalem, and as Elijah lit a sesame oil lamp and sang songs of victory and valor in a thin, solitary voice, he could not know that in those very moments the city was surrendering and the English were entering its gates. One month later, on a horribly cold day in December, he went to the portable gallows, smeared the noose with soap, examined and oiled the trapdoor lever, and climbed up to stand on the plank of the condemned. Just then a loud knocking was heard on the door, then the creaking of wood and sledgehammer blows. Startled, Elijah began shouting in Turkish that he didn't have a key; the door caved in, and two officers in foreign uniforms entered. The younger one was wearing riding boots and eyeglasses with such thick lenses they looked like transparent river pebbles. His name was Arthur Spinney, and I'll tell you about him and his exploits later. The second was a virile fellow in a general's uniform, his forehead strong and vaulted and his eyes surprisingly pleasant. He was built like a bull, his hands were broad as plowshares, and his chin was ruddy and craggy. Elijah realized at once that these were English officers, since their clipped mustaches weren't dyed and waxed. His second thought made clear to him that this man was certainly General Edmund Henry Hynman Allenby, whose name he had often come across in the pages of German intelligence he had translated.

The two Englishmen were amazed to find the strange Turkish soldier with a rope wrapped around his neck, surrounded by canned goods, stuffed animals, and military documents. Elijah was trembling with cold and fear, for he knew that if he had to explain, he would get himself in big trouble. Fortunately for him, he noticed the eyes of the distinguished general wandering to the stuffed fowl, and he knew his salvation had come. He threw the noose off his neck and rushed to introduce him to every single one of the birds by its English, Arabic, German, Hebrew, and Latin name.

Allenby, a great lover of winged creatures, was very impressed with him. "Keep an eye on that fellow, Arthur," he said to the nearsighted cavalryman before they sent Elijah home. "Seems to me we'll be able to make some use of him."

Chapter 8

A braham went back to work in Ergas's bakery. The baker was glad to see him, bought him shoes and clothes, and taught him the mysteries of his art; the secret of the proper dose of salt and sugar that enabled the baker "to harness the yeast *como cavaillikos*," the precise movements of the baker's shovel for shooting the bread in and bringing it out into the light of day, and the Ashkenazi style of braiding challah. In a gesture of trust, Ergas also taught him the hidden secret of "Armenian spitting" on the blazing bricks and deciphering the whisper of the vaporizing saliva.

Abraham would come to the bakery at one o'clock in the morning, stir the yeast to life, and light the wood in the oven. Ergas the baker came two hours later, his eyes red with weeping and sleeplessness. In the long nights of baking he recounted to Abraham his disaster and his grief. Ten years had passed since his wedding night, and he had never touched his wife. Evil tongues said that when the sour smell began coming from the bakery, Ergas's wife knew the dough was rising and could not be left alone, and then she entertained men in her house who weren't of the Covenant; but the truth was that Mansanika's bed was moistened only by her tears.

The poor baker's wedding night lived in his memory, and with a candor bestowed only by prolonged pain he told Abraham every detail, no matter how embarrassing. "She had there inside her a kind of mouth of a suffocating fish," he said, searching desperately for similes to explain the secret of his wife's internal clasps. With one hand he cut slits in the loaves of dough "so they won't explode wherever they like," and with the other he described how the old women scorched "G-O-D" on his bedclothes and scattered baits of *dulce le leche* under his bed.

The aim of these potent remedies wasn't precise, and they cured the wrong ailments. Ergas's bald pate sprouted shoots of curly hair, his baker's cough disappeared, and his backaches moved down to his big toes. Only his dread, his erection, and his pallor remained intact. At a certain stage the old women placed on his member two white doves who specialized in softening and calming, but they stood there cooing comfortably, in perfect balance until the baker was filled with disgust and despair. He washed the corrosive bird droppings from his flesh, and bought a long, broad band of Egyptian cotton to bind his loins, and fastened his rebellious member to his belly to make it stop beating and stirring up the front of his pants; and ever after, the Arabs called him "Abu el-Hizam"—Father of the Belt.

Sometimes the lame Mansanika would come to the bakery and give Abraham her buck-toothed grin, evenly split between seduction and embarrassment by the cleft in her lip. Her skin emitted pleasant smells that reminded him of the delicacies of the table at Rosh Hashanah. He turned his bewildered back to her, and for a long time after she left the bakery he still imagined he felt her eyes and hands, but he wrenched his thoughts away from her and escaped to his own torments, which, though bothersome and painful, were at least familiar to him down to the last detail. Ever since he returned to Jerusalem, a recurring dream had tormented him, a dream of black rocks, white spots of geese, pouring rain, and a big girl. Her wet head soared to the sky, her breasts breathed as she ran, and every night her fair, strangling thighs rose above his wide-open eyes. When he walked in the stone passages of the city, he saw again the broad shoulders moving in front of him, those legs running and leaping on the alley stairs, saw the remote and frightened eyes, smelled the fragrance of wet earth rising from her hair, heard the coarse, childish voice saying "Sarah" and "twelve" and shouting "di katchkes." At last he went to Elijah Nathan and confessed to him, bled secrets and tears as if he were cleansing his flesh of poison.

Elijah smiled. In those days he was gripped by a mania for the cinema, and the silent actresses of the twenties reinforced his belief that there is nothing in love except pretense. "Amor ez solo una palabra," he quoted the famous saying of Saporta the matchmaker, and prophesied that one day "a new Louis Pasteur" would arise to discover the secret fluid that stirred the torments of love in the human body and to inoculate against it. He read Abraham Enlightenment books about the physical and spiritual dangers of exhausting the vital force of the testicles, described to him the well-known depression after coitus, which affects everyone, though only the Yemenites admit to its existence; and then he amplified, maintaining that traits are passed on in both the father's semen and the mother's milk.

"*Nada da nada que disho Kohelet*," declared Elijah on the vanity of vanities of love, and Abraham left his friend's room and went to the bakery.

"Shame!" he hurled at himself. "Shame!"

In spite of Bulisa Levy's poverty, matches were proposed for him, for he was a good and loyal worker and was known as a descendant of fifteen generations in Jerusalem. But Abraham paid no heed to the girls he was offered, just as he ignored the yearning looks of Mansanika, the sermons of his mother, and the gossip of her neighbors.

Elijah invited him on an automobile trip. Arthur Spinney, the English cavalry officer who had freed him from the cellar of Kolarasi, and was now finishing his military service, decided to stay in Palestine, opened a general store next to Jaffa Gate, and hired Elijah to work in it. Across from the store, among the cabs of Jaffa Gate, was parked a rattling little Ford, part van, part diligence. Elijah declared, "There's nothing like a trip in an internal combustion automobile as a proven means for erasing memories"; and after he paid the driver he said, "Smell, Abraham—the smell of gasoline, that's the smell of the world." But the smell of the world made my father's head spin, and at the Garden of Antimos he jumped out of the car and threw up.

Elijah didn't despair. He took him to the workroom of the distinguished micrographer Bekhor Nathan. In those days, Elijah's father was trying to write the Ten Commandments on the head of a pin, and thus to create that absolute point "that is smaller than all smallness," which Lucretius extolled and Diogenes worshiped and Democritus said was indivisible.

Bekhor Nathan despised "the wisdom of the Greeks" and said that Lucretius was wrong, that the point was not a geometric entity but a verbal one. "Only the word has no physical existence, and only it is indivisible," he smiled.

Abraham looked around and was filled with admiration. The miniscule words fluttered before his eyes in a dance of black points that hid the converts' daughter from the Galilee for a moment. But when he and Elijah emerged from the room, he returned at once to his longing. He was disgusted with himself for allowing the awkward girl to penetrate his dreams, and irritated with the parents who had bequeathed him in their semen and milk his characteristic of sleeping with his eyes wide open. At night, when he came to the bakery and lit the twigs and wood in the oven, he saw the straw-colored hair burning in front of him in the flames, like a photograph engraved in a heart that won't be consoled. In the special misery of lovers, using the system of point diminution, he withdrew and compressed inside himself and into the leaden heaviness of his infinite yearnings, and even Elijah couldn't get him out of there.

Thus he tortured himself for three years, and then he got up and announced to his mother, his boss, and his friend that he was "going to take the woman." Bulisa Levy raised a cry of despair, his sister Duduch smiled, Mansanika didn't say a thing, Elijah laughed and said, "How are the mighty fallen," and Ergas the baker looked at him sorrowfully, adjusted the painful belt fastening his shame to his stomach, and told him he would do well to marry "a woman of the Covenant," and stay in the bakery. But with the same firm and surprising strength that had kept him going in the desert, Abraham packed some food for the road, took a stick to keep off snakes and dogs, and went out of Nablus Gate heading north.

He passed Saint Stephen's monastery, spit three times at the site of Titus's camp, "as befits that evil man," and passed the wall of the Calvary, where furious Catholics and Greek Orthodox threw stones. Three hours later, when he reached the rocky hill where Shem, Ham, and Japheth are buried, he garnered his courage and sat down to rest. A bad place that was. Here the Crusader knights of Siena killed Rabbi Jacob Aaron, who came out from the city wall to curse their armies, trusting in the prayer he prayed and the priestly breastplate he wore. Here Rizpah daughter of Aiah lamented her crucified sons, and in the morning you can still see her tears glittering on the rocks, the tears of a bereaved mother that never dry.

"And they didn't harm me." He was still amazed at his good luck even in the days when he told us the story. "Neither man nor beast, neither fiery serpent nor scorpion."

The hyena and the snake observed his progress, smelled his sweat, the sweet sweat of lovers, got out of his way and let him go. The cassia, the cactus, and the caper withheld their thorns from his skin. Fellahin working in the fields looked into his eyes, offered him water, fed him olive oil and tomatoes, and onions, grapes, and bread, and their gaze followed him as he stood up, thanked them, and went off to the horizon of his love. All along the road he saw the spot of yellow hair quivering before him like a doe's tail, the long legs stepping, kicking the stumbling blocks out of his way.

In Wadi el-Haramin, mounted bandits burst forth from the rocks, tore up his rucksack, broke his stick, and stripped him naked.

"Where are you going, One-condemned-to-death?" asked the head of the gang, a short, thin man with one blue eye and one brown eye.

"To take a wife." Abraham covered his privates with his hands.

The armed bandits laughed, reared their horses, and fired gleefully in the air, but as his words penetrated the coarseness of their bones and the wickedness of their flesh, they were stricken with yearning, fell serious and silent, and gave him back his clothes.

"Open your mouth!" the bandit leader ordered.

Abraham closed his eyes, opened his mouth wide, and waited for the metal gun barrel that would break his teeth and the slug that would slice through his brain. But instead of that, he only felt two rough, warm fingers smelling of *samna* and sage, the ashes of bonfires, and rifle oil touching his lips, spreading his jaws, and poking into his mouth. Under his tongue, the bandit put a heavy gold coin and kissed him on both cheeks. Then he gave him a big block of dried dates, a new stick, and a striped cloak, sat him on a horse, and the whole gang rode behind him for a long stretch, for two days, until they came out of the mountains into the plain and Abraham asked them to leave him, for he didn't want to come to his beloved surrounded by "highwaymen and Gentiles."

When he reached the village, he went first to the home of the mukhtar, Yakir Alhadef, a sharp, fat Bulgarian Jew with his thumbs permanently stuck in his belt.

"What is your desire?" asked Alhadef.

"Arrange me a match with the maiden Sarah Nazaroff," said Abraham.

Alhadef almost choked with laughter and amazement. "You don't need a matchmaker," he told Father. "The poor converts would give their daughter to a monkey if he was a Jew of the seed of Our Father Abraham. She doesn't even want to go to school, the filly." Then he grew serious. "Hey, you're one of us, why do you go to them?" he asked. "There aren't any virgins in Jerusalem?"

But Abraham assumed the blank countenance of one firmly in love, and Alhadef, understanding that his guest saw and heard nothing but the reflections of his own imagination, rose and took him to the Nazaroff house.

The old convert, his wife, and his oldest son were sitting at the table. Sarah was serving water, bread, vegetables, and cheese. She pierced Abraham with lowered gazes and aromas of rain that would never dry. His flesh melted. She had now turned sixteen and hadn't changed a bit since he had seen her three years before, for she had continued growing up in his dreams too. He controlled the trembling in his knees and contented himself, I imagine, with a small smile full of honor. Mikhail Nazaroff asked how he was and questioned him about his occupation and his family, and Abraham answered every one of his queries with a detailed and respectful reply, though he knew the old convert had already decided to give him his daughter for a wife. But before he and Alhadef left the house, the brother suddenly approached with his mighty body, bent down, and said quietly into his truly terrified ear, "You be nice to Sarah, or you better watch out. We are Tartars!" And he went on his way.

The next day Abraham went to the Abulafia family in Tiberias, the "good people" who had taken him in on his return from the war; he brought them regards from their relatives in Jerusalem and spent about ten days with them. He stayed in the Alhadef home another week, until all the necessary preparations were completed and Rabbi Joseph Abulafia came from Tiberias, tied up his donkey in the converts' stable, and married my parents in the courtyard of the village school.

After the ceremony the young couple withdrew to the room prepared for them in the Nazaroff house. For a whole hour they lay next to one another, throbbing with love and yearnings this first encounter couldn't assuage, and then my mother got up from the bed and led my father to the field. Terrified and barefoot, he walked behind her, the soles of his feet recoiling from the clods and thorns. Her white nightgown showed him the way, her hair gleamed in the darkness, and as they lay on the ground embracing, as her body gathered him up from the mire of his torments, my father suddenly began weeping. Neither a weeping of joy nor a weeping of love, but the weeping of men when their first child is born. "Weeping that draws tears out of the bones," as Mother would say years later, whenever she recalled it. That night my father touched her with his eyes, heard her with his breast, saw her with the palms of his hands, and at sunrise, when he was awakened by the singing of warblers and the dews of the cold earth, he found her lying behind him, his body cupped in the hollow between her chest and thighs, her breath warming the back of his neck, one hand supporting his cheek, and the other covering his rib cage and his heart.

Chapter 9

Who am I?

"I was born at Blunderstone, in Suffolk, or 'thereby,' as they say in Scotland. I was a posthumous child. My father's eyes had closed upon the light of this world six months, when mine opened on it."

"I was born in 1910 in Paris. My father was a gentle, easy-going person. He owned a luxurious hotel on the Riviera."

"My name was Tommy Stubbins, son of Jacob Stubbins, the cobbler of Puddleby-on-the-Marsh."

"My poor father owned the firm of Engelbert Krull."

"Never was there real peace between me and father. He seemed to treat me harshly from the moment I was born."

Nearsightedness thrust me into the arms of memory and reading. There, among the pages, I discovered clearly drawn people, comprehensible ambivalence, and the horizon that is never blurry, the one that stretches behind the eyes, not in front of them.

Even today, I impress my interlocutors with quotations from Dickens and Melville, Tschernikhovski and Hoffmann, Vasari and Saroyan, Nabokov and Fielding. But friends I didn't find among their lines. "For what do we seek among the pages of books if not the sight of our own face?" wondered Robert Louis Stevenson. It was Jules Verne, of all writers, who had a lot to tell and little to say, who introduced me to Marfa and Nadia, showed me the image of the mother and the features of the beloved. But, even then, tears didn't come to my eyes. "*Si vis me flere*," said Horace to the novice poet: "If you would have me weep, begin the strain,/ Then I shall feel your sorrows, feel your pain." I suspect all those writers never weep.

The big, fair girl filled the little room with a good smell of milk and field. Quiet prevailed. Between Bulisa Levy's fat knees, damp husks of watermelon seeds piled up on a rag.

"*Tfu-hamsa-mezuza*," she finally exclaimed. "That's the woman, Abraham? That's the bride of your dreams you brought us? Every one of her dresses will cost twice as much. With the fabric we'll buy for that one, you could clothe a whole family."

"The first word she said was *tfu!*" Mother grumbled over and over in years to come, staining her memories with anger and accusations. "They didn't want me there. Only the Duduch, she loved me."

Tia Duduch was about fifteen years old then. She looked at her new sister-in-law and was breathless with admiration. Mother's good smell, her strength, the rippling muscles under the white skin of her arms—all stirred love and longing in the girl. Sarah, who was only a year older than Duduch, smiled at her shyly and surveyed the room in astonishment. She was a simple girl, a gooseherd who couldn't read or write, and now her eyes opened wide, trying to take in more and more. In her father's house moldy hues of brown, gray, and black prevailed; here a colorful carpet was spread on the floor, embroidered cloths and gleaming cushions adorned the sofas. Two big ironclad *kashas* to hold bedclothes stood against the wall, and a *canoon* of coals glowed red in the middle of the room. Her admiring eyes didn't notice the splotches of moisture on the walls, the empty oil cans that propped up the sofas, or the patches on the upholstery.

A large mirror hung on the wall, with two wings that reflected the other side of whoever looked into it. Sarah, who until that day had seen her face only in the small hand mirror of the principal of the village school, and her full body only in the serenity of big puddles of rainwater, approached the mirror curiously, saw that her goose was still clutched in her arms, and immediately became embarrassed and let go of him. The goose panicked, beat his mighty wings, and smashed the mirror into thousands of slivers.

A shout came from Bulisa Levy's mouth. Terrified, Sarah knelt down and began gathering up the sharp glass splinters of her reflection. Duduch sank down beside her to help, and their bleeding fingers quickly began touching one another. When they finished, she smiled and offered Mother roasted chestnuts, almonds, and hot, sweet wine.

Abraham went out to the courtyard, and his mother hurried after him. "There are things that will never mix, Abraham," she said to him through the wooden wall of the common toilet. "A cat and a dog don't mix. An orange and spinach don't mix. And us and those don't mix."

In her terms, "they" were the arrogant leaders of her own community, and "those" were all the foreigners. Abraham, squatting on the crapper, moved his bowels and didn't answer, but his mother knew that lines of dread and distress were etched on his mortified face. She raised her voice so all the neighbor women could hear and remember what she said.

"When I see white ravens, you will have it good with that woman. She isn't your rib, Abraham, she will only bring trouble on us."

At night she and Duduch slept in one bed, Abraham and Sarah in the other.

"And what did the *cabailla* bring? One crazy goose." Thus Bulisa Levy complained about the dowry her daughter-in-law had brought. She knew everyone was lying there in bed and no one was sleeping. Her voice sawed the darkness of the room: "Big as a mare, white as a sick sheet, and breaks everything she touches."

The next morning the rest of the necessary facts were delivered to the women of the courtyard, by evening the whole Jewish Quarter knew, and it took two more days for Jerusalem to fabricate all the rest. The coloring, the eyes, and the gait of the gigantic girl stirred the gossips and filled their mouths to bursting. More than once, the female relatives said, she was seen crossing herself at the table. During her menstrual period, the neighbors huffed, she isolated herself in a locked room and received her food through the window like one of the Karaite women. On *Dia de banyo*, the old women spluttered, right after she came back from the *mikve*, she pushed Abraham to the floor and rode him with that bold and loathsome gallop that brings untimely births and ghosts to the world.

The gossip filled the courtyard and overflowed it, sloshed along with the filth of the sewers and preceded the victim wherever she went. Winter came in her wake, and with it the thin, stinging Jerusalem rain, the wind that erupts from the burrows of the city, and the cold that pukes out of the crevices of her walls. All summer the stones emitted dust, and now the rain swept it away in turgid, frozen streams that clogged the alleys. The lizards crept off to the desert, the little songbirds migrated to Jericho, and only the big ravens in the pines of the Armenian Quarter remained in the city, flying across her skies and shrieking ancient abuse in all the languages their forefathers had learned from the soldiers and pilgrims.

A year after she came to Jerusalem, Sarah gave birth to a big, handsome daughter. The midwife put a wedge of wood between her teeth, and all through the delivery a wet spot on the ceiling dripped water onto her forehead. The great poplar moaned in the courtyard, the cistern filled up, and the burning embers whispered in the *canoon*. The little girl had marvelous blue eyes, long, sturdy legs without a single fold of baby fat, and a devil's coat of fine red fur that covered her whole body. The red mantle of hair frightened the entire Jewish Quarter, especially Abraham, who was calmed neither by Elijah's genetic explanations nor by the declaration of Dr. Korkidi, who had returned that year from medical school in Paris: "It falls off!" He heard the whispering about the *creatura* he had sired, and believed his mother was right. "Then I understood it was all a mistake. That my mother of blessed memory was right. White ravens never come, oil and water never mix, a bull and a donkey don't plow together."

But Sarah loved her little daughter dearly, for beneath her red down the baby had her coloring and proportions, and to Sarah she wasn't only a daughter but also a sister and an ally. She tied the baby to her back with a sheet, and carried her like Arab peasant women do, not parting from her for a single moment. When she nursed her, she recounted all her suffering, and when the baby was four months old and died in her cradle, all Jerusalem trembled with her awful lament, which held the terrible keening of mountain wolves, the dread of winter winds among the folds, and the stunned bleating of the slaughterhouse.

"She made noises like a beast." Father dredged up a rare memory. In my childhood, when I asked him about our older sister, he usually denied her existence, scowled mightily in refusal, pretended to be deaf, and finally, when I persisted, offered to make silhouettes on the wall for me. Only many years later, in one of his letters to me in the United States, did he write that "your mother" lay in bed for a week with the tiny corpse, shouting "Not to the Olives. . . . Not to the Olives. . . ." The goose didn't let anyone approach, "and it was lucky it was winter and her little one didn't stink."

In the end, Dr. Korkidi kicked the goose, entered the room, stroked Sarah's hair, and persuaded her, putting his two small warm hands on her wet temples. She held his wrists, got out of bed, and let Jacob Parnas the gravedigger come in and take her daughter to her grave. Parnas's mother purified the infant, swaddled her in a shroud, and tied the little corpse, which was hard as a rock, to the wooden board used for carrying dead infants; and Jacob Parnas bore it on his broad shoulders to the children's section on the Mount of Olives. That was how they buried children in those days, in the most horrible of funerals, the funeral of a dead child no one accompanies out of fear and guilt, who has no name carved on the tombstone.

Like a public judgment, the child's death confirmed the suspicion and resentment everyone felt for our mother Sarah, and now Abraham's soul was pierced too. Chenou Apari, a woman I'll tell you about when her time comes, said a long time later that you don't kill love with a sword. Oh no! You torment love with pinpricks. And love never dies. *Jamais!* It only shouts, does love, and crumbles, and melts, but never does it cease to exist.

Chapter 10

On days when her suffering overflowed its banks, Sarah would run away and seek an open field to breathe in, grasses to wallow in. "To smell flowers," she said, "to smell flowers and see trees."

Barren fields and rocks stretched around the city, and the few neighborhoods outside its walls looked like tiny frightened islands floating and drifting on wasteland and boulders. Sometimes she would go out Nablus Gate and walk past Mea Shearim. To the northeast, a small lake had been forming all winter, reeds crowned it, toads sang its hymns, stray storks landed on its shores. Sometimes she walked on Jaffa Road to the Garden of Antimos to peep through the stone wall at the orchard and the villas, and I imagine that was where she first saw the Greek Patriarch's carriage. Then she hastened to Ganjiria, where houses were just springing up in those days, and beyond she discovered the valley that became her shelter and refuge. She would call the goose, go out Jaffa Gate, pass Spinney's general store, and look in to say hello to Elijah Nathan, because she knew that Duduch dreamed of him; from there she walked along the Moslem cemetery, with its pervasive stench of stagnant water; with frightened step she ran up the path at the mouth of the ancient cave, for an old lion lived in its depths and guarded the skeletons of the righteous that had fallen apart, and to this day no one knows how to put them back together. Panting, she reached the ridge of the hill where the Franciscans built their new college. To the side stood a marble Virgin with bent head, leaning against the wall and waiting for ropes to lift her to the roof.

Opposite was a windmill, and next to it the pioneer stonecutters were building the first houses of the Rehavia neighborhood. They were sure that Sarah was only a Russian pilgrim in local clothing, and they talked about her in Hebrew. When they saw her blush and realized that she understood, one of them stood up and invited her to share their lunch, but Sarah got scared and took off. I sometimes think she might have done well to respond to that fellow, who might have loved her with a love worthy of her—of her devotion, her physical force, her integrity. But Mother, it seems, pays no heed to my thoughts and heads west from there down a gentle slope to the valley and the monastery that dwells in it.

All around grew old olive trees with twisted trunks, pocked and pitted like corpses eroded by the soil of their graves. She was always amazed at these dead-looking trunks with such fresh silvery-green treetops rejoicing on them. A narrow railroad track curved in the valley then, and a shiny little military locomotive would sometimes appear and rumble boldly to the north. From here the riverbed descended to the south and vanished among bare rounded mountains. In the afternoon a pleasant wind blew in the ravine, rustled in the olive trees, scattered dry yellow seeds, and rippled the garments of haze that turned pink in the light of the setting sun. In the distance two mighty oaks were seen, and once, when she walked to them, she saw the Arab peasant women of Malha dancing between them, lifting big dolls of cloth and straw and praying for rain; and though they called to her, she didn't dare come close and dance with them but only smiled at them from a distance.

In the center of the valley stood a huge building—the Monastery of the Cross, which the Arabs call Mutslabi, the biggest and most ancient monastery in the whole country. Enormous buttresses had been built against the walls; covered with lichen and mold, they looked like the legs of some prehistoric beast that had turned to stone in its flight. There was one tiny door in the wall, shut like an eye under brows of climbing plants. Beyond the wall appeared the sharp black crest of a cypress that looked to Mother like a prisoner stretching in his cell. There were also a few peepholes in the wall, and sometimes the monastery blinked: a tiny window would open and close again at once.

Sometimes the place filled with students and priests from Greece, but most days of the year only one monk lived there, a man from Kandia in Crete, along with his sister and mother, a spinster and a widow. The two women cooked his meals, mended and ironed his clothes, warmed and perfumed his bath water, scrubbed and toweled his flesh. A few times Sarah saw the pair of short women, dressed in black, creeping along the path like a pair of drone beetles, carrying baskets to the monastery. Once she also saw the monk himself, a tiny energetic man, emerge from the small door. He stretched, panted, stamped his foot, and burst into a trot. Like a rubber ball, he bounced around the walls of his prison, shedding robes and cries as he ran until he was down to a short white skirt and sandals with red thongs, leaping and shouting incomprehensible verses whose special rhythm made clear that they were ancient poems.

In springtime the soil of the little valley put forth a profusion of lush grass, and the Arabs of Malha and Sheikh Bader grazed their lambs there. The burnet turned red in myriads of tiny flowers that looked like the clay pots that earned it its name. Crab-apple trees blossomed in a white raiment, a pleasant smell of soap wafted from them, and wasps circled them. The wasps too had by now adopted the angry Jerusalem buzz, a buzz of envy, threat, and possession.

Jews gave the valley a wide berth, but no one did her any harm there. The inhabitants of the monastery thought her an eccentric pilgrim, the shepherds feared her height, the knob of her stick, and the goose that hopped around her. She loved to feel the sap of trodden stalks of asphodel on her toes, to spray the purple heads of briars with childish kicks, to catch and release lizards and locusts. Here she gathered the dried fruit of the storksbills and sat for hours watching them curl slowly and drill into the earth or the cloth of her dress.

On her return, everyone greeted her with dark looks. They didn't approve of a woman walking around alone and daring to go outside the city walls. Only Duduch welcomed her warmly. The two women were good friends and found consolation in each other's company. Duduch told Sarah what they said about her in the courtyard, and Sarah gave Duduch the gift her parents had sent her: a colored wooden doll containing another doll that also had a doll inside—four wooden dolls with the same smile and the same eyes and the same red cheeks and the same strange sweet name: Matryoshka.

Duduch was already known as a *nikogira*—a good and clean housekeeper; and she had bold black hair, and I can't tell of its blue sheen without recalling Laura, Laura Luthy, Thomas Tracy's and William Saroyan's girl. At that time, Duduch married Elijah Nathan, the love of her life, and discovered that marriage turned her beloved into a different man, a man of sick jealousy who forsook his calculations and his stars and didn't even allow her to stand at the window or go alone to the outhouse in the courtyard. She and Sarah played together a lot, like two little girls, and complained to one another about the death of their husbands' love, one under the silken sandal of the fitting and proper, the other under the tramping boot of jealousy and madness.

Chapter 11

On Dr. Korkidi's advice Sarah got pregnant again, and this time twins ran about in her womb. After she gave birth to me and Jacob, she purchased some goatskin bags and some bowls and opened a little dairy. She bought milk from the shepherds of Lifta and Abu Ghosh and specialized in day-old yogurt, ricotta cheese, and kefir. The smell of milk boiling in its kettle drew customers, cats, and furious competitors, and deposited a sourish ancient stratum of sediment in my memory. I am not drawn to smells, but I am gifted with the ability to reconstruct them. "The pleasures of sound are more magical to me than the pleasures of smell," said Saint Augustine, and added, "With the attractions of odors I am not much troubled. When absent I do not seek them; when present I do not refuse them; and am prepared ever to be without them." I swore to myself that I wouldn't put in a lot of quotations here, but sometimes I can't curb my desire. At any rate, because of my sharp nose, my soft brain, and my weak eyes, most of my memories of Jerusalem are smells and sounds, and only a few of them are pictures.

Even when we were infants, Mother noticed that Jacob and I couldn't recognize her from more than ten steps away. Yet when she told Father we didn't see very well, he responded with his favorite word of dismissal: "*Puntikos*." He declared that most of the inhabitants of the city had sick eyes of one kind or another, and concluded with one of his impenetrable sayings about sharp sight, which in Jerusalem had been nothing but a handicap from time immemorial.

Mother wasn't assuaged. Her long arms, her anxious shouts, and the stone walls of the courtyards and alleys kept us from going far from her. She also put her white goose in charge of us and, following the local custom, pinned notes to our shirts with our names and the name of our father written on them. A lot of children walked around Jerusalem like that in those days, and when I recall it now, I chuckle to myself, because we all looked like delegates to the biggest Jewish congress of them all: the congress of fearful mothers and their children who threaten to go astray.

Like many natives of the city, we too developed traits of orientation and recognition that had nothing to do with the sense of sight. The eye furnished us only a general and foggy view, while the nose and the ear, divination and memory, gave it an anchoring and a means of identification. Jerusalem presented her opaque curtains of stone to our weak pupils, beguiled our ears with bells and wails, laid us down on ponds of her smell. Despite that ability I mentioned, few are the smells I miss, and above all I have no wish to recapture the repulsive smells of my hometown. But in America—"the lovely trustful, dreamy enormous country," remember?— where I live and where many of the women have only one smell, the lack of stimuli sometimes leads me to recall that desperate, violent, and hopeless blend of kitchens, latrines, and the sweat of worshipers' toes. One by one, they rise up before me. From the stench of rot and blood in the butcher shops to the sweet aroma wafting from the tiny alcove of the hashish roaster. And sometimes, just as I enter some air-conditioned American store, a memory of the good warm smell of the miserable donkeys of Jerusalem will suddenly rise to my nose, those heavily laden donkeys with sores on their rumps and ankles, the skin on their necks and backs scraped to bleeding baldness by whips and bridles, and with it the smell of the dust that collects in the prints of their little jet-black hooves.

A bitter green smell rose from the wall where the cattle drovers urinated. They led the herds of the Steel brothers from the highlands of the Sudan, and the tremendous thundering of countless hooves raised clouds of haze that could be seen a week before they arrived, tinting the eastern horizon with red dust. The black drovers rounded them up with shouts, drumming, and goads of palm thorns, and they burst into the city with their mighty humps, roaring and nicking the walls of the alley with their horns. Like all who come to the gates of Jerusalem, these enormous cattle didn't know they were being driven to their bitter end until the walls of their fate rose high, closed on them, and led them to the slaughterhouse. Right after they coralled the herd in pens, the drovers were free for their ceremonial urinating on the wall of the Tower of Storks. They had so much urine, and it was so strong and pungent, that it melted karstic cavities in the chalky stone; and the Christians made fun of them, saying they had restrained themselves all the way, a journey of several months, so they could scrupulously observe the commandment of their *Mahdi* to make water on the holy stones of Jerusalem.

Warm and vibrant, the smells swept us off to the El-Atarin *souk*, a dim covered trap where no one saw well except those who blend mixtures of cloves, nutmeg, and coffee, and those who deal in drugs and perfumes. They had sat there for so many years that some of them had already gone blind, and the rest had pupils as wide as coins and the eyesight of an owl. In one of my earliest memories, a blurry image appears of a tall, stolid English soldier entering the *souk* with a confident step and tottering out the other end to fall on his face in the open sewer, where his beret sailed off like a small boat. Even after the tiny poignard was discovered stuck between his ribs, people continued to argue that he hadn't been murdered, since they were used to seeing foreigners emerge from the perfume *souk* with shaky knees, a dopey smile, and eyes rolling from the rich conjunction of smells and darkness.

There were other smells, because water was doled out in small quantities and the daily washing of the whole body was a luxury of the rich. In a blend of nausea, rage, and nostalgia—which, by the way, is the correct filter for photographing Jerusalem—I restore them today. The smoke of dung bonfires rose from the cloaks of the shepherds, sweat from the cracked necks of the stonecutters, a maternal smell of *kishek* cheese, lemon buds, and lamb fat from the hands of the Arab peasant women. I remember incense wafting from the priests and clinging to our bodies like a dark, hidden threat, the smell of bread trailing from the old Armenians, and the sour vapor rising from the fur hats of the Hasids, who wore them even in summer, and our father called them "*gatos muertos*," dead cats, because of the way they looked and smelled. A nice smell came from our neighbor's young bride when we all went out to see her coming back from the "*banyo de b'tulim*," the virgin's bath, and labdanum of the wounds of her body rose up, mixing with the rainwater smell of the women's *mikve*.

The Maman and Teitelbaum families, who were also in the dairy business, took up arms against Mother, and she didn't flinch. There were fights that ended in broken vessels and teeth, spilled milk and blood, and split goatskin bags and sacks of cheese. But when they falsely accused her of touching the milk during her period, mixing camel's milk with yogurt, and using an impure part of a calf's stomach to make cheese, the rabbis banned her products and she was forced to sell them to the hostels for tourists and pilgrims. When Jacob and I were two years old, she started climbing the Mount of Olives every morning and selling to the nuns of Mary Magdalene.

From there she went north on the ridge and sold kefir to the workers who were laying the foundations of the university on Mount Scopus. Sometimes she took us with her, and when we returned, riding together on the donkey halter she hoisted onto her broad back, she brought us to Reina de Geron and the refreshing perfume of her flowers.

On her sun-drenched balcony above the street of the Karaites, Reina de Geron placed pots of wood, earthenware, and tin, and grew flowers that overflowed the balcony ledge like cascades, flooding the alley with cool flames of smell and color. Aromas wafted from her courtyard night and day, from the *reina de la noche*, the fragrant white night-blooming flower; from the multihued blossoms of the tajuri, the purple sultan's daughter; from the profuse white butterflies of the jasmine, the purple sweet basil, and the chalices of the white lily brought here by the wives of the Crusaders who left them so their sons could find their way back to the Holy City.

People were always clustered at the wall of Reina's courtyard, seeking in her flowers a balm for their anguish, consolation and hope for the bitterness of their soul. By now they had despaired of the promises of the city, of her whiny prophets, her tarrying messiahs, her leaders puffed up with wealth and pride. Some of them lost control, took ladders, and climbed up to stick their heads in the petals and pick bouquets; and Reina de Geron, like generations of besieged Jerusalemites before her, prayed and cursed, pushed their ladders off the wall, and poured slops on them from her dishpans and the *basiniko* under her bed.

Mother, Jacob, and I stood in the alley and raised our heads. In our weak eyes Reina de Geron's flowers looked like distant clouds and colorful foggy lamb's fleece, but the smells of the lily and narcissus, the rose and dianthus, were sharp and clear, and every movement of the head changed their nuances and enhanced their richness. Many years later, when I was living in the United States, I once swam in a warm lake where cold currents moved like snakes' tongues. I recalled the smells of those flowers, which also moved side by side but didn't merge with one another. A memory of a smile rose in my heart and spread from there to my face. My hands grasped the waist of the woman swimming at my side. A young woman, she was, a redhead, handsome and tall, who constantly bemoaned the fact that she wasn't a boy. I hugged her, I laughed with a mouthful of bubbles, and plunged the two of us into the water so my beloved wouldn't see my tears.

Chapter 12

A nother summer came to an end. In the evening a wonderful breeze blew in the alleys like a prophesy of consolation, caressing damp necks, penetrating the stink of *abbayahs*, *capotas*, saddles, and cloaks, and calming man and beast. The Days of Awe stood at the gate, and with the approach of Yom Kippur everyone took care to improve his relations with his fellow man.

"The Creator-Blessed-Be-He says to man, Why do you come to me? First go to your fellow man," the neighbor women explained to Sarah when they came to apologize for offending and insulting her. But the impending holidays filled her with tension, and going to the synagogue was her Via Dolorosa. In the women's section, she knew, everyone would still look at her as if she were a man who had snuck in, and the sight of Abraham's back through the wooden partition wouldn't comfort her either. She didn't know the melodies of the prayers, nor did she understand their strange words.

"May we enjoy a good and sweet year." Abraham smiled at her when she brought to the table the plate of dates, the bowl of pomegranate seeds, apples in honey, *prasa*, pumpkin, leeks, pears, and beets. He explained to her that beets symbolized the beating of the foes, leeks stood for the blood that would leak from our enemies' veins, and pears for the repair of the evil decree against us.

When my brother's daughter Romi was bat-mitzvah, Father told her the same stories, and Romi, who looks a lot like her grandmother but is wiser and more wicked, suggested he serve poppy seeds at Purim in memory of Mordechai "speaking peace to all his seed."

"*Satanika!*" Father raged at her.

"And dates at Passover, Grandfather." She didn't let up. "For the Lord brought us out of Egypt with a mighty hand and an outstretched palm."

But Sarah loved those simple legends and the flavor of the holiday dishes. That year, after they had tasted and blessed the fruits, Bulisa Levy got up and, grinning broadly, went to the kitchen corner, and as Abraham declared, "May we be the head and not the tail" and "In memory of the sacrifice of Isaac," she returned and placed a lamb's head on the table. Everybody gasped in admiration. As for the head, it gazed drowsily at Sarah with eyes sleepy from baking so long and a smile of horror spread on its roasted lips. A lump of nausea gored her throat, her eyes rolled. She landed amid slivers of crushed fruit and broken glass, sticky webs of honey and vomit. A horrible commotion arose. Bulisa Levy shouted, "Shame, shame!" Abraham's whole body shook, and Sarah ran out of the courtyard.

That night, for the first time, she told Abraham she wanted to move somewhere else and open their own bakery. But Abraham, whose fear of new places and willful women silenced him, and whose main asset was his seat on the back of fifteen generations in Jerusalem, told her there was an economic depression in the land and this wasn't the time to leave this place.

"Never mind what happens, people will always eat the bread," she pleaded, but to no avail.

In spring, when everyone was busy cleaning and whitewashing their houses and doing laundry, and doors and windows stood wide open, the Nawarites, roving fortune tellers from India, began appearing in the courtyards, sowing anxiety among all the mothers of the city. They were known as thieves, carriers of disease, and kidnappers, and mother was no longer satisfied to pin notes to our shirts. When we went to play in the courtyard, she tied long strings of red wool to our wrists, and these twisted up to her wrist, got tangled, and made all three of us stumble. But it was because of those wool strings that we finally left the city.

The Nawarites, black and grimy as the sides of a kettle, with forked tongues, clad in rags, lived in the ancient cells of the jail of Habs el-Abid and among the tombstones at the Gate of Mercy. They knew all the tunnels under the city, and when English archaeologists excavated and discovered the Jebusite sewer, to their surprise they found two old Nawarites sitting there playing cards.

Equipped with empty sacks, nimble fingers, and dancing bears, they appeared in the courtyards. They pulled wheezing doves out of the *lapa* turbans wound around their heads, perfumed silk handkerchiefs from the buttocks of surprised donkeys, and hen's eggs, still warm and damp, from under the cloaks of blushing priests.

They tamed bear cubs in a very cruel way. The animal was made to stand on a hot tin, and then they played tunes on a violin and a noisy little bagpipe while four female dancers circled him in a ring of clasped hands. The miserable cub hopped and danced on the blazing tin, shrieking in indescribable torment and amazement. Everybody thought he was trying to imitate the dancers' movements, but the truth was that the ring of girls kept him from fleeing. Finally, one of the dancers would bend down and take him up in her arms, caress his bristly back, and dip his scorched paws in a pan of cold water. Thus the bears learned their lesson, and like people smitten by love, all it took was the sight of a violin or the scent of a dancer to revive the memory of the tune of pain and make them dance.

As soon as the tinkle of their earrings and the groans of their bears were heard in the alleys, Mother's white skin would turn red, then dark brown with anger.

"Dance, dance, *ya-ta'ban*," sang the bear tamer, and the bear would grimace and launch into a clumsy step that looked so much like the wedding dance of the Ashkenazi Hasids that the whole crowd burst into laughter and applause. When the bear tamer saw that attention was focused on his performing animal, he sent his wives, brothers, cousins, and children to steal food and pots from kitchens, babies from empty houses, and garments from clotheslines.

"Back in the Astrakhan," said Mother, "they teach children to walk on high wire and play the cards. Here they kill the child."

And indeed, a child who fell into the snares of the Nawarites did not return to the land of the living or the home of his father and mother, and even the English police detectives and their dogs couldn't find him. The kidnappers would abscond with their victim to one of their hidden burrows and smother him with a soft pillow of silk and down, so nice to the touch that it left an expression of bliss on the face of the murdered baby. Then they would slit the belly of the little corpse with a knife, fill it with potent drugs, and baste it with embroidery thread spun, said the Jerusalemites, from the webs of glowworms. One of their women would carry the dead child in her arms, deep in sweet dreams to all appearances, and thus they smuggled drugs from one country to another.

The city weighed ever more heavily on Mother's shoulders. Hatred swelled inside her, and when we were four years old, there was that incident with the red string that made her steal the Patriarch's carriage, kidnap her family, and flee Jerusalem.

It happened on our first day of school, when we were brought to the Talmud Torah of a little rubbi, cruel and loathsome, whose name I haven't managed to forget, but I don't want to mention it. Mother was very excited. True, she was illiterate, but unlike the other illiterate women of the courtyard, she didn't accept the rule that ignorance is destiny. "Need to learn," she kept telling us, "need alef-beit."

The classroom was half cellar, half pit, and its crumbling cement floor was covered with torn reed mats. All day long the boys knelt on the mats on numb legs, reciting their lessons. At that time Jacob and I were still tied together with that red wool string, and when we came to heder, we refused to untie the string and part from one another. When the rubbi pulled out a pair of scissors and was about to cut us apart, we raised a racket, got tangled in the string, and fell to the floor together.

A commotion started. The rubbi took his cow's tail lash down from the wall. "This is the *razon*, justice!" he said, hitting Jacob on his back and head and pinching my ears something awful.

In the afternoon Mother returned from Mount Scopus and hurried to heder to pamper us with *kantoniko*, a heel of bread dipped in salt and olive oil. When Jacob refused to eat and burst into tears, Mother's suspicions were aroused. She interrogated him until he went to the wall and showed her the whip. Mother took off his shirt and saw the red lash marks.

I remember the slow turning of the broad shoulders, the hands stretched out in the air, the deep flush that rose from her chest to her throat and face. A loud hiss was heard, and the white goose suddenly appeared flying heavily over the wall of the courtyard and landing in its center. A strange and bitter frost rose in the gleam of Mother's eyes. The rubbi immediately understood that trouble had overtaken him, and was already preparing to dart from his *bankita* and flee for his life. But the goose planted himself at the rubbi's legs, and with two long lioness strides Mother caught the man and pushed him down on his knees. She grabbed him by the nape of his neck and lashed him with the "*razon*" so hard even she couldn't stop herself.

The rubbi's shouts of fear and pain drew the denizens of the whole alley. The people were afraid to stop Mother, for dreadful was she in her rage, and the goose didn't let anyone get near. Here he is: his neck is twisted between his shoulders, his big wings are spread to half their span, curved like scimitars. Can you see him, my dear? He walks around Mother, his beak is orange and wide open. His voice rises in my ears. Seeking a quarrel. Whispering and hissing, keeping watch over his mistress.

Mother was like a woman possessed. Molly Seagram and Diana the Huntress all in one. She jumped on the swooning rubbi with her wooden clogs, screaming "I'm the Tartar! I'm the Tartar!" and other words nobody understood. She vomited up all the rage massed inside her. She picked the rubbi up, propped him on his waxen knees, and pounded his head against the wall. The thud was dull and pleasant. Crumbled plaster stained with blood dropped to the floor.

If Father hadn't been summoned, the rubbi would have been a dead man. He approached Mother, and everyone could tell that he too was in awe of her. But the moment she saw him she grew calm, sat down on the floor like a baby, with her legs spread out in front of her, rolled her yellow head, and began crying and striking her breast with her fist like an Arab mourner, both from shame and from the anger that wasn't completely slaked. Meanwhile, Dr. Korkidi also came and started tending to the rubbi. At last, pale and shaking with the enormity of the disgrace, Father managed to persuade Mother to stand up. She hoisted Jacob onto her shoulders, picked me up in one arm, laid the other on Father's narrow shoulder, and thus we returned home.

In the evening Dr. Korkidi came to us, scolded her for her violence, treated Jacob's wounds, and said things to Father that we couldn't hear.

As she told us later, when we were young men, it was then that she decided to flee Jerusalem. "The camel is already broken straw in back of all of 'em," said Romi, and burst out laughing. She loves to mimic her grandmother's broken Hebrew and to repeat some of her sentences. Just yesterday she asked me, "Make up your couch?" Sometimes it scares me that they look so much alike, and then I remind myself of what Henry Fielding said to the literary critic: "Another caution we would give thee, my good reptile, is, that thou dost not find out too near a resemblance between certain characters here introduced." That's what I tell myself, and I smile, calm down, and am consoled.

Chapter 13

On the night of the big quake, July 12, 1927, we ran away from the city. Everybody was sure that Father, Mother, Jacob, and I were buried under the rubble. Only two weeks later, when they cleared the heaps of stones and linked one fact with another, memory with gossip, and crumb with crumb, did they understand what had happened. But by then we were already far from Jerusalem, from the dairy, from Tia Duduch, and from Bulisa Levy, whom you are indeed correct, my dear, I should call Grandmother, but I have no desire to do so.

In the bowels of the carriage Mother hid the foundations of our future. A red-gray heating brick she had secretly removed from the depths of the baker Ergas's oven, to place as an amulet on the floor of the new oven she would build. A tiny leather bag of sour milk, properly fermented—oh, a small and quenching revenge—by a nonkosher piece of calf stomach. A piece of *levadura*, an aromatic sourdough starter, swaddled in cloth and breathing like a baby. Many years later, Jacob told me that the progeny of that starter dough Mother brought from Jerusalem still continued its leavening in his bakery, like those immortal molecules of albuminous sperm sprayed from generation to generation. But by then I knew my uncle Elijah was right. Human characteristics aren't content with the routine paths paved for them by heredity. They also pass in milk, in stories, in the touch of fingertips and the saliva of a kiss.

It was a hot night, but Mother didn't let us take the cover off the carriage. Right after we got out of the city she abandoned the highway and turned left onto the mule path leading to Dir Yassin; about a kilometer from the village she turned right and landed in a narrow, steep ravine with a winding road paved with stones. As we passed the smooth rocks of the ravine, a distant barking and a strong, unfamiliar smell filled my nostrils. A few weeks ago I went back there with Romi and peeled away all the new houses, streets, tombstones, and highways off the ground, and I found that road again and went down its slope. An old man picking Blood-of-the-Maccabees—what you call cornflowers—told me it had been paved by Titus when he went up to destroy the city and that no one could build roads like the Romans. There's an abandoned quarry there, and the sound of shooting rises from it, and that same smell came back and called to me from grape skins fermenting in the nearby winery, intoxicating proof of the quality of my memory.

Jacob and I glued our eyes to the pinprick holes in the carriage cover, flared our nostrils to smell the wet wildflowers, bent our ears to the noise of the wheels, to the heavy breathing and the tread of the wingèd sandals of our mother Sarah. Accompanied by the barking dogs of Kolonia, she crossed the cool bed of Shoreg Brook, and climbed the seven sharp twists of the mound of the Castel. We didn't marvel at her speed or her strength. Everybody knew that the mysteries and forces of another land and another people were forged in Mother's body.

A small village sat atop the mountain then, and beyond it Mother started groaning and stumbling with the effort to brake on the downgrade. From the foothills, not far from a grove of gigantic plane trees and the pallid ruins of a monastery, we heard the braying of scared mules, the grunting of camels, and the shouting of merchants. A pungent, startling smell of fish came from the mountains, where those who brought watermelons and fish from Gaza would park before ascending to Jerusalem; everything had been scattered by the quake that struck their camp. Amid chunks of broken watermelon and ice and wide-mouthed fish carcasses, nobody paid any attention to a carriage harnessed to a woman.

From here on out, opinions are divided. Jacob claims we hid among the vineyards of Abu Ghosh with a family that supplied milk to the dairy, while I maintain that Mother continued her assault on her road that same night, passed the village of Saris like the wind, and galloped along the bank of a deep riverbed with dark gloomy mountains on either side and a *khan* at the end.

"I remember clearly that we came to a big vineyard," Jacob tells me.

I also remember the vines, pruned and laden with fruit, but in my opinion those were the vineyards of the monastery of Latrun and the fields of Dir Ayub.

The sun was about to rise, Mother collapsed between the shafts as if an invisible scythe had lopped her off at the ankles. A thick smell of dust and burdock rose from her torn clothes and her wounded feet.

"Now shout," she whispered, her mouth full of dirt, "now shout, hit. To the Rusalem I don't go back."

And Father, scared by the darkness and the goose, with a cloth gag in his mouth, didn't answer.

For a week we were on the road. By night we traveled and by day we hid. The tones of the earth changed, its smell grew richer, and the tramp of the foot was answered by a soft rustle of flesh, and not the beating of boulders. Stars changed their places. Ruined wayside shelters and cactus hedges sprang up along our route. Mother's flying thighs never flagged. Mountain and valley, field and wasteland, brook and swamp, oleander and sycamore. The plain welcomed us with the open, shorn fields of August, warm, soft smells, and crushed plowed earth that held no stones or promises, and no memories or graves were rotting in it. I remember the scratching of coarse leaves against the side of the carriage, the bright silhouette of a distant Arab town with ancient olive trees turning silver all around, a muezzin singing, turrets and palm trees rising. I remember our arrival in the village, Mother arguing there with amazed people who didn't wear hats or sport beards. She was very agitated, stamping her foot and shouting, and Father sat on the side like a bundle of rags and didn't say a thing. By now Mother had removed his fetters because she knew he wouldn't run away. Shame and honor were the strongest chains his world knew, and they wouldn't let him return to Jerusalem to be an object of derision.

Slowly the argument and the shouting died out, and a woman invited us to eat and spend the night in one of the huts. The next evening a loaded wooden wagon appeared in the village, harnessed to a big ox, and with it came Mother's father and brothers and a mule with a terrified, bleating heifer tied to its back. Mother fell on their shoulders, wept with joy, hugged the ox's neck. "He was little, he was little," she repeated, and beat the animal's forehead fondly.

I was surprised to discover that Mother wasn't the only one of her species in the world. Her brothers were big like she was, with wrists as thick and strong as hers. But my attention was riveted on my grandfather, the convert Mikhail Nazaroff, whom I saw then for the first and only time. He was even taller than Mother and her brothers, and his countenance—"that masterpiece of force and melancholy"—immediately touched my childish heart and was seared there like a brand.

His face pink, like a youth filled with the sap of life,
His beard long and gray, each hair steeped in silver,

Falling in curls on his torso and vaulted chest;
Eyebrows too are silvery, hairy, and thick,
Taut like arches, joining each other, a boundary to his delicate forehead.

When I was twenty-one and Jacob took Leah away from me and I ran off to the United States, I made a few literary pilgrimages. I didn't get to the Crimean Peninsula, but I did visit Hannibal, Fresno, Walden, and Nantucket. In the library in Camden, as I was looking at a picture of Walt Whitman, two things occurred to me. One was that Whitman's face looked a lot like my grandfather's, even though Whitman, being a poet, had to look more sensitive. And right after that, as if taking hold of the heel of the first memory, was born the knowledge that I had seen the picture of Whitman back in my childhood, on the wall of the village library, and the line Yehiel Abramson, the librarian, selected to put under the picture floated up in my mind: "Behold! I do not give lectures or a little charity,/ When I give I give myself." But back then, in the presence of Walt Whitman's picture in that library, I wasn't reminded of Dyedushka Mikhail.

Grandfather wore a gray cap and a shirt belted with a rope; big blue patches adorned his trousers, and his hands were as enormous as baker's shovels. I was about five years old then, couldn't fathom his expression, and didn't understand what I do today—that Dyedushka Mikhail wanted to experience again the pain of his circumcision. Two years later he died in an awful catastrophe. Walking barefoot in a field, he cut his toe on a sharp, flinty rock, and the infection poisoned his blood and killed him in horrible torment. "He's not live," Mother lamented her father, and then she whispered to us, "He had the dreadful death."

Grandfather drank three glasses of boiling tea one after another, his eyes shut, his lips taut, and with every mouthful he sighed and said, "Ah . . . that's good. . . . Ah . . . that's good. . . ." When he saw Jacob and me watching him, he smiled and picked us up in his arms, and even then I could feel that like Mother, he too was drawn more to my brother, for Jacob is built like Father and has his coloring. "Little Jew," he called him proudly, and laughed, tears of joy glimmering in his eyes. He caressed and hugged me too, but out of simple affection; jumbo redheaded children were no novelty in his family. After he finished his tea he went to Father and said, "It will be good, Abraham, it will be good." But Father, sitting off to the side with his head bowed, didn't extend his hand to him, and the old convert said no more but turned and began telling his sons what they were to do that day.

Summer reigned, and Mother's brothers quickly erected a big hut of cloth, branches, and posts for us. From the wagon they unloaded sacks of cement and gravel, tools, wooden beams, and molds for making bricks. They had the wisdom of peasants. First they built the oven, because the oven for a family, they said, is like the anchor for a ship and the roots for a tree. "Once upon a time," Grandfather told us, "trees didn't have any roots and they could walk." But then they didn't give fruit because they were too busy with wars, expeditions, and courtship. So they got together and decided to have themselves planted in the ground.

Every morning, the men in Mother's family proudly wrapped themselves in *tallises* too narrow to cover their broad shoulders and fastened the straps of the *tefillin* with a force known only to ascetics, ox drivers, and barge haulers. Veins thick as ropes stood out in their flesh. They prayed hesitantly, with slow, heavy words that got tangled in their beards and brought an expression of contempt to Father's face. Afterward they spat noisily on the palms of their hands and got down to work. The oven they built looked like a giant belly with a chimney sprouting from it. The uncles rigged up a heavy black iron door that could be raised and lowered with a mechanism of cogs and sprocket wheels. Beside it they introduced an innovation: a peephole with a thick glass pane so you could shine a light through and watch the loaves as they baked. They attached an oil burner to the door, the acme of progress and perfection in those days, seen only among the German bakers in their villages; it had a long arm that turned on an axle so you could direct the spout to every corner of the oven's belly. A steam bellows fanned the fire inside, and there was a black cast-iron boiler and a three-headed Swedish Primus stove. At the bottom of the door, they dug the baker's pit, where the oven man plies his trade, and floored it with stone tiles.

After the oven was completed they built the bakery itself around it, with a workroom and a storeroom with thick masonry walls, and only then did they build us a small house with two rooms and a kitchen.

"What a good hands my brothers have," said Mother proudly. She worked alongside them, she hauled, dug, erected, and cast, and also made us meals in a pot that hung over a fire in the yard, planted trees, and put up a fence. She loved borders, and she loved even more the area they circumscribed. Our new neighbor brought us a jug of milk. "Pay me later with bread, Frau Levy," he laughed, in an accent brand-new to us. His name was Isaac Brinker, and I'll tell you about him later. Mother made sour kefir for us all and invited Brinker to have some too, and all the while Father sat with a melancholy expression, like a prisoner among his wardens, the white kerchief of torment bound around his forehead, but here in the new place no one understood what it meant.

When the work was done, we all gathered at the oven, and even Father stirred from his place to come to the first lighting. Dyedushka Mikhail grabbed his shoulders and said, "Please, Abraham."

Father puffed out his lips in perfect imitation of a child trying to blow out the candles on his birthday cake. He lit the big Primus stove, and when the steam was compressed in the tank, he opened the cock of the oil spigot and put a burning rag to the spout of the burner. How well I remember that moment when the fire laughed and the steam burst and shot the flame inside. For a long time Father listened to the roar of the burner, turned the spout first to the right and then to the left, then fired the center of the oven, and went on like that until it grew dark outside and the bricks glowed with a dark and pleasant redness reflected in all our faces.

Father turned off the burner and an awful silence prevailed. He put a finger to his lips so no one would utter a word, went down to the pit, and listened for the rustle of the bricks cooling. A few cracks were heard, but not a single brick slipped out of place. Everyone stepped back, and Father put his hand inside and turned his palm here and there to test the quality of the heat and its feel, and studied the nature of the new oven. Then he gathered saliva in his mouth and spat inside as Isaac Ergas had taught him in Jerusalem, bending his ear to decipher the vaporizing whisper with incomparable expertise. Years later, when I wanted to explain to my readers the fact that every brick oven has its own personality, I described the construction of that oven, but there I chose to write that it was built in Jerusalem, not by Mother's brothers but by the famous oven builder Gershom Zilberberg, a Polish Hasid who never really existed.

When everybody went to sleep, Father remained at his new oven. All night he lay near the door and stuck his hand inside from time to time, stroked the blazing bricks, and closed his eyes.

In the morning the brothers took simple carpentry tools out of their wagon, and following his instructions, they planed and smoothed boards for the work table, built the *gareh*, as they called the rising chamber, and made sieves, kneading troughs, and long and short baker's shovels. Then the youngest of them harnessed the ox, and in the evening he returned with sacks of flour, yeast, sugar, salt, and cans of oil. After the brothers unloaded the flour and sifted it, they asked Father to bake bread.

Jacob, who doesn't remember anything from that night, and I, who remember more than what happened on it, huddled together on the side, and those moments when the Primus stove and the burner roared and the sourish, living smell of the yeast spread in the air—I remember them well, even though Jacob claims I'm taking Mother's stories apart and reconstructing them. "What else have you got to do there in America but sit and waste time and make up memories?" he grumbles. I admit he's right. I'll tell the truth: sometimes I lie.

Father emptied the sacks of flour into the kneading troughs, added water and sugar and salt, and poured in the yeast mixture. The dough began to rise and give off its sour smell, and Mother rolled up her sleeves and started kneading—folding, beating, pulling, pounding. Tears spilled from her eyes onto the dough, and sweat and snot joined them. Her face blazed from the effort, and deep groans rose from the valley between her breasts. Barefoot she was, and whenever her hands raked the dough, the big muscles in her legs bulged, the Achilles tendons in her heels stretched taut, and her toes clenched hard, gripping the ground. When the dough rose, Father cut it into pieces, shaped them into round loaves, and put them in the new *gareh* to rise some more.

Half an hour later he turned off the burner, closed the chimney, sprayed a quarter of a bucket of water on the white-hot bricks, went down into the pit, grabbed the shovel, and started shooting the loaves into the oven with fine, precise hands. When the smell of baked bread filled the air, everybody got excited and smiled at one another. Father took his bread out of the oven and immediately sprinkled glaze on the hot crust. Mother took the first loaf, broke it, and gave everyone a piece. "For he who made us live and exist and brought us to this time," said Dyedushka Mikhail, dipping his hot morsel of bread in the plate of salt, and we all ate.

Less than two minutes later a tumult arose outside. The village people came running, their heavy shoes clumping. The smell emanating from the new bakery hovered like a cloud of sweetness over their poor huts, flooded their dusty street, burst through walls of wood and tattered blankets, and struck their nostrils. They brought cheese, tomatoes, and olives, they even found liquor and herring somewhere. Isaac Brinker, the friendly neighbor, spread a tablecloth on the cutting boards, and everybody smiled and laughed and sang, patted Father on the shoulder, hugged us and each other. It had been only a year since they settled on the land, and their happiness filled the space.

"Now we've got a bakery," they said. "May it bring good luck for all of us."

Mother sliced bread for everybody, Father smiled, and for a moment he even looked content. We didn't know back then that he would never recover from the humiliation—from the kidnapping, the binding, the building of the bakery by the "Russkies." Even though he knew that if not for "her," her strength and energy, he would have remained a baker's apprentice to the end of his days, a miserable and wretched Jerusalem *orniro*, he nursed a hostility for her that rose and flourished until it took on a life of its own and no longer needed tending since, like all hatred, it was sustained by its own leaven.

And Mother, whose big body hid a grateful twelve-year-old gooseherd, wet with rain, throbbing and smitten with love, never stopped loving him for a single day.

Chapter 14

A nd here, here's a picture of Jamila I see in my mind's eye, blurry and tremulous as if emerging in a pan of developing fluid. Here she comes—coins tinkling on the embroidery of her bodice, the ring green in her nose—bringing us a wicker basket of homegrown Baladi apricots, the most wonderful fruit in the world if you know how to get the worms out. Here's Mother, giving her stale bread to feed her chickens. Father would fume and say we had to feed our own chickens first, and Mother would answer: "There's enough for everybody, Abraham. For us and for thems too." Jamila had a big Cypriot she-ass, white and light-footed, and when she got pregnant by our donkey, Father declared, "Congratulations, now the Arab woman and the Russkie woman are in-laws."

Apparently Mother poured her heart out to her in-law, for the Arab woman came to her aid. It was springtime, rain was still falling now and then, and Jamila told Mother to take vats into the yard and collect the spring rainwater in them. The next day she gathered an enormous bundle of camomile in the hills and told Mother to soak it in the water she had collected and shampoo her hair with it. That's what Arab peasant women do, she said, to revive love.

Mother followed her instructions, and I still remember the wonderful effect of that shampoo on her hair. A pungent smell, full and seductive, rose from her head, and her fair braids shone with a new intensity. That day she walked around as if a crown had been put on her head, naïvely believing the fragrance of rain and field would lead Father to love her again. Jacob and I peeped out the bakery window as she heated the rainwater on the Primus stove, took off her blouse, and, weeping mutely, bent over the big basin. It was the same basin she used to wash Jacob and me, and say, "Shut your eyes," when she lathered our heads with the stinging Nablus soap.

She had a fair neck, the arms of a wrestler, broad white shoulders, and the pale, delicate nipples of a little girl. Her fair skin gleamed in the permanent gloom of the bakery, muscles rippled in her back and her long, prominent shoulder blades. Her hair, in choked serpents of red and gold, floated in the perfumed water. Only now, as I dredge those pictures up from the darkroom of my memory, do I begin to understand them—the tremor of her fingers when she brought food to the table, her extinguished looks while kneading the dough, her frightened smile when she looked in a mirror, her childish, coarse, repentant voice: "Abraham, Abraham, Abraham . . ."

I spent my whole childhood and youth in the shadow of my brother's love for Leah and in the shadow of my father's hatred for my mother. At first I didn't understand, then I refused to understand, and finally the knowledge swooped down on me, grabbed me by the scruff of the neck, and hurled me from this house to the ends of the earth.

Chapter 15

Early in the morning, compunctions rise from my father's room. Should he have slept all night with the window open? Should he put on his shirt before his pants? And what is "the good way" to button it? From the bottom button up or vice-versa?

From the kitchen comes the clatter of dishes. Tia Duduch is already putting on the pots. From the bakery comes the noise of my brother Jacob and our cousin Simon working, dragging crates of bread and preparing deliveries. Leah, my brother's wife, is sleeping in her room. All of their three children are where they belong. Michael, their little son, is in the nursery. Benjamin, their firstborn, is in his grave. Romi has already slipped off to the city.

How loud and orderly is the singing of the awakening birds. First—as in my childhood—come the bulbuls, clustered like dark balls on the branches of the lemon tree and the electrical wires, their feathers puffed out and bristling with the chill of dawn, the yellow trim under their tails mocking the gravity of their black skullcaps. The crowing of the roosters and the lowing of the hungry calves are no longer heard in the village, but the bulbuls, as in the days when we first came here, still chatter every morning and tell their unchanging dreams. When the sparrows join the conversation, they start singing, and their voices roll up their throats like transparent marbles. Then the male blackbirds stir, opening their orange beaks wide in song, or whistles, or imitation prayers, until the sun rises to the shrill screams of the jays, the graceful and violent hoodlums of the gardens.

Father, from his room on the other side of the house, is still debating aloud with himself: "Now I'll put my feet out of the bed and put on my house slippers. Then I'll go to the toilet, and then I'll drink coffee, and then I'll shave." And after a brief silence: "No! First I'll shave, and then I'll drink coffee, and I'll walk around a little, and then I'll have a good bowel movement."

"Either you come take care of him or I'll throw him out of the house," Jacob wrote me. "You know I never got along with him, and now I've had it up to here. He shouts all the time that he has pains. No doctor finds anything wrong with him. I can't stand him anymore, I never could stand him, and I've got enough troubles without him. He's your father too, so please!"

And I, who didn't go to my mother's funeral or my nephews' circumcisions, packed three suitcases that very day, left a note on the door, a stupid joke addressed to no one in particular—"The baker will be away for a month. If knead be, please apply to Dr. Norstrom, Boulevard Haussman 66"—took the train to New York, and flew home. On entering the village, I told the cab driver to go on and unload the suitcases at the gate of our yard, and I got out and walked down the street.

Groping, recognizing, my memories strode ahead of me, barking with excitement. It was very early in the morning, and the old rumbling of the palm dove rose from the vistas of casuarinas and fig trees, as if it had been there for years and had only now managed to burst from the foliage.

The little houses of the peasants had changed owners, added years and floors and wealth, and become splendid villas covered with cold carapaces of marble and furs of vines. Smells and gurgles of first pots of coffee filtered through the fragrant hedges, and farther away, signals of my brother Jacob's fresh bread beckoned me, telling me I had returned, reminding and tempting with their sweet siren song.

In a photograph of an old landscape, I ascended to my house, walking toward my brother's hug, my father's weeping, and my own tears. Return home, you are surely chuckling, my dear, return to the hardships? The storms? And the rocks tossed by the giant? And who are your Circe and Scylla? And who is the woman waiting? And what is more hackneyed than the return home? "Only a book about the return home is more tedious than the return itself."

The gate to the yard was already wide open, and a rickety-looking truck, its doors gaping, was maneuvering to back into it to load the crates of bread. Only now did I remember that at the entrance to the village I had passed the cemetery and hadn't gone to Mother's and Benjamin's graves.

Inside the yard, the old pickup truck was also parked, the one painted a dreadful yellow that belonged to Romi, my brother's daughter; and for a moment my heart stopped because Romi herself appeared on the porch. Fair and tall she is, handsome and broad-shouldered. A cruel prank of yearning. With a single jump she leaped down all four steps and wound her strong arms around my neck. She kissed me on the mouth, tilted her face back, and looked at me with pleasure. She has the face of a boy; her lips are soft and expressive, and her eyes, wide-set yellow-blue pansies, "a blossom of sky and a blossom of gold," are laughing under her thick fair eyebrows.

"What did you bring me, Uncle?" she breathed into my neck.

As soon as I went into the bakery the flour dust tickled my throat again, and the smooth smell of the glaze and the strong, sour taste of the *levadura* grabbed me, and my brother Jacob's arms bound my shoulders. What is more emotional than coming back home? Not even the book that will be written about it. Hugging and crying, we crossed the yard, climbed the four steps to the porch, entered the house, and went down the long corridor to Father's room.

Lying on his bed, his shirt white against his skin, his thin hair combed back, my father's smile melted into a thin quiver, and became real weeping at the corners of his mouth. His two withered, hairless hands stretched from the bed as I knelt there before him, pitying, and embracing.

The *shakikira de raki*, the handkerchief soaked in arak, was wound around his forehead as a banner of misery, and under a veil of anise the smell of the glue on the envelopes of his letters snuck over to me, the smell of brown age spots blossoming on his hands, the smell of creases etched in his singed neck by the white-hot baking oven and the love fire of Sarah our mother.

"Well, he came, Father," Jacob announced impatiently. "He came, you can take the rag off your head now. Everybody sees you've got pains, you don't need to cry. I told you he'd come."

A thin, delicate little boy was hiding behind my brother's legs, peeking at us as his fingers played with an old pearl necklace he was wearing. Up to now I had seen him only in the pictures Romi had sent me.

"And here's Michael," I called. I bent down and picked him up.

Jacob, I saw out of the corner of my eye, grew tense. He almost jumped to take his little son away from me but immediately mastered the storm assailing his body, smiled, and said, "Come on, I've made up a room for you. You must want to eat and wash and rest up."

He fixed a salad and omelets, sliced his bread, made sweet coffee with milk. "I'm as happy as thirty pigs," I said, and Jacob asked affectionately what book I was quoting from now.

"Quick, outside, for a picture in honor of Uncle!" Romi shooed us onto the porch. "An automatic family picture," she said, all frenzied activity. She dragged armchairs and little spotlights, stretched sheets on the wall. "You stand next to your brother," she scolded me. Simon, on the other side of Jacob, held Michael in his arms. Romi took the big pictures of Mother and Benjamin and propped them on Father and Duduch, who sat in the armchairs. She herself stood next to me. All of us fell silent. "Look at the camera!" The hum of the mechanism was heard. The tiny hourglass in it emptied. The blade of the shutter held its breath.

"Don't laugh. Don't move. Don't breathe," ordered Romi. "Whoever moves will turn old in a second."

The picture was taken.

Afterward I distributed gifts. I brought Father four kinds of aftershave, two white cotton shirts, and a pair of sealskin house slippers. For my brother Jacob a Stanley toolbox and a state-of-the-art radio that could pick up the distant programs of the early morning hours. As he requested, I brought Michael two costumes, one of the Angel of Death and one of a "regular angel," and all kinds of magic tricks. For Romi, aside from the little Olympus she asked for, I also brought a new tripod, photograph albums of William Klein, Ansel Adams, and Helen Levitt, and a numbered copy of the series *Life and Landscape in Norfolk* by Emerson, which, as you can imagine, cost me a small fortune. For Tia Duduch—"the ugly dwarf," Romi calls her—I brought a new black dress and black shoes to make her life easier in old age, and for her son Simon a cane and three kilos of assorted candy.

Jacob had prepared the room we once shared. Romi lugged my suitcases there and examined my clothes as she hung them in the closet.

"I love the way you dress," she said.

When she saw me groping around, she burst out laughing. "They're hanging on your neck, dummy." She came and put my glasses on my nose. She's as tall as I am, her hair is red like mine, and when she stands in front of me, a sweet breath blows from her mouth straight into my face. She calls me "Uncle," and when she's in a good mood or wants to please me—"Unk the Hunk."

"Let's pretend," she said, "that you're a fragrant mouse and I'm a hungry cat."

"Let's pretend," answered Unk the Hunk, "that I'm a Persian rug and you're a teaspoon."

"When will you bring me a dress instead of a camera?"

"When you learn how to behave."

"I haven't stopped messing you for a minute," she said. She knew all the stories about her grandmother, even though Sarah had died before she was born, and imitated her with a precision that was scary because they looked so much alike.

"And you're not nice to me," she announced, turned her back, and went on arranging my clothes in the closet.

Chapter 16

Fifty years passed. Mother—sturdy and healthy as an ox—is dead. Father—small, sickly, and pampered—is still alive. The goose has been devoured, the Patriarch's carriage is crumbling in back of the bakery. Jacob and I grew up, and each of us went his own way. He, to sum up briefly, married the woman I had destined for myself, inherited the bakery my father had destined for me, sired three children, and lost his firstborn son. I went to the United States, didn't get married, didn't sire children, and didn't lose any. That, in fact, is the whole story. But—and I apologize to you again, my dear, for my tendency to quote—"detail is always welcome."

Fifty years passed, and the hands of fate didn't make me and my twin brother any more alike. Only the lenses of our glasses remained identical as they grew thicker. I am still a head taller than Jacob, broad and strong and more reserved, and while my thick red hair is laced with only a trace of white, my brother's black hair is falling out. The years I have spent in a pleasant house, in a comfortable and detached country, in a temperate seashore climate in cotton clothes from Lands' End, in the arms of amused, amusing, and grateful women, my brother has spent at a blazing oven, at his son's cold grave, at the closed door of his wife's room.

Like my father and my brother, I also make my living from bread, but I don't bake it anymore. I write about it. I jettisoned the family tradition of suffering, the inferno of the oven, the heat of the pans, the dead weight of flour sacks. When Mother was alive, she cursed me and called me "traitor," and indeed, I am a man of words and recipes. Farewell, cracked eyelids and scorched hands. Take away from me the baker's cough, the fetters of dough. A burner roars, Get out. I'm sorry if I seem to be apologizing.

Chapter 17

N ow I'm turning my shirt inside out," Father announces from his room. "Here . . . like this . . . first right and then left."

Old age is returning my father to the fierce battles of children against the rest of the world. He resumes the discussion of questions everyone else has answered as a baby—which arm is to be thrust into the sleeve first, how to aim the sweater so the front faces front. With trembling fingers and weak eyes, he reports for combat. He fights rebellious shoelaces that refuse to be threaded through their holes, mocking shirts that won't be buttoned, people who are taller and smarter than he is, who know what's good for him.

Bitterly and at length he consults—with me, with himself, with the heroes of his memories—about his tendency to toss and turn in his sleep. "What's the good way to sleep? Only on the side of the heart." He imparts his lesson to me. "If you sleep on your stomach, it gives you gallstones, and if you lie on your back, kidney stones."

"What a terrible thing happened to such a little boy," I heard him murmuring to his reflection in the mirror. I couldn't help laughing, despite the obvious anger in Father's voice. Even his body—that crumbling clod of treacherous malcontent flesh—deserted to his enemies, lay in ambush for him at the Ford Jabbock of his old age, and surprised him every day with new deceits: shaking fingers, shortness of breath and memory, dams of constipation not even his fig-in-olive-oil marinade could loose. And, above all, the pains. Wicked, with no rhyme or reason. "An old man," he said to me, "doesn't see well and doesn't taste well and doesn't hear well, but pains he feels just like a youth."

He prepares like a demolition expert and chronicles his activities. The mumbling words seem to ooze from his skin: "Now I'm going to the table. . . .

Slowly, slowly. . . . I cut myself a slice of bread. . . . Carefully. . . . Put margarine on it. . . . Like this. . . . And now I'll sit down to eat. . . . Chewing slowly."

Worst of all are the domino games he always loses because he won't stop describing his stratagems aloud, along with which tiles he's holding in his hand.

"Why do you do that?" I say, flying into a rage and sweeping the tiles off the table. "That's a secret. The whole point about dominoes is that I'm not supposed to know what tiles you have."

"Why?" replies Father joyfully. "It's not what you think. It's because I might die any minute, and I want everybody to know what my last words were."

His memory is like mine, alert and strong. Yesterday the spirit moved me, and I went into the kitchen and magically revived Mother's fruit compote, the one with black plums, slices of lemon, and quince. "The compotes is very got," Romi said, and we all laughed. That's how Mother herself would laud her own compote, because Father never bothered to praise it. This time too he ate it eagerly, but its taste resurrected ancient terrors in him, and he kept squinting to either side as if "she," the Russkie mare, was lying in wait for him in some corner.

He's a terrified man, anxious and haunted. Every descent from bed is liable to turn into a nocturnal adventure many times more dangerous than his trek through the desert. The dark of night, the frailty of his body, and his poor sense of direction combine to turn the house into one gigantic labyrinth where he can't get his bearings. One night, he told me in an embarrassed and furious whisper, he went to the toilet and groped his way back from door to door until he found his room and lay down. A few minutes later he felt a body next to him and was petrified. All night long he lay awake, not daring to move a muscle. Only when the sun rose and its beams penetrated the cracks in the shutter did he look over and see that he was lying in his dead grandson's bed with his daughter-in-law Leah at his side.

He gradually turned his room into a small apartment so he didn't have to go out and encounter other people. It was easier for everyone that way. Simon made him a marble tabletop, shelves for dishes, and a sink. Here he inspects his body, listens to his memories, makes countless cups of coffee on the small gas burner, and offers them to me proudly: "You don't have coffee like this in America."

As we drink, he tells me again about the dwarves of pain who have invaded his body.

"The first ones to know a human being is going to die are his pains," he said, "and then they leave him and go look for somebody else. That's the way they found me, and that's the only way they'll leave me."

"They come from outside?" I wondered. "I thought pains come from inside."

"Outside," Father affirmed.

Later he interrogated me about my own house. "Describe every room in it," he asked.

"And all that comes from your books?" He was impressed. "Pictures and television and cabinets and sofas?"

"It's not so much, Father."

"And women of the Covenant, you meet there?"

I smiled. Father saw that a roundabout approach wouldn't work, and he attacked: "Now maybe you'll want to get married, maybe you'll want the bakery?"

"The Leah and the bakery are the Jacob's." I imitated Mother too, and Father screwed up his face.

"*Pustema*," he said, lifting his hand. "Don't let her come into my room," he ordered.

I felt thin blades of compassion pierce my chest. His memories of Mother were so strong and fresh he sometimes forgot she was dead.

"She isn't here anymore, Father. When will you understand that?"

She died one year after I left for America, from a quick virulent cancer, the kind only a body like hers could engender, and I didn't come to her funeral.

"I understand, I understand. She can hug me, break my rib, and then the rib cuts the lungs and the spleen. She can choke with her kisses, the *cabailla*, she's not like our women. I didn't tell you about Mr. Nissim Alkalay? How he died from a woman's kiss?"

He lies on his back in the middle of the bed, and I sit at the foot. His ankle is on my thigh, and I'm cutting his toenails. In this bizarre position I see that his nostrils have sprouted a fringe of fresh black hair.

"Shall I cut the hairs in your nose, Father?"

"Later," he answers. "First the nails, then the hairs."

The nails of his big toes are yellow and recalcitrant as bone, and Mother's old pinking shears are the only thing that can cut them. When I finished, he sat up and cut his fingernails. Very slowly he cut them, his tongue poking out and retreating in time with the scissor blades. Then he gathered the crop of cut fingernails into an ashtray and burned them on a tiny pyre of matchsticks—a remedy against a host of evil spirits that congregate around anyone who cuts his hair or his fingernails.

Finally he got up with a groan and aired the room of the stench of his little fire. "Nothing happens the first time anymore, and nothing happens only once in a life. What's easier to think about? What will be or what already was? Now put my shoes on my feet and let's go to the doctor. Let's not be late."

I kneel down before him, pull his socks up on his calves, tie his laces with a double knot, as he likes. His conversation, like the endless spaghetti of Saroyan's barber, unfurls into my ears.

In the pain clinic patients were already waiting. "Now I sit down. . . . Carefully. . . Straighten my leg . . . ," Father murmured, collapsing gloriously into an armchair, smiling at his neighbors with the gracious benevolence of a victor. They replied with frozen, angry expressions.

Like men at a urinal, the patients glance at one another covertly, as if comparing the size of their pain. Each is enveloped in the coil of his torments; their lips move but their voices are not heard. Migraine sufferers, their pupils tiny as pinheads the only hint of their illness. People with backaches, faces contorted in anticipation of the spasm. People with pancreatic cancer, bent like pocket knives, chests glued to their knees, faces hot and white. Masons of torment, hewing the deadly gravel of bladder and kidneys from their own flesh. Some of them are young, and their pain is training their bodies for distant death; some are old and their pain is the only relative who still visits them in their isolation. They touch and stroke themselves with such concentration that it's hard to know if they want to calm the pain or encourage it.

"Pain is the *razon*," Father explains to me with solemn decisiveness, "justice," and suddenly, fifty years after the rubbi whipped Jacob, I understand that for Father pain is merely an instrument of punishment destined for man by the nature of his creation, "like honor and love and memory."

The doctor came out of his office and smiled at Father. He likes him, praises his Hebrew and his appearance. Father's black trousers are always ironed. His shoes are shined. His shirt is white. You won't find old-age spots of soup and urine on his clothes, no faded sediment of sweat or drips of egg yolk.

"Come on, Father," I said, "it's your turn now."

The patients lifted their faces in envy and resentment, and the doctor, like the angel in charge of torment, raised his hand.

"Everyone is in pain," he said, "everyone. Please, Mr. Levy."

I went in too.

"How do you feel, Mr. Levy?" asked the doctor.

"No good, no good."

Father's finger slid up his leg and moved from his groin to his stomach, sketching the route of the new pain. Jacob had warned me in advance of the visit. "Just give him an audience," he said, "and you'll see what he can do." With the precision and pride of an inventor, Father described for the doctor the paths of his agonies and their wiles. "First a flicker in my foot, here, a nothing, a little *lampa* goes on. But by now I know the bastard. Very slowly he creeps, circles, climbs up to my thigh, and from there, with tiny steps, he steals into my guts, settles down, makes himself right at home. A *ziara* of torments."

"How does he creep?" asked the doctor. "How does the pain creep, Mr. Levy?"

All patients, he told me later, have a hard time describing their pain in words. Every account begins with "like"—"like a knife, like fire, like a saw, like black dots in my flesh." He has an interesting collection of such metaphors which he records from the patients: "Like a cloud in my stomach, like an animal's teeth, like small explosions in my head, like black smoke in my liver, like the pain of love but in my leg. Nice, isn't it? Nice and not clear. There's an absurdity for you to ponder, Mr. Levy: the metaphor is such a personal thing you're sure the whole world must understand it."

"There are some things I say that everybody understands. For example, pain is like chains on my hands," said Father. "But there's also a pain like a lemon in my shoulder, and there's a pain like a disgrace in my flesh. My sons don't understand that, and Your Honor does."

"In fact, pain turns them into poets." The doctor was moved. "For one upright walk to the grocery store, for one night of sleep, they open their most hidden treasure to me. The treasure of metaphors."

A naïve and friendly man, my father's doctor, a fool who believes everything.

Chapter 18

A hedge of passion flowers quickly twined around our house. Big blue eyes blinked in it. Beyond it stretched expanses of open, blurry fields, and beyond them a soft, evasive horizon played with our sight. There were mountains too, not far away but yet invisible to our weak eyes; the only evidence of their existence were the wadis that descended from them and the wind that brought their wild smell.

In the new place everything was different. The village was only three years old, its trees had yet to bear fruit, its people had yet to see a blessing from their labor. But for us refugees from Jerusalem delights and wonders were prepared here. New sounds were heard: squeaking mice from the field, trilling falcons from the sky, mooing and neighing from the barns. The hoarse toads of the Jerusalem cisterns gave way to jolly frogs frolicking in the nearby riverbed; they had bright shapely bodies, they leaped like dancers in the shallow ditches of water, and they could sing in two voices— and when the heron's beak caught them, in three. The most colorful birds—the common roller, the bee-eater, and the kingfisher—who in Jerusalem, nested only in the glass cabinets in that story about Ernst Grimholz's taxidermy collection, here hopped among real wild trees near the brook. The crickets, who in Jerusalem sang lonely songs of poverty, here chirped loudly and gladly "a very lovely song of one that hath a pleasant voice." Blackbirds whistled in field and garden. Jackals and wolves howled in the mountains. Flowers glistened on the earth instead of drying between the olive-wood bindings of albums for pilgrims.

Mother was happy. Her hands never stopped working. She didn't seem to need any rest or sleep. All night long she kneaded and baked, and during the day she tended her garden and her house. Every morning I woke to the sound of her slurping tea and sighing with pleasure in between: "Ah . . . that's good. . . . Ah . . . that's good!" In my weak childish eyes she looked mature, strong, and wise, but now I know that she was not only young and ignorant—she was twenty-four years old in those days—she was also childish by nature. More than once she went out to the field to play hide-and-seek, tag, and dodge ball with the village children; she was very fast and hurled the rag ball boldly and accurately. Her ways were not to everyone's liking.

"People are talking about you, *pustema*," Father grumbled. "A woman shouldn't play like a child in the street."

But Mother pranced around the yard with a surfeit of happiness and strength bubbling up in her flesh, lent her voice to illiterate and funny songs, and chased us when she saw us watching her, pressing us to her heart with the crushing might of her arms. She never understood Father's hatred and loathing, nor did she sense the distrust she stirred in everyone, a distrust that stuck to her like a shadow, followed her from Jerusalem, and slowly took shape again in the conversations of the peasants' wives in our new place. Jealous eyes began glaring at her, and clenched mouths began hissing out their gall.

Behind the bakery she planted a small kitchen garden that gave off smells of garlic, green onions, and tomatoes. She took the heifer to the bull because Father was scared to go near him. Four brooding hens and a rooster pecked around under the young mulberry tree. "The rooster has lot of wives," she explained the ways of the world to us, "and the goose has one wife." Isaac Brinker, our neighbor, gave her a white solution, and she plastered the trunks of her seedlings with it. She set useless traps for the rats that were drawn to the bakery storeroom, and cursing loudly she pulled up the weeds that dared grow in the soil of her yard. She had a terrible hatred of thieves and parasites. In the yard were several anthills whose inhabitants paved themselves paths of plunder to the storeroom. One day, I'm ashamed to tell you, I saw her standing over one of the anthills in her loose work dress, hands on her thighs, eyes closed, feet wide apart, a strange expression on her face. When she walked away, a foamy puddle remained on the anthill. I hid, and Jacob, stunned and embarrassed, asked her if she "made peepee on the ants." Mother glared at him, confused, and finally laughed and said, "No money we got for kerosene, children."

In the new place, no one practiced blowing the *shofar* and no beadle woke us for penitential prayers before the High Holy Days. Instead, shrieking swallows and flocks of butterflies with black-and-white wings fluttered to us to announce that autumn was coming. Then Mother took us to the fields to see how Isaac Brinker plowed the soil. Holding her hands, we tramped along as hard as our legs could go, half running, half dragged, as she strode between us. Her shoulders and breasts rose and fell as she inhaled the smell of the plowed earth with pleasure. The dark furrows swallowed the light of the sun and spat it back out soft and dull, velvety and sweet to the eye. Brinker walked behind his Yugoslavian mule, and when he saw us, he began singing in a loud voice.

A host of stars is in the sky,
Which one gives a sign?
So many lads are passing by—
Which do I choose for mine?
Oh, yes, you're the one who's spoken,
Yes, yes, you my heart have broken.

He nodded to us with his pleasant face and smiled at Mother. A good neighbor he was. He gave her seedlings and seeds, taught her to prune, and at her request spent a few nights, armed with his hunting rifle, lying in ambush for the rats that raided the bakery storeroom. He had one son named Noah, who was bigger than we were and could sing harmony for every song he heard, and a dried-up wife whose name was Livy, but in the village they called her "Dead Livy" because the stench of carcasses emanated from her. A faint smell, but undeniable and ineradicable. "Dead Livy" didn't leave her house much, but her smell certainly did. Later on, when I started reading books, I called her Madame Thenardier, unbeknownst to Brinker.

A few weeks after we arrived in the village, Brinker brought us a copy of the newspaper *Davar* and read us an item about a meeting between the High Commissioner, Lord Palmer, and the Greek Patriarch, Demianus. The Patriarch did indeed complain to the Commissioner about the theft of his carriage, "and the two also discussed current affairs and the feuds between the Christian denominations in the Church of the Holy Sepulcher."

Brinker and Mother laughed, but Father was scared. He wanted to set fire to the carriage right away. Until that moment it had been merely a shameful memento, but now it also became the Most Wanted exhibit of the Mandatory prosecutor general. Father was always afraid of the authorities, of anyone who wore a uniform, of punctilious officials and health inspectors who invaded the bakery on Friday morning, of all days, to look for rat droppings and signs of cockroaches. Like the greedy kashrut inspector, with his scraggly beard and teeth, and his filthy looks and clothes that got on Mother's nerves, they too made official records of sins and took a tithe of the challahs. Now the detectives of the C.I.D. joined the ranks of those who were after Father's life.

Years later, when I was in America, the last of the English left the country, and Father breathed a sigh of relief. But in a few months, during one of his fights with Mother, she told him with unexpected cunning that the High Commissioner had left one plainclothes policeman in Israel just for that purpose. For years, in Father's imagination and nightmares, a ruddy undercover detective would appear in the village, his thick, freckled, hairy arms concealed beneath a nun's habit that hid his sex and his mission. The detective would confidently stride straight to the carriage, take his penknife and scrape off the peeling gray paint Mother had smeared over the lacquer insignia of the Patriarchate, grab Father by his fringe of hair, and hurl him into the deep dark cellar of the jail in the Russian Compound in Jerusalem.

We all laughed at his fears, but one day such a detective did appear at the house and we held our breath even though he was wearing a cap and a vest, not a nun's habit. The man asked in English about a "woman from Jerusalem," and I, who knew a little English by then, said, "No! No!" with great authority, and he left. Mother was certainly bolder and more practical than Father. She had pulled the velvet bench out of the carriage and made it into a small love seat for the living room; she had cut off the folding canvas roof, and Brinker, who was an excellent craftsman, had turned it into an awning for the porch. He also took the wooden wheels off the carriage and replaced them with a pair of old rubber auto tires; and inside the carriage he installed shelves for bread and screen doors. "That's for you, Frau Levy," he laughed joyfully. Over the black lacquer and the emblems of the Patriarchate, Mother drew a gigantic ugly loaf of bread that looked like a cross between a potato and a houseslipper. Thus the traces of incense, rosewater, and the chocolate mint candy the Patriarch used to suck on his travels all disappeared. She harnessed the donkey her father had sent between the shafts, and the holy carriage became a bread cart.

Chapter 19

D o you know the Ansel Adams photograph of a hand, an ancient white palm sketched in stone? On the threshold of our bakery two palms are imprinted in the cement. One is big and missing the little finger, the other is small and childish, and next to them it says, "Jacob Levy and Son Benjamin, Bakers, April 1955."

"He calls this hand The Memorial," Romi told me.

In one of the most terrible pictures she took of her father and sent me in America, Jacob is on his hands and knees, his face to the floor like a dog lapping, his cheeks puffed out, and his eyes shut. Every morning, after taking the bread out of the oven for the fourth and last time, he kneels like that on all fours, takes off his thick glasses, bends down to the cement floor, and blows away the flour that has accumulated in the hollow of Benjamin's palm; and every morning Romi lies in wait for him with her camera, as she lies in wait for him in the house, in the kitchen, in the yard, at the graves, at his work, at his rest, in his thoughts, and in his grief. "Someday I'll do an exhibit," she told me. "I'll call it My Father." She doesn't hide her intention from Jacob either.

She looked at the Adams photograph book I brought her and laughed: "My hand is better." In her picture the cloud of puffed flour looks like a light mist of fog.

The chairman of the Committee of Bereaved Parents, a thin, pleasant man whom Jacob calls the Head Mourner, asked him to participate in erecting a memorial to the dead of the brigade. "They've got a sculptor from Tel Aviv. A locksmith of junk. Rusty rifles and twisted machine guns. An honest-to-God shame."

Jacob took the Head Mourner to the bakery and showed him the imprints of the hands in the cement. "There," he said. "That's him and that's me, that hand is the memorial and the memorial book, and that's all, thank you very much."

They had pressed their hands into the cement the day a new floor was poured in the bakery. Everybody was surprised that Jacob made an imprint of his wounded hand, the one with the little finger cut off, because he usually hides it in his pants pocket, and by now that's not a conscious act but a habit the hand has acquired, to hide like a mole from the light of day and the eyes of its fellow creatures.

In the good times, when Jacob married Leah and took over from Father and waited for Benjamin to grow up and inherit it from him, the bakery was a source of pride for the village, and was famous all around. Jacob's standard white bread, rolls, and challahs were known far and wide. For village celebrations, circumcisions, and weddings my brother baked challahs glazed with egg yolk and sprinkled with poppy seed, breads as big as a baby, delectable and sweet. Those were his gifts to the grooms, the parents, the brides. But ever since Benjamin was killed and Leah closed herself up in his room and went to sleep, Jacob had stopped baking those challahs. At first the people begged him to bake them again, and when they despaired of him, their pleas turned into angry complaints for depriving them of their pride and joy.

"I don't care about that," he told me. The stump of his little finger turns red and quivers when he's mad, and Jacob stuck it in his pocket. "We're bakers! Always strangers. Always alone. Always night people."

The years I spent in America, comfortable years of tedium and distance, had painted the village in yearning and nostalgia. Memories celebrated their power in me, creating and fostering pictures of shining light and green space, of a happy childhood, of joy and friendship, of the pretty poem Yehiel Abramson, the village librarian, used to teach me English. Here it is, without opening a book and with my eyes closed.

The days may come,
The days may go,
But still the hands of memory weave
The blissful dreams of long ago.

But to myself I admit that Jacob is right. We always were strangers. We clearly sensed the superiority the farmer feels over the baker, tomorrow over yesterday, people of the field and sun over toilers of the oven and stars. Once Father told Brinker that he was "the fifteenth generation in

Jerusalem from the seed of Abrabanel," and Brinker said, "That's very nice, Mr. Levy, but we're all sons of Our Father Abraham."

Offended and frightened, short of build, pupils wide, our father baked his nocturnal bread and lived his owl's life. When the village woke up he went to sleep, and when the village went to sleep he got up for work. And, in fact, without any dealings with my neighbors, that is how I live today in America, though I don't bake a single loaf of bread. One afternoon we saw him, my brother and I, standing in the baker's pit, his shoulders shaking and his head stuck in the oven, and when we approached we heard a terrible shouting, or maybe weeping, swallowed up by layers of brick, mortar, and sand as soon as it came out.

And Mother—mighty, beautiful, foreign, aggressive—here too, she stirred the dull ferment she roused everywhere. At the time we couldn't decipher the real nature of the looks people gave her. I thought the women loved her and the men lusted after her. Only now do I understand that the women wanted to kill her and that she didn't stir desire and love in the men but instincts much darker and more primeval: of hunting, harnessing, domesticating, taming. Every morning she sold bread from a window at the back of the bakery. Customers would stare at her as they pawed the bread and squeezed its flesh. "You could get crazy from thems!" she would thunder through the window. "What you want from poor bread? Why you squeeze poor bread?"

Chapter 20

At the crossroads twines
A rose with eyes of red . . .

It is Father's voice, coming from a bench on the street. Jacob, at the breakfast table in the kitchen, dandles Michael on his knee and scowls.

. . . And she begs
All passersby:

Please, good people, hear my cry,
Keep your steps from brushing me
Lest your feet go crushing me.
Please, hear my cry,
Oh, passersby,
Pluck me from the brush
Lest your feet me crush.
Take me to my garden bright,
Garden of my heart's delight.

"Listen to him," says Jacob angrily.

"Who is 'him'?"

"Stop lecturing me."

"Why do you call him 'him'? Didn't you always get mad when he called Mother 'her'?" I say. "And what do you care if he sings? Good morning, Romi. I didn't know you stayed here last night."

The kitchen is filled with the force and light of my niece. She stands at the sink and drinks her coffee with milk; only then does she join us at the table.

"Maybe you'll be nice, Father, and let me photograph you in the studio?"

Jacob doesn't answer. He sits Michael on a chair, and Romi stares at him, amused and teasing. "And who is this little boy?"

Jacob grows tense. Michael shifts in his seat, filled with that blend of anxiety and anticipation only children can conjure up.

"Hey, little boy, what's your name?"

"Michael," he says, innocent and smiling.

"And mine is Romi," says Romi. "Romi with a T, not a Th."

Michael giggles. "But I know you're Romi. You're my sister." He looks around, enjoying the confusion the game has stirred in him.

"Tell me, Michael"—she dips a piece of bread in Tia Duduch's tomato juice—"where do you live?"

Michael's look lingers on Jacob, who is trembling with anger but hasn't exploded yet.

"Here."

"Here?" Romi is amazed. "So how come I haven't seen you here till today?"

"You found somebody to play your games with?" roars Jacob. "Did you come here to get on our nerves or to eat?"

Michael is silent, relishing the titillating dread of the moment.

"And do your parents know you're here in our house?" asks Romi. "Maybe you should tell them so they won't worry about you."

"Here's my parents," says Michael. He gets up and stands next to Jacob.

"You're his father?" asks Romi. "How come you didn't tell me you had another child somewhere?"

Jacob gets up and opens the door: "Get out!"

"And who's his mother?" she shouts from the porch. "You got somebody new on the side?"

"Why does she do this to me?" Jacob groaned afterward. "Why these games? Why does she photograph me all the time? Who did she get this cruelty from? And you still think she looks like Mother."

"She looks very much like her, only she's sharper," I tell him.

"Yes." Crumbs of bread and omelet spray from Jacob's mouth. "If Mother had had half of that evil, her life would have been easier. But that's your specialty, an easy life. We don't know about such things."

Chapter 21

I'm one of those who believe that the squawk of a seagull at the Cape of Good Hope can sink a ship in the English Channel at the end of a chain of events. Thus, protein molecules traveled to the origin of my body, sketched the pictures of my childhood, and plotted the course of my life. What if rain hadn't fallen that day in the valley? I shudder at the thought. And what if the nymph butterflies had delayed their journey in the desert by one night? And what if our older sister hadn't died? And not only the annals and nature of my parents and my brother. Also the ringing of the ancient bells, the weeping of a beaten child, the migraine in the head of a man who died before I was born—these too reach me and rend the webs I spin around me.

In our first days in the village we still went around tied together by the red wool string. Later, Mother ordered us to throw it away. "The Rusalem's over," she said, proclaiming her own declaration of independence. We walked to the new school hand in hand, like two blind seeing-eye dogs, each of us leading and being led at the same time. Our teacher, whose name I can't remember for the life of me, held a bright spot in his hand, and passed it over the blackboard with strange rasping noises; not until recess, when we went up to the board, could we read what he had written on it.

"Maybe we don't see good," Jacob said to me, and I said, "What are you talking about?"

Two weeks later, when the teacher—Shimoni? Maybe Dr. Shimoni? It's been almost fifty years—gave back the first arithmetic test, he also gave us a "letter to your parents."

"What's this?" asked Mother, embarrassed. Even though we had both tried to teach her everything they taught us in school, she still couldn't read and write. Father took the letter from her, and when he read it his face grew dark. Dr. Shimoni—what's so bad about Dr. Shimoni?—wrote clearly and explicitly, and somewhat aggressively, about our nearsightedness; using rude expressions like "blind as bats" and "don't see beyond the end of their noses," he mentioned "serious neglect" and added ironically: "They copy from the board what their eyes see." Father understood that the authorities, who had only been sticking their noses in his business so far, had opened a new and insulting campaign against him over his sons' nearsightedness. "Go over there and tell them a baker doesn't need to see any farther than the end of his shovel," he ordered Mother.

All night long the argument raged between them, their voices drowning out the roar of the Primus stove, the dirge of the burner, and the screech of the pans they dragged. The next morning, when the two of them came home from work, tired and angry, Father stood at the window to sell the bread, and Mother harnessed the donkey to the bread cart and took us to the eye doctor.

A cool wind was blowing. Jacob and I opened the screen door, hung our feet from the back of the cart, and let our toes graze the passing weeds. Mother closed her eyes and opened her mouth as if trying to gulp the air, and when we looked at her in amazement, she laughed and said, "Ah . . . that's good . . ."

The eye doctor asked us if we knew all the letters of the alphabet. When we said yes, he asked if we saw well, and we nodded. Then the doctor pulled back the curtain concealing the official version of the truth: a white board with rows and rows of blackish blurs. That board, which didn't give off any helpful sounds or smells, proved the claim of the authorities: Jacob and I couldn't see a single one of the letters on it.

"And the missus?" The doctor turned to Mother. "Does the missus also want to read the board?"

Mother turned pale. "I see very good," she said.

The doctor put a wooden box on the table, took out round metal frames that weighed heavily on the bridges of our noses, and began inserting lenses in the grooves, asking: "Now? Now?" The tiny nebulae on the board grew clearer, taking on shape, turning into letters, and the whole world became sharp along with them. As if out of twilight, invisible, unimportant details were born, bursting into my brain, threatening to flood it. My head started to spin and scan, with a force I couldn't resist. In the middle of the room the air suddenly crystallized into a pair of tiny specks that turned into two hovering flies. Smoke stains blossomed on the doctor's teeth like illustrations of the bad smell coming from his mouth, and the square on the wall of the clinic turned into a picture of a strange woman, though even with the help of the new lenses you couldn't tell if she was naked or clothed.

A dreadful, sweet pain swelled behind my eyes, balled up under my forehead, wound around my temples, and drew me from the board to the picture of the woman. I approached her with hesitant steps as Jacob bounded to the window to peer outside. "Look! Look!" he shouted ecstatically, pulling me by my shirttail and pointing upward.

The chirping we heard had turned into a little scarlet bird hopping on a tree. Three distant dots became people. Two of them curly-haired, in wide khaki shorts, suddenly raised their hands and struck the third until he fell to the ground. From the depths of the sky something floated up and took shape, a yellow-red kite that hadn't been there before. I looked at the distant beaten man lying on the ground, and then beyond the kite, and I vaguely understood that the new lenses sharpened my vision but shortened its range. Until then, the sky had had no limits, but now it became a clear and opaque shell that even the new eyeglasses couldn't penetrate.

"But you don't see the string," I said.

"What string?" asked the doctor.

"Of the kite," I said, returning to the woman in the picture, and I saw that her breasts, ashamed and fearful under the new force of my eyes, were wide apart. Today I don't remember if she was a redhead or a brunette, if she was in a low-cut gown or was bare-chested and wore only pants, and a few days ago, when I took the reproductions of Venus of Urbino and Odalisque à la culotte grise out of my suitcase and asked Jacob which of them had hung in the eye clinic, he said, "What are you talking about? What picture?" Sometimes I wonder if our memory is really so different or if we simply divide it between us.

I turned my face to my mother and my grief increased. Whenever she took me up in her arms, I delighted not only in the touch of her body but also in the sharpness of the lines of her face. Until that visit to the eye doctor, that sharpness had seemed a reward for my love. I knew I would never again have to put my face up close to hers to see the little lines at the corners of her mouth and her thin, fair lashes.

The doctor brought us back to the table, put drops in our eyes that dilated our pupils until we looked like a pair of owls, peered at us down the knife-like beam of his flashlight, and ordered us to follow his finger with our eyes as it moved from right to left, leaving an almost imperceptible trail of tobacco, chocolate, feces, and soap. Finally he said that despite the external differences between us we were genuine twins. Both of us, he found, needed lenses of identical strength, four diopters.

"That's pretty strong to start with," said the doctor, "and it will get even stronger." And he too scolded Mother for neglecting our health and not bringing us for a checkup sooner.

On the way home we saw Isaac Brinker on top of Asphodel Hill, and when we approached he came running down to us. Mother reined in the donkey, and Brinker's eyes lit up. He climbed into the cart and said, "What's up, boys?" Then he gave Mother some autumn crocuses he had picked, and we drove him to the village. I asked what he was doing on the hill, and Brinker said that he went there in the autumn to see the straight lines the squills sketched on the fields. "The ancients marked the borders of their land with those squills. Because the squill always grows in the same place its parents grew and nothing kills it, right?"

Asphodel Hill was a treasure of flowers. Blue anemones and yellow buttercups covered it, and at its foot irises blossomed in the spring and crocuses at Hanukah, and a lot of other flowers whose names I don't know. On its western slope grew the shoots of asphodel that gave it its name. Nettles also flourished there, and in school the teacher told us that the nettle is evidence of the existence of ancient life on the land. "It grows where there were houses and people and graves," he said, and then he smiled and added, "Maybe that's why it stings." Mother took us here for walks on Saturday to pick camomile for her shampoo, and sometimes we went as far as

Skull Rock, an enormous, scary boulder, with clefts that made it look like a human skull from a certain angle.

Now an ugly house stands on that hill, clumsy and white, the kind they call "Spanish style" here. I need all the powers of memory and imagination to identify in its coarse contours the lines of Leah's house, which used to be here. Some merchant bought it, tore down most of it, and rebuilt it in his own bad taste. Most of the village fields are sprouting such houses now, and except for Brinker, none of the old farmers are still here. As I walk through the streets of the village, among the poincianas, the araucarias, and the hedges gardeners have trimmed into balls and pillars, past stone fences, lawns, and swimming pools, I nod a greeting to people I don't know. But they, it seems, do know me, and have invited me in a few times, introducing me as "a native, an American writer and gastronome,—you won't believe it, but he's one of the Levys from our bakery." Once I was forced to carry on an unpleasant conversation with three loud men who assaulted me with their vulgar aftershave and tall clinking glasses, and demanded that I convince my brother to sell the bakery so it could be torn down.

"You know how much that land is worth today?"

"He can live for years on that money . . ."

"Instead of ruining his health . . ."

"And ours."

The bakery, which had been built at the edge of the village, is now surrounded by villas, and looks like an ugly mole on the neighborhood's spanking new skin. Years ago Jacob wrote me that "complaints of the rich" were beginning to be heard—about the roaring of the burners and the noise of the kneading belt, which disturbed their rest, about the shouting at work, about the "aesthetic aspect," and even about the good smell of the bread that burst into their houses, reminding them of their weaknesses and robbing them of sleep.

"They never liked us here. Didn't give a damn about us. What were we to them, after all? Half Frankists, half converts." And my brother pronounced the word "converts" with the accent on the wrong syllable, the way they were mocked in Mother's old village.

"Believe me, I still remember what they said when I married Leah," he added, reminding me of what I knew very well, that the villagers didn't respect anyone who didn't work the land.

"That didn't bother you. You threw away the eyeglasses, you sat in the library and read books. But I saw everything. Father, who worked only at night, so nobody knew what he looked like, and Mother, who drove them totally crazy with her body and her Hebrew and her hair and those eyes, and Simon and Tia Duduch, with the way they looked? Did you ever see any of the farmers come visit us? Except Brinker? And even he, you know, only came to look at Mother. What did you think—he loved you?"

Then my brother said something terrible. He said that Benjamin's death was his entry into the society of the village. "Only then was I worthy in their eyes, only then did they say to me, 'You are our brother.'"

In the evening we heard the shrill squeals of the rats from the holes they dug in the wall of the storeroom. Here and there they left demon's clawprints on the floury floor and demon's droppings that spotted the flour. They ruled over the bakery from nightfall to midnight, when the work began. They gnawed sacks, stole flour, gorged themselves on bread and dough, befouled the storeroom, and drove mother out of her mind. These weren't the village rats of the chicken coops and the silos, but vicious, tough city rats full of their own self-importance, who hated the whole world and especially one another. I guess they reminded her of the Jerusalemites, the abomination of her soul. She used to say that a pair of "ratses" snuck into the carriage on the night of the quake and came with us to the village, "'cause the curse of the Rusalem pursues you everywhere."

Father was so scared of the rats that he denied their existence. "It's a cat," he said when I showed him a rat running across the bakery. "There are cats with thick tails, there are cats without any tails, and there are some like that, small with skinny tails. There are all kinds of cats. I didn't tell you about Jacob Uziel's blue cat?" That Uziel, by the way, was a valiant Saloniki man whose approaching fist was the last sight seen by two Janissaries who touched his sister. He was a descendant of Aaron Luis Levy Montezinos, a distant uncle who discovered the Ten Lost Tribes in South America, and "Menashe Ben-Israel himself wrote a book about him titled *Hope of Israel*." Father has a host of relatives—uncles and forefathers who wrote books, concocted medicines, defended widows and orphans, "knew all the good ways," recited prayers, "cured the queen of Spain of her husband's pains," and always wore red coats when they went to battle so their blood wouldn't be seen. But Father himself didn't fight, didn't struggle, didn't overcome, and didn't dare make war even on the rats.

When Mother saw a rat in the bakery, her hatred knocked her off balance. With the force of an animal reflex that circumvented the obstacle of thought, she pelted the creature with anything that came to hand, a piece of dough, a glass of milk, a loaf of bread, one of the iron weights from the scale. Like a daughter of Queequeg or Tashtego, she cast baker's-shovel harpoons across the bakery, threw oil cans and glaze brushes, and since none of those objects was meant for the slaughter of pests, she did quite a bit of damage and infuriated Father. Despite his fearful mutterings, she scattered strychnine in the storeroom, but in vain. She brought Brinker's cat to the bakery, and the animal returned from battle after suffering grievous losses. She set traps, but the rats waited until a mouse got caught in them, and then they ate it along with the bait. A few times Brinker came to sit with her in the darkness of the bakery, but he didn't manage to catch any rats either. One night she borrowed the hunting rifle he used to clear jackals and porcupines out of his vineyard, sat down in the yard, and started shooting. In the morning we counted two owls, a big puddle of water from a perforated pipe, three shattered windows, and one dead rat, but nobody understood what had happened to it because it didn't have a single wound.

Only once did Mother succeed. One night, a minute or two after Father lit the burner, a rat passed by the pit. Mother noticed it, but she was empty-handed. The abominable animal assessed the situation correctly, sat down on its behind, and tranquilly cleaned its roguish whiskers and front paws, all the while observing its enemy with a mocking look. A pink blush began climbing from Mother's collar, growing redder and darker until her face was scarlet with rage. Very slowly her feet slid toward the oven. Four eyes, two big gray ones and two small black ones, never left each other. When she was close enough to the pit it happened, and even today I have a hard time believing it. Mother flung out a long, powerful hand, grabbed the arm of the burner, tore it off its base, and aimed the tongue of fire at the rat.

Two shrieks were heard through the roar of the burner. One, thin and short, came from the rat, now a reeking firebrand; and the second, longer and coarser, was the roar of vengeance and requital that turned into a terrible wail of pain when Mother's fingers felt the heat of the burner arm. She flung away her weapon, dipped her hand in the can of glaze, and worked with the other hand all night long, groaning and laughing.

It took two weeks for the new eyeglasses to come, and Father and Mother went on arguing and shutting up whenever we came within earshot. Jacob, the Vasco Da Gama of sight, dreamed of the new world that would be revealed before him and ran around prophesying happily, while I withdrew inside myself, preparing for the invasion of that world into my eyes. Neither of us imagined what was to happen, and I know you'll be surprised too. Eyeglasses cost a lot of money in those days, and the new equipment for the bakery had used up all our parents' savings. Father, who regarded eyeglasses as an indulgence from the beginning, decided to buy only one pair for the two of us.

Now I look at that miserable, pitiful old man whose bed I was summoned to, and I tell myself that I don't know anyone else who would have dared to come up with such a wicked idea—to force two nearsighted children to share one pair of eyeglasses.

"At last you remember something right," said Jacob when I reminded him of that. He called Father "a cheap creep," but I am grateful to him. I have no doubt that with that decision my father set the course of my life more than any other person. More than Mother or Jacob, more than Leah, more than Yehiel Abramson, the librarian, whose time to enter the story is approaching, and more than all the women who have shared their souls, their beds, their lives, and their hearts with me. I am grateful, and full of love for those women and for Father, who by dint of that tight fist of his brought me together with every single one of them.

Two weeks later, we got our one pair of eyeglasses, with round steel frames. As if we had decided in advance, Jacob put them on immediately and strode outside like a conqueror. The children called him "four-eyes" and "glasses-head," but he paid them no heed, just as he paid none to me. I was left content at home, and I was relieved when I realized that our parents weren't intervening in the way we shared our eyeglasses.

My brother devoted most of the next weeks to learning the world anew. He stood close to every object, took off the eyeglasses, and put them back on, comparing the familiar blurry sight to the sharp and alien new one. I accompanied him as he mastered the way from home to school and back. He skipped and ran around me, enthusiastically describing all the new details of our route, which were completely superfluous as far as I was concerned, oppressing my eyes with their claims, demanding constant attention, competing with imagination, and exhausting thought. I suppose the animosity I feel for sharp-sighted people, those arrogant tourists visiting my hazy world, was born in those days. To this day I think that blurred vision is the proper vision for a civilized human being, who no longer needs the eyes of a hawk, the ears of a bat, or the nostrils of a dog. Eyeglasses, which I still wear little and lose a lot, seem like a pair of superfluities fit only for hunters, peeping Toms, and rich people.

We looked like the two puppies of Lycurgus of Sparta. Jacob played with his friends in the yards and fields, wrestled, hid, stamped, and leaped among the new sharp sights that surrounded him, and I let him live in his world and didn't interfere with his happiness. Even after summer vacation, when we went back to school, we didn't fight. In the classroom we sat next to each other and passed our one pair of glasses from nose to nose, to the great anger of the teachers and the laughter of the children. At recess, the eyeglasses were Jacob's, because he would play in the yard and I would read books.

The only time fights broke out between us was when the man who showed movies came in his pickup truck. Once I was even forced to exercise my superior physical strength to gain the eyeglasses. Jacob started crying and insisted I describe to him what I saw. After that he didn't demand the eyeglasses anymore because he said that the movie, blurry as it was, was more interesting accompanied by a story; and the little children, too, whose impatient parents weren't willing to explain things to them, gathered around us to listen to my description. Once, at a Buster Keaton Indian movie, I couldn't resist temptation and told him the Indian bared his belly and put it to the ground. "That's how Indians listen for horses galloping or a train coming from the distance," I explained to him. A year ago I got a letter from him that began with the words "You liar, you." He wrote me that Romi had taken him to see *The Blue Angel* in Tel Aviv and he saw that it was Marlene Dietrich who showed her legs in the wings of the theater, not the professor, as I had told him then.

For two years my brother and I shared one pair of eyeglasses. And until they bought us another pair, the common pair served its purpose. No longer did we walk hand in hand; each one of us went his own way and lived in his own world.

Chapter 22

The village library. Joy of my childhood, sanctuary of my youth, my heartbeat. I almost added: Light of my life, flame of my nights, but there has to be a limit even to courting you. A large library it is, strange and rich. It's still standing today near the community center, but now the center has been turned into a big club humming with young people, and next door there is a small splendid shopping center built on the ruins of the silo, a twinkling of neon and glass, indicating the passage of time.

For a few minutes I stand there, enjoying measured doses of excitement and examining my memory. Here Leah passed by on her bike, a laughing, youthful Persephone, her braid bouncing on her back and her smile rising on her face. Here the donkey used to rub his back on the pillar. Here stood Isaac Brinker, who was so impressed by the goose's devotion to Mother that he declaimed Rilke's poem on Leda and Zeus to her in German, in the middle of the street, concluding with a fervent explanation: "And only with her, Frau Levy, did he feel he had feathers. Yes? Only with her!"

Most of the other farmers have already slipped my mind. Reading and baking aren't occupations that create a loyal circle of friends. The path my feet trod was short and clear, stretching from the house to the bakery and the library. Here and there rumors penetrated the walls of flour and the bookshelves. We heard the gossipy conversations of those who bought bread, but we didn't take part in their plowing and harvesting, their quarrels and loves. We knew that Binyamini grew the biggest beets for fodder and that Slutzki was persecuting his neighbor, threatening to kill him with a pitchfork, but we didn't interfere. We were bakers, enclosed in the narrow realm of night and oven, defended by a wall of fire and bricks, in another time, in thick darkness.

"Such sociomaths, the two of you," Romi teased her father and me. "And you're getting to be just like him," she added. "Standing still in every place that reminds him of something with Benjamin. Can't you two remember and walk at the same time?"

She came up to me, thrust out two deft hands, and suddenly took the glasses off my nose. "You look better without," she said. "So we can see your beautiful eyes."

"Give them back," I said. "I don't like these games."

"Right away, Unk. You're a real hunk like that."

"Don't make me resort to violence, as the diner said to the oyster who refused to be opened." I smiled, but anger was rising in me, dim and blunt.

"Right away, okay. . . . You're hurting me! Here! What's with you?"

In the library there was no need for eyeglasses. All you had to do was put your nose to the shelves and push it along the rows like a plow. Small and sharp, the words soared to my eyes, and the good smell of the paper mingled with the pleasure of its content. This is how I read even now, though I have my own eyeglasses.

"I grew up, a happy, healthy child in a bright world of illustrated books." Thick ivy covers the walls of the library. Under a brow of green leaves the closed wooden door looks like the eye of a sleeping animal. "Monday and Wednesday," says a note taped to the old brass sign, "from four to six p.m." It used to be open every day from three to seven, and on Friday from ten to one. Almost all the books in it came to the village with Yehiel Abramson, and many of them were sold or stolen or disappeared after Yehiel was killed.

Yehiel Abramson—"Founder and First Librarian"—was a friendly, generous man, tall, with muscular white hands and a lean, bespectacled face. He immigrated to this country from New York and was so unlike the people of the village that as a child I thought he was different from all humanity. But when I came to the United States, I saw many people like Yehiel, and for a moment I thought I had landed in a country of librarians, until I remembered Emerson's saying that air and land, principles and diction determine the lines of a man's face no less than his parents do.

Yehiel came to the village a few months before us, driving a green Dodge truck loaded with five enormous wooden crates containing the forty thousand books of his late father, Judge Mordechai Elijah Abramson. Out of the crates came volumes in Hebrew, English, Yiddish, German, and Russian, along with ancient manuscripts added to his wonderful collection by this talented autodidact, a Monastirial born by mistake in the Ukraine, endowed with insatiable curiosity, fine literary taste, and a practical knowledge of binding and moth control. "In one and the same year we got bread and books," said Brinker, who, like me, was a constant patron of the library.

"Take a book for your mother too," said his voice from beyond a shelf, but I was ashamed to tell him that Mother didn't know how to read and write. I often read to her. She would listen attentively, mouthing the words, and keep asking for the part in *Michael Strogov* where Ivan Ogareff heats his sword, the gypsy girls of Nijny Novgorod dance, and Michael stares at his mother Marfa.

"Look while you may, look while you may . . . ," she repeated after me. "Look while you may . . . " And her own eyes filled with tears.

In the two years before he came to us Yehiel Abramson wandered through the country in his green truck of books, trying to interest libraries and institutions in his father's legacy. Many wanted to take parts of it, but in his will Judge Mordechai Elijah Abramson had stipulated that his collection was not to be dismantled. Yehiel explained that to his father, an observant Jew, that would be like performing an autopsy on his corpse. His areas of interest were many and varied, and libraries interested in the research of

Faïtlovitch and Shatner on the history of the Falashas had no desire for the pamphlets of Israeli and Feldman on artificial methods of fertilizing dates. Someone who wanted *Karaite Vocalization* by Simha Pinsker and *T'udat Shlomo* by Shlomo ben Moshe Hazan, in the rare and expensive edition of 1718 printed in Amsterdam, did not want the complete *Almanac of Utah for the Mormon Farmer* by Jefferson Hope. Those who desired *Ma'aseh Tuvia* by Tuvia Hacohen of Metz and *Even Bohan* by Kalonymus had no interest in the rare and terrifying copy of the *Kalevala* written, as Yehiel whispered to me, on parchment made of human skin.

He was a pedantic librarian. Everyone who took out a library card had to raise his hand and swear an archaic loyalty oath and agree to weird prohibitions—not to drip candle wax on the pages, not to dog-ear them or dry flowers between them. On the wall of the library Yehiel hung the tablet of "House Rules" and next to it a portrait of his father. The oil painting of the judge was done by the artist Max Weber. Yehiel showed me a marvel: the painter's face reflected in the space between the twinkle of the judge's eyes and the glint of his glasses.

With polka-dotted bow tie, white goatee, Druze mustache, and abundant curly gray hair, Mordechai Elijah Abramson peered through round gold eyeglasses at everyone who came into his library, proud of his wonderful collection, his devoted son, and his great resemblance to the poet Shaul Tshernikhovski. He and his son were both very fond of Tshernikhovski, whose books, signed in his own hand, are still here, in a cabinet with locked glass doors. For my bar-mitzvah Yehiel gave me a book of his poems, in the splendid "Moriah" edition of Odessa, and when I opened it a small brass Yale key fell out. My heart stopped. It was the key to the library, and I knew that would be the happiest moment of my life. Do you know many people who can say as much about a moment of their lives?

Forty-two years later I take the old key out of my pocket and go in. A dim silence reigns in the library. The sense of smell—trigger of memories—is released in me when I enter and walk around among the shelves. From both sides of the ancient House Rules, two countenances now look at me, the old one, painted and familiar, and the second a painful photograph of Yehiel, "who gave his life for the defense of Jerusalem in the battle for San-Simon in the War of Independence." I went there too, with Romi, on a pilgrimage of memory. A small green bell tower stands there, surrounded by cypresses and pines, and to the side the wreckage of a tank, monkey bars for children, and Yehiel's name on the memorial plaque, among the other dead. Youngsters in wheelchairs were riding back and forth. "Take my picture, take my picture," they called to Romi.

The first book Yehiel gave me to read was *Wild Animals I Have Known*, by Ernest Thompson Seton.

"*Wild Animals*," he read. "You know English yet?"

"No," I said.

"Why don't you wear glasses?" he asked when he saw me stick my nose between the pages.

"'Cause this is how I like to read," I answered.

Every day I came to borrow a book, sometimes twice a day. One day Yehiel said to me in his American accent, "Approach. Do you read all the books you take?"

"Yes," I told him.

He examined the book I was returning. "This is a bit too advanced for you." His face grew serious, and then he smiled and opened the book to its last page. "Tell me, what were Peter's last words?"

"'Friends,'" I declaimed, "'confess that with us perishes—'"

"Then what?"

"It doesn't say," I answered in embarrassment. "He dies."

"Fine," said Yehiel. "And Nero's?"

"'Here is faithfulness,'" I quoted.

"Last words," Yehiel informed me solemnly, "are the most important. All wisdom, and all truth, and all sincerity are just compressed into that inappreciable moment of time in which we step over the threshold of the invisible."

I was too young to understand, but I was very moved; and a few years later I discovered where the sentence came from and about whom it had been written. You surely remember Kurtz's last words: "He cried in a whisper at some image, at some vision—he cried out twice, a cry that was no more than a breath—'The horror! The horror!'"

I browse through the old books. On the inside of the covers appears that plate with the fat chicken wearing glasses, hatching a closed book. Yehiel explained to me that that was his father's *ex libris* and said, "That is the most faithful reflection of him."

"That chicken?" I asked, fearful and amazed.

"That's not a chicken. That's an owl, symbol of wisdom," laughed Yehiel. "But Father insisted on drawing his *ex libris* himself."

He told me that his father had steeped himself in reading from his earliest childhood, and that books destroyed first his eyes, then his relations with his wife, and finally his vertebrae. "My father," he added proudly, "came from Kharkov to New York when he was five years old and learned English all by himself."

When he was six, Mordechai Elijah Abramson asked passersby where the public library was. He entered and fearlessly asked the librarian for the first book on the bottom shelf. When he brought it back the following day, he asked for the book next to it, and then the third and the fourth, and thus he read the whole shelf. The library was arranged alphabetically by authors' names, and by the time the librarian had discerned this strange method of reading, the child had already read Aasen's *Norwegian Dialectics*, Abbadie's *Twelve Years in Upper Ethiopia*, and a considerable part of the hundred and eighty books in Abbott's dreary Rollo series. From then on the librarian took him under his wing and taught him to be more discriminating. "If every youth would make friends with a librarian, a science teacher, and a tall and indulgent woman, the world would look completely different," said Yehiel.

The judge amassed his own library with persistence and talent. He aided Jewish immigrants in exchange for the books they had brought with them, he bought, he traded, he found, and he stole. And when he died, he left his son that legacy—to move his library to the Land of Israel. Yehiel bought the green truck, loaded it and the books on a ship, immigrated to Palestine, and embarked on his trek of trials and tribulations. He despaired of the National Library at the Hebrew University in Jerusalem, which was interested in only a small part of the collection, slammed the door on the way out of various municipal libraries, and was expelled from Degania and Tel Yosef after the kibbutz members found "harmful bourgeois material" in his books. For a time he put his trust in the people of Rishon Le-Tsion, until he discovered that they weren't interested in the library but in the truck. In the end, weary and angry, he came to our village. Under Brinker's pressure, the village administration agreed to accept the complete collection and to give Yehiel accommodations and regular work as librarian, but they imposed a condition on him: he would have to sell a few rare books to finance the construction and maintenance of the library. Yehiel had no choice and consented, writing a letter to England that brought an arrow dispatched in the form of a mustachioed nun who was none other than a secret agent of the Bodleian Library of Oxford. For an enormous sum the man bought the *Mishneh Torah* of the Rambam, printed in Venice in 1550, the *Sefer Torah Or* of the Ba'al Shem Tov, the *Esperanza de Israel* of Menashe Ben-Israel, Amsterdam, 1650, the *Sefer Haikkarim* of Yosef Albo, printed in Soncino (Albo was also a distant uncle of my father's, if you can believe his stories), and the *Voyage de la Judée, la Samarie, la Galilée et le Liban*, by a scholar named Cardinal Beaudoin of Avignon, a book that wasn't so ancient but was an extremely precious find, with a strange, very thin bookmark of delicate, shining skin preserved between its pages.

After the deal was concluded and the five rare books sailed for England, hidden in a corset under the black habit of the Oxford agent, Yehiel took pains to divulge publicly the fact of their sale and derived great enjoyment from the shock of the important gentlemen of the National Library, who hastened to the village in a private cab and inveighed against "the pursuit of lucre and the delivery to foreigners of inalienable goods of the culture and legacy of our people."

"You could have got them for nothing," said Yehiel to Professor Heinrich Reiss-Levy, head protester, a short, pale man who hopped around like a crazed locust, flared his nostrils, and demanded that Yehiel let him into the library. Three years earlier that very same man had gone over the list of Mordechai Elijah Abramson's books, wrinkled those very same nostrils, and stated that he wasn't interested in the complete collection.

"Despite a few impressive items, your father's collection is simply an example of the delusions wealth is liable to engender in the soul of a talented dilettante," said the professor to the embarrassed son, and when the latter protested the insult, Reiss-Levy rang the sort of little bell Berlin children use to call their governesses on stormy nights, and had his guest shown out. That epithet—"talented dilettante"—made a great impression on me because Yehiel spat it out with a special grimace whenever he told me the story. Only years later did I understand that it was censure and not praise, but at the time I was old enough to understand that I was also a talented dilettante, and I'm not angry that you've discerned that too, my dear, and even used the same word about the description of Alexandria in the story of Zoga and Anton. But if Mordechai Elijah Abramson hadn't been a talented dilettante, the Hebrew University library would have been glad to accept his books, and then Yehiel wouldn't have come to the village and I wouldn't have known him or found refuge in his library and become a talented dilettante myself. Thus the ship sinks in the English Channel because of the seagull's squawk at the Cape of Good Hope, and thus my life too revolves, and here I am before you—a dilettante. A cunning hunter. Who makes savoury meats. A talented man. In love, in memory, in deceit, in repentance.

Chapter 23

A t the end of the corridor, behind the last door, in the room that was Benjamin's room, in the bed that was his bed, Leah sleeps. From time to time I pass by the closed door, and I automatically lower my voice and tread softly, as you do when you pass an infant's cradle or a dead man's tombstone. But nothing rouses Leah from the netherworld of her slumber, and the room is closed, as Jacob grumbles, because her sleep disturbs those who are awake.

"Go on, go in and look at her," he told me when he saw me lingering and wondering at her door. "You were friends once, weren't you? Maybe you'll manage to wake her up."

When Michael was two years old, he went into his mother's room and asked Jacob, "Who's that?"

"That's Leah," my brother said.

That answer, the cruelest, most logical reply, satisfied Michael completely, and for a year and a half he didn't ask for any further explanations. Sometimes he'd say, "I'm going to sleep with Leah," and he'd get into her bed, huddle against her back, put his cheek on her shoulder, and fall asleep.

"I hate when he does that," Jacob wrote me. "I hate that he gets close to her at all."

Not until he was three and a half did Michael ask where his mother was. They were eating lunch, and before Jacob had time to open his mouth, Romi said, "Leah is your mother, Michael, and mine too." Jacob flew into a rage, and Romi said to him, "You could have thought about that sooner, before you told him, 'That's Leah,' and before you raped her."

Jacob slapped her. Romi flushed and said, "You watch out, I'm the Tartar too," and this time, though the imitation was perfect, she didn't laugh.

A week after I came, I dared to go in.

Leah lay like a big sack under the shroud of the blanket, amid the hovering particles of flour and dust, faded posters of actresses and motorcycles, a pair of army pants she had laundered for Benjamin, and no one came for them. The thick smell of a cave hung in the room. Naturally she didn't wash much. One day, my brother told me, he ambushed her as she was groping her way on her daily sortie to the toilet, tore her nightgown off, thrust her into the shower, and stood there with her in his clothes under the stream of water. He scrubbed her furiously, almost flaying her, and she leaned her wet head on his shoulder and let him soap and rub her, shampoo and dry her. Once, the water had raised a good smell of rain from her skin and hair, a smell that used to rouse my brother, make his heart stand still, and fill him with love. "But now," he said, "she stinks like an old mop."

A stifling dimness silenced the room. I pulled the blanket back a bit and looked at her face: that mummy of my love, preserved in the amber of her grief. Once, Leah had had a long thick braid; I had never seen one like it before and I never saw one like it again afterward. Later, she cut off her braid, but now her hair has grown again and lies in bed with her like an independent living thing. Her skin is white and spongy because of her prolonged contact with the dark, her cheeks are pasty from the stagnant air.

"The bright Tammuz . . ." I seek refuge from my sorrow. "The bright Tammuz, the Tammuz is dead." The first time I saw that face it was framed in the window of a moving car. I was twelve years old, and every morning I would go out to deliver bread. The donkey dragged the Patriarch's carriage through the sand, his little hooves digging in and pulling out, while I stuck my nose in *The Pickwick Papers*, my whole body shaking with laughter provoked by the sayings of Sam Weller. All of a sudden an elegant car appeared, a Ford coming toward me, raising reddish dust in the main street of the village. A little girl's face looked at me from the back window. The tires made a pleasant hiss in the sand, and a smell of gasoline and hot metal came from the body of the car. Children burst out of all the yards and ran behind it, and I prodded the surprised donkey, rushed home, grabbed the eyeglasses, and climbed a tree. The car reached the end of the street, turned onto the rutted path leading to the fields, and easily took the grade of Asphodel Hill. A man, a woman, and the little girl got out and observed the view. Even from a distance you could see that the man was very tall, thin and fair-haired, and the woman wore a suit and leaned on him too much. The little girl, in a flowered dress with a white collar, pranced around them. That was Leah.

Sleep split her face into youth and old age. Her forehead is arched and smooth, still shining with that gleam, but the slope over her mouth is a map of fine ravines. Her lips are covered with a transparent layer of parched skin, like the lips of a thirsty child, and the two hairs in the small mole on her chin, which she used to ask me to pluck out with tweezers, have grown long and thick, as if they were pushed out by the pressure of her pain. There is no sorrow on her face, only a weariness even dreams despair of and no sleep can satisfy.

> I paid you with my sad heart's blood,
> With despair and belated solace,
> With the soul of my longing mood—
> I paid you everything you gave me.
> Please, from your curse, now save me.
> Please, from your curse, now save me.

I grabbed the blanket and yanked it off. Leah stirred, groping as if she wanted to get back under its warmth, and then she huddled up, drawing her knees into her belly and clasping her hands between her thighs, as if she was trying to turn her body inside out like a glove, to gather herself into her own womb. Her eyes opened for one moment, and I felt like I'd been struck in the groin. Only a shining cataract lit them, like the gleam stretched over deep dreams. The eyes looked at me, went out, and closed.

"It's you? When did you come?" she whispered.

"A few days ago."

"Don't be mad at me."

"Get up, Leah," I said.

The door opened and Simon appeared. "What are you doing here?" he asked.

"Get lost, Simon," I said. "This is none of your business."

"Why did you uncover her?" He came up to me.

"Don't worry," I told him. "I didn't do anything to her."

"That's Jacob's wife," said Simon. "I'm gonna tell him."

"Simon." I sat down on the edge of the bed. "You can tell whatever you want to whoever you want."

"I saw you then too, when Jacob went to Tia Sarah's family," said Simon. "I saw and I heard."

We have always been suspicious of one another, from the day he came to us, a misbegotten child, crippled and ugly, and time, as we know, far from erasing first impressions, only reinforces them and supplies them with proof.

"Listen carefully, you dummy," I said to him. "I didn't do anything with Leah. Not then and not now. More than thirty years have gone by. We're all grown up now, we all know everything, and anyway, what are you doing here, in this room?"

"I came to change her sheets," said Simon. "I do that every week, and my mother washes them, and now you go take care of your father. That's why they called you to come, isn't it?"

"Don't be fresh, Simon." I stood up and approached him. "I punished you once, in case you've forgotten. If you want to find yourself tied to a tree again, just say so. I haven't forgotten how to do it."

Simon's neck became wet. The pain of his crushed thigh makes his sweat smell like the sea. His shoulders and ribs expanded. He leaned forward, looking like a direct descendant of Cherokee the bulldog and Quasimodo the hunchback.

"That's what family is," he said. "You protect and take care of. You don't go to America."

He stooped, not taking his eyes off me for a minute, picked the blanket up off the floor, and covered Leah.

"Get out of here now," he said. "I have to go get Michael from school, and I won't leave you alone with her in the room."

Chapter 24

So many people have confided in me. My brother wrote me amazingly candid letters. Tia Duduch entrusted me with the secret of making masapan. For attorney Edward Abramson, Yehiel's old uncle, I catalogued hundreds of love letters by woman, date, and "miscellaneous." Oh, that "miscellaneous"... Two days ago Michael revealed to me the "magic words that explode stars," and it seems to me that you also entrusted a "little secret" to me in your next-to-last letter. But I have never forgotten the day when Yehiel lifted the hinged counter in the library and said, "You can come in now and choose your book yourself."

In the blurry village street, children ran around, had dust-ups in the dust, and poked fingers in each other's faces, shouting "Hands up!" And in the library Yehiel told me riddles, taught me the English alphabet, and trained me in techniques of repetition and memorization. Even now, when I read a book, I list in the margins the names of the characters in order of appearance, sketch family trees, and draw lines and arrows of relationship. I recommend you do the same. The investment is small and the profit large, as the flower vendor said, advising the suitor to bring his beloved a single rose instead of a pair of diamond earrings.

A short time later Yehiel allowed me to return books from the tables to the shelves, dust them, and air them, and started teaching me to read and write in English. Together we read *The Little Engine That Could*, and Yehiel was amazed at how fast I learned the language. He introduced me to the books of his native land, and when I came to America I didn't come as a foreigner, like Mottl the son of Peysi or Karl Rossmann. He quoted to me from Emerson and Thoreau, decreed that Mark Twain's best book was not *Huckleberry Finn* but *Pudd'nhead Wilson*, said he "respected" Whitman and Faulkner, vilified Louisa May Alcott, and announced that an "important young talent" was growing in America and his name was William Saroyan. I let him mold my taste, and thus many books and authors have escaped me, as have entire branches of literature, but who can read everything? Even you, my dear, didn't identify more than a third of the quotations and allusions that appear in the pages I have already sent you.

Yehiel's own favorite books were a saccharine novel about the suicide of Crown Prince Rudolf in the lodge at Mayerling and the myth of the miner of Falun, in Hoffmann's version, which he forbade me to read. "That's not a story for adolescents in love with their mothers," he told me. But Brinker said, "That's a nice story for children who love their mothers," and he took the book out for me. On the way home he explained that it was a true story about a Swedish miner who perished in the collapse of the famous copper mine of Falun, and whose body was discovered fifty years later, embalmed in vitriol of copper and preserved in its youthful vigor as on the day his soul took wing.

Yehiel memorized *The Sorrows of Young Werther* and envied Brinker for being able to read it in the original, and I even suspect him of secretly holding on to a blue-yellow "Werther suit," like other devotees of that bothersome, bawling, tedious lover. One day Yehiel denounced and defamed the mocking poem by William Thackeray about Werther's love for Charlotte. Years later, when I reprinted in my bread book the passage in which Charlotte slices the loaf of bread, I also included Thackeray's poem. Suddenly I was gripped by a great uneasiness, even though Yehiel was dead by then and perhaps precisely because of that, and so I didn't use the last mocking stanza, only the first.

Werther had a love for Charlotte
Such as words could never utter.
Would you know how first he met her?
She was cutting bread and butter.

There were some subcollections in the library: photos of movie actresses, not all of which he let me see, as well as a set of beautiful ink drawings and watercolors of wild animals of North America, the work of Ernest Thompson Seton. First editions of all of Seton's books are still in the library, and rouse instincts of theft and redemption in me. To you I shall reveal that I have already made use of the old key, and a few days after my arrival I filched the drawing of the American fishhawk, the osprey. That was merely the closing of a circle, since in my childhood I would stare at it in the library, and now I follow it from the window of my house in Cape May on the Atlantic coast as it plucks its prey from the sea and washes its murderous claws in the waves.

But more than anything else Yehiel loved his "Collection of Famous Last Words." I was too young to understand when he declaimed to me, in his New York accent, the verses of Shakespeare he recorded in his fine handwriting at the beginning of every one of the albums of his collection.

O, but they say the tongues of dying men
Enforce attention like deep harmony.
Where words are scarce they are seldom spent in vain,
For they breathe truth that breathe their words in pain.

He recited in English, then closed his eyes and with a shy smile declaimed his own Hebrew translation of Shakespeare's words. He was so excited about that translation of his that he hung it on the announcement board at the entrance to the library, between the list of new books that had arrived and the library hours. The next day an inscription appeared underneath: "Don't let Yehiel Abramson translate me into Hebrew—the last words of William Shakespeare."

Yehiel was outraged. "Coarse brutes!" he cried. "They've got no shame and no culture!" And he took his albums out of the metal cabinet, leafed through them like a madman until he noticed me watching him, and began reading to me from them. My childish brain absorbed and preserved, collected and guarded. Lines, stories, sentences, and facts—unintentionally I even remember most of the last words I heard back then. Not only well-known sayings like "Let me die with the Philistines," or "To bring you down at the hands of Aeacus great royal son ... Achilles!"—but also curiosities like the words of the opera composer Rameau to the priest who heard his confession: "Stop chanting your prayers, you're off key!" Or of the zoologist Georges Cuvier to the nurse who applied leeches to his skin: "Nurse, it was I who discovered that leeches have red blood," he said, and died.

With a broad grin, Yehiel read me the last words of Benjamin Disraeli and with tears in his eyes quoted the ornithologist-poet Alexander Wilson: "Bury me where the birds sing."

"Go play with the children a little," he said finally, and put his albums back in the cabinet. "It's not good for a child to be among books all the time."

Chapter 25

I've been home a few weeks now. With Father, who never stops complaining about his torments, I go to the pain clinic. With Jacob I talk a lot. With Romi I laugh and fight.

"Let's play that you're raw lettuce, Uncle, and I'm a crazy rabbit."

"Let's play that you're Dolores Haze and I'm Dolores Dark."

"Stop trying to impress me, you pain in the neck."

"Your mother would have understood that."

"So go to my mother."

You understand too? Don't you?

A few nights ago, as I lay cradled in the last flickerings of wakefulness, the door of the room suddenly opened, and Father's small, bent silhouette groaned on the threshold. He stood still, and it took me a few seconds to realize that he didn't see me at all. He coughed, put his hands on the wall, and groped his way along, and when he came to the closet door, he opened it, dropped his pajama bottoms to his ankles, and peed inside. The scant, continuous stream, accompanied by sighs and pauses, lasted a few minutes, and I didn't dare disturb him.

I didn't sleep all night, and in the morning I drew a shiny white stripe on the floor from the foot of Father's bed to the door of his room, and from there down the hall to the toilet.

"Follow this line, you see?" I said to him. "It will lead you to the toilet and back."

Jacob, to my surprise, didn't say a thing about the stripe except to ask, "What's that?" and when I explained it to him, he smiled.

Tia Duduch caresses me, gives me her wonderful masapan, cooks me her delicious meals as if I hadn't eaten a thing since the day I left home.

Sometimes she grabs my hand and puts it on her chest, which she suddenly bared one evening, as she used to do when we were kids, and I was startled. The teeth of time, which have gnawed all her limbs, haven't touched her breast. The awful scar, a memorial to its amputated sister, is still there next to it, but the breast is beautiful and shapely, and its glow hasn't vanished. When I gave her the black clothes I brought her from America, she beamed. She went to her room to put them on, and Romi photographed her as she slowly twirled in front of the picture of Uncle Elijah, whose insanely jealous eyes have never stopped following her even from beyond death and behind glass.

Their son Simon glares at me with the grudging eyes he glared at me with thirty years ago. He didn't inherit the curiosity and lust for knowledge ascribed to his father. His temperament is loyal and gloomy, his body strong and cunning like a pit bull. Every day he takes Michael to school and brings him back home, leaning on the new cane I brought him and leaving deep holes in the sand. At recess he makes sure Michael doesn't participate in rough games and doesn't get hurt. One day I saw him waiting there for school to let out. He crouched on his crippled thigh in a corner of the school-yard, reached into his shirt pocket for the plastic soapbox in which he kept a blue pack of cheap Silons, pulled a cigarette out, and tapped it on his thumb-nail. His eyes rummaged around, and smoke belched from his mouth. "He's the last man in Israel who still smokes those stink bombs," says Jacob affectionately. "I think they keep an assembly line at the factory just for him."

Whenever Jacob and I laugh, Simon shrinks. Whenever I approach Leah's closed door, he rushes up and glares at me.

"It's hard for him," says Jacob. "He thinks you're trying to join the family again."

Sometimes I have to remind myself that my brother is wiser and crueler than I think.

From the yard the joyous shout of Michael returning from school is heard, and Jacob hurries to the door. Michael has a merry gait, a combination of a forward step and a sideways hop, and he waves both arms as if he's trying to take off. "We're angels!" he calls. "We're flying." His fearsome guard limps behind him, chained to the ground with the weights of his pain and disability.

Jacob knelt down and hugged his son, then straightened up and opened Michael's schoolbag. "You didn't finish the rolls I made you," he said. "I'm very offended." Every night he bakes two small, funny rolls for Michael, with raisin eyes, yellow sesame-seed smiles, and big poppy-seed mustaches.

Then he said to me, "Give us a few minutes," and disappeared into the bedroom with Michael.

"He's all right," he said when they came back, and served us lunch. He warned Michael that the soup was hot, and he didn't take his eyes off him, chewing and swallowing in time with his son.

"The child looks like Elijah," Father said, chuckling maliciously. "They named him after the Russkie, and he turned out like the Monastirial."

Michael is a thin, delicate boy whose body is stronger than it looks and much stronger than Jacob thinks. Every morning he bursts out of the house barefoot, in a thin nightshirt, runs across the yard holding his clothes and his shoes, and comes to get dressed in front of the oven, which is long dead by then but still gives off heat. He goes down to the pit, takes off his nightshirt, and stretches. Darkness reigns in the small bakery. The low sunbeams sketch lines of silver and gold in the flour dust, which never settles, and illuminate blotches on his body. When he saw me he didn't say anything, but he smiled at me from the pit, and I was embarrassed. Where did that child take shape? I can't figure him out. His countenance is open and pleasant, but his smile is a transparent wall I can't get beyond. His face is the face of someone who knows how to enjoy himself, serious and very pensive. He has none of Mother's and Romi's stormy power, none of Leah's soft gleam, and none of Jacob's scorched taciturnity. He's not like Benjamin either. His back and rib cage remind me of Father, of all people, but Father keeps claiming, "The boy is like Elijah of blessed memory."

This week Tia Duduch started teaching Michael the art of making masapan. Don't make light of this. The women of the Levant keep the secrets of masapan from two interested parties: hateful women and loving men. But Jacob and I, Benjamin and Michael, each in his turn, won this lesson of grace and even learned the most arcane secret of all—to recognize the *punto de masapan*, the moment when the ground almonds are to be added to the melted sugar.

This *punto* is a slippery sliver of time that can't be captured by the hands of a clock or cut by a camera shutter. In his book *Meats and Sweets* Adolph DeVine wrote that the time between taking the piece of meat out of the pan and carving it on a platter is the shortest long time, while the *punto de masapan* is the longest short time. But DeVine always looked for meanings where they were yesterday, and in his *Big Book of Stuffings*, he wrote this nonsense: "We mustn't forget that the eggplant lends a framework to the stuffing but the stuffing lends significance to the eggplant." I much prefer good old Konrad, the pastry chef from Lübeck and self-styled "technician of sweetness," who researched and confirmed scientifically that the duration of the *punto de masapan* is "like the duration of a thought about a wink."

One way or another, it's the moment when the cooked sugar syrup reaches the right stage between liquidity and viscosity, one of the most ancient compromises the human heart has pondered, something you, I am sure, will understand better than I. After all, it was you who wrote me about reading as opposed to memorizing, about the millstone as opposed to the film projector, about the charm of wooing as opposed to the dead weight of jealousy.

A few days before making masapan, my aunt is like a nervous brood hen. She walks around counting in Turkish on her fingers, which is how everybody knows she's beginning to calibrate her body for the necessary calculations.

"Like a pregnant eunuch." Father contributed his own simile.

She took Michael to the kitchen, picked up a wooden spoon, and gave him a taste of the water the almonds were soaking in. Pressing them between finger and thumb, she slipped their brown skins off and set them to dry on her special soft white masapan towel, laundered only in rainwater and hung to dry in the shade. Then she ground them in a mortar, with soft, circular strokes of the pestle, stopping now and then to stir the grains and feel them with the wisdom of her old fingers, for masapan isn't just a flavor, but also a texture, and the way it feels when it rolls between the palate and the tongue is no less important than the way it tastes.

Not needing scales, she poured a precise quantity of sugar into the pot, added a little almond water, and put it on the stove. Then she took the boy's hand, and together they left the kitchen to contemplate the dissolving of the sugar, returning to the pot right on time. As if an hourglass were releasing sand into the hollows of her body, Duduch could return to the melting sugar just before the genuine *punto*. Then she inserted a wooden pick into the pot, raised it to her eyes, and examined the web of congealed silver left by the falling drop.

I remember how she would close her good eye and wait an immeasurable beat, like the time between pressing on a piano key and hearing the sound dissolve, and when she opened the eye again, she stared at the face of the child, who learned the nature of the moment from the dripping of the sugar into his hand and from the gaze of his great-aunt.

Each of us in his day yelled *"Punto da masapan!"* and Duduch added the ground almonds and turned off the fire. *"Abasho!"* cried the child, "Down!" and Duduch banged the pot on the floor, knelt, mixed and mixed and mixed, and put the masapan on the marble to cool.

A few hours later, when the almond dough had cooled and set, they shaped little hills together, and Michael was allowed to stick the sharp pale nipple of a peeled almond in the summit of each of them.

Chapter 26

We were seven years old when Tia Duduch came. She was blind in one eye, and had been widowed, raped, and maimed; one of her children was dead, and she was so stunned by her catastrophe that she didn't speak at all. In her arms was Simon, her surviving baby, a crippled, crooked remnant of her family, and she carried him so that his body would conceal the awful mutilation that had befallen her. She left behind the destroyed dairy, four shattered Matryoshka dolls, an insane mother who never stopped groaning "Somos Abrabanel," and two fresh graves—of her husband Elijah, and of her firstborn son Bekhor Ezekiel.

When we left Jerusalem, Mother had entrusted the dairy to Duduch, who found herself surrounded by a host of bowls, goatskins, *mandilas*, and mysterious tins she didn't know what to do with. Every one of them reminded her of her beloved sister-in-law. She was still sobbing bitterly when a young woman appeared in the courtyard, her splendid face framed by the wimple of a Pravoslav nun; she came to Duduch as if she had known her all her life and beckoned to her to follow.

My uncle Elijah was insanely jealous, as I've said, and jealousy, the lowbrow sister of collecting and love, also infects its victim. Not until the nun rolled up her long habit and proved she wasn't a suitor in disguise did Duduch go with her to the Church of Mary Magdalene, where another nun awaited her, an old woman with a bass voice and the stooped, laborious gait of pilgrims walking against the wind; she gave Duduch precise instructions for the preparation of all kinds of yogurt and cheese, which made the dairy she had inherited famous.

Duduch was a great success in her new business. Bulisa Levy announced, "When I see white ravens, the *chapachula* will get the dairy back." But fate decreed otherwise. Duduch's world fell down around her, and she came to us.

It was the same day Yehiel sent me outside to get some air, and I joined the children on their way to the field to look for antiquities. Brinker was doing his fall plowing, and the blades, as they did every year, turned up reddish and yellowish pottery remnants, glass fragments that gleamed green and blue, marble shards, and colorful floor stones. A mixed group of crows and children walked behind the plow. The crows hunted for earthworms, snails, and seeds, and we scouted for mosaic tiles, the best thing for playing jacks, and for coins we sold to Mr. Cocosin, who ran the village general store.

Mother called him Cocosin because of the stinking coconut oil he sold. He was mad about the greenish coins the plow turned up, and we were just as mad about candy. In the evening Cocosin would receive us in his house. His wife and his plump daughter also waited at the table, along with our payment for the merchandise: Cadbury chocolate from England. He haggled with us for a long time over how much the ancient coins were worth, since we had no idea of their real value. "You got holes in your teeth from candy, and the Cocosin go to Tel-Aviv to build himself big house with the

Bar-Kokhba's pennies," as Mother summed things up a dozen years later, when the manager of the general store had disappeared without a trace.

A silken dusk fell on the fields. The stillness was so soft and deep that Brinker's giddyaps and the mule's braying were swallowed up in its folds. The sun and the earth came together and radiated a pleasant, friendly heat back and forth, and we hovered in the rosy space in between.

I heard the cries of the swallows above us, the beating wings of the cattle egrets as they soared over the cows and landed like blurry handkerchiefs on the willows in the riverbed, where they assembled every evening to spend the night together. A small, dark figure appeared walking down from the hills beyond the plowed land not far from Skull Rock. I, of course, couldn't see anything, but something in her movement attracted the children's attention. They fell silent and fixed their gaze on her. I pressed two fingers to the corners of my eyes to improve my vision a little, but she disappeared in the riverbed, in the shadow of the willows, where the egrets sat like snowflakes in the foliage. A few minutes later the tiny black nebula reemerged at a bend in the riverbed, exhausted and stumbling on the smooth pebbles, climbing and laboriously extricating herself from the thickets on the steep bank.

I remember that picture well because Jacob suddenly got excited, took off our eyeglasses, gave them to me, and asked me to tell him what was happening.

The figure came closer and turned into a short woman wearing a black dress, holding a dark, simian-looking baby in her arms. She passed us, crossed the field slowly, stopped at the edge of the village, right where a Sonol gas station with a Chinese restaurant now stands, looked around until she made out the chimney of the bakery, and headed straight for it.

"She's going to your place," the children shouted, and we ran after her. To this day, when I look at my old aunt, it seems to me she's still walking like that, wounded, weak, a suckling infant in her arms clinging to her one breast, with a noisy flock of curious children at her heels.

"What's she doing?" Jacob asked impatiently.

We were hanging on the fence, only our heads sticking out. The minute the woman opened the gate and entered the yard, her legs began shaking. She took no more than ten steps and collapsed like a top in its last fluttering.

"She fell down," I told Jacob. The door of our house opened immediately, and Mother appeared on the threshold.

"Mother's going to her," I reported.

Mother leaped over the four steps, rushed to the guest, and stood over her.

"She's lifting up the baby and giving it to Mother," I went on.

Now that they were relieved of their burden and responsibility, the woman's hands dropped to her neck, and to my amazement, I saw her rip open her dress. From the corner where I stood I couldn't see the exposed chest, only the two big black buttons that came off and rolled from her collar to the sand, only the chalky whiteness of Mother's eyes wide with terror and her fingers turning pale on the baby's back.

The shattered weeping of the woman in the dust rose in the air.

"That woman's got to be completely crazy," I said to Jacob.

"Just say what you see, not what you think," he answered sharply.

"What did they do to the Duduch?" Mother shrieked in a strange voice, kneeling down next to the woman, weeping along with her, hugging her.

"What's going on?" Jacob inquired.

"Mother is throwing that woman out of the courtyard," I said cold-bloodedly.

But this time I didn't fool him. Jacob glared at me, forced me to the ground, and took the eyeglasses away from me with unexpected strength. For a few moments, I lay there, and then I got up and went home.

Many years have passed since then, and Tia Duduch hasn't left us for even one day. She has nursed dozens of infants, made thousands of pieces of masapan, cooked tons of ratatouille, concocted barrels of jams, baked acres of pastries, and didn't say a word. Only one sentence kept emerging from her mouth, a souvenir of the fears of the 1929 slaughter: "Ibrahim, what are you doing?" She announced these words to the family, whispered them to the kitchen utensils, shouted them out the window to amazed people passing by the house, and murmured them into the pillows she would throw out every week, asking for new ones because her nightmares melted deep holes in them that only she could see.

But that day in the field we didn't yet know all that had happened. That day we only learned who the woman was. Duduch Nathan, Father's sister, Uncle Elijah's widow, a reflection who broke out of Mother's yearnings and Father's stories and came to us.

Chapter 27

The splendid Ford, the little girl, the woman, and the man were already forgotten when a green truck came laboring up the hill. Jamila and Mother were gathering flowers on its slopes because camomile didn't work and Jamila suggested other solutions: narcissus to strengthen weak love, mandrake to kindle flagging lust, crab apple petals to assuage desire for another, and asphodel buds to focus scattered fidelity. By the way, Jamila herself was loved very much. Her husband, a shepherd who could read the ground like a book, had seen the tracks of her bare feet on the lane one day. The prints of her toes and the pads of her heels were so perfect, and the spaces of her arches were so noble and attractive that the fellow abandoned his lambs and followed the tracks until he came to the feet that had made them, and dropped down on the ground they had trod. A few months later negotiations for the dowry were completed, and Jamila came to her husband's house near our village. With the rest of his money he bought her shoes so she wouldn't leave tracks anymore, and in exchange he didn't take any other wives but her.

The truck stopped. Panting workers in caps and undershirts unloaded building materials, molds to mix cement, black rubber pails, and tools. In the following days they measured, thrust pegs into the ground, stretched strings, and then excavated and wounded the flesh of the hill, uprooting the asphodels that gave it its name, leveling the summit, and mottling its flush with heaps of plaster, gravel, and stones. To me they looked as if they were setting the stage for a play.

"Take the Simon too," shouted Mother when she saw Jacob and me leaving the yard and heading toward the hill.

"Then I'll stay here," I grumbled.

Jacob said that "Simon is family" and we had to take care of him, but I said that I had neither the strength nor the desire to carry him. Even though he was short, Simon was very broad-shouldered, and his torments compressed his flesh, making him dense and heavy as lead. Mother sewed him a hammock from an empty flour sack, and when she saw that his weeping was about to burst the barrier of his teeth, she'd shout to us, "Rock the Simon!" Simon never bothered anyone with his agony, but would put a wedge of wood in his mouth and clench it between his jaws until it cracked. Mother, who fostered the legend of the wooden wedge Dyedushka Mikhail bit during his circumcision, said that biting calms pain. But whenever his pain relented, Simon got upset, as if he had lost both the reason and the proof of his existence.

As if he wanted to show that it wasn't only an alleviation but also a dialogue with the world, he started testing his new teeth on all possible material. He left strips of bark turning white on the trunk of the mulberry tree; he poked round holes in the soles of work boots; and one morning he crawled to the bakery and shortened the baker's shovels. Mother was sure that rats' teeth had had a hand in it, but Yehiel said there was only one animal that could gnaw wooden poles like that and it couldn't be any of the animals of this country. Simon's habit quickly turned into a compulsive desire for perfection and improvement; it smacked of that infuriating experimentation of a growing boy who always produces a hard-on, as if challenging it: who would give in first.

He didn't let his mother leave him for a single moment. If she disappeared from his sight, he would bellow dully, with that sorrowful grumble of old lawyers when you take their bookmark out of a place. Slow and steady, he dragged along behind her through the yard and the street, leaning on his knuckles and one knee, spitting crumbs of leather and sawdust, dragging his crippled leg after him. When he was two and a half, he still couldn't stand upright and walk, but his torso developed the muscles of a wrestler, and the plump pads every baby has on his palms became horned hooves on him. Jacob made him rough crutches and taught him to stand and walk, and Simon conceived a devotion, love, and loyalty for him that continue to this day.

"He had a strange nightmare. He complained of seeing black spots penetrating his body," I told Father's doctor about Simon during one of our conversations about Father.

"Interesting," said the doctor. "He cried a lot when he was small?"

"Almost never," said Jacob, who had come along on that visit at my request and had been silent up to that moment.

"Tolerance for pain is different in each person," said the doctor in the pedagogical tone assumed by kindergarten teachers, preachers, insurance agents, and everybody else who comes into contact with dependent people. "Pain, after all, is a processing of the sensation and not the sensation itself, and the processing is first of all a matter of personality, circumstances, and values. Some people yell when you stick them with a pin, and others don't make a sound even when they're broken on the wheel. There are women who shriek in childbirth, and there are women who only groan."

"I knew a woman who screamed even during fertilization," I told him, but the doctor scowled at me and returned to the pleasant course of instruction and explanation.

"As for pain," he continued, "there are several errors. Pain doesn't always have a purpose, it isn't always at the right intensity, and it can never be measured. You have probably noticed that in reply to the question 'How much do you love me?' men spread out their arms and women press them together. I ask the patient to rate his pains on a scale of one to ten, and you'd be amazed what a good indication that gives me of the success of the treatment. Or I ask him to compare a pain he had in the past, an especially strong pain, to his present suffering."

Suddenly he turned to Jacob, pointed to his hand, and said, "For instance, if you were my patient, I'd ask you to compare your present pain to the cutting off of that finger."

My brother's face contorted and turned pale. He doesn't want people to notice his defect. He feels that the stump publicly reveals some weakness. Sometimes he hides it in a fist clenched so tight his face takes on a violent expression.

Now he hurried to cover the lopped-off finger with his other hand. "It didn't hurt when it happened," he growled.

"It probably started hurting afterward?" inquired the doctor.

"I don't remember anymore," said Jacob reluctantly. "It was a long time ago."

Chapter 28

We were far away from God and man, up to our knees in dough and earth, and the house under construction became a focus of espionage and outings. On Saturday farmers' families climbed Asphodel Hill, the children played in the piles of gravel and sand, and the adults went inside, wandered around the gaping spaces, and made estimates—how much money, how much time, how many cubic meters, how many people, who would live where.

Every new event or visit from a stranger became a topic of conversation, guesswork, and a very definite kind of hope. The itinerant doctor, the bus driver, the cattle dealers, the general store suppliers. Sometimes haberdashery peddlers also came. A pleasant smell emanated from their boxes, and the abundance of small items they contained won your heart. But when one of them knocked on the door, Mother would chase him away and watch him suspiciously because they reminded her of the Nawarites of Jerusalem.

One day a strange peddler appeared. A tall, skinny man with lusty moist eyes and hair so thin and stringy it could have been the raveled edges of his black skullcap. In the wooden box hanging around his neck was the usual display of razor blades, soap, shoelaces, combs, and a dozen vials of perfume, "essences" he blended with alcohol to order.

Jacob and I peeked into the haberdashery box, and Mother, to our surprise, offered the peddler a glass of water from the icebox and picked out *ridoma de colonia* as a gift for Father. Then her real intention was revealed. She took a tube of blue eye shadow, put it in her pocket, and started haggling over the price.

As she was arguing, Father woke up from his daily nap, came in, and also started touching and sniffing the vials of essences. Mother was embarrassed, pushed him aside, and said, "There's no money for the shoes for children, Abraham, and you buy cologne?"

The peddler shot her a look of hatred, licked his lips instinctively, and uttered one clear word: "*Goyete.*"

No one in our family knew Yiddish, but Mother knew that word very well. It wasn't the first time she had heard or thought it. Jacob looked at me and I looked at him, and I think we even exchanged a small smile and retreated to make way for the fight that was about to break out.

Mother trembled "like a Bukharan cobbler spit on by a snake." The insulting syllables burst through the bones of her temples and penetrated to her brain, where they exploded. A terrible flush of anger was kindled in her chest and mounted to her throat and face. She bared her wolf's teeth, and the veins of wrath swelled on her neck, descending from her jawline and disappearing under her collar. She thrust out two strong, precise hands, grabbed the leather straps of the haberdashery box, and tightened them around the peddler's neck. The man's face turned purple, his arms and legs jerked, and his mouth gaped open. Not until his whole body was writhing on the floor did Mother let go of his throat, and only then did a few broken curses manage to creep out.

She put a broad, bare foot on his frightened stomach and said: "Who you call *goya?*"

"Nobody," groaned the peddler.

"You watch out yourself, I'm the Tartar!" declared Mother.

We all hid behind her back. Jacob rocked slowly from one foot to the other, waiting for the next round. I wondered if the curses creeping out of the peddler's mouth were uttered at that moment or had been stuck in his throat until Mother let go of it. Half hidden by her body, Father tapped her shoulder warily, soothing and entreating. Duduch looked at her from the side with a mute and admiring eye, a rare smile of pleasure beamed on Simon's face, and the goose strutted around making sure no one disturbed his mistress.

"My father, a rabbin with beard down to here converted him!" Mother announced. To the peddler, to us, to the whole world. She shifted all her weight to the foot treading on him, and gestured to indicate the size of that beard. "A bigger beard than the *berdaleh* on your rabbin," she went on heatedly. "And eyes he had like the Elijah the Prophet. And my father was grown up when they made him a circumcision. Everybody else they tied with ropes because there wasn't no anesthesia, and my father wanted it without no ropes, and he didn't holler because the circumcision wasn't no pain for him."

-"Enough, enough," grumbled Father. "We heard it already."

Mother took her foot off the peddler, bent down to grab his shirt, and pulled him back onto his quaking legs. "We're better Jews than you," she concluded; "and the blood of Our Father the Abraham is flowing already in my sons."

With that she pushed him back out into the dust and closed the door. Now her knees buckled, and her eyes—tired, despairing—slowly closed. The wall she hurried to lean on shook with her weight and her weeping. Jacob made her a cup of tea, and Mother sipped it until she calmed down and uttered her refrain—"Ah . . . that's good . . . "—so we'd know she was better.

The next day a short woman with the face of a prematurely aged goat, hands like a bird, and a small wooden valise came to us and asked, "Where's the lady of the house?" Without waiting for an answer, she went to Mother, took out two blue combs, and swept the hair off her temples.

"It's much prettier like that." She took a step back, the better to observe her handiwork. "*Chez nous à Paris* that's the latest thing."

In a flash she pulled a blue velvet ribbon out of her pocket and fastened it around Mother's neck with a white mother-of-pearl pin. Mother laughed a loud, self-conscious laugh, but her eyes closed with pleasure. The whole picture was strange and wonderful, and even then I knew I would never forget it: Mother, a head and a half taller than the strange woman, beautifully transformed by the cheap trinkets. Jacob and I gazed at her in admiration. Suddenly, in our eyes, she looked like a different woman; her big face, wide-set gray eyes, and broad shoulders lost their coarseness and became so splendid they frightened us with their foreign new force.

With a delicate shove the guest sat Mother down in a chair. "*S'il vous plaît, Madame*," she said. "*Chez nous à Paris*, with the *formidable* face and hair and shoulders like yours, you could have been the very very most beautiful queen."

She opened the valise, took out a comb, scissors, a black hairnet, a hand mirror, and bobby pins, and said, "Yesterday there was somebody here who behaved very not nice, and I came to ask . . . "

As she was speaking, Simon's incisors closed on her foot. Fortunately for her, the teeth sank into her shoe and not her skin. There was an awkward silence, but then the woman leaned down, stuck her hand under his shirt, and stroked his back with her fingertips. A miracle occurred. Simon's eyes closed, his muscles relaxed, his jawbone let go of its prey.

"Men and boys," laughed the woman, "they're all the same, lovely little dogs. *Chez nous à Paris* they bite when they're forty, too." And she ordered

Mother to sit still in the chair, spread a big sheet over her shoulders, and started cutting and combing her hair.

That was how Mother met Chenou Apari, the wife of the obnoxious peddler. She was a devout Francophile, an expert in affairs of the heart, and Mother's good friend from then on. She had a little beauty parlor in the next village and a small and adoring circle of customers who considered her the last word in curls, permanents, and love. She was indeed a gifted hair-dresser and succeeded in making those hardworking women beautiful. All of them were worn down by monotonous years of poverty and toil, and had no one to make themselves beautiful for except their oafish husbands.

The nickname Chenou Apari stuck to her because she was always say-ing those French words which mean "back in our Paris." Of course she also had a real name, but it had vanished through disuse and no one knew what it was anymore. She herself had lovingly adopted her nickname and would introduce herself proudly, "Chenou Apari, *enchantée*."

She would reinforce every one of her definitive diagnoses with the expression "*chez nous à Paris*":

"*Chez nous à Paris* love is like the bread of the people."

"*Chez nous à Paris* people kiss in the street."

"*Chez nous à Paris* even the very very most dirty *clochard* knows how to pamper a woman."

Once a month Mother went to her for her beauty needs, and once a week for her social and emotional needs. Here she sat with her new women friends, exchanging recipes and complaints, leafing through magazines full of gorgeous women accompanied by handsome, visionary poets, involved in aviation and banking, who wrapped their throats in silk cravats.

Chenou Apari ruled over these convocations of women with a hand both firm and gentle, and was as generous with her own secrets as with those of other women.

"Here comes Rosa," she would declare. "Well, Rosa, we all want to know what happened last night. Did the ointment help your husband?"

To give her her due, I must say that she didn't gossip about anybody behind their back, so the sessions in the beauty parlor turned into work-shops of confession and absolution that the women were passionately devoted to. They believed in her so much that even her prematurely lined face didn't keep them from buying the wrinkle creams she concocted to rejuvenate their skin.

"It doesn't do a thing for me," she once told a woman who was hesitat-ing and examining her dubiously, "but you don't have to suffer because of that, right, *ma chérie*?"

Chapter 29

A few faded postcards from school: in fifth grade we had a substitute teacher whose left hand was always stuck in his belt. In science class I threw up once because the smell of formaldehyde reminded me of Brinker's Dead Livy. In contests of general knowledge—synonyms, rivers, books, capital cities, or who said what to whom—I always won first prize. But school memories aren't the kind that want to resurface in me, and none of my teachers left a mark on me that hasn't healed.

When I was eleven, I volunteered to deliver the bread. Every day I got up at six in the morning, loaded the cases of bread into the cart with Father, harnessed the donkey, and left the yard on my adventures, heir of Hector and Ben-Hur. The red dust road was still damp with dew, and the soft, worn rubber tires didn't even make a murmur. Achilles and Messala were nowhere on the horizon, and since the donkey knew the way and the houses where he had to stop, I put the reins around my neck and buried my nose in a book. I managed to read three or four more books a week that way. I would linger at Isaac Brinker's for a few minutes despite the depressing presence of Dead Livy. Brinker would just have come in from milking, and the two of them would have finished their morning quarrel, which always revolved around the same subject: food. Brinker loved omelets with parsley, but the smell of parsley gave Dead Livy an itchy rash on her neck. On the other hand, Dead Livy would make cockscomb soup, which nauseated her husband to the depths of his body and soul.

Brinker knew why I was hanging around and would take the piece of amber he had brought from Germany out of the drawer. Inside the amber a million-year-old fly was embalmed, as fresh and surprised as the moment he died. I would put it up to my eyes and take a deep breath. In the book on old Uli-Buli there was a block of amber like that, and there too the children held their breath at the sight of it. The light was refracted in the gilded arches and magnified the image of the fly, and the faculty of the nearsighted to see clearly at short range made it very sharp.

"How is your mother?" Brinker asked, stroking my neck.

"Fine," I said.

"Give her my regards," he said. "Tell her to come take the chicken droppings for her garden if she wants to."

I got close to Yehiel too. My studies with him turned into private lessons based on a deal of "English for bread." I liked the English language. I know now that I found in it the qualities I would someday discover in the women I loved—clear intelligence, the humor of the victors, as well as the gracious generosity that greatness and diversity bestow on their possessors. To this day I am impressed by the plethora of its synonyms, its waiver of gender, and its strictness of tense. Ten years after those lessons from Yehiel I talked with his old uncle about the love of English. Edward Abramson sneered contemptuously: "Yes, yes, that's a language for Franklin and Hardy, not for Ecclesiastes and the Ten Commandments. Three hundred words for all kinds of sheep and pliers, and only five words to die with precision."

I loved those lessons, which also included coffee and cookies and the conversation and affection of a grown-up man. And thus, as my classmates endeavored to declaim, "Once there was a wizard, he lived in Africa, he went to China to get a lamp," with Yehiel's guidance I could already read Fenimore Cooper in his own language, the fondly remembered *Pudd'nhead Wilson*, and later on *Tracy's Tiger*, my favorite love story of all, as I have taken pains to hint. Thus, Yehiel also made his contribution to my withdrawal, my consolidation, and ultimately—my trip.

Bachelorhood suited Yehiel well. He wore tweed jackets, the only jeans in the country, and yellow American work boots. Every now and then he'd buy cheese and vegetables from the farmers and eggs from Jamila, who also learned a few words from him. When Yehiel asked her, "How do you do?" she would laugh with her big teeth, tinkle her jewels, and repeat after him, "Hadidu, hadidu."

In time he opened up to me, and one day, he revealed his secret dream: to formulate his own last words now.

"I'm nothing but a little librarian in a little village in a little country," he told me sadly.

His dream was to formulate a last utterance so important and beautiful it would be worthy of inclusion in a distinguished anthology, along with those of the prominent dead. He made up last sentences, tested them on me, and recited them incessantly to observe how they rolled between the palate and the tongue so he wouldn't forget them in the mists of dying. He quickly despaired because none equaled the marvelous sentences of his collections.

He enviously quoted Beethoven's last words: "In heaven I will hear." He melted at Goethe's death rattle: "more light. . . ." "What simplicity," he cried, "what humble optimism in such great human beings."

Only when he had almost given up hope did an idea flash in his mind that was so brilliant it made him impatient and his death suddenly seemed too remote to be realized. He decided to laugh between his final words, whatever they would be. He would laugh softly but clearly, thus expressing his full scorn for the black face of death.

At dusk I would go with him to watch the laborers working on Asphodel Hill. Even before the construction was finished, you could sense that the house emanated intelligence and wealth. From the room on the roof Yehiel concluded that the owner was a poet. Dead Livy announced that a poet didn't need two bathrooms and decreed that a rich Englishman was building the house for his Jewish mistress and his illegitimate son. In the general store Cocosin said he had already met the inhabitants, a family of Jewish industrialists from Dresden who had rented the entire Pension Saltzman in Haifa until the house was finished, and were going to set up a porcelain factory in the village. But I, who had already seen the little girl who was to live here, knew she wasn't a son, legitimate or illegitimate, and that she didn't look like the daughter of poets or of porcelain makers, but I didn't correct anyone.

Meanwhile carpenters came and installed thick doors of wood and glass, glaziers put in windows, the walls were plastered and whitewashed, tiles were set. Two gardeners planted shade trees and fruit trees, flowers and grass, and the green truck brought crates and furniture. Workers unloaded the shipment, and I, who had been given my own eyeglasses by then and broke them the next day and Father honored me with a slap in the face, pressed my fingers to the corners of my eyes and went out to see the show.

They carefully carried wrapped pictures, goblets padded with wool, metal trunks, and wooden crates. The tables were heavy and polished. The armchairs were cumbersome and plump, and when they were hurled in the air, they looked like heavy dowagers caught *in flagrante delicto*, swollen ankles kicking and panties waving.

The next evening the Ford returned. The tall man, the leaning woman, and the flowery girl entered their new house, and all night long lights shone and wonderful merry music poured from the open windows. A few years later, as a young man, I heard exactly the same music again just as I stepped off the ship in the port of New Orleans and went to look for a meal and eyeglasses. I wasn't surprised. Even then I knew that Emerson was right, that old smells, sounds, and pictures lie in ambush for you no matter where you go.

Chapter 30

Strangers sometimes show up at our house and ask for "Mr. Abraham Levy."

"We got a letter," they say. "We got a letter and we came."

Father takes them to his room for a short talk, and a few minutes later they go off, downcast and ashamed.

"They failed the test," Jacob laughed when I asked him about it. For years, my brother explained, our father has been sending letters to people he suspects of being relatives. "He's building himself a new family, better than the one he's got. That's why all the telephone books are in his room. He won't rest until he writes to every Levy in the book."

"One son went to America, and one son is estranged from his father. A human being has to have a family," Father replied to my questions.

"Can you live with relatives like that?" He pointed to Simon. "Look at that. Where's all the intelligence of his father of blessed memory? Elijah, who had the wisdom of King Solomon, Elijah, who observed all stars and read all numbers and spoke all languages? Gone, all gone. The gloss is gone, the dross stays on."

I look at Simon and see tempered flesh and forged pain. Hephaestus bent over the anvil of his own body.

"That's not the child of Elijah of blessed memory." Father continued his laments. " That one, when he was little they gave him to a Georgian wet nurse, and her milk made him stupid."

And to prove the wisdom of Elijah, he quoted a poem his beloved brother-in-law wrote at the age of six.

And the stork, with heavy wings,
Body pearly dew,

In her path far above
Cuts the sea of blue.

"Let him fool around with those poems all he wants," Jacob fumed. "Old good-for-nothing. I rely on Simon, and on myself, and that's all."

Father even looked askance at Simon's mother, his sister Duduch. I don't know if he was still angry about her friendship with Mother, or if he blamed her for her husband's death, or if he was just one of those men who can't forgive a woman for being raped. He always scolded her a lot but nevertheless kept asking her to make him the unforgettable salad of their childhood, tomato juice, slices of green onion, and olive oil, which the *orniros*, the baker's apprentices, would dip their bread in and eat with black olives and shots of fig arak.

In those days Duduch was weaning Simon because she was afraid of his emerging teeth. Suckling, even more than love, demands complete trust, and well do I remember the wretched child crawling to his mother, rounding his lips and curling his tongue into a tube, wanting to nestle and suck and being rejected. But my aunt's breast didn't stop producing milk. Groaning with pressure and yearning, she began looking for a new baby to nurse. She followed pregnant women around, peered into houses where infants were heard crying, climbed fences into yards where diapers were hanging on clotheslines. And once Father was even summoned to the hospital in the next town because his sister had snuck into the nursery with the newborn infants and wasn't caught until she had suckled four of them.

Ashamed and angry, he brought her back. "*Kipazelik!*" he screamed. "What more disgrace will you bring on us?"

She suffered such painful congestion that Isaac Brinker suggested consulting his brother, Herr Professor Ludwig Ephraim Brinker, the famous gynecologist from Jerusalem. Every summer the professor came to the village. A tall man with a high brow, whose name and title were whispered by everyone with respect, except for his brother the peasant, who called him Fritzi, wrestled with him in the yard, and rubbed his face in the dust, laughing as *yekke* peasants do when they throw their professor brothers to the ground.

Along with Professor Ludwig Ephraim Brinker came his twin sons. They often visited the bakery, with their smooth tow-colored wavy hair, their ironed khaki shorts, their white teeth, and their perforated shoes.

Brinker told his brother about my mental powers, and he examined me with the pedantic quizzes of the Heidelberg medical school.

"I'm a flower and inside me is a bird!" he cried out. "Who am I?"

"Hibiscus," I said, and won a precise tap on the forehead.

"I'm a bird and inside me is a queen. Who am I?!"

"Gannet," I answered, and received a gift: a gigantic steel syringe.

I could tell him where the copper mines of Sweden were, when Halley's Comet had appeared over Jerusalem, and the name of the Roman soldier who put his hand into the fire before the eyes of the Etruscan commander. "'And in the dark of night, without bow or javelin . . .'" said the professor, and when I recited the following lines of Tshernikhovski's ballad about King Saul, he gave me a pat on the shoulder and an old stethoscope.

Yehiel plied him with questions about Tshernikhovski, for Professor Brinker and the poet had studied medicine together. "Yes, of course," I heard him chuckle, "very much, like stockings." Yehiel wanted to know who "Miriam" was and what sin the poet had committed against her, but Professor Brinker didn't know. "If he published a poem about her and dedicated it to her," he said, "apparently that's really a great secret." Such was his diagnosis, which stunned Yehiel because disguising reality that way never occurred to him.

Professor Brinker was also an enthusiastic phrenologist, an expert on the writings of Lombroso and Kretschmer, and like—well, like who?—asked for and was granted permission to measure Mother's skull with a measuring tape and calipers he took out of a special leather pouch.

"A fine head," he said admiringly. "The skull fits the brain like a glove."

He explained to her the difference between long faces and round faces: "Saint Francis of Assisi as opposed to Martin Luther, Don Quixote and Sancho Panza, King David and Nabal the Carmelite, Dante and Goethe." Mother, who didn't know these personages and was not well versed in the ways of the academic world or in German nicknames, called him "Professor Fritzi" with an embarrassed little curtsy of respect. Dead Livy snorted as corpses do just before they roll into their graves, Father blanched with shame, and Professor Ludwig Ephraim Brinker blushed with pleasure.

In exchange for letting him measure her head, she asked him to relieve Duduch's pains. But by then the poor woman was so strongly identified with her late husband's jealousy that she wouldn't let him examine her even if he were blindfolded. He prescribed pills to stop the milk, but they didn't work; and when he returned to Jerusalem, he sent her an awkward rubber and glass pump that didn't squeeze a single drop from her nipple.

She would walk around the house, stooped and groaning, and even now I have trouble believing what happened one day. Out of a bewildering sisterhood that eludes the understanding of men, Mother closed herself up with Duduch in a room and tried to suck from her, but to no avail. Duduch required the tongue and gums of a baby. At the family table she would suddenly bare her breast with a strange and touching gesture, for there was both generosity and supplication in her.

Swollen, lonely, and ashamed, terrifying in its orphanhood and splendor, my aunt's left breast bursts into my memory and lights up the room with its beauty, its freshness, and its nostalgia for its amputated twin. Time made my father into an old man. My brother into a grown man. My mother into a dead woman. . . . Me? What did it do to me? Only my aunt's breast remains as it was, preserved in the amber of its youth. "Like a photograph of the second breast," as Romi said.

"Good God!" Father lowered his eyes, and his chin trembled with anger. "What are you doing? There are big boys here."

Jacob and I, who were past bar-mitzvah age by then and starting to sprout signs of a mustache, looked at the silken mound with round eyes and dry palates. Jacob couldn't resist, stuck out a hand, and touched it with his fingertips. Father hit his arm and shouted at her, "Get away from here! Whore! *Putana!*"

"Leave the Duduch alone, evil you!" Mother rose up beside Duduch's chair. "You didn't understand nothing? She doesn't want man, she wants baby."

Her big hand fluttered over the hair that had lost its Saroyanesque blue luster, traced the eternal lines of wonder etched in the face, arched for a moment over the empty eye, then caressed the neck, descended to the bud of the nipple, which looked as if it had been painted on with a purple brush, and covered her sister-in-law's nakedness with a panel of her dress.

Tia Duduch shivered, leaned her head on Mother's hip, and a dark wet spot spread on the fabric of her dress.

"Ibrahim, what are you doing?" she sighed.

Father shuddered with wrath and left the room, and Jacob said, "Now he'll go yell into the oven for sure." But Father returned with the *shakikra de raki* wound around his forehead to show that he had *dolor de kabesa*, that they got on his nerves, that they should all get out of his sight now, that they should leave him alone.

Duduch wasn't the only one who disgraced him. None of us managed to satisfy him. He hated Mother for her behavior, her origins, and her looks; Jacob was a "stubborn and rebellious son"; I was easy-going and polite, but I had already withdrawn into my own blurry worlds, and Father was the first to understand that salvation would not come to him from me.

Simon was also an inexhaustible affront to honor. That year he was in fact promoted to the third grade and surprised everyone with his diligence, but at the same time he graduated from biting to a mad passion for sweets. Dead Livy had a separator and a Hoskvarna hand churn, and sometimes Brinker would smuggle Mother a little butter and cream, and she would make us a treat of cocoa, cream, and sugar. Simon, who could hear the whisk beating from any distance and any place, would materialize in the kitchen with his twisted hyena's gait, and stare at Mother with pleading eyes, salivating eagerly.

She would bend down, show him his portion and say, "Don't bite!"

We would laugh as Simon, pale with yearning, carried his spoils to a hidden corner. Not until long after we had finished ours did he sally forth again, and give Mother back the bowl and spoon, which were carefully licked clean.

Mother was fond of Simon and pitied him because she understood his distress. Not his pain, but the supressed animality that dwelled in him just as in her. Sometimes she would save up a few pennies and buy a chocolate bar from the English soldiers who came to get bread for the base. Simon would pop the chocolate into his mouth, but despite the tremendous temptation for strong and instant gratification, a temptation both little boys and grown men have a hard time fighting, he didn't chew it or even suck it, he just closed his eyes and his lips and let it melt in the warmth of his mouth. Still as a stone he was then, immersed in his sensations like a fakir, his whole body wrapped around the strip of pleasure between his tongue and his palate. I could see how the sweetness dissolved in his mouth, infiltrated the sorrow of his tissues, consoled his flesh, and planted hope in him.

"Chocolate makes the black spots go away," he once told Jacob.

"Give him, give him a lot of *chocolada*," said Father. "Let all his teeth rot, the *perro*, and then let's see how he bites."

Chapter 31

One morning when I went out to harness the donkey, I found him already hitched and my brother sitting on the cart.

"I'll come with you to deliver the bread," he said, and on the way he suggested we stop at the new house.

"Forget it," I told him; "I really don't think they eat bread, and anyway they're not from the village."

"Everybody eats bread," said Jacob, "even them." And he turned the aggrieved donkey—a diligent and loyal worker but a sworn enemy of change—to the new house. In the distance we saw the Ford gliding down the hill. The tall man passed us in a quick cloud of dust, scared the donkey, and disappeared. Not until some time later did I understand that I had witnessed a man's escape from his home and family, and that he would never return to them again.

We crossed the field, climbed the hill, and went through the open gate into the yard. Small piles of building material still mottled the red loam, and plaster dust turned the leaves of the saplings and flowers white.

"Bread! Bread!" shouted Jacob, ringing the big brass bell to announce our arrival.

The house was silent.

"Bread! Bread!" Jacob went on ringing.

The woman peeped out the window. "Come in, boy, bring two loaves." Her voice was tearful and choked.

Jacob selected two loaves and went inside. Two minutes later he returned, his eyes shining.

"Why was she crying?" I asked.

"I saw the new girl," Jacob answered.

That night he talked with Father, who laughed and said, "You're still children, Jacob, make her *pasharikos*." And he showed him how to bake

139

rolls in the form of birds, and to use raisins and onion skins for owl eyes and hoopoe fringes.

The next morning Jacob insisted we go to the new house first. He rang the brass bell with great ceremony, and Zivia Levitov, Leah's mother, called to us to come in.

"Come with me," said Jacob. "And put on the eyeglasses. I want you to see her."

Leah was eating breakfast. She hadn't yet plaited her braid, and the abundant cascade of hair stunned me.

"This is for you," said Jacob bravely, approaching the table and putting the birds down in front of her.

Leah withdrew into the mantle of her hair and didn't say a thing.

"What is it?" Zivia was amazed.

"A gift."

"From who?"

"From me," said Jacob. "For her."

"And you? Did you bring something too?" Zivia turned to me. She looked so sad I flinched.

"What?... No. No ... I'm just his brother." And then, since I didn't know what else to say and my sentence didn't seem to come to an end on its own, I added, "We're twins."

"You don't look like twins," said Zivia. And to Leah, "Say thank you, Lalka."

Leah glanced at Jacob's rolls, smiled wanly, and said thank you.

"Lalka, Lalka, Lalka, Lalka," Jacob kept repeating all the way home in the cart. "Lalka, Lalka, Lalka, Lalka." His jaws moved, Lalkas took wing in his mouth, melting pleasure lit his face.

Chapter 32

==

That week, as Isaac Brinker was working his vineyard, the blades of his cultivator hit a hard, heavy block hidden under the ground. The startled mule braked as if the hand of fate or of a giant had stopped him. Brinker unhitched him, hoed all around, and exposed a carved marble capital. Greatly excited, he went on digging, and by evening he had discovered a few more broken capitals, stumps of pillars, and some floor tiles. Restlessness gripped him, the uneasiness of a man who hasn't yet found what he wants, but doesn't even know what it is. At night he continued digging by the light of two oil lamps and a yellow moon, and kept on past dawn, and in the afternoon he exposed a small Hellenistic mosaic and knew why he hadn't stopped digging. Narcissus and poppies bloomed in the mosaic, two faded geese twined their necks at the edges, and in the center was the dull image of a beautiful woman whose eyes and pale stone nipples followed you wherever you went. Brinker knelt down and couldn't get enough of the sight. Then he covered the mosaic's nakedness with soil and ran to the library to tell Yehiel Abramson.

Relations between Yehiel and Brinker were best described as bonds of mutual tension. Brinker was older than Yehiel, smarter and better educated, and Yehiel suspected him, correctly, of being the man who had hung the announcement mocking his translation of Shakespeare. But Yehiel ruled the library and Brinker couldn't live without it, so there was a balance of power.

Yehiel and I were sitting in his office during one of those pleasant hours devoted to English, quoting the openings of books and ranking the rivers of Africa according to their annual flood rate. We were drinking coffee with milk and eating American chocolate chip cookies, and Yehiel recited from Emerson—"Man does not live by bread alone, but also by catchwords"—and asked me roundabout questions designed to test whether I had picked up the double irony in the sentence.

He wanted to know who the new people were who had come to live on the hill. "I hope for their sake they don't have anything to do with the Hebrew University," he said gravely.

Then he showed me famous "last words" that had more than one version and complained of being unable to decide between two sayings of Archimedes to his Roman captor: "Stand back, you're hiding the sun," or "Wait until I finish the equation." I loved his hesitations and knew he would include all the versions in the end, because like all collectors, he was excited more by quantity than by quality. The two versions of Vespasian's last words were also among his treasures, and both seemed equally authentic because both had an equal measure of military stupidity.

The three conjectures concerning Rabelais's last words nagged him especially, and he examined them aloud.

"I am going in search of a great perhaps." He waved his hand solemnly.

"I'm greasing my boots for the last journey," he whispered.

"Ring down the curtain, the farce is over." He clutched his throat and sank to the ground.

All three sounded fake to me, and the first quite stupid as well, but Yehiel preserved them with the same thrill and tenderness old opticians feel for their children's first pair of shoes.

Dusty and sweaty, Brinker burst into the library and told us about the mosaic. The dying Rabelais got up from the floor, put on his tweed jacket, hung the box camera on his shoulder, and invited me to come along.

I remember Brinker's expression as he put his finger to his lips to silence us, knelt down among the vines, and dug with his hands in the soil that covered the buried woman. First a shoulder was revealed, then a neck and a cheek, and I was overcome. I sank to the ground on all fours, pain constricting my vital organs and flooding my eye sockets, the expression of a desire I hadn't known until then, the desire to see better, which has since returned to me so sharply only four more times, and I'll tell you about two of them later.

Brinker's broad hand exposed the other shoulder, caressed the neck, slid over the breast, and climbed to the face. A veil of reddish dust covered the Hellenistic girl. Brinker pursed his lips and blew hard, and her face floated up from oblivion. Pure and comely she was, and her cool beauty illuminated the vineyard.

The librarian was excited. He began walking around and around her in a marvelously precise circle, as if bound by a string to her gaze, all the while murmuring in English, "Unbelievable, unbelievable," for the girl followed him too with her nipples and her eyes. Brinker called my attention to this phenomenon, which roused great wonder in me. Only as time passed, with the help of my *Venus of Urbino*, did I decipher the secret of that roving gaze. I discovered that for all her charm and sexuality, her reddish hair, her girlish nipples, and her strong hands, she is squinting. Please don't argue with me, my dear. I don't think there is another man in the world who has spent more hours than I in front of her picture, except maybe Titian himself.

Yehiel went to the pump and filled a bucket with water, and when he poured it on the mosaic, the girl came to life. All at once, the color returned to her skin, the warmth to her flesh, the suppleness to her breasts, and the gleam to her eyes. The yellow of the narcissus glowed, amorous hues blossomed on the gander's neck, and the two men sighed. Not until years later did my own flesh teach me that that was the sigh of men whose embalmed love had returned and awakened before their eyes. Then Yehiel photographed the mosaic from various angles and advised Brinker to cover it again with soil and not to tell anyone about it.

Three days later a truck came loaded with picks, sieves, and excited scholars from the Hebrew University in Jerusalem. Yehiel blazed with the rage of a betrayed librarian and announced that he wouldn't join them. Brinker led the guests to the red pennant he used to mark the girl's grave, and they dug but found nothing except fragments of capitals and pillars. The mosaic had disappeared. They rushed to the library and demanded that Yehiel hand over the roll of film he had taken. Scornful and insolent, Yehiel didn't even deign to show them out. The angry archaeologists went back to Brinker and accused him of playing a joke on them; he was offended and threw them out of his vineyard.

The loss of the maiden gave Brinker headaches and the kind of agony "that story tellers call wounded love." His suspicions muddied the atmosphere in the village and stirred up a sea of conjectures there. Some claimed that Yehiel stole the mosaic to get even with the Hebrew University; others pointed a finger of blame at Jamila's husband from the neighboring Arab village, since he had already been caught stealing antiquities; still others accused Mr. Cocosin of the general store; and there were those who remembered children playing "jacks" with small stones.

Brinker himself suspected his own wife, who was so jealous she didn't even trust women in portraits. But the weeks passed, time sank the rumors, and Brinker calmed down. Finally almost everybody forgot the mosaic, but when I went to the library, I would sometimes see Yehiel sitting there looking at some picture he had taken, and I knew I mustn't disturb him.

"How, of all the men in the village, did you get close to those two who fell in love with Mother?" Jacob said to me yesterday when we saw Brinker

143

in the street. The old man was leaning on the nursery school fence, listening to the little ones singing, and didn't recognize me.

"I can understand what they saw in you. You were a key for them, and a cover, and a pretext. But what did you see in them? That's what I just don't get."

Chapter 33

At night people would come to the bakery. There were field guards, men who sprayed the groves, hungry workers getting off the night shift. But there were also those I privately called "the condemned": the smell of bread reached their noses, looped around their necks, and drew them to us.

One by one they rose up out of the dark and took shape. On especially hot or especially cold nights, when many people came, the bakery looked to me like a remote field clinic for those infected with yearning. Each one and his own flaw, each one and his own grief, each one and his own pain sat in the yard and chewed his bread. We didn't know many of them, nor did we know their names or their homes. Some were great insomniacs whose memories wouldn't let them fall asleep. Some were in love, and their pain was doubled by Hypnos in his cruel mirror dreams. Some were ugly and emerged from their houses only under the veil of darkness; some were seeking consolation; some were lunatics who wanted to burn their wings at the grace of the oven.

They ate the bread with tremendous concentration. Those who were experienced and addicted would bring something to spice the bread—cheese, a pickle, a herring. And they brought a thermos of coffee and a book to read. Sometimes they came inside and asked permission to dip their bread in Dyeduskhka Mikhail's ancient salt cellar, or they peered through the window to watch us at work. Father's precise and measured movements, the warmth of the oven, the iron laws of fermenting and rising—all this calmed their soul.

Mother, the practical and excited one, wanted to add another room onto the bakery, put tables and chairs in it, and sell butter and cheese, olives and tea. But Father couldn't bear the nocturnal guests. He claimed that when they came in and went out of the bakery, the door slammed and the dough fell because of the banging.

"You won't make a café of Italians here!" he announced, and told Simon "to throw those good-for-nothings, those *indehiniados*, out of the yard." Simon, who knew in his own body the soothing labor of the bread, was confused; he cast a questioning glance at Jacob and didn't budge.

"They came to look at Mother," said Jacob. Even today he claims that I was even blinder than they thought back then. "Brinker was in love with her, his brother the professor was in love with her, your Yehiel couldn't take his eyes off her, and all those poor souls were thinking about her while they chewed their bread."

"You're talking nonsense," I told him, surprised at the blunt rage his words aroused in me. Of course I remembered that Yehiel came too. He was a bachelor, and the nights sometimes assaulted him with stabs of loneliness, stupor, and restlessness. I knew he sometimes went to the city because Dead Livy would greet him the next day at the door of the general store and ask loudly, "Well, Yehiel, an intellectual like you went to do a mitzvah?" But Yehiel usually came to the bakery to eat fresh bread and look at the photograph of the stone maiden as he chewed.

"I thought you understood those things better than me, with all your women there," Jacob mocks me. He was always surprised at how many lovers Benjamin and I had. But he despises me, and he boasts of his son. "So many girls came to his funeral," he repeats proudly.

Once he saw Leah, he joined me every morning. He started wearing a white shirt to deliver the bread and carried a small comb in his pocket. His hair—thick and wavy in those days, soft and thin today—made him unhappy. Chenou Apari had given him an old wooden comb, and as soon as we left the yard, he started running it through his stiff curls to make them assume some sort of shape. Sometimes he was steeped in prolonged meditations, and a smile suddenly played over his face as prophecies and supplications of love kept forming inside him. Every morning he drove the Patriarch's carriage into the Levitov yard, rang the bell hard, selected a nice loaf of bread for Zivia, took the *pasharikos* he had baked for Leah the night before, and knocked on the door so they would invite him in.

"Lalka, Lalka, Lalka," I heard him sating himself with that ancient oath of men—the name of the beloved.

"Look," he said and pointed to something only he saw. "Those are her footprints in the sand. See how pretty they are." And he took off his right sandal, put his bare foot in Leah's print, and closed his eyes. "It's like

145

touching." He took off the other sandal and walked in her tracks until they rose onto the grass and vanished.

How strong is the love of a boy, hotter and more desperate is it than all other love. When my brother came out of the Levitov house, I knew from the way he walked down the steps whether he had seen her or not. I hoped he wouldn't notice the bread birds he had brought her yesterday scattered among the freesias in the garden. The sun had already dried their flesh, the ants had hewn burrows in them, the jays had pecked out their eyes. Jacob didn't linger over them and didn't say a word about them, and today he even claims that such things never existed, but I can't forget those dead birds in the flower beds. A dozen years later, when I started writing my first bread book, I invented in it "an ancient Jerusalem custom" of greeting the beloved with such rolls. I called the book *The Bread of Jerusalem*, and I wrote the whole thing from memory and reconstruction leavened with imagination and fiction; between bread recipes, I embroidered documentary fabrications and authentic falsehoods that were very popular with readers. Who knows better than you, my dear, that it is easier to invent a fact than to discover it, and I have been an expert in that profession for so many years that I no longer know which of the facts in my books are really true. I either concealed or delayed a few details, as I am doing at this very moment, but the biggest lies were the ones I wrote in my private diary. Do you remember what Miss Prism said to Cecily? "Memory is the diary that we all carry about with us." And Cecily answered, "But it usually chronicles the things that have never happened." I don't understand how Oscar Wilde could have endowed such a stupid girl with so much perspicacity, but in any event, it is the nature of private diaries to show up at a time that is very inconvenient for their owners—after their death—and I can't trust that Jacob will live long after me and destroy my diary when the time comes. I'm not Goethe and my brother's not Max.

An American woman whose broad white shoulders I remember well told me on the one and only night she spent with me that a liar has to have an excellent memory. "More excellent than yours," she said, and then she laughed and got up and left. "A viper in a basket of figs," she called me. Bitter and cool was her laugh, too tormented for me to endeavor to recall the reason for it, but if I do say so myself I have an excellent memory. I've already told you that as a child I always won the school contests, and in the United States too I once gave in to temptation and participated very successfully in a public contest of quotations and general knowledge. But I distinguish between memory and memorization, remembrance and recollection, and whenever I need my archives their content changes. This quality, which I euphemistically call "creative recollecting," I inherited from my father, who was and remains an adroit prevaricator without any malice. "That book was made by Mr. Mark Twain, and he told the truth, mainly. There was things which he stretched, but mainly he told the truth," Huckleberry Finn testified about his creator. About my own father I can say that if Agathon had known him, he would have changed his famous maxim and said, "Even God can't change the past, but the baker Abraham Levy can." So, Jacob can't bear Father's fabrications and similes, while I just want to enjoy stories whether they're true or not.

I was struck by nostalgia in my writing, the kind of calloused nostalgia nothing can extirpate from the soul—for the home I had left; for my mother, whose awful curse has stayed with me to this day, more than thirty years after she uttered it; for my brother; for the blurry landscape of my youth; for my brother's wife, whose love I didn't fight for as I should have; I even missed the rats in the bakery. Struck with remorse I was, for my trip, for its nature and its reasons. And struck with rage I was, for the young shoots torn off, hanging flaccid from the soles of my feet and giving me phantom pains in the limbs amputated even from my memory.

Grief filled me as I wrote. "And an uninvited wave of tears will also come, and choke the throat, and try to hang on the eyelashes." I often raised my eyes from the desk and looked at the pictures of my women on the wall. Meanwhile, I had already thrown away the pages I had torn out and stolen from Yehiel's albums the night before my trip, and with my first paycheck in America I bought myself beautiful reproductions of the *Odalisque à la culotte grise* and *Venus of Urbino*. The truth is that I prefer Gauguin's *The King's Wife* and *Leda and the Swan*, but like a gosling who follows the first creature he sees when he hatches, so I want the woman I saw then, when my virgin eyes hatched.

"Your books are loathsome scribblings," Jacob wrote me. "I don't have enough time or enough English to finish them."

I wasn't offended. My bread book was a great success. Newspaper reviewers wrote about "the erotic mystery of the loaf of bread" and "the fragrant allure of the history of the bakery," of bread "that accompanies the human race from the dawn of civilization, and the individual from birth to death," and about the author, "scion of a dynasty of Jerusalem bakers" who "kneads before our eyes a wonderful Mediterranean blend of mythology, gastronomy, and history."

In a little while, I'll tell you about my bread, the "bitter bread of banishment." In a little while, later, when this pain that gnaws and digs in my chest subsides.

Chapter 34

"She's so beautiful," Jacob said to me. An ice chip was between his teeth, freezing the *b* and the *l* as he sucked it ardently. The ice man had passed by in his cart covered with sacks, and Mother had sent us to get a half-block for the icebox in the kitchen. The ice man, who was almost toothless, gave us a terrible smile but let us gather up the slivers his ice pick sprayed from the blocks. All the children loved the ice man, and all the parents warned them against him because of his habit of washing his hands in every faucet he saw on his way. When we were little, Noah Brinker told us that the ice man had murdered his wife and children with this pick and that their blood still stained his skin, and when Noah saw our panic he added that, on the birthdays of the victims, blood dripped from the murderer's fingernails.

Unwittingly Jacob had hit on the ancient distinction that beauty, in all its varieties and degrees, is merely "what evokes love." But we were adolescents then and didn't understand the difference between beauty solely as a physical quality and grace as a physical and spiritual quality. Years later, when I read Giorgio Vasari, I was surprised to see that I had heard all his refinements on that issue from Father in my childhood. He watched Leah, was fond of her, and delighted in calling her *"Ijika con Gracia."* A few years later, when he was urging me to fight Jacob for her, he said, "Grace, stupid. It's like love and it's like pain. It's not beauty or weight or height or something you can measure in centimeters."

Leah was also interested in all kinds of collecting. I really don't understand how all these collectors have gathered in my life—Father with his relatives, Duduch with her sucklings, Yehiel with his father's books. Sometimes I think Romi is just a collector too. She crucifies her victims on atoms of silver and light, and exhibits their portraits in cages of frames, like her mother in those far-off days. Leah collected dried flowers, stamps, napkins, dolls, and postcards her father sent her from all over the world. Unlike Yehiel Abramson, who hid his collection of famous last words from strangers, she used to invite her girlfriends to show them her collections, and she did it in such a way that none of them felt jealous, not even over the picture of the actor John Gilbert that came from abroad with his signature sparkling at the bottom.

The girls said that the collections were arranged in hundreds of small polished boxes of wood and glass, and that Leah enjoyed other advantages of being the only child in a rich family, aside from a tormented and distant father whose guilt drained a stream of gifts from him. She had her own room on the roof, with her own clothes closet, containing an abundance of blouses and skirts, and even a few ensembles from the exclusive Ilka boutique, with rustling sachets of rosemary and lavender nestled among them. Now, at her bedside, Jacob shows me the faded remnants of the old collection of butterflies and says in a broken voice, "Remember her then? Remember?" Back in those days he claimed that when she crucified the butterflies with pins, they sighed in gratitude at being found worthy of her attention, and I know what's going through your mind now. You're wrong, my dear. I'm not a collector. Neither of memories nor of quotations and facts. Willy-nilly they collect in me. Like Father's pains, like Jacob's sufferings, like Romi's photos, like all those women, harvested, gathered, collected into my life.

Outside, spring cleared out, summer came early, the blaze of August prevailed in early May. In the bakery time revolved, not deviating from its cycles. In the library Yehiel showed me a photograph of the Hindenburg Zeppelin blazing on its anchor and read me an article from the *New York Times* about the Peel Commission so I would also learn "newspaper English," and when I asked him why he didn't get married, he laughed and quoted two maxims from Robert Louis Stevenson: "Married life is a long, straight, and dusty road to the grave," and "The cruelest lies are often told in silence." One I understood even then, and the other one I don't understand even now.

I remember that on May Day that summer we sat in the library gluing bindings. Outside we heard the drums of the parade beating to a song that made Yehiel grimace.

On mountain, on vale,
From here to Bombay,

All cheer and all hail
The first day of May.
The worker is free
All over the world,
On land and on sea
His banner's unfurled.

"The kulaks sing about workers," said Yehiel contemptuously.

In the few hours I spent outside the bakery and the library, I saw that the grass in the fields had turned yellow, the level of the brook was low, and the little fish caught in the puddles in the riverbed had died from the heat of the water even before it evaporated. Birds mad with anxiety fought over every dripping faucet, filled their beaks with water, and sprayed it on their nests, beating their wings over them in vain. A stench rose from the nests, where chicks were baked alive and unhatched eggs boiled and rotted. And in the hottest hours you could suddenly see Leah coming out of her house on the hill.

A child of the sun she was, and the sun didn't turn her skin red or burn her, but gave her a good smell of fruit and made her the brown color of Florentine bronze. (Florentine bronze? Florentine? Even I don't remember what I'm quoting.) Her hair shone. When she rode her bike, her dress would cling and billow in turn on her gilded legs, and from the right angle you could see the white flash of her thighs. I could sense Jacob's muscles tense and his heart quicken, but back then I didn't understand why. He would go up to the roof or climb a tree to observe her, and I would go to the library to bring him "nice sentences for letters."

Yehiel sat at his table pasting stamps on letters to be sent abroad. He had taken to writing to the families of "prominent deceased" to ask them for the last words of their loved ones. Among his addressees in those days were the relatives of Lawrence of Arabia, Kemal Atatürk, the writer Scott Fitzgerald, the painter Paul Weber, and the composers Gustav Sterner and George Gershwin. Incidentally, when Virginia Woolf's last letter to her husband Leonard was published, Yehiel sent the widower a letter of condolence, informing him that he had decided to include "Mrs. Woolf's lovely sentence" in his collection: "I don't think two people could have been happier than we have been." But Leonard Woolf didn't answer Yehiel's letter either.

In his despair the librarian told me he would have to murder some famous person to hear his last words with his own ears.

"Albert Einstein," he said, "he's the best choice."

I told Yehiel of my brother's request, and he directed me to Peter Altenberg: "Your flesh is like a delicate poet's song." "Here, you bathe in light and air," and other such blandishments that made Jacob so happy he hurried to weave them into a letter he sent with Simon.

Leah was sitting on the balcony when the crippled boy crossed the fallow field and lurched into her yard, waving the letter at her.

"Get out and take that back to whoever sent it, you black monkey," she told him.

Simon put the letter between his teeth, grabbed the banister of the balcony with both thick, filthy hands, and swung himself up. Leah was so scared by the crushing force of his fingers on her wrist that she took the letter from him. Simon stood next to her to make sure she read it, and then he said, "And now you'll write an answer and I'll take it."

"I'll just go get pen and paper. Wait here," said Leah pleasantly. "Meanwhile, have a drink of water from the faucet."

She got up, went into the house, and locked the door behind her. Three years later, lying on her bed, she shifted her cascade of hair from her shoulders, asked me to stroke her neck with my fingertips, and told me that Simon had waited on the balcony for ten hours. Not until one o'clock in the morning, when he heard the burner lit in the bakery and smelled the sourish rising of the dough, did he leave his post to go help at work.

She showed me my brother's old childish letters, and the two of us, without any malice, read them and laughed.

"You're both so pathetic," she said. "You shouldn't have tried so hard. All you had to do was kill a lion with your bare hands and bring me his carcass."

I never experienced those torments. I was steeped in my books, and along with my nearsightedness they defended me like Perseus's polished shield. I didn't take my first real steps in the love of women until a few years later, at a relatively advanced age, and then with great ease. I was twenty-two the first time I went to bed with a woman. She was a few years older than me, was built like me, and she won my heart with her habit of writing authors' dedications to herself in her copy of their books.

"*In the crow's nest, between the deck and the sky, I sought your bounty.*— Herman."

"*Beware of Sofia Grigorievna.*—Leo." ("I expected a somewhat more original dedication from him," she told me plaintively.)

"My black Tartar, eat me berry by berry.—William."

"Remember the blue anemone?—Victor."

"My fatso, hoo hoo hoo hoo—André." (With a line under the third "hoo," of course.)

There were also the usual dedications from Hemingway and Wassermann, and another one, surprisingly long and direct, from—you won't believe it—Miguel de Cervantes, who kept having detailed erotic visions of her in his prison cell and declared that he wrote the book there only to try to forget her.

"The first time you do it in the dark," she told me. "And take your glasses off by yourself and remember where you put them."

She guided me with her words, routed me with her laughter, and directed me with her sighs until I was inside her, surprised at the simplicity of the act, which had looked very complicated in my daydreams.

But Jacob, an emotional, humorless, and short young man, with his thick glasses on his nose and his whole body throbbing like a heart plucked out of its ribcage, was too young to see the laughing face of love. In despair and crushed he was, and he plunged into the dark depths of his suffering with all the levity of a block of lead. Father told Mother: "Your son is as heavy as the head of an Albanian," and threw him out of the bakery because his presence there was enough to kill the yeast.

He often climbed to the top of the mulberry tree to see the love of his life skipping in her winged sandals over the fields, brandishing a butterfly net; and he immediately ran after her, gave her brown beetles that secreted a stinking defensive fluid, scorched by the sting of impatient bees, whose toil and sterility make them hate all lovers, and he gathered the abandoned larvae of swallowtail butterflies that Leah raised in her house. He even asked me to steal Brinker's amber block because he knew she longed to add it to her collection, but I refused.

"Borrow it from him and tell him it got lost," he pleaded.

"I'll swipe it," he warned.

"And they'll blame you," he threatened.

With a persistence and courage only amorous boys can muster, he tried to strike up a conversation or catch a glance. When Leah was prancing around with her girlfriends, he felt their sharp looks pierce his back and heard their laughing, venomous hornets' buzz. Mother recognized in him all love's obstacles and clumsiness, which she knew so well from her own life, and when she saw him bare his stomach one day and lie prone on the ground, she was terrified.

"What did you doing?" she shouted.

"I'm listening to her footsteps. That's how the Indians do it," said Jacob; and when he saw me laughing, he got up and chased me, hurling stones and clods of dirt at me.

Worst of all was the knowledge that there was no one anywhere around who could give him advice. I was as young and inexperienced as he was; Tia Duduch's education in the area of love was summed up in yearnings for Elijah's jealousy; Mother was even more pitiful than he was in her awkward wooing of Father; and Father regarded the conduct of his wife and son as "*una granda palabra.*"

In his distress Jacob went to Chenou Apari, the expert on "relations."

When Chenou Apari said the word "relations," she meant an all-purpose term for the whole collection of rules of intimacy, from the precise pitch of first looks and opening lines, to the color code governing the sending of roses, to degrees of whispering and endearment and various kinds of kissing on the way to the "act." And when Chenou Apari said the word "act," she always said it with the definite article, the way Mother said proper names, and her voice grew husky and dropped a full octave.

"First of all, straighten that hair of yours," Chenou scolded my brother. "What are you, the king of Africa?" She sat him down on a chair, smeared an oily green liquid on his hair, and combed it. "*Chez nous à Paris,*" she went on, "men have smooth, soft hair and the fingers of a pianist." And she decreed that "in love the very very most important thing is to know where to put a period and where to put a comma."

"And start shaving every day," she said, "or it's like dirt on your face. You're not a child anymore. Any minute now you're a man."

She stood in front of him and took his crimson face between her hands. "*Chez nous à Paris* men are not animals," she declared. "They have patience. They know it is forbidden to skip any stage on the way to the act."

Chenou's husband—"The haberbashery peddler?" laughed Romi years later in America when I told her the story of her parents' love—would sit at the back of the beauty parlor filing his fingernails, smoking foul-smelling Maluki cigarettes, and sometimes playing oriental tunes on an old clay ocarina. Chenou Apari amused all the women with her juicy descriptions of their bedroom habits. "The very most he loves it with *très-très* Nivea," she bleated out a big guffaw. Sometimes she laughed softly with the guttural dove's coo Hungarian women use to signal one another that they intend to reveal a secret: "His little thing, when he was young, it would watch him brush his teeth, and now it watches him brush his shoes."

Now and then the husband would bestir himself, make tea and serve it to the waiting women, then sweep up the piles of cuttings. He too was a kind of collector, the most repulsive kind, for he collected the women's hair on the floor of the beauty parlor, and people said he sorted it by color, stuffed pillows with it, and sold them in the Nablus *souk* to old Arabs who came from Transjordan just for that.

Mother couldn't stand him. Sometimes she mimicked his way of sticking a cup of tea in her face, saying, "Drink, drink," and staring at her. But Chenou Apari hinted to anyone who was cool to her husband that behind his shabby exterior was a sensitive lover who was never sated, an expert and connoisseur in all *manières* of love and seduction in vogue in Paris, who wasn't afraid to try anything, and whose main asset was that he "laughs during the act."

"*Chez nous à Paris* they laugh a lot during the act," she commented; "because after all, the act is a comical thing, *non?*"

She never said it explicitly, but you could surmise from her words that she also had a lover. Sometimes she went to Tel Aviv "to buy a corset from Mrs. Goldstein" and to restock her supply of Komol hair dye; and the next day she would yawn noisily and hum Christina Bennet songs, or sniff her fingertips conspicuously to hint at the aromatic events she had experienced.

Once she came to us and asked for a little yeast to make her rejuvenating creams.

"There's a store," Father told her angrily. "Go buy it there."

Chenou Apari gave him a long, contemptuous stare, walked around him and examined him very carefully, and finally said to Mother: "Now I understand exactly what bothers you about him." She spun around to him. "You have a *formidable* wife," she said. "*Chez nous à Paris* she could have been a queen, and you don't even understand that, cretin!"

"What *chez nous à Paris*, which *chez nous à Paris*?" shouted Father. "When were you ever in Paris, *pustema?*"

"*Pardon,*" Chenou retorted with all her charm, and turned her back on him.

"*Pardoon macaroon,* she pretends like she knows French," grumbled Father. "That one knows French like a donkey from Tiberias."

She said *alors, bon jour, comme ci,* and *merci* a lot, but Father scored a direct hit on Chenou's weak point, because all her French was summed up in those words, and even though every year on "Bastille Day" she decorated her beauty parlor with "tricolors," she had never been in France in her life.

"It is for me an honor that a young gentleman in love comes to ask me for advice," she told Jacob after he finished relating his distress. Then she interrogated him at length about Leah and said, "She doesn't pay attention to you? That's a good sign. When she finally does pay attention to you, it will be the very most biggest attention."

"The wisdom it is to give the woman exactly what she wants," she explained. "And it is even greater wisdom to give her what she wants before she knows what she wants. Only when she gets it for the first time does she say, Oooh . . . How could I have lived without that before?"

On July 13 that year, Mother told Jacob to go help Chenou Apari "clean the fours and widows of the beauty parlor to honor the holiday of the Paris." When my brother climbed the ladder to hang banners over the lintel, Chenou Apari suddenly said, "Come down a minute, Jacob, and show me your eyes."

"Red like *rouge*," she diagnosed. "A sign of love. You're not blinking, right? You're scared that the minute you blink, she'll pass by and you'll miss her, right?"

Jacob nodded in embarrassment, and Chenou Apari kissed his cheek. "Now you're a real man, Jacob," she said. "You'll give her the sun as a gift."

To this day I don't know if she was speaking literally or metaphorically. Jacob, at any rate, took her literally.

Chapter 35

Father's bad old smell permeates the toilet, though Jacob was the last one to come out of here. Suddenly I am gripped by an awful weakness, as if my blood were pouring out of me. Sharp, tiny slivers of glass are pressing into my bowels so much I am forced to lean on the wall with both hands, and I dribble around the toilet bowl.

Once I used to close myself up in here and read. Father's smell prevailed around me like a proclamation of ownership. His hands drummed on the door. His mouth shouted for me to come out. At night, when the sour smell of fermentation rose from the bakery and I knew the dough was beginning to rise and Father couldn't leave it anymore, I would come in here and latch the little hook behind me. Sometimes I meditated here. Sometimes I daydreamed. Such a repulsive little room, but it has isolation, and it has a lock, and that is enough to let you engage in the "four occupations of solitude," which are, you surely recall, "reading or day-dreaming, secret tears or sensual gratification." The strong fresh smell of first semen spread in the air. "A faint stream of perfume, which flowed through the tide of bad smells without being absorbed by it." Father's fine copper pitcher with the long spout is still on the windowsill. "*Papel par el kulu ez por los Ashknazis*" was his mocking answer when we asked him to explain the pitcher. "And newspapers are for the head, not the bottom," he added. He was very fastidious and never forgot the common toilet of the Jerusalem yard, and in his batch of "good ways," there is also a "good way" to purify smells. He takes a long strip of toilet paper and lights the bottom like a wick. The paper blazes, crumbles to a curl of ash, and the flame, says Father, "burns the bad vapors." But Jacob shouted that if he continued this practice of his, he would set fire to the whole house. To calm them down, I brought him a dozen jasmine scents. Father tried it once, and went back to his own ways, claiming that "this thing, excuse me, smells like somebody took a crap in Joshua Edelman's field."

Jacob laughed when I reminded him of the jasmine fields of our youth. Strange, it's when he laughs that I can hear a crying creep into his voice. "What would I do without your memory?" he asked. Loving, candid, credulous, and mocking. We are so different from one another, and so close and connected. "You're right," he said to me a few days ago at the cemetery. "We're not twins anymore. Since the day we got one pair of glasses, we haven't been twins. You read, write, fly off above us, don't want to know, don't want to get involved. And me, I'm just a baker, burned at the oven. What's simpler than bread? What do I understand? Who knows now who won, who was smarter?"

Restrained and reclusive is my brother Jacob, but when he bursts, all his bitterness pours out. "That they didn't tell me how he was killed, that I had to go investigate and examine and discover it by myself—never mind that. But that platitude, that 'he-fell-in-the-performance-of-his-duty'— that's what drives me crazy."

Hand in hand, we stood at the tombstone, and the stump of my brother's finger burned in my hand. "He fell in the performance of his duty," he said with bitter contempt. "Like a clerk who slipped on a puddle of tea in the office. He fell in the performance of his duty, too, didn't he?"

And then, lowering his voice, he added, "And he didn't fall in the performance of his duty. He fell in the performance of their duty. Because of a few stupid officers who didn't know how to get a patrol out into the field, and because of a few hysterical soldiers who first shot him and then couldn't find him until he didn't have any blood left. So now they tell me it doesn't matter, that everyone who's killed is a fallen soldier. It doesn't matter if it's in battle or in training or in an accident. I don't need them and their ceremonies! I'm not in their business and I don't plan to play their games. I don't want their memorials, and I won't let anybody tell me what to do!

"You know how many memorial days a family like this one has in a year? The national Memorial Day, the brigade memorial day, the unit memorial day, and the command and the school and the village memorial days, so we won't get bored for a single minute. And my own memorial days, what about them? The day he was born, and the day he died, and the day I saw him for the last time? And what about the memorial moment when you pass by a tree he fell out of when he was six? And the memorial minute of silence when you see somebody in the street who was in his class at school, and the memorial second because of some blond kid who looks like him? And the places? How trite and terrible that is. It's not only the grave, it's the village monument and the brigade monument and the command memorial and the monument here and the monument there and the memorial plaque in the school. And on top of that there's the place where he was killed—and in this country that's never far enough away from home—and there's his place at the table, and whenever you set the table, you think about whether to put out his plate too. And when they ask you in some government office how many children you have? What do you answer? Two or three?"

"Stop it, Jacob, you're exaggerating," I told him.

"My dear sir," my brother exploded like the old smoking bellows, "how the hell do you know when I'm exaggerating? When your big America makes a war, it's far away. Your sons aren't killed close to home. Here everything is so near, everything is so dense. Separations are never forever. Wars are wars of neighbors. You see and hear the smoke and the shouts from your house. This whole country is one crappy *kortijo*. Everybody craps together, everybody knows everything, everybody hangs their laundry in each other's face. That's what it is. Crowded shit. One on top of the other, the living and the dead, all of them together. Everything in range of your hand and everything in range of your eye, and everybody who's killed is killed at a distance of two or three hours from home. Four at the most. Then you go there. And I'm not the only one who's exaggerating. I've heard that about other parents. I know exactly. You go see the last view the child saw and the last piece of ground he lay on. And suddenly you understand about the blood that shouts from the earth. Not just understand, you hear it."

We left Mother's and Benjamin's graves. Jacob apologized for shouting and suggested we also visit Yehiel's grave.

"After all, he was your good friend when you were a boy, wasn't he? You should know that I also visit him sometimes. Not much. Every time I go to Benjamin's grave. I wasn't a friend of his like you were, but I always go to those who were killed in the War of Independence and the Sinai campaign. Almost nobody takes care of their graves anymore. Most of the parents are dead by now, the brothers and sisters are old, live far away, want to live their own lives. They don't come much."

He bent over, brushed a few pine needles off the tombstone, and pulled out a few shoots coming up at the edges.

"Only once a year for them, before Memorial Day, some Arab worker from the village council suddenly shows up to get things in shape," he said. "All the petunias and little cactuses and violets are dead by now. Nothing grows on their graves but hardy wildflowers and weeds. Black and red ants have already built their nests under the ground, among the bones, and the tombstone isn't white anymore, it's covered with moss and bird shit and pine needles, and the names aren't so sharp and clear anymore. And that's how it should be, that's how a grave should be."

Chapter 36

Joshua Edelman was one of the regular nightly customers of the bakery. He was one of a group of new immigrants from Poland who had plots of land and huts at the edges of the village fields. The settlement institutions, in a moment of whimsical Zionism, had sent them here to grow jasmine for the French perfume industry.

In Kraków Edelman had been an expert in casting platinum, and there he lost his wife and oldest son. One night I heard him telling Father his tragedy and though his mouth was full of bread and tears, I understood that the accident that killed his loved ones involved two locomotives, two engineers, one lineman, and four bottles of vodka. "They were drinking all the way they were drinking," he kept saying over and over.

The grief that never dissolves, the yearning for his dead son—"He was so much like me he was"—the longed-for smell of his wife that even the jasmine flowers couldn't erase from his memory or his fingertips, drove him out to our bakery every night. He would buy a loaf of bread and ease his sorrow in it. He'd sit on the bench and chew very slowly. Absentmindedly he would bring his fingers up to his nose and smell the memory of his wife with his eyes shut. Only then did he dare to return to the jasmine beds, for only love and yearning could immunize him against the seductive venom of the flowers.

The jasmine growers woke their children at three in the morning so they'd have time to help gather the flowers before the heat of the sun robbed them of their perfume. When they got to school, they were so drugged and weary they fell asleep at their desks. One of them was Itsik Edelman, Joshua's remaining son, who was in the same class as Jacob and me, and even then had the disgusting habit of talking about himself in the third person. "Anybody talks like that is the cheat!" declared Mother, adding that Itsik had another very unfortunate quality: "The face of a Gypsy." Which meant that even now you could see he'd grow up to be a thief. The years proved Mother right, but in those days I didn't know that was what a future thief looked like. On the other hand, I did discover that Itsik looked amazingly like Philip II of Spain; Yehiel Abramson had shown me his portrait by Antonio Moro, to make me understand Till Eulenspiegel.

Joshua Edelman was an inexhaustible source of stupid wisdom of life, and was always proffering maxims like "The dog barks but the cat meows" or "He who has money doesn't need charity," and weighty truths like "You mustn't believe a person who lies." One night when he bought his loaf of bread, he said to Father, "He who doesn't eat remains hungry in the end." Father, whose feelings of goodness and brotherhood were always stirred by such clichés, answered, "How true," and Joshua smiled and got up and helped him drag a sack of flour. Since he wasn't rebuffed, he began coming every night, and also helped load the pans, sift the flour, and even knead, and Father paid him a salary of two loaves of bread, an attentive ear, a pair of shoes, and work clothes he didn't use because he preferred his enormous gray underpants.

"Put on your glasses and look at the worker," Jacob whispered to me, and the two of us burst out laughing since, because of the heat, Edelman's testicles hung down almost to his knees.

Two years later, when he had become part of the bakery, Joshua asked Father to take him on as a regular worker. "I don't sleep at night anyway I don't sleep," he said. He settled right in and suggested that Father bake a roll called *Knipele*, and when that proved to be popular, Father raised his salary and let him bring Itsik along, "so he can help and learn."

Orphanhood had sharpened Itsik's senses in dealing with adults. He and Mother became enemies. "That there Itsik is snake," she kept repeating. "He's just like the Ibrahim of the Duduch." But Itsik was a diligent lad and a devoted son. He cooked meals for his father, played checkers with him, and laundered his work underpants, as if he read a softness and weakness in him no one else could see.

"I have the best boy in the world I have," Joshua Edelman would say proudly, and his boy would hug him and say, "Itsik loves his daddy."

Chapter 37

For a long time Jacob pondered Chenou Apari's strange instructions, and finally he took Father's shaving mirror from the bathroom, waited in the street for Leah, and when she came he aimed the mirror at her and blinded her. Leah bent her head, turned away, and covered her face with her hands, but Jacob danced around her and kept beaming the sunlight at her.

"You ugly son of a bitch," she finally screamed at him with startling coarseness. "My father will come back and take off your stupid head!"

Jacob smiled, skipped back to the yard, and lay in wait for her from that day on, surprising her with his salvos of sun. His new method and his devotion to her made Leah so mad she shut herself up in her house. Jacob took the mirror, climbed up on the bakery chimney, and aimed the sunbeams at her window from there. But the distance was too great, the mirror was too small, and the capering spot of light dwindled and vanished.

Jacob came down and walked around for a few hours, immersed in thought, and the next day he went to Simon and whispered a plan in his ear. Simon was eleven years old, and he already had the hands of a black-smith and a heart that knew neither fear nor hesitation. He went into our parents' room, yanked out the middle door of the clothes closet, the one with the mirror attached to it, and helped Jacob take it up to the brick chimney of the bakery.

The big spot of light ran groping over the field, slid across the red loam like a shining tablecloth, flickered on the grasses, and climbed trembling up the walls of Leah's house until it caught her window and broke into her room on the roof. A moment later the small amazed figure was standing at the glowing window, shading her eyes with one hand and waving furiously with the other. She knew where the light was coming from, but she couldn't see Jacob because it dazzled her. The shutters of her window banged together so hard we heard it in our house.

"She doesn't see you anymore," I said.

"That doesn't matter. She knows I'm here, and here I shall stay," my brother replied smugly.

But now he encountered an unexpected obstacle in the person of Mother, who had bought new hairpins on the advice of Chenou Apari, and wanted to see what she looked like in the mirror.

"I'm coming up to you!" she threatened Jacob. When he didn't answer, Mother climbed up to the stolen mirror and sat next to him on the edge of the chimney, combed her hair and put rouge on her cheeks.

Father's rage flared. "Get down from there, *putana!*" he whispered madly from the yard, trying not to rouse the neighbors to come look.

He stamped his feet, panted and gnashed his teeth, and finally, when he couldn't contain his temper anymore, he ran into the bakery, stuck his head in the oven and screamed into it, as usual. But this time he forgot to close the flue, and his curses, amplified by the echo chamber of the oven's belly, rose up through the chimney like a tremendous wave, and the mirror tottered and broadcast them over the whole village. All the neighbors came out of their houses, and Brinker ran to our yard scared and angry, as if he were about to attack Father, but as fast as he had come, he turned around, went back, and disappeared.

"Get down, Mother, just get down," Jacob pleaded, for he knew that Leah too saw and heard.

But Mother laughed, examined her reflection in the mirror again, patted his shoulder, and went down. That evening, when she told Chenou Apari about Jacob's new method, Chenu clapped her hands and shouted, "*Preparez la mouchoir*, we soon will have a wedding."

Thus Jacob began his days on the chimney. Father was fit to be tied. He simply couldn't bear the "idle sitting," the atmosphere of aimlessness the love-stricken mother and son spread over the house, and as usual with him, he kept expanding his circle of rage. He called Duduch "stupid as a cow at Hanukah prayers"; he said that Simon had "iron teeth and cotton brains"; that Mother was "the belle of Albania"; I was "a *pashariko* studying arithmetic in a beehive"; and Jacob was *pezgado kurshum*. He claimed we should go back to the days when the right of courtship wasn't in the emotional hands of lovers but in the experienced care of matchmakers, "who know the good way," and have fluent tongues, neat brains, and hearts that beat at a moderate, even tempo.

The arguments about the mirror continued until two police motorcycles roared into the yard one day, followed by an official black Humber, and Father was terrified. He was sure that the High Commissioner, Harold MacMichael in person, had found him out and come to arrest him for stealing the Patriarch's carriage. And, in fact, the same English detective who once asked me about the woman from Jerusalem did get out of the car. Now he stared at me sternly, laughing at the same time, and behind him emerged a thin man with thick glasses and a pleasant expression. That was Arthur Spinney, who had rescued my uncle Elijah from the gallows many years before along with General Allenby. Tia Duduch recognized him immediately, grabbed Simon by the hand, and went to him.

"Mrs. Nathan," said Spinney excitedly.

He gave her a splendid package containing a few bolts of fine English wool, a black dress, and black shoes. His assistant, a tall, balding Englishman, opened the trunk of the car and took out cardboard boxes full of Lipton tea, Columbian coffee, canned pineapple from Natal, tubes of Nestles, bottles of Cabri water, and chocolate whose smell overwhelmed Simon.

Duduch's eye opened wide in admiration and bliss. "Ibrahim, what are you doing?" she whispered her motto in a brand-new tone. She grasped Spinney's hand, showered kisses on it, and burst into tears. Arthur Spinney had a heart that was soft, Christian, and large, and mists of pity and emotion quickly fogged the thick lenses of his glasses. It's interesting, I don't remember what his face looked like, but only the fact that he was very nearsighted. I suppose his vision was even worse than mine and Jacob's, and I am amused by the notion that it is because of his nearsightedness and not my own that he is preserved in my memory as such a blurry image.

"They assigned me to the cavalry because a horse's eyes were better than mine," he used to say about himself with the humor of Anglican clergymen he had inherited from his forefathers.

Palestine transformed Arthur Spinney from a cavalryman into a merchant. In the first battle for Gaza he won a medal and attracted the attention of General Allenby, who attached him to his staff and, after the surrender of Jerusalem, put him in charge of evacuating the wounded by train. The front moved north and the trains of the wounded went south to Egypt, leaving behind trails of sirens, shrieks of pain, and columns of smoke. Like many others, Arthur Spinney aspired to leave his mark on the chronicles of the Holy Land, but the good places in history were already taken by those who had elbowed their way in, and Spinney knew he would never ascend to royalty, establish a new religion, utter a prophecy, or lead a regiment. Instead he invented the milking car: he bought a few milk cows from the Mikveh Israel agricultural school and put them in a freight car padded with straw and connected to trains crossing the desert. Now, he announced proudly, the chaps could enjoy "a decent cup of English tea." The milking car didn't change the face of history, but it did make Spinney's name famous in the British army and in the London newspapers, and they made him manager of all the army canteens in this country. When he was discharged from the army, he opened his first general store at Jaffa Gate in Jerusalem and hired my uncle Elijah, first as a salesman and then as manager.

That was the beginning of the nicest empire of all those that have ruled the East. Spinney's department stores sprouted up one after another in Jerusalem, Nablus, Tel Aviv, Alexandria, Beirut, Baghdad, and Limassol, pleasant islands of decency, sobriety, and reliability in a region that traded in lies, anguish, and honor. Spinney attracted a lot of customers to his stores. His motto was "Fine merchandise at reasonable prices." He sold cheese from Hebron, chocolate from Liège, wooden buttons from Damascus, tin forks from Portugal, mineral water he bottled himself from the springs of Cabri, horsemeat sausages from Hungary, lace tablecloths from Normandy, and butter from Lithuania.

Every morning Elijah would come to the store, sprinkle attar of roses in a gleaming copper bowl, and prepare piasters and pennies and shillings to make change. And at a quarter to eight he would open the doors. He spoke with every customer in his own language, and at the request of his boss he covered his premature baldness with a tarboosh.

"And in my innocence I thought you were paying me for what's in my head, not for what's on it," Elijah protested, and Spinney laughed and patted him on the back.

Every now and then he recalled the strange day he and Allenby took Elijah down from the portable gallows in the Kolarasi cellar, and was glad he had heeded the general's advice and taken the young man under his wing. When Elijah was killed in the pogroms of 1929, he decided to look after his widow, but Duduch disappeared from the city and it took the detective he hired eight years to locate her with us. He had done fine work. Arthur Spinney knew every detail about us. He brought Father two bottles of raki, white handkerchiefs, and essences to blend his cologne. He brought Mother a blue flowered dress that had short puffed sleeves and went splendidly with her hair and eyes and the long line of her hips. For me he had a real surprise. That month Orson Welles had broadcast the radio play *War of the Worlds*, and Spinney brought me a gorgeous edition of the book with the original illustrations by Walter Ernst, which wasn't even in Yehiel's library. And he brought Jacob a leather case with a blue "Katav" fountain pen, blotters, paper, and envelopes, for writing love letters.

"Happy hunting." With a smile, he quoted Kipling's wolf pack.

"But I want a mirror," Jacob whispered. "He brought everybody what they want, and I want a mirror."

"You got a present," said Father. "Where's your dignity?"

"But I need a mirror!" cried Jacob. "Not paper."

"Shame! What kind of son are you raising!" Father shouted at Mother.

Spinney was embarrassed. Even though he didn't understand Hebrew, he sensed that he had chanced on a quarrel between husband and wife. But by that time, Father had lost a considerable part of his manners. He no longer bothered to disguise his hatred and contempt, and didn't hesitate to berate Mother in front of us, in front of the neighbors, even in front of strangers. "A cow on the seventh candle of Hanukah," he now aimed a new and obscure insult at her.

"All I have to do is breathe, and even that isn't right," said Mother.

Embarrassed and pale, she turned around, climbed the porch steps, and disappeared inside the house.

I hope I succeed in describing my mother as she was. She was the most complex simple woman I've ever known. Other women always had trouble understanding her, and each and every man understood her in his own way. She was a child held captive in the mighty body of a woman, fearing my father with an unimaginable fear and loving him with the worst love of all—the love that has no reason and lacks hope. Awkwardly, blindly, with an explosive force without measure or restraint, she wooed him and didn't understand that their life together had made him a hunter of faults. He trapped, identified, and described them in such a way that she could never guess the next insult and fortify herself for the impending blow. He found fault with the food she cooked him, the way she walked, the defective syntax of her speech, the way she sliced bread, peeled cucumbers, hung laundry. With her smile, the movement of her comb, the way she sat, and the sound of her sneeze. Even the childish position she slept in—on her back, arms and legs spread out, as he had first seen her in the valley where they met—roused his fury. "How do you lie there?" he sneered. "Like a Yemenite baby they threw into a *basiniko*."

But now Father was embarrassed, because he had read on Spinney's face the rebuke he deserved. "Tell him, tell him something in English," he urged me, but I didn't know what to say. What should I tell that amiable man? I turned and followed Mother, who was already standing in the kitchen grinding meat. What didn't she do to win his heart? She was turning the handle of the grinder, wiping her nose with the back of her hand, closing her eyes so as not to see the meat—in vain. She wanted me to teach her to read and write, and she couldn't learn. Pencils broke between her fingers, black flowers bloomed on her tongue and lips, and the paper was strewn with holes, slivers of graphite, and tiny Rorschach blots of ink and tears. Her hope melted away. In despair she waited for her encounters with Chenou Apari. In despair she combed her hair and made herself beautiful. In despair she bought a new dress and washed her hair in Jamila's rainwater—all in vain.

And all that time my father seeks her in her body, walks to her on the mountain paths, the spot of her hair flickering in front of him, bandits all around him, deer rush up the mountains. Her picture above his eyes, her long legs next to his head. The wet coils of your hair. The surge of your body. So much rain.

Chapter 38

A week later the mirror arrived, packed between two upright boards in the back of the pickup truck, padded with cardboard and cotton. Jacob made a frame of iron bars for it and mounted it on a hinge on the chimney so he could move it and aim it.

He was beside himself with happiness. At two in the afternoon, when the sun reached the proper angle, he put on a straw hat, took a bottle of water and half a loaf of bread in a bag, packed up some paper and books so he could do his homework there, and climbed onto the roof of the bakery. Later on, he made himself a little bench on the chimney, because one day he almost flew off in a sudden gust of wind.

Days went by and rumors of my brother's love were known all around. Even strangers would come see the fellow on the chimney. Once a newspaper photographer tried to take his picture, but Jacob noticed him and turned his mirror toward him. An awful shout of pain was heard, and the man fled with his hands over his eyes.

He spent most of the afternoon hours of his youth there, persistent as a nesting stork, beaming without being consumed. The window of Leah's room didn't open, but Jacob knew that she was there and that she knew he was on the chimney, and he knew that I was there too.

"That's not nice what you do," Mother told me.

"She invites me," I said.

"The Leah is the Jacob's."

"The Leah is nobody's," mocked Father.

"Not to worry." Chenou Apari smiled prophetically, with a nod of encouragement. "She acts like that only to excite Jacob's love."

"I'm not worried," said Jacob. "If she invited him, let him go to her. In the end she'll be mine."

At night, in our room, I asked him if he really meant it.

"Why should I care?" he answered. "I already told everybody, in the end she'll be mine."

My meetings with Leah started in the library. One day she came in as I was spreading moth poison in the cracks of the shelves. "Recommend a book to her," Yehiel said, and I suggested *Thaïs*. When she got to the chapter where Paphnutius goes and sits on the high pillar, she brought the book back and told me angrily that if I was trying to help my brother, I would do better to mind my own business. She was about fifteen then, but living with her mother, an abandoned woman, had enriched her perceptions and made her mature. We stood facing one another in the aisle between the big bookshelves, Leah ran her hand through the billows of her hair, and I fell in love with her.

The signs were simple and clear, depressingly normal. Dryness. Heartbeats. Pressure and limpness. I assume you know them too, from your own flesh, from the flesh of your lovers, from books you've read. But I felt one more sign, a special one, because I had expected it ever since I heard

Chenou Apari tell Mother: "And there's also a kind of man whose knees talk to each other in rhymes when he falls in love."

In the days to come I displayed my best wares to Leah. I quoted poetry to her, I stole Tia Duduch's marvelous masapan from the pantry for her, I showed her the albums of ancient art that Yehiel didn't lend anyone, and I told her to read the *The Story of San Michele*. Two days later she said, "Let's play that you're a bear and I'm a Lapp girl." Suddenly she spun around and, with both hands, waved her skirt at me for a dazzling sliver of time. I didn't have my glasses on at that moment. Her bare thighs gleamed like the halo of a distant cloud, the fog of her flesh seeped into my retinas. For a moment I thought I felt Jacob's pains, but I understood immediately that it was my own torments that were searing me.

Someday, if we meet, my dear, I'll seduce you with Duduch's masapan, too. At the Miriam Deli near my house, I once came upon that sticky deceit called Masapan of Toledo, and I teased the owner of the shop about it until she burst out laughing and put her hand on my arm as if inadvertently. A woman of about forty, she was, jolly and handsome, much like me in height and coloring, and I told her about my aunt's masapan—the pale pleasure, the great consoler, the ultimate indulgence, the only sweet that makes women laugh when they taste it.

"Masapan is the purest, simplest, and most sublime of all sweets," I quoted from the *Small Encyclopedia of the Kitchen* by Otto Gustin, and then from Gregory VII before he became pope and was buried in the library of his mother's palace: "Among the sweet sins, the confection of Lübeck is well known, composed of only two ingredients—almonds and sugar— which are not naturally opposed, except for the purpose of their common existence." Even though he didn't mention it specifically by name, most researchers agree that he meant masapan.

On the shop owner's forehead, I saw a row of red dots that looked like the painful tracks of a centipede or the pricks of thorns. She felt my eyes staring at them and was embarrassed. When she was thirteen years old, she told me, she went to mass with her parents and accidentally chewed the holy wafer the priest put on her tongue. Her mouth filled with hot saltiness, the collar of her blouse turned red, and twenty years later the blood spots appeared on her forehead.

"You could have made a career as a saint," I told her.

She laughed. "I'm not a saint," she said, and a bitter, long line was suddenly etched between her eyes. "God knows I'm not."

I bought almonds and sugar from her, all night long I conjured up Duduch's lessons, and the next afternoon I went back to the shop. I waved the little package at her and said, "The ideal match is a man with masapan and a woman with stigmata."

Of all the women I've met in America, I love her the most. When I enter her house, she collects the sweet tithe I bring her, and still chewing and laughing, she strips off all my clothes, takes my hand, and leads me to the shower. There, with complete faith I entrust my glasses to her, and when she scrubs my limbs with soap and pours scalding water over me, she doesn't discriminate between poor and rich, is neither put off nor turned on. "Close your eyes." She shampoos my hair, towels me dry with her strong hands until my skin turns red, and leads me to the bedroom.

We always make love the same way. "He who knows what is good no longer needs experiments," she laughs. Afterward she lets me sleep in her bed a bit, and when I wake up she urges me to come eat. She makes me wonderful French fries. One day she revealed her secret to me: she fries them in coconut oil. When she took the can of oil with the ancient label out of the pantry, I burst out laughing. Ever since then, even though she doesn't like it, I call her "Madame Cocosin."

One day I made her a *mezelik* from delicacies I garnered in her store: black olives I removed from their can and dried with coarse salt, fat cheese I soaked in Tuscan olive oil, small hard pretzels, Zoga anchovies, sharp, dry San Sebastian *cabanos*. We spent two hours of contentment over a few glasses of raki. I hope you're not laughing now and suspecting me of nostalgia. Even that table of delicacies was merely an exercise in memory, like the platter of jewelry with which Lurgan Sahib tested Kim's memory. So many facts with neither rhyme nor reason are amassed in me that I must become a merchant of antiquities of myself, burrowing in attics, sifting through heaps of garbage and dust, until a Mnemosyne rises in my mind's eye and waves her skirt at me.

Speak, Memory. Speak and don't stop. Draw from the deep well of Thomas Mann's past, float on Melville's warm sea, cut into the living flesh of the prophet Jeremiah. Lie in amber, swim in vitriol. Joseph Conrad, in the voice of Marlow, told me, "I thought his memory was like the other memories of the dead that accumulate in every man's life—a vague impress on the brain of shadows that had fallen on it in their swift and awful passage." Saint Augustine compared memory to a warehouse, to a spacious field, to a large temple where he encountered himself.

I'm constantly reexamining the burrows of my memory, shoring up its shifting sands, cleaning its gutters of fallen leaves. When we were children, Mother would turn on the faucet in a thin stream to encourage me and Jacob to urinate. Now too all I need is the slight stimulus of one taste bud, of the auditory labyrinth, one olfactory cell, one retinal cone. All I need is one lock of hair, blurry and chestnut, plundered by my glasses from the head of a woman passing by, or the gleam of her white shoulder. All I need is a red column of dust, the dull copper ring of a bell.

Leah loved to weave wreaths of blue flowers, to hear stories, to laugh, and to put puzzles together. The fields supplied her with flowers, I provided laughter and stories, and the puzzles came to her in packages her father sent. He was still "abroad," and no one really knew whether he was an important figure in the Jewish Agency, a famous violinist, an English spy, or a diamond merchant. She refused to talk about him, and I didn't tell her I had seen him the day he fled.

Because of my nearsightedness I would put my face right up to the puzzle. "You're in the way," she would say and push me. We wrestled, laughed with delight, rolled around on the floor. A fruity vapor blew from her mouth to mine, the cascade of her hair poured over my chest and tickled my palms, a terrible eternal flame from the love light Jacob beamed at her window glowed in the room.

"Your brother's crazy," she said. Lying on her stomach, her face buried in a pillow, she moved her hair aside so I could stroke her neck. Suddenly she jumped up and pushed the slats of the shutter aside a bit to relieve the heat. Then she opened them a bit more to be sure, and finally she opened them even more to be blinded. All the while, she was muttering reproaches very very softly—but it wasn't clear if she were cursing or prophesying—with the seriousness and proficiency of a street urchin, out of harmony with her beauty: "Drop dead, go get buried, you stinker, you ass, may crows peck out your eyes, may Gypsies tattoo your prick, may the Mufti come visit you every night, may you drown in pig shit, may all your fingers fall off."

Once, after four hours of Jacob's light salvos, when the sun at last went down, I went for a walk with Leah, and Jacob approached us. He stopped to tell me to come help unload a truck of flour sacks, but he didn't say a word to Leah. The two of them ignored one another completely, as if they could converse only by way of the mirror. He didn't tell her about his sleepless nights, and she didn't tell him that she watched him through the cracks in the shutter, but his red eyes and her eyes always squinting, and her face always tan even in winter, betrayed their habits.

Flour sacks are heavy and limp as corpses, and when you carry them you have to run at the right speed, a compromise between your force and the force of gravity: if you run too fast, you'll stumble and fall down. If you walk slowly, your knees will melt like candles.

Jacob and Father stood on the truck, loaded the sacks onto Mother's and my shoulders, and we carried them to the storeroom. Particles of flour were crushed in my mouth and mixed with spit and sweat. Lead was poured into my limbs. What I should have understood back in Yehiel's library became clear to me in Father's pain clinic: that it is better to describe what the other person already knows so he can concentrate on the nature of the description and not on his understanding. I assume you are not yet experienced in the labor of unloading flour sacks from a truck; so, if you need a literary description of this task, you will find that too in *Tracy's Tiger*, although Saroyan describes sacks of coffee beans, which, heavy as they may be, will never equal the dead weight of flour. At any rate, running with the sack always ended with a brief, tormenting climb on the piles of previous stacks, and when I stumbled there this time, I discovered a cloth bag hidden behind one of them. That evening, I went back and found the bag with a green book inside, and on the binding, it said: *Cent manières de la séduction française*. In it were pictures that gave me an urgent need for a blood transfusion. I quickly returned the book of seductions to its hiding place and ran to get Jacob so we could enjoy the loot together.

Marvelous, strange women paraded through the pages. Plump ones with cat masks covering their eyes, tall ones with ostrich feathers on their behinds, short ones with thick eyebrows and disheveled curls. They were costumed in provocative transparent corsets; they drank pearls dissolved in vinegar, ate nacre and asparagus, and wore net brassieres that penetrated us with an observant double gaze. Pearl eyes winked from their navels, and mustached, toothless smiles peeped from their wide-open muslin panties.

"Chenou Apari must have given that to Mother," I said.

Jacob assaulted me, but I grabbed him violently. Even though I was stronger, I had trouble restraining him. We fell onto the sacks in a clinch, and I was forced to squeeze him in my arms until he coughed and cried and begged me to stop.

In those days Mother was all of thirty-five, but she looked very old to us. Only now that I'm much older than she was then, and I look at the four pictures of her that were kept after she died, especially the one Isaac Brinker took of her—and I'll say more about that later—can I see that despite the hard work and Father's indifference and mockery, she was at the height of her beauty, and that Romi looks more and more like her every day. But Jacob, who hadn't yet won Leah's heart then, was terrified of one thing—the enormous distance that suddenly gaped between him and the real magicians of seduction.

He sat down and banged the book shut. "How ugly that is," he said. "How disgusting."

I told him the famous joke about the algebra teacher and the ski champion, but Jacob didn't laugh or say anything. I thought he was in despair—over me and over love—but the next day my brother went back to his mirror, and persisted.

Chapter 39

Time passed, did its work, and didn't pay any attention to us. By now, the two of us knew how to identify the snares our bodies set for us, but love refined the urgings of flesh. Jacob found refuge in glass, and I in paper. He went on blinding Leah and sending her his heliographic letters, and I went on bringing her books written by other authors and sentences of love written by me with hovering fingers on her back.

"What does that mean—'we were friends'?" Romi asked a hard question. "And what did Dad say?"

I kissed her with a dry throat and a yearning heart, I breathed the air from her mouth, I covered myself with her braids, and I dared to stroke her young breasts through the cloth of her blouse. My thighs tasted the throbbing warmth of her flesh, but I didn't sleep with her. Even now I don't understand why. The possibility didn't even occur to me.

"Why don't you break that mirror of his?" she asked me one day.

"Why should I?"

"You're weird," she told me. "The two of you are really weird. I should throw both of you out and look for other boys."

We were walking through the field between her house and the village on our way to the library, with Jacob's spot of light running ahead of us. He memorized the times of Leah's comings and goings and the routes she took. When she left the house, the big spot of light was waiting for her on the threshold, moving and quivering in place, and wherever she went it accompanied her and capered in front of her, dragged at her feet like a bright rag of devotion, scaled her dress, and convulsed on the ground.

"You think Yehiel's got somebody?" she asked when we reached the door of the library.

"I don't think so, but sometimes he goes to the city." And then I laughed. "You know what Edelman says about Yehiel? 'He who doesn't get married ends up a bachelor.'"

By then I allowed myself to see Yehiel not only as a guide and friend but also as a source of amusement.

"Only one man ever understood me, and even he didn't understand me." He quoted Friedrich Hegel's last words to me.

"That's nonsense!" I told him. "Come on, Yehiel."

Yehiel was shocked and furious. "Nonsense?!" he shouted. "Nonsense?! Hegel on his deathbed is nonsense?!"

"That's like saying, 'That's the end, or maybe the beginning,'" I said. "Or 'Will they forgive me up there for not being myself?'"

"Who said that?" Yehiel got excited.

"Nobody. I'm just giving you examples of more nonsense."

"Yes, but who said it?" The librarian was frothing.

"Nobody, Yehiel." I was angry. "I made it up right this minute."

But Yehiel didn't believe me. He recorded my last words in his notebook, and next to them he wrote, "Anonymous."

When we came out of the library, Leah and I saw the guards' pickup truck flying down the street. It was going so fast we jumped onto the side of the road in panic. A cloud of reddish dust rose in its wake; Noah Brinker was driving, and his father was lying in the back, bleeding and unconscious.

Brinker, we found out later, had been hit in the head by an irrigation pipe. "He was wounded by love," Chenou Apari enthused; only it wasn't Brinker's own love that hit him but the love of his son. Noah Brinker was attached to Mr. Cocosin's daughter, whose name I've forgotten by now, but I still have a clear memory of what she looked like. From a fat little girl she grew up to be a lascivious dwarf whose enormous Ishtar-like behind tried to compensate for her total lack of a neck. For several months Noah had been telling her constantly that she was beautiful, until she believed him. "Apparently," said Leah, "Noah Brinker has the ability to persuade," because that Purim his beloved went to the carnival in Tel Aviv and attempted to enter the Queen Esther beauty contest. Dead Livy, who had an inordinately elevated estimate of her son, abhorred the girl and said she devoted herself with equal ardor both to the men of the Hagana and to the members of the dissident organizations, and gave the English their due as well. I suppose she also granted Noah Brinker her favors; otherwise I can't understand the longing she roused in him.

Noah loaded a length of irrigation pipe on his shoulder, and as he was walking, out of the corner of his eye he caught sight of the elfin figure of his beloved—rattling along and desirable as she was—between the trees of the next plantation. He spun around to see her better, and the heavy pipe on his shoulder whistled a quarter-circle in the air, struck his father's left temple like a clapper, and laid him on the ground with a split skull and a mouth full of blood.

When he woke up in the hospital, Brinker couldn't get a single word out of his mouth. Professor Fritzi was already at his bedside, where he stayed all night, and the next day he came and told Mother that his brother was afflicted with aphasia. Brinker's blood, as was explained in the village, had flooded an entire part of his brain, drowning and choking the words in it.

"Frau Levy." Professor Fritzi cleared his throat softly and didn't look her in the eye. "Even we in medicine don't understand everything. If you could visit my brother, as a neighbor, of course, that could help very much."

Mother went there and came back sad and gloomy. Dead Livy sat at her husband's bedside and didn't say a thing when Brinker recognized Mother and his hand groped until it found hers. He shook all over, sweated, groaned, but couldn't get anything out of his mouth except weeping and bleating.

Chapter 40

My brother's hand is in mine. The stump of his finger twitches like a fledgling. The bread truck has gone out now, and we are sitting next to the oven pit.

"You know, I never told anybody, but once I went to a workshop—you know, the kind they set up for bereaved parents. They called me from the Ministry of Defense and recommended it. At first I didn't want to hear about it. I told them, I finished with you the day you sent me a form to fill out so you would recognize me as a bereaved father. You kill him, and then you've got the nerve to make me run after you. And that word, 'workshop,' also pissed me off. For me a workshop is a place where you work—blacksmiths, mechanics, not all kinds of psychologists. But I don't know, somehow I went.

"I went and it was terrible. There were people there who had never met each other. It was our dead children that brought us all together in the same room. There was one mother who had lost two sons. Did you ever hear of such a thing? Two sons in one war. What is this? God's jumping over his own bellybutton? And there was a father, a policeman, came in uniform, broken into pieces, as if they had put him through a meat grinder. A beautician who brought along her surviving daughter, a little ten-year-old girl with terrible facial tics, and she kept talking about her son and how successful he was. 'Peach,' she called him. 'My Peach.' Everybody started in right away, everybody had his own Peach. What should they do—keep quiet? And all the time the psychologist is telling them: Talk, get everything out, let it all out. That's what they say: Let it out. I couldn't stand it. That Peach of hers, but I didn't say anything. I thought maybe I'd tell them how I made myself Michael, how much I wanted another child and how I did it. But I'm not used to talking to people anymore, and anyway, they were talking about the dead children, not the living ones, and I don't have much to say about Benjamin, and what I do have I'd rather not. After all, we know what he was. A good boy, but that's it. Nothing special. Romi is superior to him in every way. Her heart, her mind, everything. And Michael's a dream. A little angel. Leah should have gotten up to see him. I didn't even make a memorial pamphlet for Benjamin because he didn't leave anything in writing. Maybe I should have made a booklet with pictures of all the girls he had."

"Daddy? Are you in there?"

Michael's voice comes from outside and paints a watercolor of pleasure and love on my brother's face.

"I'm here, Michael. Come here, son."

The sun is still low. A long, thin shadow anticipates its little owner. Jacob got up and hid behind the door, and when Michael came into the bakery, he swept him up in his arms, rocked him, and swung him in the air.

"Now we'll make you into a sweet challah."

He put his son into the old kneading box, squeezed him delicately with soft, tickling fists, lifted him up, and laid him on the worktable. He sprinkled fine white flour on him and kneaded his belly, stuck gentle fingers in his back, pressed his thighs and the muscles of his calves, and Michael laughed and wailed and squirmed with pleasure.

"Who do you belong to?"

"Daddy, Daddy."

"This is my child," Jacob tells me over and over. "Look at him. I made him."

The longing for a baby, he recalled, was too hard to bear and too sweet to contain, hardening and softening, blazing and freezing. The village children knew that if they got to the bakery early, they would get a roll, a gift from the melancholy baker who worked there. Young women walking toward him on the street were embarrassed and angry because his eyes ripped off their dresses and stared at their bellies and crotches.

"Even at Benjamin's funeral I thought about that," he said. "I couldn't help myself. There were so many women there. It was amazing. I never saw so many pretty girls as at his funeral. Who would have guessed such a thing? Like a flock of colored butterflies had landed in the cemetery. Like the flowers that crazy old Arab grew, the one who had all those pots on the balcony in Jerusalem, remember? In the military sector. Girls from the agricultural school, girl soldiers, girl students. Even his history teacher from high school was there. Not with the other women teachers, but with the girls. Even two fifty-year-old bags who came together from Tel Aviv in an American convertible and hugged each other and cried and cried and cried, like two cats at night. Cried over my child who must have done with them all the things I don't dare do in my dreams and won't ever do again in my life."

His fist clenched in his pocket. "And Benjamin wasn't even in his grave before I wanted a new son. Like Tia Duduch. I had to have a baby."

My brother's expression was soft and proud now. "They loved him. He had something I never had, that ease with them, the knowledge that a woman isn't a sprite or a witch or a demon or an angel. Things I understood only one night, and that most men don't know and don't understand until they have a daughter and watch her grow up. But by then it's too late. And doesn't do anybody any good."

Suddenly he laughed and blushed. "And when I say 'daughter,' I don't mean Romi."

And the women, who were familiar with charming flirtatious winks, blinking flesh, and the pain of a dry palate, couldn't interpret my brother's look, in which the sadness of entreaty blended with the pain of urgency. They wanted to savor their sense of common mourning of beloved women and their pleasure of belonging to the dead, which is lugubrious indeed, but not unbearable. They shuffled their feet uneasily, hugged each other, and wiped each other's black and blue tears.

A few years later Romi brought a friend home from the army, a full-bodied, friendly girl, ugly to look at, yearning for touch and love. The two girls made dinner together, and that night, when the bread started rising and spreading its smell, she suddenly appeared in the bakery.

"That smell wouldn't let me sleep," she said, embarrassed. "I'm not used to it."

She stood next to the *gareh*, looked at Jacob, Itsik, and Joshua, and when the first loaves cooled, my brother sliced some bread for her.

175

"She held it in both hands and ate like an animal."

The girl stayed in the bakery all night, laughed and gorged herself as if she were ravenous, and Jacob kept thinking of that fecundity, so touching because so obvious to everyone except the girl herself. With those breasts, whose nipples hadn't yet been stretched and darkened by pregnancy. That womb-clock, pink and young, whose muscles weren't yet flaccid, pouring out its own hopes and others' dreams every month.

"You won't believe it, but I almost propositioned her. At most, she would have said no. But I was scared she'd tell Romi, and Romi really isn't capable of understanding such things. Or she would have come and photographed us in bed for her exhibit."

He turned Michael over again, braided his arms and legs, and the child dissolved in loud, shrill giggles, and gurgled and cooed when his father tickled his back with the big glaze brush. He covered Michael's nipples and eyelids with raisins, sprinkled poppy seeds on his belly, knees and chest, filled the hollow of his navel with yellow sesame seeds, and stuck a bakery label on his forehead.

"So they'll know who you belong to," he announced.

"To Daddy, to Daddy," squealed the child.

"Now you're ready," said Jacob. "Now we'll bake you."

He put his son in one of the black tin bread pans, picked it up, and carried it through the bakery.

"Where to now?"

"The oven . . . the oven." Michael babbled, laughing.

Chapter 41

Brinker stayed in the hospital a few weeks, and when he came back home, he dragged his right leg, had trouble understanding the news on the radio, and spoke nonsense. By now he managed to get a few words out of his throat, but he couldn't write, and he had forgotten most of the nouns he once knew. The rules of syntax and usage were erased from his brain. He spent a lot of time pointing his finger, saying "this" like a baby, and searching for synonyms.

"To open . . . this . . . transparent in the wall," he growled at his son when Noah didn't understand that he wanted him to open the window.

"Bring . . . well . . . five, bring . . . sweet-sweet."

He was educated enough to understand the nature of his illness, wise enough to suffer depression, and diligent enough to try to recover as fast as possible. A few weeks later Noah Brinker came and inquired obsequiously if I wanted him to take me for "a ride on his Matchless motorcycle"; when I refused, he asked if I wanted to "make a few cents," proposing I teach his father the words he had forgotten.

I had always liked Brinker, and now an unexpected devotion to him arose in me. Every day I gave him a lesson.

"What's a pen, Brinker?"

"Pen . . . pen . . . to see . . . " He searched in a drawer, pulled out a pen, and his face lit up. "Here, I see. . . . Pen. To write."

"What's a house?"

He closed his eyes. "I see it. . . . Live in a house."

"Is there also a house in Jerusalem, Brinker?'

"Maybe . . . no . . . No see . . . Jerusalem."

After a few lessons a malicious idea took shape in my heart: to teach Brinker new words that were wrong. But since every lesson vanished from his brain in five minutes, I gave up the plan.

"Once you used to come to me," Leah said, "and now you spend all day with that idiot."

"You can join us," I told her. "It's very interesting, and he won't get mad."

"I don't have strength for him," she said.

"And he's not an idiot," I explained. "He understands everything and has every ounce of his sense."

"Really. The Vilna Gaon." And her face clouded over. "Such strange weather," she said. "Scary."

A hot haze blew from the southwest, made the sea turgid, and covered the gleam of the sky. Salty air grated between your teeth and scratched your lungs.

Brinker was as restless as an animal. He looked at me and said, "Mother . . . mother."

"Very good, Brinker," I said. "What is mother?"

"Mother," Brinker repeated, "mother." And suddenly tears and words and sweat burst out all over his face. "We would also go fifteen and then you don't know the day before yesterday, in the field because nobody and only mother."

He rummaged like a madman in his desk drawer, took out the amber block with the fly, and stuck it in my pocket without a word. "For . . . for . . . now," he said. An awful grief was reflected in his eyes, and a gratitude and love he wanted me to understand and convey.

> *A host of stars is in the sky.*
> *Which one gives a sign?*
> *So many lads are passing by—*
> *Which do I choose for mine?*
> *Oh, yes, you're the one who's spoken,*
> *Yes, yes, you my heart have broken.*

That's what I sang to him, but Brinker only shook his head no and didn't say a word.

As I returned home, the setting sun looked like a sick eye through the reddish curtains of dust. Dogs stuck their tails between their legs and howled, cats licked themselves incessantly, and even the shabby crows whose noisy insolence isn't distracted by anything were silent and kept their heads bowed.

That night, Father told us to add a little sugar and hot water to the yeast to reinforce it in its war with the salt and dust. He turned on the motor of the kneading machine and said to Jacob, "You haven't got a chance with her, stupid. You sit on the roof like a bird while your brother visits her."

Jacob smiled. He never attached much importance to Father's diagnoses, and in this particular matter his confidence had been growing all by itself ever since he got the mirror, while Leah's indifference grew stronger. Contrary to convention, he didn't waste away, no lines of grief were etched on his face, his feet didn't stumble, and his eyes didn't sink into their sockets. Love beamed from his eyes, stubbornness smoothed his skin, and hope strengthened his flesh, but didn't grant him the gift of prophecy.

Even now, when I recall that night, I still see things from the side, though at that moment when Leah entered the bakery I was in the picture. I was struggling with a sack of flour that refused to be dragged to the sifter, Itsik Edelman was arranging pans, Jacob and Father were standing at the kneading machine cutting the dough into chunks, Joshua was in position at the table. Mother and Simon weren't working that night.

Jacob's job was to lift the dough out of the big bowl of the kneading machine and stretch it so Father could cut it with his knife. You must know, my dear, both for this incident and in answer to your question about Duke Anton's decorated rolls, that dough is a cunning and deceitful material. It may look spongy and submissive, but it is elastic and strong, heavy and rebellious, and when it starts rising, even steel doors won't stop it.

Jacob leaned over the bowl, thrust his hands into the dough, straightened up forcefully, pulling out a decent chunk, and Father sundered it with a long, old butcher's knife the ritual slaughterer had sold him because its blade was nicked and so it was declared unfit for that purpose. Every day the knife was honed on a barber's strop, and it was so sharp it passed through the dough like a cold wind. Joshua Edelman waited at the table, pulled the big chunks Jacob put down, and with a loud bang of the cleaver, he chopped them into smaller pieces each weighing exactly "nine decos," as Edelman called nine hundred grams. He was so experienced he didn't bother using the scales sitting next to him. Wielding his cleaver, he would cut a piece that was somewhat bigger than necessary, and, after a quick, precise, appraising squeeze, he pinched off a tiny strip, and smiled to himself with pleasure because he knew that he now held a loaf of exactly nine decos in his hand.

The moon rose in the window with its soft, pink, whorish light. "Why doesn't he weigh it on the scale?" Jacob got mad. The haze made him jumpy and irritable, and he had more faith in measuring instruments than in the worker's experience and the wisdom of his hands.

Father chuckled. "Edelman's hands are like the scales of a Bukharan goldsmith," he said.

"He who works precisely never makes a mistake." Joshua smiled at Jacob, and another wave of rage passed over my brother.

"Someday they'll come from the inspector's office to weigh the bread, and there'll be hell to pay," he grumbled, and bent over the kneading machine again, and with an effort, pulled another chunk of dough for Father to cut off.

Then, in that sweaty moment, as Father was brandishing the knife and I was dragging the sack to the sifter and my brother was lifting the load of dough and we were all groaning with the heat and the strain, the screen door suddenly banged and Father shouted, "Who did that? Now the dough fell!"

We all turned around and saw Leah coming into the bakery, light and fresh as a nocturnal flower.

Silence fell. Leah was carrying a covered pan, and in the dim heat of the bakery she looked like a princess who had come down to visit her slaves in a mine. The oven fan drew the good smell off her dress and spread it through the dense space.

"Hello, Leah," I said. In those days, even though Yehiel didn't approve, we were reading Damon Runyon together in English, and we greeted each other with "hello." Leah smiled at me, put down the pan, and uncovered three big white rolls of strudel.

"Mother would like to put these in your oven," she said to Father. "We're having company for the Sabbath, and there's no room in our oven."

Father usually didn't allow people in the bakery during working hours. "A knock, a whistle, and a menstruating woman makes the dough fall," he kept telling us. He let the village women put their cakes only in the "last oven," on Friday morning, but he accorded Leah, the *izhika con Gracia*, special treatment.

Sixteen years old she was then, her thick braid was wound around her head in two and a half circles, and she wore a blue cotton dress with short sleeves. When I put on my glasses, small white flowers with yellow sepals bloomed on her dress, and a strong, fresh smell of saffron filled the air. Leah's eyes wandered around the bakery, and she suddenly aimed her first look straight into my brother's eyes; and even though it was a very brief look, it surprised him and lasted long enough to open gaping spaces in Jacob's flesh and threaten to overpower him under the load of his feelings and his dough. His hands were fettered by a big, heavy chunk, and Father, who was already waving the knife over the dough, looked at him and was afraid because he knew what was about to happen, and knew there was no way to prevent it.

"Hold the dough, dummy!" he cried in terror. Five thousand years of baking have turned the baker's movements into a category of fate. Father knew he couldn't stop the knife midway in its course.

"Hold on tight!" Father pleaded. "Jacob . . ."

But Jacob was looking at Leah, and felt particles of irritating flour drying his throat, his bound hands getting wet with love and losing their grip on the heavy dough.

"Don't move, Jacob . . ."

The thick layer of dough swallowed the terrible clamor of the blood, blocked the flesh, and hid what happened: the fingers of Jacob's right hand moved blindly in the dough, trying to improve their hold, and the slaughterer's knife lopped off the littlest one of them.

Jacob didn't make a sound. Only I—watching his face turn pale and dropping to the ground along with him—understood. Before he passed out he put the chunk down on the table, and when his body hit the floor, the stump of his finger popped out of the dough and gushed blood like the throat of a slaughtered cow. Leah leaped back in fear, and you could see her own blood pounding under the thin skin of her neck. Father dashed over to lean on the wall. I, who was lying on the floor next to Jacob, got up, threw off my eyeglasses, and went to the window. Itsik Edelman turned white, and Joshua was the only one who didn't lose his head. He rushed to Jacob, wrapped the terrible wound in dough, tied it up with the filthy rag of the glaze brush, grabbed the knife, and shouted, "We've got to find the finger, got to!"—and fenced with the bowl of the kneading machine like a clumsy Cyrano.

"Good that he didn't shout, good that he didn't shout," Father kept mumbling into the wall, but his hope was deceived. Within a minute, the old goose landed in the bakery, hissing and panting, with Mother and Brinker in his wake.

Jacob lay on the floor in a puddle of blood. Leah's pale neck was still humming and throbbing. Father was shaking all over.

"They killed us the Jacob!" Mother screamed at Leah and Father, and to my amazement, despite the catastrophe, I felt a smile rising on my face, because I never imagined she would quote the beginning of a book.

Once again the broad shoulders slowly turned, the arms opened, the flush rose from the chest to the throat and the face, deep and menacing. The stunned girl fled the bakery, and Mother grabbed the heavy pan she had brought, pitched it after her, and the strudel wriggled in the air like thick pale corpses of snakes, opened up and dropped their sweet innards to the ground.

She ran all the way home. She went up to her room, opened the window wide, lay down on the bed, and pressed her screaming mouth into the pillow. A wise and comely girl she was, but young and inexperienced. The knowledge she suddenly came into, knowledge that, in a normal life, is learned and processed and amassed over many long years, was heaped on her all at once and choked her throat with pincers of sobs. It wasn't bad enough that the stubborn, clumsy son of a baker surprised her with such a terrible and vile sacrifice, but in the very same second it dawned on her that she would be his, that she would bear his children, and that in their future battles of love she would never win.

Elijah Salomo and Miriam Ashkenazi

(A Story Close to the Truth About People
with Fictional Names)

O n June 22, 1913, a few minutes before sunrise over Jerusalem, a *vali* from Hebron appeared at the Gate of Mercy in a good humor, riding on his mare. The rising day was the longest of the year, and every summer it was the *vali*'s habit to circle the holy walls on that day. It was a ceremonial circuit, slow and stately, that began as the sun leaped up and ended precisely as it was sinking, and lasted long enough for him to recite the entire seventeenth *surah* of the Koran.

Here we should stop and explain that there was no mistake concerning the aforementioned date and the *vali* wasn't tardy. In the rest of the world the longest day of the year is June 21, but in Jerusalem it is a day late because of the enormous gravitational pull of the foundation stone of the Temple. These facts are well-known, and have been recorded and described in many books, including *The Shape of the Country*, by Rafael Haim Levi of Ofeibach, as well more recent treatises, the most famous being *Voyage de la Judée, la Samarie, la Galilée et le Liban*.

The *vali* looked to the east, and the moment the sun flickered above the Mount of Olives he shifted his mare to the left, tapped her neck, and began circling the city at a pace so perfectly attuned to the rotation of the earth that the common shadow of horse and rider grew neither longer nor shorter. And so it was that near ten o'clock, when the *vali* passed Nablus Gate and approached the mosaic of Orpheus, something terrible happened. Far away from there, near Baalbek, a Maronite peasant set fire to a pile of dry briars he had pulled out of his vineyard. The flames caught the edge of the next field, leaped into the grove, and a great conflagration quickly spread on the slopes of the mountains. The heat whirled the air, a great quivering rose in the Lebanon valley, a wind stirred over the east, and its sudden gust moved the Greek windmill at Nablus Gate. One of its blades struck the *vali*'s mare and broke her neck.

The stunned holy man whose horizons were narrowed by his piety, and who didn't quite understand cause and effect, extricated himself from under the carcass and poured out his wrath on the closest sinner—he waved his hand and cursed the windmill: may its blades dry up and never move again.

The blades stopped as if struck by thunder; they were still all that night, and at dawn the sobbing miller saddled his donkey, tied two mules loaded with tributes to it, and rode to Hebron to appease the holy man and ask him to lift the evil decree. But when he reached Hebron, he found that the *vali* had returned to his own town, made his will, and was lying with his forefathers. An old man he was, and because of the intense effort of the curse, the veins of his heart burst, and he died.

The windmill of Nablus Gate, incidentally, was famous for its beauty, and is mentioned in the writings of many travelers, including Gustave Flaubert, who called it "a lovely delight at the edge of that heap of rot called Jerusalem." To those who are amazed at the style, we shall only say that in Flaubert's relations with Jerusalem there is indeed something obscene. The distinguished writer even took pains to state that he broke wind from his behind the moment he entered the city for the first time, and that she, with her exquisite sense of justice, gave him in return a fine dose of syphilis through that same behind; and these things are also known, and the delicate soul will understand them well even without going into detail.

The mill stood still, but not time. Seven bad years came and went. There was a war, hunger and disease ruled the city, its masters changed, many of its sons left and didn't return, and all the while, the mill was embalmed in its curse, immortalizing the moment of its death. The *vali*'s sorcery was so potent that people would gather there on winter days to see that the blades didn't move, even in storms that made roofs fly off and bells ring.

On the advice of the Greek Patriarch, the miller decided to dismantle the windmill, invert its stones, and build it anew. But as he was figuring out his calculations and preparing his steps, an Italian named Salvatore Benintendi came to Jerusalem, a film projectionist from Alexandria who was wandering all over the Levant in camel caravans and on steam engines. The Italian toted boxes of silent films around with him, as well as an enormous projector whose system of gears could be connected to the pump in the citrus groves, the water-wheel of a well, Circassian dancers, the ox working an oil press, or any other Oriental machinery that rotated. Jerusalem, with her stylized lies, her infinite stone memory, and her touching attempts to terrify her visitors, captured his heart. Salvatore Benintendi investigated, asked around, and quickly rented the arrested windmill. As soon as the first movie was projected there, a miracle occurred: a terrible screech was heard, and the blades of the mill began moving again.

Salvatore Benintendi wasn't only a lover of silent film, he was also a pious Catholic, and by virtue of these two qualities, he loved miracles and believed in them. To the joy of the audience, the Greek miller allowed him to continue his shows, because he was a wise man and understood that, even if the strange projectionist belonged to the wrong church, without him and his movies, the mill would come to a stop again.

In an amazing display of fraternity, the heads of all the millets in the city imposed bans and prohibitions on viewing, the blades of the windmill set up a terrifying racket, clouds of ground flour whitened the faces of actors and spectators—nevertheless, the audience flocked to the cinema. The most persistent and enthusiastic of them all was a Jewish lad named Elijah Salomo, a youth of the Monastir community. He was incorrigibly curious, devoted to excitement and novelty, and like all Monastirials, he too was known as an astronomer, philosopher, linguist, and mathematician. But he was chiefly famous as the first Jerusalemite to ride in an automobile.

This matter demands some specification, for in a city that has seen all kinds of death, foolishness, miracles, and pain, it is hard to create wonders; but the first automobile surprised even her. It was a daring little Napier that was unloaded from a ship at the foot of the Carmel and galloped across the country confounding the eyes, ears, and noses of the inhabitants with the wild, mad world of internal combustion. Its polished mahogany trim, the heartbeats rising from its body, the lack of nuisances—no grousing carters, no tangled reins, no daydreaming horses—delighted everyone who saw it. On a lovely summer day it reached Jerusalem, burning the strange frankincense of gasoline and caoutchouc, leather and hot metal.

The driver, an American of about fifty, a tall man with a moustache, adorned with an equestrian coat, gigantic teeth, and a visored cap, parked it at Nablus Gate, not far from the windmill. He took off his dust goggles and driving gloves, mixed fearlessly with the gathering crowd, shook hands and said, "Mister and Missus Charles Glidden of Boston." Missus Charles Glidden, a smiling redhead, increased the amazement. She also shook hands, and she also wore riding boots. Her freckles and eyes gleamed, a silk scarf around her neck fluttered in the wind, and her tweed trousers proved to the agitated audience that her legs were attached to one another. Until that time, the religious leaders had succeeded for generations in convincing every man in the city that his wife was the only woman in the world whose legs met, so that he wouldn't lust after the junction of any other woman's legs. They made up lies, issued threats, and sewed dresses that blocked the light and the truth. And here came the American, his wife, her trousers, and their automobile, and stood the order of things on its head.

Elijah Salomo was a ten-year-old boy at that time, but he was already clever enough to regret that Missus Glidden had come to Jerusalem before he became a man. That night he couldn't fall asleep, and after midnight, he slipped out of his house and went back to Nablus Gate. The crowd had dispersed, only a few onlookers were still standing in the distance, and two guards assigned by the American consul were walking around the automobile. In the misty dead of night the child crept into the trunk and closed the top over him.

The next day, when the Gliddens went to take a dip in the Jordan, they heard a muffled cough from the wrong end of the automobile. They stopped and discovered the child, asphyxiated by the exhaust fumes, expiring with admiration and heat. They immediately took him out into the air, gave him food and drink; and in the evening they brought him back to Jerusalem, sitting in the lap of Missus Glidden's trousers—safe and sound, in love, and speaking fluent English.

He didn't fall asleep that night either, and the next morning he rushed to Nablus Gate and saw that the couple had disappeared, leaving behind only tire tracks in the dust and a faint aroma of perfume and combustion. Elijah never saw the Napier or Missus Glidden again, except in his dreams. Then, as they are wont to do, the dreams split into regrets, hopes, and memories, and Elijah Salomo was once again steeped in study, observation, and cogitation, and after Salvatore Benintendi came from Alexandria—also in silent movies. He quickly made friends with the projectionist, learned Italian from him, and assisted him in his work for free, without any money. He swept the flour and the spittle off the floor, sold tickets, and rewound films. This friendship raised a number of eyebrows among the Monastirials, for Salvatore Benintendi was suspected of loving men, and those suspicions, like all suspicions that have ever been raised in Jerusalem, were true. Somebody even heard Benintendi say with a shrill laugh, "I don't care if they talk about me as long as they talk behind my back." But Elijah wasn't worried, because he knew that his friend was a homosexual of the Platonic variety, and that any kind of physical contact—either with women, men, or animals—was repugnant to him.

Like most Monastirials, Elijah Salomo was also graced with a talent for tinkering, and in time he perfected the monstrous apparatus of wooden wheels, shanks and straps that connected the projector to the millstone. The transmission had no coupling or flywheel, and so strong winds sometimes accelerated the plots of love films, while funny movies brought clouds and rain to the city. And that, too, of course, infuriated the believers.

Elijah saw every film several times and quickly learned to read the lips of the silent actors. His grasp was so sharp and fine that he succeeded in reciting their speeches in total synchronization with the picture. Even in the worst storms, when the actors began running around on the screen "like *cucarachas* when a scribe spills ink on them," in the words of Salomo Salomo, Elijah's father—even then he didn't fall behind them, and by imitating the movements of their lips and the expressions on their faces, he also unwittingly acquired a perfect American accent.

A few years later, when the first talking picture came to Jerusalem, the spectators set up a racket of howls and laments, demanding that the machine be silenced, and they all wailed that Elijah Salomo's synchronization was better, and his voice was more dramatic and pleasing than the voices of the speaking actors, but Elijah himself was dead by then. The story will revolve around that, and here begin the details.

The Monastirials traded in fabrics, olive oil, arak, and herring, and prayed in a synagogue that was the only wooden building in Jerusalem. Their forefathers were Romaniot Jews, a bold ancient race that came to Macedonia in Roman times. A thousand years later the redheaded Jews expelled from Hungary mixed with them, and ever since, they have given birth to fairhaired girls with a wonderful sense of humor. Not many of the exiles from Spain who came to Monastir a hundred years later dared to marry them, because those girls were graced with sharp tongues and dazzling beauty, unlike the stupid, delicate gazelles lauded by the poets of Seville. But the few who did venture to do so didn't regret it. This union brought children into the world whose fame spread all over the Mediterranean.

Elijah looked very much like Salomo Salomo, his father, for among the Monastirials the features of the father passed only to the oldest son, his firstborn, while the rest of the children resembled their mother in body and soul. Even today in Jerusalem you can still hear the expression "As alike as a Monastirial and his firstborn son." And indeed, all the oldest sons were marked by insatiable curiosity, and afflicted with unfathomable boredom, all studied astronomy to understand the secrets of infinity, and all were endowed with perfect night vision. That vision had developed over long years of observing the stars, and was passed from father to son not only through training but also through inheritance. In fact, every firstborn Monastirial resembled the man who was thought to be the father of the community, the great theoretician of infinity Issachar Modrukhi Monastirali of blessed memory, and they all looked like living memorials to him, or like attempts to resurrect him.

Issachar Modrukhi Monastirali lived in the sixteenth century. He knew all the stars of the sky, and their orbits were as familiar to him as the back of his hand. In his childhood, he had discovered the formula for summing up an infinite geometric progression many years before it was formulated by Friedrich Gauss, but proving the formula bored him so much he decided to pigeonhole it, thus keeping the fame of the world away from himself and his city. Everyone admired him and honored his memory, but even he didn't succeed in settling the great controversy that tore the community of Monastir Jews apart, the controversy over the right way to that desired infinity. The "reducers" claimed that the way of absolute reduction is the right way, while the "magnifiers" preferred the way of enlargement. We may state that this was the continuation of the Minoan controversy about the infinity of space versus the infinity of the point, which still echoes in debates of our own day about the creation of the universe.

Even among the Monastirials, known for their sharp wit, Elijah Salomo was considered a genius. By the time he was four he could solve in his head any mathematical problem presented to him; at the age of nine he could explain why the white and the yolk don't get mixed up in the egg. At fourteen he recited the laws of Kepler and Baum and the tables of Mendeleyev and Brand, and at seventeen he began going bald because of the intense heat inside his skull.

In logarithmic and numerological calculations, Elijah Salomo even triumphed over the twins Zerubabel and Nehemia Teitelbaum, who were nicknamed Zerubuzzel and Zebuzzabel in Jerusalem because everyone who stood next to them could here the constant humming in their heads. Those two could look at you and tell you the sum of the letters in the sentence in your mind even before you said it aloud, and they no longer talked to one another in words but only in numbers. They say that at Passover, 1869, when Zerubuzzel and Zebuzzabel sat at their father's seder, an awful quarrel erupted between them right after the second cup of wine, when Zerubabel suddenly stopped humming, looked at Nehemia's wife, and said, "2652." Nehemia flushed with offense, left the seder in a rage, and didn't talk to his brother for four years, until Zerubabel knelt before him at their father's funeral and, with a tear-stained face, whispered, "6467." And Nehemia raised his brother up, pressed him hard to his heart, and forgave him with "575," which adds up to "we be brethren."

The *Kortijo de dos Puertas*, the courtyard where the Salomo family lived, was also inhabited by a widow named Bulisa Ashkenazi and her growing daughter Miriam. Once, when Miriam was still a child, Elijah Salomo was crossing the courtyard on his way to the street, and gave her a sliver of blue glass through which to look at the world. He gave her the glass casually and didn't pay any attention to her afterward, just as he didn't pay any attention to any woman except two: Missus Glidden on earth and Aurora in heaven. But Miriam loved him ever since with the sharp, hot love of children, and whenever she looked at the blue world he had bestowed on her, her heart would flutter and her knees would grow weak. She grew up into a quiet, good maiden, whose black hair sparkled with a deep blue gleam, and whose chest was flat as a board. All the girls her age had already puffed up and become convex, and they mocked her with the nickname Wailing Wall. Her breasts waited in her rib cage like the pair of white ravens in the famous Turkish adage, the white ravens that will never come, and their dilatoriness worried her mother. But neither Bulisa Ashkenazi's prayers nor the Hebron amulets nor the Saint Jacob ointment of the old Armenian women did any good.

Then, when Miriam was sixteen years and seven months old, she woke up in the middle of the night with a pain she couldn't describe or compare with any other pain—not a stomach ache or melancholy or *dolor de kabesa*, or a dream of love, or anything that had ever happened to her before.

For a few moments she lay excited, her eyes wide open, but not scared, because the strange pain lodged in parts she had never had before, and so she decided that the pain didn't belong to her but had gotten lost, the kind of pain that has departed the bodies of dead men and are seeking new hosts. Years later, on nights when she felt the phantom pains sawing the memory of her right breast, she would recall the pain of that night. But then, when she suddenly woke up, she only smiled to herself, turned over on her back, and fell asleep again, and in the morning she saw that this time the breasts she dreamed about every night hadn't disappeared when she woke up.

"*Dos miraculos*. The right one of soft porcelain and the left one of hard silk," reported Bulisa Ashkenazi to the astounded neighbor women, and they hurried off to Hamam-el-Ayn, where the bath attendant let them peep in at the pair of miracles Miriam's body displayed; and as they left, they shook and turned green with their envy and her beauty.

One of those women was the wife of the matchmaker Shaltiel, who appeared at Bulisa Ashkenazi's house the very next day, and told her he had taken the liberty of pondering the unique case of Miriam and wished to propose a "match *speziale*."

Bulisa Ashkenazi pretended not to hear, and brought cold water to the table, along with roasted almonds, quince jam, and coffee cups.

"Your daughter requires somebody special," said Shaltiel, who didn't forget to praise the refreshments either.

"Why?" asked Bulisa Ashkenazi.

"I've already heard about your daughter," said the matchmaker, wiping his lips on a white cloth napkin he pulled out of his coat pocket.

"What did you hear?" asked Bulisa Ashkenazi, with a cleverly acted suspicion.

"Never mind," said the matchmaker, "but what I did hear was enough. For her we need one of the Monastirials."

Despite the gravity of the matter, a smile spread over Bulisa Ashkenazi's face. Conjectures and legends about the conjugal life of the Monastirials were rife. The qualities that made them fit for a life of observation and contemplation—that is, curiosity, wisdom, a methodical mind, and patience—also made them splendid lovers, but their lust for knowledge and research was stronger than the lust of the flesh, not to mention drives like hunger and thirst, which dropped into third and fourth place. Which was why they remained thin as children and slept with their wives only on cloudy nights. Even today in Jerusalem you can still hear this analogy for utter despair: "Like a Monastirial woman who returned from the mikve and found her husband looking at the stars."

The Monastirial women did indeed hate the summer because its days burned the skin of their white faces and its nights, sprinkled with the seductive winks of the stars, took their husbands away from them; and it's a known fact that in 1911 they didn't give birth to a single child because Halley's Comet had appeared in the skies of Jerusalem the year before and all the Monasterial men were busy.

"For instance," said Shaltiel the matchmaker, "for instance, a fellow you know, for instance, Elijah Salomo."

"For instance, what about him?"

"Elijah Salomo has a great many important things in his head. Silent movies, automobiles, calculations, sunrises, languages, numerology—the wisdom of King Solomon. Your daughter wouldn't do Elijah any harm."

Bulisa Ashkenazi was happy about the matchmaker's proposal, but for the sake of honor and good order, she hastened to point out that Elijah was prematurely bald. Shaltiel, bald himself, smiled as if he hadn't heard the remark, and quickly mentioned the affluence of the father of the intended bridegroom, the micrographer Salomo Salomo, one of the best-known Monasterials in the city. Salomo Salomo was an expert in the miniaturization of holy scriptures, and sold Christians the Epistles of Paul to the Corinthians written on seashells, Moslems the seventeenth *surah* on harness buttons, and Jews the Blessings of Dawn on fifteen grains of wheat. By virtue of his profession he belonged to the "reducers," and took pride in the fact that his principles guided his life and earned him his bread, for the art of tiny writing, he claimed, is the correct way of coping with the menaces of infinity.

Salomo Salomo's interest in micrography began when he was nine years old. During a class in the Talmud-Torah, out of the awful boredom only wise children can feel, he started looking for something to do. He recited the list of names in Genesis 36 until he knew it by heart backward and forward; he secretly drew the imaginary portraits of the daughters of Zelophehad, who for some reason looked alike in his mind; he devoted a few minutes to wondering whether there was some meaning to the fact that "dad," "mom," and "sis" are palindromes but other family members aren't. Then he plucked a thin hair from the neck of the boy dozing in front of him, inserted it in a slit in the end of his writing quill, stuck out his tongue, and wrote Genesis 32:3-7 on his fingernail.

This feat provoked great excitement in the Talmud-Torah and in the courtyards of the quarter, and came to an evil and bitter end. The Mutasaref's deputy, a vile, cruel Turk, an admirer of miniatures and a dwarf himself, heard that same day of "the little Monastirial's fingernail," sent for him, and after a brief examination ordered the nail sent to the museum in

Istanbul. The screams of the tortured child, when two Anatolian soldiers dragged him to the portable gallows and an officer of the guard guillotined the top part of his finger, were heard throughout the entire city, but in Jerusalem that was considered merely a drop in the bucket. Besotted with holiness and madness, her stones familiar with the taste of the blood of children, virgins, lambs, soldiers, and old people, the city wasn't impressed by the affliction of Salomo Salomo. His father and mother, waiting near the fortress until their bleeding, unconscious child was thrown out, loaded him onto a litter, carried him home, and tended to his awful wound until it healed. But that pain was erased neither from his memory nor from his flesh. At night, he said, he could hear the missing joint of his finger; and whenever he chanced upon a person in torment, he asked him to describe his pains, listened patiently to his metaphors, and then decreed, "That hurts less than a finger" or "That hurts more than a finger."

Salomo Salomo persevered with his art, and when he grew up his fame spread throughout the world, spawning claimants, imitators, and admirers of his tiny writing. Equipped with watchmaker's loupes, wide pupils, and brushes made of a single hair plucked from the eyelashes of a fly, he created his works and obtained high prices for them. As a matter of course vicious tongues began to wag, and when Salomo wrote the five books of the Pentateuch on five goose eggs, the slanderers said he didn't write anything there but had only pricked dots that hid their fraud with their pretension, since their extreme tininess made it impossible to examine them.

Salomo Salomo's rage was inflamed. He immediately took Rabbi David Altman, who knew the whole Torah by heart and was the only Ashkenazi Jew to teach in the Beth El Yeshiva, to his English friend Dr. James Burton, whose clinic housed a microscope so powerful "it showed you the lice on lice."

In those days Dr. James Burton had come from India to Jerusalem, and unlike other characters mentioned here, he was a real person. A few old-timers in the city still remember his custom of playing tennis with lips painted scarlet, eyes shaded blue, and a tight hair net on his head. (And he always won, because the lacy skirt he wore fluttered on his bullish thighs, perplexed his opponents, and deprived them of their power of concentration.)

Rabbi David Altman examined the goose eggs under the mighty lenses, compared the tiny letters on them with their identical twins in his photographic memory, and six hours later, straightened up and confirmed that the entire Pentateuch, including the apostrophe on the s of "And his sons and his sons' sons with him" in the Book of Genesis, and the comma before Esau's kiss of Jacob and before "and Aaron" in Numbers 3—appeared on the shells, and not a single dot was missing. Salomo Salomo's glory soared to new heights.

Bulisa Ashkenazi knew well the sublime excellence of Salomo Salomo and the exalted importance of his son, but she mentioned to Shaltiel the matchmaker his own great failure in another match, which had started out with great expectations and ended with the husband's incurable priapism. Shaltiel heard and smiled and said, "The fool is scared of good things, and the wise man loves to read the stars," leaving Bulisa Ashkenazi to interpret the maxim by herself. He rushed to the Salomo house, and the moment he entered, Elijah announced, "I agree," because the birds of the sky and common sense had already brought him the rumor. He knew the bride and didn't fear the beauty attributed to her breasts, because his love was given to Missus Glidden, and Missus Glidden had the three virtues every Monastirial man desired in a wife: she was far away, she was married to somebody else, and she didn't know she was loved.

The wedding was celebrated with joy and splendor. The wedding contract was written on a loquat pit, the challahs of the offering provoked the expected admiration, the dried salt fish swam in pools of arak, the Monastirials rejoiced and danced, and demanded that the bridegroom and his father follow tradition and conduct a public debate.

So Salomo Salomo stood up and maintained that absolutely infinite miniaturization would be achieved when "YHVH," the four letters of God's name, were written on the point of a needle—thus compressing the globe and its inhabitants into one incomparably heavy point, and because of the infinity of its smallness and the smallness of its infinity, every person dwelling on the globe could carry it in the smallest pocket of his trousers even though in the nature of things that person would also be reduced so that he would be even smaller than that point on which he stood while it was in the pocket of his trousers. The audience applauded, and a few lads fainted because these kinds of circular meditations accelerate and reinforce themselves, and in young men, as we know, intelligence is already at its peak, but knees and eyes and heart are still awkward and have neither coordination nor experience.

Then Elijah stood up, and while honoring the Fifth Commandment, he proved to his father that even if he succeeded in creating that incomparably heavy point, the point would sink through itself, dragging everything after it, and thus turning the entire cosmos inside out like a glove, from the trousers pocket to the great seas and mountains, and would come back to its previous size but from the other side. Elijah explained all this while standing on one foot to prove his maturity and stability.

Again everyone applauded, and his father said "You won, my son!" The members of the bride's family—poor cloth dyers who didn't understand a single word their new relatives spoke—were embarrassed but also happy.

Catastrophes are wont to be born taking happiness by the heel, and thus it happened that the catastrophe of Elijah Salomo befell him that same night. The father of the groom and the mother of the bride reminded the young couple how important it was to keep the nuptial chamber dark, and Bulisa Ashkenazi sighed with nostalgia, and said to Miriam, "It's better for a woman to lose her virginity in the dark so she won't be able to find it afterward."

But in his great curiosity Elijah Salomo lit the oil lamp in the nuptial chamber and thus brought the evil down on himself with his own hands. The light illuminated the walls of the room, the carved headboard of the nuptial bed, and Miriam's joyous smile. She had heard such contradictory and evasive descriptions of the wedding night from the women in her neighborhood that she had decided it was merely a game of hide-and-seek. She pushed aside the sheet that covered her, and remained in her modest nightgown. Then she lifted one hand to take the pins out of her hair, and two supple ripples of flesh, almost imperceptible, rolled under her nightgown.

Never in his life had Elijah seen a movement comparable to the dance of cloth of his wife's breasts. Like river cats hovering on wings, like a dream slipping through wisps of fog, like the Spirit of the Lord blowing on the white petals of a rose. But even the absurd metaphors scurrying around in his brain didn't put him off. He hung the oil lamp on the wall, approached Miriam, and opened the tassels at the low-cut neck of her nightgown without understanding the danger floating above him. His eyes descended the slope of bared skin, glided down and climbed up, and discovered that all the conjectures and rumors widespread in Jerusalem about his wife's breasts were all true. "Like stars," he muttered to himself, and already wanted to turn and record this in his notebook of observations, but even before he sensed his whole body shaking, he felt a sharp sword slicing his brain, his pupils shrank to the size of louse eggs, his legs gave way, and he landed on the floor with a cry.

Miriam was sure that her husband's contortions were simply part of the nuptial night games, and was already shouting, "I saw you, I saw you, *uno, dos, tres!*" But the miserable Elijah, with the last of his strength, dragged himself to the courtyard, crawled through the gate to the street of the Karaites, crossed the alley on his knees, collapsed on the threshold of the house of Elhanati the apothecary, and when Elhanati came out, Elijah told him someone had thrust a rapier into his head. The apothecary examined Elijah's pupils, sighed, and informed him that he was afflicted with *la migraine du jaloux*, a rare but well-known headache that strikes the jealous, an individual illness with no remedy or early symptoms, and everyone who is afflicted with it is doomed to seek his cure all by himself.

In the morning Bulisa Ashkenazi brought two old Yemenite women from the village to examine the wedding night sheet. They found a sheet as white as snow, a bride who said, "Elijah yelled a lot, but it didn't hurt me a bit," and a tormented bridegroom who didn't dare blink, wailing like a slaughtered camel, and clutching his wife's hand hard. Elhanati the apothecary came, said he had read books and thought thoughts all night, and explained that the source of the ailment lay in the blood vessels, because "jealousy influences the small capillaries and love the big ones, and an equilibrium is necessary." But Elijah threw out the medicine he brought, because beneath his pain and jealousy he was still a devotee of logic, and the apothecary's superstitions, learned as they may have been, were not acceptable to him. He knew that migraines, shortness of breath, love, and allergies are all considered part of the same group of plagues, and so he deducted one component after another from his meals and one piece of clothing after another from his body, lest one of them contain the guilty element, and by dint of the same logic, he also omitted one consonant after another from his speech. Within six weeks he had reached a state of walking around the house only in his socks, living on grass broth, and calling Miriam "i-ah." Then he understood that the only medication for his torment was the constant presence of his wife. And when he described to his father the terrible migraine of jealousy, Saolomo nodded his head for the first time and said, "That's just like a finger."

On Yom Kippur that year Elijah didn't dare go to the synagogue because he knew they wouldn't let him into the women's section with Miriam. Thus his catastrophe was known, and the wildfire of rumor spread throughout the whole city. A week later, when everyone was sitting in the *sukkah* and Elijah cut the pomegranate with his sharp pocketknife, he looked at the pictures of the patriarchs, especially Joseph and Aaron, and saw them looking at his wife with their ancient eyes and lascivious smiles concealed in their beards. In mighty rage and amazement Elijah cut his finger. The wound was very deep, but Elijah didn't pay it any attention; he just went on looking at the pictures of the guilty saints and sawing his flesh, and didn't feel a thing. A white bone was exposed, and an incredible stream of blood flooded the tablecloth. Miriam screamed and bandaged his hand, but blood immediately burst from his mouth too because, as he ate, he kept biting his tongue over and over. Miriam began crying, and Elijah told her to calm down and drank a full cup of boiling coffee in three big gulps. Thus it was clear that even saints in pictures lusted after another man's wife and that the migraine of jealousy ruled Elijah so totally it closed the gates of his consciousness to pain from outside. If he was stabbed or cut or pinched or seared—he didn't know it, didn't feel it.

"Pains don't save us from death," Bulisa Ashkenazi consoled her daughter, "they just make sure we'll die in torment." And the neighbor women laughed and said that now Elijah could remove the *canoon* embers without a shovel or a coal pan. But Salomo Salomo was extremely worried and took his son to his old friend Dr. Burton.

At that time the physician was renting an apartment in the Moslem quarter. Foreign music incessantly poured into the street from the gramophone in his house, and twice a week he went to the *souk* in embroidered Persian slippers and a silk sari to buy calf's lungs for his three cats. He was known for his love of Wagnerian opera and he even taught four Russian nuns to sing parts of *Die Meistersinger* in four voices, including bass, contributed by the Mother Superior of the Convent of Mary Magdalene. This feat, incidentally, was to be documented a few years later in Ronald Storrs's memoirs, and Dr. Burton's name also appears in the *Book of Quotations* by Sir Bernard Harvey, who attributes to him the mocking line: "The only two bearable places in Jerusalem are the bed and the bathtub." That, of course, is an error. The author of the saying wasn't James Burton the physician but William Burton, Storrs's predecessor as governor, who hated the city and its people and spent the two years of his rule in those two bearable places, where he lay supine reciting lines from *Paradise Lost*. This anecdote is also related in Storrs's memoirs but has nothing whatever to do with Elijah and Miriam.

Dr. Burton was stunned. In India he had seen people who felt no pain, people who felt only pain, and people who felt other people's pains, but never had he seen the *migraine du jaloux*. He said that Elijah's malady was very dangerous.

"Pain is neither punishment nor insult, it's a gift from God!" he declared. "A human being who doesn't feel pain can die from a tooth cavity." And he instructed Miriam to examine her husband's body every day from the bottom of his feet to the top of his head to see if he was wounded or burned or cut, and to take his temperature every morning and every night, lest he be afflicted by some internal inflammation.

Miriam sewed thick clothes for her husband to protect his skin, hid all the knives and needles, and made him stay in the house. But like all who suffer from the migraine of the jealous, Elijah didn't trust his consort. He leaped to the conclusion that she wanted to put him in a cage so she could go out and run wild in the streets with her lovers. By now he had proof that every man in Jerusalem—from the lowest donkey driver to the High Commissioner, from the smallest tyke in the Talmud-Torahs to the Moslem Mufti—were all thinking about her, because he himself couldn't think about anything else.

Like a slow river of mud, the migraine of the jealous closed on the brain of the magnificent Monasterial, filled all its compartments and threatened to push out whatever contents had been in them before. He felt the pain swelling in his soft temples, rising and encompassing the bones of his skull, and rolling back to the ancient depths of consciousness. His torment grew so tremendous that even inside the house he wouldn't let Miriam leave his side or stand near an open window and show herself to strangers.

Now that his nerves were exempt from the need to conduct and transmit the insipidities of the outside world, they concentrated on really important things. He trailed her everywhere, a flaccid shadow who never allowed himself even the respite of a blink, for he knew that the hands of groping men were even faster than the flick of an eyelid. And every morning he secured his pair of contumacious treasures with a girdle of Arab cloth wound around them ten times that flattened their defiant flesh and didn't let them breathe.

In his *Book of Jealousy*, aside from possession of the body of the beloved, Father Antonin also enumerates a man's hatred for the life of the woman before she became part of his life, his dread of her thoughts, his loathing of her memories, his hostility to her lingerie, the spoon she eats her soup with, her old pictures, the uncles who dandled her as an infant on their defiled laps. Then Father Antonin mentions the famous murder known in the literature as the case of the Jealous Man of Beirut, a Maronite goldsmith who beheaded his wife because she let air into her lungs and light into her eyes. But Elijah's jealousy for Miriam was greater than all those and was the hardest of jealousies, the most painful and refined of them all—to wit, prophetic jealousy. Despite all our sympathy for the poor Maronite woman, it cannot be denied that that sinner did indeed let air and light penetrate the pores of her body; but the sins that tormented Elijah were worse than that, worse than anything: the sins that Miriam was going to commit in the future, not the sins she had never committed in the past.

Now that his jealousy had destroyed the remnants of his savings and his sanity, the young couple was forced to move to the courtyard of Widow's Border, a courtyard of paupers whose floor was layered with dirt, trash, and pigeon droppings, that formed a breeding ground for cunning rats and cats who could pick locks and were so desperate they even stole potatoes. The rooms were musty and dark, and the water in the cistern was polluted through the cracks that appeared in it. Under the big poplar in the center of the courtyard, whose wild roots had already pushed up the tiles on the ground floor, the impoverished women gathered for neighborly gossip. Here they would strain the cistern water through a diaper, shrieking at the sight of the wet red sewer worms that wriggled on the white cloth.

In the winter Miriam cooked *sahleb* and roasted watermelon seeds she had hoarded all summer. In the spring she made *hamle-m'laneh*, and during the heavy *hamsins* of May and July, when the *barad* and *sus* vendors appeared, she made *pepitada*, a refreshing drink of melon seeds, and she and Elijah sold it in the streets.

Elijah loved the children who gathered around him with their excited faces and copper pennies. They were little and hadn't known him in his days of greatness, but they were fond of the tattered, filthy man who kept racking his mind with visions that had burned what was left of the hair on his head. He poured drinks for the children, posed riddles with four unknowns, and rhymed sayings and maxims for them, but his lips smiled in fear, and his eyes were always darting about in their sockets. He always returned hurt and wounded, because passersby stabbed him from behind with needles and put lighted matches to his earlobes to see if the rumor about his malady was true.

By that time, he had imposed a strict discipline on himself too, and treated Miriam's breasts by "only looking" at them, and thus their nights of love became extremely frenzied and provocative. A year later their first son was born, endowed with the features and wise eyes of his father and grand-father, and they named him Salomo Ezekiel Salomo. He was an alert and curious child, and at night he and his father would howl in harmony, one voice of hunger and one voice of pain, for the baby also yearned for the breasts, and his father tried to keep him away from them.

By those days, the miserable jealous man had turned into an invalid, without one single part of his body intact. His tongue, which he kept biting unawares, was now forked like the tongue of a snake; fractures he didn't know about made his limbs swell up, his rotting teeth poisoned his blood, and his eyes—which didn't sense foreign objects—became cisterns of red pus. Dr. Burton warned him again and gave him medicine, but even though he was completely crazy by then, Elijah had not lost an ounce of his lucid Monastirial logic. The razor sharpness of his own diagnoses easily defeated the medicines the doctor gave him, for, like all of medical science, they too were based on the assumption that all human beings are alike, and Elijah knew from his own flesh and the flesh of his wife that that was not so.

Now there was only one obstacle separating Elijah Salomo from complete devotion to jealousy, and that was his great obsession with recording the sunrise. Ever since he turned thirteen, he had climbed Mount Scopus at dawn to record the exact time of the sunrise. He wanted to do that for forty-nine years, prepare tables and study the cycles of sun and time. But ever since he had discovered and cultivated his wife's treacherous nature, he no longer dared climb Mount Scopus and leave her alone in the house during the dangerous hours just before dawn, the darkest and most capti-vating of all times. He tried to persuade her to climb the mountain with him, but Miriam refused, and her ostensibly ingenuous argument—that if human beings had to get up with the roosters, God would have created them with a cockscomb—only increased his suspicions threefold and brought a bitter smile to the corners of his mouth.

He wrote to Salvatore Benintendi asking for a loan to purchase two big mirrors. The Italian was surprised. In Alexandria they used to hang such mirrors on the walls of whores' cubicles, to multiply pleasure to infinity. He came and questioned Elijah, and when the broken man revealed his plan, the Italian said that "as a lover of men and films," he deplored his friend's willingness to destroy his life utterly for "two swellings of fat like millions of others all over the globe."

"Do you know how many new breasts join the world every year?" he exclaimed.

But Elijah smiled sadly and said that other women's protrusions didn't exist for him, and if Benintendi thought in the right cinematographic mode, he would also reach the conclusion that they didn't exist at all, and that in the entire world there was only one pair of Miriam's breasts and all the rest were only reflections and copies of them, reconstructions, memories, mirages, and prophecies; something that gave you an understanding of the circular course of time, but he no longer had the leisure for such lightweight problems.

"Breasts are nothing but physical clichés!" yelled Salvatore Benintendi, determined to prove to Elijah once and for all that human beings are all alike—a uniformity that does indeed have something melancholy but is imperative and provides doctors, whores, priests, and tailors with a respectable living. "Everything rests on that similarity—trade, cinema, art, faith. Everything!" he shouted bitterly, and insisted stubbornly that that was why so many people could earn their livelihood from inserting suppositions and prophecies into cloth goblets or projecting a *fata morgana* on a sheet.

Elijah waited patiently, and didn't answer because he knew that every attempt to argue with a madman was a waste of time. But Benintendi grabbed his shoulder and announced that breasts are "infantile organs" added onto an already existing body, and therefore are younger and dumber than the other limbs and never catch up to them. "A twenty-year-old woman," he shook his friend, "has six- or seven-year-old breasts! Two children! Did you ever think about that?"

But ultimately, Miriam managed to persuade the projectionist to lend her husband the money, and Elijah hired two Arab boys, entrusted them with the mirrors he had bought, and sent them to the mountain. One of them stood near the tower of the German hospital, and as soon as the sun rose on the Mountains of Moab, he caught its glow in his mirror and cast its beams to the mirror held by the second boy. The latter stood near the Church of Mary Magdalene where he beamed the light straight into the Jewish Quarter, to Elijah sitting at his window, his left hand shading his eyes, and his right holding a notebook of observations, one eye looking at the mountain and the other peering suspiciously at the sleeping Miriam.

Within a week, the detectives of the C.I.D. turned their attention to the flickerings from the mountain. They put on habits and dyed their mustaches, and thus disguised as nuns, they traced the course of the sunbeams, quickly tracked down Elijah and his lads, and arrested them for signaling to some enemy. Elijah was thrown into the dungeon of the Russian Compound and treated with a modern blend of cold water and electric *falakas*, the contribution of the British secret police to the repertoire of urban torments. To their surprise the prisoner continued to scream even after they stopped torturing him and when they examined him, they understood that their efforts were in vain. Their work was done by the *migraine du jaloux*.

Meanwhile Salomo Salomo had decided to open a small business for Miriam that wouldn't require his son to go out into the street. He bought her equipment for churning butter and making cheese, along with a dozen sheep. Miriam entrusted the small flock to a loyal overseer named Ibrahim, a tall, lean shepherd from El-Azariya with startling blue eyes and a strong dry smell of tobacco wafting from his clothes. For forty *mils* a day, one *abiya*, a pair of Galilean shoes with red tips, and a seventh of the offspring, the wool, and the milk, Ibrahim tended the flock. He knew the subterranean maps of underground water and the hidden network of grazing paths sketched in the desert by the feet of shepherds and the hooves of herds for thousands of years. He knew the ways of the flock, piped hoarse tunes that drove away the vipers and predators with their boredom, and taught the sheep to identify poisonous plants that make their wool fade and their milk bitter. During the day he grazed Miriam's sheep in the lushest pasture, and at night he brought the little flock in behind stone fences and burnet hedges. The ewes didn't miscarry, didn't lose their young, and weren't devoured. Their milk was rich and creamy, and their wool thick and supple.

Before dawn, Ibrahim got up to do the milking, and then he loaded a full goatskin on his donkey, and to keep the milk from getting hot and turning sour on the way, he took care to climb up to Jerusalem between the high banks of the Kidron, where the frozen night air still lay. At sunrise he came to the courtyard, unloaded the goatskin, and sat down to drink a big cup of coffee, but no one read in its grounds what was to take place in the future.

One day Ibrahim was late, and when he did come, he was upset, reminded Miriam four times that he hadn't yet gotten the shoes he was promised; and suddenly he jumped up, warned her that pogroms were on the way, and suggested that she and her family come and hide with him in the village.

"The colonial office will protect us," said Elijah, who, ever since his arrest and release, considered himself close to the colonial authorities and an expert in the ways of the British Empire. Incidentally, whenever Salomo

Salomo heard his son talking about political matters, he wanted to rend his garments and mourn for him, because to the Monastirials that was the lowest stage a man could sink to. But by that woeful time Elijah had lost all shame and honor, and had even begun escorting his wife to the common toilet in the courtyard. It was only her pushing him away and the scolding of the neighbor women that prevented him from joining her inside. He would wait nervously at the closed door, listen, and look suspiciously at everyone passing by; and the women of the courtyard shook their heads and recalled the rule that a man must not enter the toilet after a woman, but only before her, especially since men mustn't know that sounds like that also come out of the *kulu de la mujer.*

"So from her caca they make cement, from his *kokoni* macaroni!" they said.

That Friday thousands of worshipers came to the mosques on the Temple Mount. Under their cloaks they concealed clubs and axes, sharpened shears, and rods spiked with nails. For hours the voices of the preachers droned on, and the hum of the faithful grew so thick it turned into that dark curtain that drops onto the city every few years and strikes the inhabitants with madness. When the gates of the Mount opened and people charged out, the residents of the Jewish Quarter closed themselves in their courtyards and locked their gates and shutters.

Miriam, Elijah, and little Salomo Ezekiel hid in the cistern. At that season, late summer, the top part of the cistern was dry, and the family huddled among the boxes of cheese and the tins of milk and yogurt set there to cool. A few hours went by, and the familiar voice of Ibrahim was heard on the other side of the heavy gate.

"*Iftahin el-bab, siet Miriam,* open up," he called.

"At a time like this he comes to you?" said Elijah suspiciously. He stood up in a rage and went to the gate.

"Don't open it! Elijah! Don't!" shouted Miriam.

But Elijah pushed back the bolt and opened the heavy gate, and his skull was split like a watermelon by a swing of the shepherd's sword. Elijah's first thought was that he had been struck again by the migraine of the jealous for leaving Miriam alone in the cistern. He smiled as if apologizing to Ibrahim, turned around, and was about to go back to Miriam, and then he suddenly saw Missus Glidden, who had grown very old, standing and smiling in the space between the lobes of his brain. His knees collapsed, his body sank, and his soul took flight.

People burst into the courtyard and began smashing the milk pitchers with clubs and kicks, flinging the ricotta strainers, and piercing the bellies of the dripping *mandilas*. Three of them grabbed the baker next door, hung him by his feet on the poplar, and lit the big Primus stove for the milk kettles under his head.

Inside the cistern Miriam suddenly noticed that Salomo Ezekiel had disappeared. Frantic with worry, she climbed out, searched for him and immediately saw the berserk shepherd, her husband's body, and her child smiling and crawling on the floor of the courtyard, wanting to play with his father.

"Ibrahim, what are you doing?" she shouted.

At that moment, the moment she saw her dead husband and her living son, the obstacles fell off her nerves. The fetters of tradition, the chains of fear, the filters of custom, the bars of prohibition—everything whose choking fingers had ever bound her body and her awareness—vanished. The eye, the ear, the nose, and the mouth—gaped. Like tiny desert flowers waiting for a signal, the buds of senses rose and blossomed all over her body. With tremendous clarity in the smallest split seconds, they absorbed every detail. Her hands tasted. Her breasts saw. Her shoulders smelled. Her vagina became an ear that heard the gushing of the entire world—Elijah lying between Ibrahim's feet, his pain, her love, her little child crawling to the shepherd and smiling at him, the heavy breathing of the rioters, her own shrieks—she combined all those strips together and knew that the whole time the cheese went on curdling and the yogurt went on fermenting.

Miriam tried to grab her son and go back to the cistern. But Ibrahim crushed the baby's thigh with one stroke of his club and with a long leap, forced her to the ground. He pushed her neck back and clasped her head between his bony knees. In one moment he swung his curved blade over her throat, and in the next he gouged out her left eye as a thrush plucks a snail out of its shell.

"Ibrahim, what are you doing?" groaned Miriam, and beyond her torments she was amazed at the hardness of the shepherd's knees, which hurt her even more than his knife.

Ibrahim ripped off her dress and cut the cloth girdle that concealed her glory. Miriam's legendary breasts were exposed to a stranger for the first time, dazzling in their splendor, warm and throbbing like birds. For one moment, the shepherd's legs grew weak as if he wanted to kneel down before the splendid truth revealed to his eyes, sharper, more beautiful and frightening than any conjecture; but in the next, he cursed, reconsidered, grabbed her right breast, and lopped it off with his knife. Heavy curtains of blood and pain covered her face, hid the rapists who were already gathering around her and undoing their belts.

Two hours later, when the sounds of smashing stopped resounding among the stone walls, dropped to the dirt, and fell silent, and the last roars of murder and lust were already absorbed in the stone and were silenced too, the frightened neighbors emerged from their holes, covered the dead, searched for the missing, and the women began tending to Miriam's awful wounds and cleaning the clots of blood and semen off her. Then, suddenly, the hoarse weeping of Salomo Ezekiel was heard rising and gushing out of the netherworld of the cistern. With the cleverness of a baby rabbit, the infant had crawled, dragging his crushed leg, and hid in a tin up to his nose among chunks of Bulgarian cheese turning red. They pulled him out and brought him to his mother, who clutched him as a drowning woman clutches at a straw, thrust the nipple of her left breast in his mouth, and didn't stop suckling him.

"Ibrahim, what are you doing?" she screamed all night, spurting blood and milk.

In the morning they brought her to Dr. Burton, who disinfected her wounds, bandaged her eye, and sewed the stump of the amputated breast. Black and blue tears dripped from his eyes, and weeping escaped from between his clenched teeth.

A few weeks later, when a scar had formed on her chest and the eye socket had closed and the baby's thigh had knitted, Miriam washed the blood out of the girdle for her breasts, made it into a pouch like the ones Arab peasant women use, tied Salomo Ezekiel to her back, and left Jerusalem. She departed from Nablus Gate, and when she passed the mosaic of Orpheus and remembered the words of the silent actors Elijah had declaimed in the nearby windmill, her heart shriveled with her enormous grief, shook the air, and the blades of the mill moved. But their movement was so slight that no one sensed it, not even the actors scampering around on the screen.

Chapter 42

I t's three in the morning, pouring rain, and all of a sudden two soldiers
come into the bakery. Half dead, soaked to the skin, shaking with
fatigue and cold. The army does navigation exercises all the time
around here, and those poor guys, when they smell the bakery in the middle of the night, they just go nuts. You know how it is when a person is cold
and homesick. They drop everything and run with their eyes closed for a
piece of bread from the oven. But then, who's the third one who comes in
and hugs me? Benjamin. Hello, Pop! The way you and Leah used to say it.
When he hugged me, I felt how he had grown, how little we had hugged
each other when he was a child, how little we had hugged each other at all.
I didn't feel him growing in my hands. I didn't feel that weight, that height,
those muscles. I ran right away to wake up Leah, to bring them dry clothes,
and when I come back, what do I see? Benjamin, wet and tired as he was,
standing there putting the pans into the *gareh*.

"I was really amazed. He was never an especially hardworking boy. Neither in the bakery nor at school. When he was sixteen he dropped out of
school, and would disappear for days. But I didn't care about that. To make
bread you don't have to have a doctor's degree. Anyway, he wasn't learning
anything there, he just practiced running and made out with girls. There
was only one thing I argued about with him all the time, that he should
keep up the bakery after me, that the bakery shouldn't die with me. And I
kept telling him, I'll leave you the bakery, Benjamin, you won't be rich, but
you'll make a living. And he wouldn't answer. He'd look at me and not
answer. Until one day he said, I don't want to, I'll decide after the army,
your brother didn't stay in the bakery either, maybe I'll want to study after
all, maybe I'll want to travel, maybe I'll just stay in the army. I don't want
to get stuck in that dough all my life.

"And I understood that it wasn't good enough for him to do what I do. And that he mentioned you as an example—I didn't like that at all. There were shouts. What do you think, you're better than your father? And what kind of talk is that—stuck in that dough? I got furious and I raised my hand to him, and he raised his hand to me and he grabbed my hand like this."

Jacob smiled. "Believe me, he was seventeen then. Not as tall as Mother, but he got all the strength of the Tartars. Too bad you didn't know him. In that way, he was like you and Mother and her brothers. I'm not weak, I've loaded enough sacks and pans, and tons of dough have passed through these hands by now, but his hand on mine was like the arm of the kneading machine."

Now he stood up and paced up and down the porch, his fingers spread out, and the stump of his little finger shaking like a lizard's tail. "Don't hit me, Dad, he said, don't hit me. He was scared. Scared of his father like a little child, but a child with the strength of a grown-up, a very strong grown-up. We looked at each other like that, and then we didn't speak for two months. Only when he started getting ready to go to the army, only then did he surprise me. Because with all his strength he was pretty lazy, and nothing was really important to him. Just dancing with girls and having a good time. And suddenly, there of all places, in that fucking reconnaissance unit.

"And I'm sure"—he sat down, and his voice grew thick and moist—"every time Leah wakes up for a few minutes that's what she's thinking about, that I was the one who encouraged him to go into it, that they'd make a man out of him. You wanted him to die, she certainly says there in the dark, even when he was little, you fought with him and didn't want him. But then, of all times, when he would run and exercise in the fields to get in shape, he also started helping me in the bakery, and we started getting close to each other. He started understanding my work, and I started understanding his life, and I stopped pestering him. And afterward, in the army, I was also very proud of him, that he could take it, that he made good, that they appreciated him there. And in the village too, when he would come home with the black beret of the reconnaissance unit, and the little silver wings on his chest, people started saying hello, how's your son, and all that.

"And all of a sudden he shows up in the middle of the night, soaked to the skin. I gave them fresh bread and coffee, and I sliced tomatoes and cheese and sausage. I fried some eggs with bread, and Leah got out of bed and ran to fix them sandwiches and chocolate and tangerines for the road. I told him, Wait a minute, Benjamin, I'll wake up the delivery boy so he can take you to the wadi in the bread truck. But he wouldn't let me. They really shouldn't have come. If anybody caught them screwing around, they'd get thrown right out of the reconnaissance unit. They left to take a reading of some latitude and longitude in the wadi of Sindiana. We used to swipe figs and apricots there when we were kids, and they call it reading a latitude and longitude. And I looked at him as he left the courtyard, and I thought, Maybe, after all, he'll come back to the bakery. I didn't say anything, but my heart was shaking. Maybe we could have been friends in the end, maybe not, and now I'll never know."

He got up again. "That's it," he said. "That's how it is. Not a story from a book, eh? You can never know."

Neither of us noticed Romi, but three days later the picture came. I'm sitting down. Both hands in my pockets. Jacob is standing opposite me, his hands stretched out in the gesture of women clerks in delicatessens when they run out of Albanian anchovies. A small bowl of fruit is on the table between us. My feet are bare, and my big toes stick up like fat antennae.

"You're such a hunk, Unk, with those stretched-out toes. What were you thinking of when Father was giving his speech?"

"He doesn't look good, your father," I said.

The picture deepened the furrows singed in my brother's neck and darkened his eyes. I read the signs of a baker's old age on his body. Like lightning flashes of distant storms over the Atlantic. The agility of his fingers, tested every Thursday by braiding challahs, was diminishing. Lines and cracks gaped in his flesh. The dust of sifting and the heat of the oven are turning his eyes red and irritating them, and tormenting him. When he stands in the baker's pit and shoots the loaves into the depths of the oven, a strange fizzing comes from his shoulder joints, a sign that the tissues are drying out. Only dexterity and experience cover the weakness of his body, only the memory of movements covers his loss of agility. Suddenly he looks into my eyes like Akela the great gray lone wolf of Seeonee Hills who can't defeat the buck anymore. And I could almost hear the baker's cough, the product of the flour's action on the mucous membranes of the lung, rising from the picture.

As for me, except for our mutual nearsightedness, I'm not afflicted with anything. (By now we have both reached nine diopters in the left eye and seven in the right, and the doctor has already warned Jacob not to dare to lift flour sacks because he's endangering his retina.) My flesh and my hair aren't yet depleted, my limbs are supple and strong, I have never known a really bad pain or—what is more important—a pain that has no cause. Just sometimes I am gripped by one complaint which is manifest physically by a sense of restrained choking, a stony pressure on my diaphragm, as if a *levadura* of cement were swelling between my lungs, and ever since I've come home, that cutting pain has attacked my groin. Sharp and short it is, demeaning but bearable.

Like most human beings, I also see my body as one piece, but Jacob is getting old in a disjointed way, like a burned match writhing in unequal torments. "Pains should be the same thing in the whole body," says Father, not knowing that he is repeating the last words of Tuvia Hacohen, the famous doctor of Padua. Jacob's hands are older than the rest of his body. His palms are hard and callused from the handle of the shovel, the tops of his fingers are reddened from contact with yeast and bromate, and the backs of his hands are singed and wrinkled from the heat of the bricks. Bakers usually wear gloves when they take the bread out of the oven, but shooting the loaves of bread into the oven is done bare-handed, to improve precision and speed up the work. Jacob didn't use gloves at all.

The years amid unchanging natural processes, of the iron laws of fermentation and rising, the eternal rituals of returning to life and of tested ancient movements had endowed him with an uncommon measure of familiarity with and understanding of his body. He saw the shovels shrinking from friction and heat, our father dwindling and mapping the way to his own old age, to the day when he will no longer summon up the strength to breathe the fiery air, fling the pans and sacks, take the unsold bread back from the shops.

"One day I'll just fall down," he said to me, "and I'll die here in the pit."

Chapter 43

For three days Jacob was in the hospital, his bandaged hand on his chest, dumb and numb, reviling and defiling. His ugly, elaborate curses drew doctors and patients and nurses to his bedside, and though they didn't understand a single word, they picked up the tone and couldn't believe their ears. His whole body shook, his temperature went up and down, his face was shriveled and concentrated, like the face of a newborn baby, and I knew he would get better and arise as a different man.

Mother, Simon, and I took turns sitting by his bed. When he woke up and saw me next to him, he grabbed my hand hard and said, "I didn't pass out. I was only thinking with my eyes shut." He smiled, and I knew I was right. The old, familiar lines of his face didn't come back.

"Love shouldn't hurt you like that," he decreed a few times, as if he were reciting a great Edelmanic truth and engraving it on his flesh.

"She came here twice to visit you, and Mother threw her out," I said.

"She did well," said Jacob, and didn't explain which one he meant.

Pale and weary he came back home, sat down in the easy chair on the porch, and took the bandages off his hand to dry his wound in the air and sun. Long hours he sat there, his eyes slowly opening and closing, the palm of his hand circling like an indolent sunflower, and the sewn-up stump of his little finger, still purple and black and red, quivering and suppurating.

The sacrifice to his love filled Mother with dread and pride. "The Jacob's got such great big soul," she declared.

Joshua Edelman came up and said, "He cut his finger for her, he cut."

"Itsik wouldn't do such a thing for any female," said his son, who smoked a lot and didn't tap the ash off with a shake, but with a disgusting, stylish flick of the tip of his index finger.

Chenou Apari, a friendly Tartarine of love, came by, clapped her hands, said "*Quelquechose*," and proclaimed that even back in Paris you don't see such things.

Duduch stroked his arm, took his wounded hand, and put it gently on her breast; and one night Simon, who was about twelve then and blamed himself for not being in the bakery at the time of the catastrophe, killed all the rats Mother had been fighting for more than a dozen years.

Even today I shudder when I remember that night. At dusk Simon stripped down to his underwear, took a slice of sausage from the kitchen, rubbed it all over his legs, and when darkness fell, he went into the bakery. I climbed up to the chimney and listened to what was going on. Nothing was heard but the frantic shrieking of the rats and the crushing thud of smashing every few minutes, as if someone were cracking nuts with his fingers. We learned later that Simon sat down across the doorway to the storeroom with his legs spread out in front of him like a gigantic, silent bait. The smell of the sausage emanating from him inflamed the rats so much they couldn't withstand the temptation. When his thigh felt the whiskers sliding in the dark and the groping teeth eager to thrust, he put forth an invisible hand and with one squeeze of his finger and thumb, he broke the rat's neck. At one o'clock in the morning, when Mother came to work, Simon presented her with a bucket full of carcasses; and later Jacob found near his chair the sweets Simon had received as a reward.

For one month my brother didn't leave the porch. In the morning he sat down in the easy chair, and late at night he retired to his bed. He didn't return to the mirror on the chimney, he cut his listening belly off from the ground, he avoided the street and the field so as not to run into Leah or her footsteps, and for the same reason he asked me to go back to delivering bread by myself.

At the Levitov house Leah stared at me anxiously.

"Don't worry, he won't die from that," I told her.

She asked me to give Jacob a letter of apology, but I said, "You don't have to apologize for anything," and I didn't tell her that my brother devoted all his time to the systematic extirpation of the crabgrass she had rooted in him. And not because he had stopped loving her, quite the contrary: now his love became as hard and hot as the floor of the oven, but now he understood that nothing could be established on such bloodstained foundations.

The strong old *levadura* of family honor suddenly awoke in him. "I don't blame anybody," he said. "I just don't want her anymore, understand?

If she sent you, you can tell her that, and if you want her, you can take her yourself now."

"Maybe you'll join the army," I suggested to him. A few of the village boys had enlisted in the British army around that time.

"That's not for me," said Jacob. "With these eyes nobody will take us to fight, and I might as well stay home as be in the rear."

That little finger of torments didn't heal; it left his skin scaly, vulnerable as a mole taken out of its burrow, and that slaughterer's knife that lopped off his finger also decreed his fate. Thus, with eyeglasses and with a knife, our father separated us.

Chapter 44

"In my droppings, excuse me, I find pieces."

"What pieces?" I grew angry. "What droppings all of a sudden?"

Father peered to the side and moved his hand helplessly to draw the attention of his invisible relatives to his slow-witted son. "Pieces of myself and my flesh," he sighed. "Of my intestines, my liver, my spleen, my own internal organs."

Apparently my face assumed a skeptical expression, and Father quickly suggested I come see with my own eyes. "I didn't flush it. I kept it so you could see."

"I don't want to, and stop that already."

My father is withdrawing into himself. His body is his world, the center of his concern and attention. Whenever I try to converse with him about any subject at all, he falls silent as we talk, his eyes fog over, and his mouth gapes a bit. I have learned that he is then lending his ears to the surge of his flesh, the roar of the striving blood, the leafy rustle of his cells. If you like, my dear, at the age of eighty-five, my father has once again become a growing boy. Frightened and agitated, he examines the tidings heralded by his limbs. Sometimes he tells me briefly, in amazement, how his body abuses him, providing eyewitness reports of observations, claims, and inferences. Torments and old age have enriched his language, treatment in the pain clinic has honed his metaphors. "A broken reed and a bag with holes," he described his situation to the admiring doctor. "My ear hears inside and not outside. I've got the noise of the sea there, as Your Honor would hear in shells when he was a child."

One day he compared his pains to "somebody else's relatives who have come to my house by mistake." When he saw the doctor recording the sentence in his notebook with an expression of pleasure, he understood that he had struck a vein of gold. Now he invents and enumerates the names of his pains for him, "The wicked bastard of the knee," "El Diablo of the back," and worst of all, the stomachache, "the Turk good-for-nothing *el dolor de istomago.*" He told him some fairy tale—"from the Book of Judges," he declared importantly—about the traitor who showed the enemies the secret entrance in the wall of Beth-El. "That's how there's a traitor in my body too, Doctor, and he shows the pains where to come in."

Long years of alienation on Jacob's part had amassed in Father an abundance of woes. Now, when my ears are open to him, he fills them with grievances. With an accusing finger, he directed my attention to the loss of symmetry in his body. The wrinkles at the corners of his mouth, he complained, the lines that grant the face its substance and character, aren't identical anymore: the right one is deeper and firmer, and the left is shallow and frail. He held out his hands, put his fingertips together, and claimed that the left hand had shrunk.

"You're the only one I can tell," he whispered to me. "Look into my eyes. What do you see?"

"They're a bit yellow," I told him, "and one is a little red."

"*Puntikos!*" Father shouted angrily. "Nonsense. You don't see?"

"See what?"

"The left one is lower than the right." He clasped my neck with weak hands, put his lips up to my ear, and whispered, "Down below too, my balls. Tell it not in Gath, the left one is lower than the right."

"It's like that with everybody, Father," I laughed. "One is always lower."

"Don't talk like that," he scolded me. "That's what you learned in America? What kind of talk am I hearing from your mouth? A mouth like a sewer!"

He pinched the drooping flesh of his chest between two fingers and pulled, as he had once examined the texture of dough.

"A corpse," he decreed.

He still persists in shaving with a straight razor, and the combination of

211

the murderous blade and his shaking hands sprouts beds of reddening paper flowers on his cheeks and chin until he looks like a pecked chick who has been wallowing in confetti. He forgets to remove the little pieces of toilet paper he sticks on his cuts, and they drop off and flutter all over the house like tiny foreskins.

Early one morning I shaved him with my electric razor. Father felt his cheeks and chin and nodded in appreciation. But afterward, he picked up the shaver and examined it carefully, turned it over in his fingers. "It hums like the fly from the Nile on Pharaoh's window!" he pronounced, and went back to his terrible straight razor and his ancient shaving mirror.

We drank our morning coffee. Outside the blackbirds sang. Through the window I saw Jacob opening the gates of the yard for the bread truck, and I went out to help him load the cases.

"Stop it, stop," he said. "Your back will give out."

The truck left, and Simon went into the bakery to clean up. I brought my brother a cup of coffee on the porch. Two men passed by the fence, and he nodded to them. They were well dressed, each carrying a briefcase in one hand and a plastic shopping bag in the other. They looked at us and nodded together in greeting.

"Good morning," they called.

"Good morning," answered my brother.

"You don't come to your son," the older one said, as if he were merely stating a fact, and the other man smiled and nodded.

"I come, I come, but not every morning," answered Jacob.

"Who are they?" I asked after they left.

"My colleagues from the cemetery," said Jacob; "from here, from the village. You haven't seen them before? Every morning on their way to work, they go there to chat with their sons. Once the younger one came to talk to me. He said, My wife and I sleep together, but we cry apart, she doesn't look in the mirror or at me anymore. She's mad at the mirror because she doesn't look like her dead child, she's mad at her husband for giving her that child. You won't believe what else he told me: You're lucky your Leah sleeps all the time and you don't have to see her eyes open."

Jacob took off his shoes and sighed. Standing at the oven for a long time, he claims, destroys your back and shortens your legs. Now he wiggled his toes and his face grew soft. "To share pleasures is no big deal. After a year together every woman knows how her husband likes to enjoy himself, but none of them knows how he likes to mourn. Why are you looking at me like that? What do you know about it anyway? What do you know about anything at all in life? There was a time when I thought I knew Leah like I know every brick in the oven. How much milk in her coffee, how much lemon in her tea. Before dawn I'd escape from the bakery for a minute to put toothpaste on her toothbrush just the way she liked it so it would be waiting for her on the sink. Everything. The little follies and the big follies. Until Benjamin was killed and I saw I didn't know anything. Mourning and suffering you don't share. That you do alone. You don't reveal it to anybody.

"All night lying awake, with your child's tombstone like a stone wall between you, every old friction becomes a terrible wound, you blame yourselves together and yourself separately, and mainly each one blames the other. And those pricks have the nerve to tell me that I don't come to Benjamin. You'd think you have to punch a time clock on the grave. But I must tell you that when all three of our sons were children and alive, those two declared war against me and tried to throw the bakery out of the village. Poor Benjamin, ever since he was killed nobody dares to touch me. Now, all of a sudden, they're my best friends. You don't come to your son. . . . Why don't we see you? . . . Come to this ceremony. . . . Come to that ceremony . . . "

"I don't go either," Romi told me. "Memorial Day is for people who haven't lost anyone in their family. For us it's a mad running to all the stones and walls his name is written on. Who needs it? Even so, not a day goes by that I don't think of him, and I make my own commemoration on the day I saw him for the last time. I even have the last picture of him. The very most last one. What are you laughing at, Uncle? You should be ashamed of yourself!"

In her apartment she has a cabinet with dozens of flat drawers: "Cytology," "Embryology," "Benjamin," "Spores," "Family," "Project," "My Father," "My Father," "My Father" . . . Fifteen drawers of "My Father," from which will finally emerge the exhibit she wants to make about him.

Her wooden clogs bang on the floor. From the drawer marked "Benjamin" she pulled out a big picture: in uniform, with his back to the camera, only his face was turned around, slightly surprised but smiling and happy.

"That was Sunday morning and he was leaving the yard on the way to the highway to catch a ride to the base, and I ran after him and shouted, 'Benjamin!' He turned around and I pressed the shutter and caught him. It gives people a very interesting expression. Because of the surprise and because of the taut neck muscles. Someday, after I finish with Dad, I'll make an exhibit of photographs like that. I've already got a name for it:

Shot in the Back. I'll call people from behind, and when they turn around I'll photograph them."

Jacob finished his coffee, went down and closed the gates of the yard, and wiped his palms on the thighs of his trousers.

"Want to eat?"

Chapter 45

One day at dusk, as I returned from Leah's house, two hummingbirds—the male in an unbelievable flicker of black-green brilliance, and the female in her grayish modesty—were knocking on the screen of the kitchen window. I opened the sides of the window. The tiny birds, who generally lived on honeysuckle and never showed much interest in human beings, fluttered inside and headed straight for my brother's shoulder.

Father watched what was going on, nodded his head, and then sniffed Jacob's bristling skin; he ran his finger over it and put it in his mouth.

"Stupid," he said, "you've got sweet skin, you know?"

Jacob got mad, said he didn't know, but fortunately for him, God had graced him with such a wise and sharp-sighted father.

"Right away he gets mad, the ornery *pelezhon*," said Father, and explained to us that sweet sweat is a "sign."

"You need a woman," he said.

"Well, whaddaya know!" grumbled Jacob, and I told the joke about the three hobbies of the governess from Berlin, and I added, "Who doesn't need a woman at our age?"

"Why do you talk like that, children?" Father was amazed.

"Here it comes." Jacob patted my shoulder. "We need a woman, and he's already got some fairy tale for us."

"Ergas the baker, of blessed memory, was so sweet that ants would climb up his legs," Father began.

"Bravo," groaned Jacob.

"Children would run after him in the street and lick him," Father went on.

214

"Maybe that's why it stood up all the time," I whispered in my brother's ear.

"You should be ashamed of yourself. Don't talk like that!" Father yelled at me, and turned to Jacob with a strange tone of pride. "Don't laugh! You brought that from Jerusalem. Nobody here has it. That one"—he pointed at me—"only himself he needs. But you, stupid, you need a woman."

"All we need now is for you to know what I need and what he needs!" Jacob shook the intoxicated hummingbirds off his shoulder and went out of the kitchen into the yard. I didn't know if he was mad at Father or at me or at his own treacherous, gossipmongering skin that gave away the secrets of his flesh.

Father stuck his head out the window and called to him, "You don't have to get mad. Who hasn't gone through that? You think you invented it?" And he raised his voice. "This is just the beginning, later it gets worse."

In the next weeks Jacob didn't talk much, and sometimes he looked so withdrawn I couldn't even guess his thoughts. He brooded for hours, gently stroking the stump of his finger, which healed nicely but even today is very sensitive to the touch, and when he went to sleep, he kept his glasses on. When I came home from school, I would find him devoting hours to useless activities in the bakery. He lined up the heavy flour sacks in straight rows, scraped the soot off the edges of the baker's shovels, scrubbed the floor and the scrapers, and announced that the walls of the bakery should be covered with ceramic tiles.

"Whatever it costs, just so all that filth can finally be washed off!" he declared.

Everyone began explaining Jacob's behavior.

Father claimed his son was demonstrating the well-known lust for cleanliness of those whose heart aches, who act "like a chicken with the Book of Job written on her eggs."

Chenou Apari said, "Leave him alone. In a love like his everybody learns by himself."

Tia Duduch thought Jacob was manifesting the nesting behavior of women in the ninth month of pregnancy, but she couldn't put that into words.

And Mother decreed that the Jacob kept busy with hard work to sweat very very much. "That is how he is cleaning out the flesh," she explained happily and proudly, for she was no longer alone in the training and battles of love.

And me? To me Jacob looked like a lighthouse built by mistake in the middle of the continent, signaling to invisible ships that weren't approaching. And I told Leah that unlike other men, who show signs of love only in certain seasons of the year or when their beloved appears within their field of vision, my brother broadcast his vague signs in his own time and in empty space. He sighed a lot like an old man, gnashed his teeth as he slept, and even asked me to recommend some books for him to read. A dull restlessness spread in his body until it resembled Mother's venerable goose, which had lived longer than any other goose and in old age even experienced a revival of the wanderlust of its forefathers. But there was no longer any need to clip its pinfeathers, because it didn't run in the yard anymore or puff up its wings, but only raised and stretched its white neck, opened its beak, shook, and fell on the ground.

"Someday a woman will come to the bakery and say she smelled our bread," my brother announced with a strange fatalism, the abominable offshoot of despair and ignorance.

"So?"

"Then I'll know it's her," he said.

Without permission he dismantled the work table and took the wooden boards to the yard to scour them with tried and true solutions of lemon juice, ashes, and myrtle oil. When he started scraping the pans, Father grew furious. Old bakers love the layers time invests in their baking pans.

"Stop cleaning already!" he shouted. "You want the bread to stick?"

"It's dirt," said Jacob.

Father snatched the pan out of his hands. "That's what gives it the flavor, Jacob. Look." He scratched the black sediment of oil, flour, and sugar with his fingernail, rubbed it into a sticky noodle and smelled it with pleasure. "That's the memory of our work, this dirt."

And the mirror, empty of love, flapped like an orphaned wing on the roof, cast the malediction of its beams on passersby. When I walked past it, I didn't lift my eyes, for its light hit me too once and it was only my tears that saved me from blindness, from the white-hot blade of the sword, from the dancing Gypsy girls of Nijny-Novgorod.

Look while you may! Look while you may!

Michael did not attempt to resist. Nothing existed before his eyes but his mother, whom his eyes seemed to devour. All his life was in that last look.

Look while you may! Look while you may!

"You want me to go talk to Mrs. Levitov?" asked Father.

"No," said Jacob.

"You know what you're like?" Father continued. "Like the old frog in Hezekiah's pool who would come to the Ashkenazim to hear Kol-Nidre every year."

Silence.

"Should I talk for you?"

"No." Jacob grew enraged. "I'm done with her."

"No good," said Father. "It could have been the honor of our whole family, and hers too."

"Don't poke your honor into this," said Jacob. "And don't play matchmaker for me."

"What is it, Jacob?" Father persisted. "First the woman should come, then love, and only at the end madness. You've got it backward."

Jacob didn't answer.

"You'll find a woman, stupid," Father tried to console him. "But you don't need to run around in circles like the black man who ate the cat's tail."

"Like what?" yelled Jacob in a dreadful voice. "Like what?!"

"Like the black man who ate the cat's tail," said Father. "You didn't hear about the black eunuch who stole loquats from the garden of Queen Roxelana?"

Jacob got up, slammed the door behind him, and went out for one of his rambles. More than once I saw him striding through the village like an Arab apothecary who ate *knaffe*, as Father put it; but to me he looked like an Assyrian scribe who lost something but doesn't know what. Whenever he passed by an open window, he slowed down, adjusted his glasses on the bridge of his nose, and looked inside shyly, like Duduch in her search for an infant to relieve the pressure in her chest.

Afterward, he enlarged the orbit of his searches, and started walking in citrus groves and vineyards.

"That's where you're looking?" Father pestered him. "In the fields? What are you, a donkey? There you'll find only thorns and mice and snakes. Go shave, get dressed up nice, comb your hair, put on cologne, go to the city, meet human beings, show yourself."

On Friday, after the last oven, Simon would go to Brinker to get a bag of bare ears of corn ejected by the threshing machine. With these ears of corn, he stoked the water heater for the weekly hot shower. The oven chimney hummed sonorously, Tia Duduch gave each of us khaki trousers and a white shirt she had ironed, and after dinner I would go to Leah. Washed, dressed, fragrant, and combed. Sometimes, when I came back from her, I saw my brother walking in the dark field. Noah Brinker, who was a watchman now and went on guard duty at night, told Mother he had seen him crossing the dirt road leading north from the village. When he was caught in the headlights of a pickup truck, Jacob stood still, shaded his eyes with his hand, and slipped away like a marten into the ditch.

Chapter 46

At the age of forty-five, Brinker, one of the pillars of the village, was as good as dead. No one could bear the stream of nonsense pouring out of his mouth, but everyone tried to take advantage of the aphasia that had struck him. Dead Livy wanted to get him out of the house. The neighbors wanted to buy his farm. Noah wanted his inheritance. And Brinker, cleverer than all of them, neither resisted nor argued. He played the dummy, went on growing his vegetables, developed his strawberry business, sold his splendid produce to the Tel Aviv branch of Spinney's, and made the most of his affliction.

When they brought him a sales contract to sign, he said cheerfully, "The day before yesterday also a pencil if not four." Then he left the room as if he were about to come right back, but he didn't, since everybody expected him to forget.

When Noah kept repeating his demands that he go someplace "where they can take care of you, Papa," he'd say, "If I sure and nobody nobody me too," blink his blue eyes, smile a vague, pleased smile of agreement, and fall asleep on the table.

As for Dead Livy, here Brinker displayed his true greatness. He followed her around constantly, entwining her in his meandering, meaningless sentences. Everybody thought he was pleading for her mercy and attention, but I was the only one who understood that under the camouflage of incessant prattle Brinker was realizing an old wish to stop talking to his wife.

Dead Livy and Noah assumed that if they left home, he wouldn't manage on his own and would give in. So the two of them moved out of the village and left Brinker alone, the happiest of men. He listened to music to his heart's content, read a newspaper at the rate of ten words an hour, was spared the punishment of cockscomb soup; and every morning the smell of parsley omelets rose and waved over his house like a green banner of freedom. Sometimes Mother would invite him to lunch, and once a week, when she cooked meat, she'd bring him a serving from our family pot. A broad, crooked grin would light up his face. I remember him well: he puts the plate down on the table, holds both her hands in both of his, his eyes beam, and his mouth keeps spouting tender nonsense.

All that time I went on giving him lessons. I read him children's comic strips because I thought the pictures might help him understand. I recited the rhymes oh-so-slowly, I moved my finger over the illustrations oh-so-slowly, but Brinker didn't laugh.

One day I saw him leaning on the nursery school fence, his eyes shut, an expression of contentment and yearning spread over his face, like the look on Simon's face when he got a piece of chocolate from Mother. From the windows of the nursery school the children's voices floated so clear. "A is for Apple, B is for Boy." And above them, loud and guiding, the voice of the teacher. She was a new nursery school teacher, the daughter of a Hasidic family, who had fallen away from the faith and fled her home. She was sure we also teach children to read at the age of three, and by the time the education committee figured out what was going on, a few babies in soggy diapers had gone to Yehiel Abramson and asked for books.

She was an unattached and good-looking girl, and for a moment I thought Brinker was interested in her. But Brinker opened the nursery school gate, strode inside with his eyes closed, as if drawn by angels singing, sat down on one of the tiny chairs, and started reciting his lost words along with them.

The children all knew and loved him because he would give them strawberries. They were glad to see him and snuggled up to him, and the teacher stopped the lesson and asked him what he wanted.

"Little is also not terrible, everything fine." Brinker was excited. "Now then like that and there is because I have places can."

I came in on his heels. "What does he want?" the teacher asked me.

"He wants to come learn words with the little children, if you don't mind," I translated.

"I don't know." The girl was confused. "This is a nursery school, after all. What will the parents say?"

"Four, four," Brinker called out excitedly. "Even where know because that is completely and also that has already then something now he said."

"He says he won't bother anybody, and that he'll fix anything that needs fixing in the nursery school," I explained to the teacher.

The next morning, when the first children came to nursery school, Brinker was already waiting for them, impatient and eager, at the entrance to the yard. A big white dunce cap guarded his skull bereft of syntax, a big basket hung on his arm, and two packs perched on his shoulder.

"Hi, Isaac," called the kids.

Brinker picked up one of them and told him kindly, "Think like that but also to sit nice on I have that because of he."

He hung his lunch bag among the children's packs. Then he went to the ice box in the kitchen, and filled it with strawberries. From there he went to the yard, took tools out of his other pack, changed the washer in the leaky faucet, and rethreaded the screws. With his firm, clever hands he repaired the mesh fence that was hanging in tatters between its poles, climbed onto the roof with a surprising feline agility and cleaned the casuarinale needles and titmouse nests out of the gutters. Then he came down, face beaming, and sat with the children for a ten o'clock snack and a lesson in the ABCs.

The nursery school became Brinker's second home. The children adored him, and the teacher got used to his presence, and learned to make the best of it. Every day he sat on one of the tiny chairs, listened with wrinkled brow to the stories the teacher read, and recited the consonants and vowels to himself.

Just recently I recalled those days, because Father's doctor suggested a new diagnosis: the language of pain isn't only a language of metaphors but also an international language of vowels and consonants.

"This is the real Esperanto, which preceded all words," he announced enthusiastically. "The groan of pain is the most universal and comprehensible sound in the world, and for that reason A is the first letter in all languages." As he spoke I thought of his "A-a-a-a," which I had already privately named "the A-a-a-a of pain," and of Mother's definite article and its buddies, the L of Love and the H of Hate and the S of Simile and the M of Memory, and I remembered Brinker playing with the children, climbing the ladders of consonants, jumping ropes of words, falling into the marshy sandbox of syntax. Within six weeks you could discern impressive improvements: colorful old tires sprouted in the playground, broken dolls once again opened and closed their eyes, well-tended grass flourished around the sandbox, and

Brinker didn't learn a single sentence. The words hovered around his skull, lit for brief moments of rest, but not one of them struck root.

But there was no one happier than he on the day he came to the nursery school and discovered that the teacher had pasted a new label with his name on one of the school bag hooks. And at the end of the year, when the photographer came from the city to take the nursery school class picture, there sat Brinker with the children, smiling at the camera, weeping strong, shameless tears of joy.

Chapter 47

One evening Jacob decided to take Father's advice and went to Tel Aviv. That night Italian planes bombed the city and dozens of people were killed. Jacob came back home the next day, dressed in strange, loud, colorful clothes, hale, hearty, and smiling. He said he had strolled on the boardwalk, eaten ice cream, and late at night had started looking for a place to sleep. He walked for hours, and when he was behind the Invalid Asylum, a name that stirs literary shudders in me to this very day, the bombardment began. A man was killed next to Jacob—his head, Jacob told us, was cut off his shoulders and rolled on the sidewalk—and my brother's shirt and trousers were soaked with his blood. An old woman came out of a nearby house, invited my brother in to wash the blood off his body and to sleep; and in the morning she gave him those clothes that had belonged to her late husband.

"What was he, a clown in the circus?" I asked.

Jacob laughed. "You see," he teased Father. "I did what you said. I went to the city, I showed myself, I was almost killed, and the only woman who invited me in was older than you."

That year, our last year of school, my brother dropped out. At night he worked in the bakery, during the day he slept, and he already wore the remote expression of a baker. Even though he and Father worked together, or maybe because of that, relations between them went from bad to worse.

Now and then, when I put on my glasses or when I got close enough, I could make out their bitter words leaping over the work boards, their faces contorted with rage.

"The camel is already broken straw in back of all of 'em," Mother defined the situation; and in the end that great quarrel broke out. It began with one of the vague insults Father was always hurling at Mother, but this time it didn't end only with shouts, but with Jacob leaving the house. Sometimes I amuse myself with the idea that I was responsible for the whole brouhaha because I was the one who asked her to tell us a story that evening.

"Now a story?" grumbled Father, who had already shown signs of going off to bed. "We don't need her *palabras* now, we need to go to sleep. We've got a night of work ahead of us."

"So, why don't you go to sleep," said Jacob, "because we love her *palabras*."

Jacob was right. Even today I can't point to a book that has given me the kind of excitement our mother's stories did. I remember the one about "how they invented bread," whose hero was a naked baby found by peasants in a wheat field and who was so heavy no one could pick him up from the ground. I still feel the sweet touch of the goslings of her childhood, even though I never saw them. I can still scream with terror at her story about "angel people," a group of flying old folks who lived among the rock ledges of the Caucasus. "Angel people" who had "eyes with light," and would snatch children, soar off, and drop them on the cliffs, just as the vulture cracks cow bones and tortoise shells.

I also loved her language, musical and defective at the same time, and the beginning, with the surprising locution—"When I was a girl"—and the gestures that accompanied her words. My mother had long fingers, so strong and embarrassed they were always playing and wrestling with each other.

"Go to the sleep, Abraham," she said to Father. "I'm coming too in little while." And to us, she smiled and said, "I'll tell you about a neighbor the Kuragin we had in settlement. The Dyedushka Mikhail had all kinds fruits, horses, geese. And in spring we saw: geese want home, to the north. Wings is flapping, neck is stretched out, home. And they couldn't 'cause my father he cut off feathers, and I, five years old, went to the Kuragin . . ."

Fascinated, Jacob and I watched her. Tia Duduch smiled, too, and the socket of her gouged-out eye pulled and twisted the corners of her mouth. Off to the side sat Simon, sucking an addictive chocolate bar, fixing his opaque gaze on Mother, and his face so relaxed he even let himself smile.

He was close to bar-mitzvah age, and despite his youth and his lame leg he was a hard worker, and neither heat nor effort disturbed the precise movements of his hands. It was only the simplest task—mixing the yeast and the flour with water and sugar—that he couldn't learn. He was always getting the quantities wrong, couldn't understand the smell, never assessed the heat and the spread of the bubbles. In his great desire to satisfy, he accelerated the yeast so much that the dough rose too fast and fell with the same speed, and Father, who was generally very careful to keep his language clean, exploded one day and shouted at him, "Your dough is like the flesh of an old whore down below."

Now his wrath broke out on his very favorite point of weakness, Mother's spoken language. "Geese want home . . ." He cleared his throat contemptuously.

"Let her finish," I said, and Jacob declared, "I thought you wanted to go to sleep." But Father had already put on his face the thin smile jasmine growers smile when their sons chant the Torah portion better then they do. "Geese!" He sat down again at the table. "I'll tell you about geese. Your grandfather's grandfather, my children, the father of the father of the father of your father Reuven Yakir Preciaducho Levy of blessed memory, had seven goose feathers for writing: one feather for liturgical hymns, a second feather for commentaries, a third feather for verdicts, a fourth feather for business, a fifth feather for letters, a sixth feather for public needs, and a seventh feather . . ."

"For tickling the sultan's ass," proposed Jacob.

"Woe unto thee, woe unto thee, woe unto thee! Boor! Stubborn and rebellious son!" cried Father. "And a seventh feather he had for proofreading. For he devoted all his time to Torah, sat in the attic where he proofread the writings of his father, the sage Jacob ben Simon Levy of blessed memory, and that *bovo*, that fool," he pointed at Simon, "is named after him, and he was the richest of the rich and a lord of lords, a lover of Zion and a poet of liturgical hymns, and they said of him, 'The scope of his piety and perfection is known by all, his plantations blossom and flourish, more delightful than gold and choicer than pearls.'"

He cast a glance of chill triumph at all our faces and continued. "His essays he wrote in Adrianopolis, 'My First Fruit' and 'The Mandrake of Reuven,' in the courtyard of Sultan Abd El-Aziz himself, one of his intimates, for whom he performed important services. And in his old age, when he immigrated to Jerusalem, he left in the Sultan's white ship with white sails and he travelled in the Sultan's white chariot drawn by six horses, and the Sultan also sent along a troop of Janissaries with bayonets and spears and striped pantaloons, to guard him on the way against demons and robbers, and to sound golden trumpets at his approach. And on Passover all of us in the family would go up to his grave on the Mount of Olives and read his inscription, composed in his honor by Rabbi Rozanis."

Here Father lifted his eyes and recited in a special nasal tone, all splendor and honor, the verses of the inscription:

> To see your face in all its glory,
> Such is the ardent wish of our soul.
> Now the rage of death concludes the story.
> To the end, carcasses resurrected whole.
> But even in the Garden of Shaddai, you live, memento mori,
> Honor and splendor shall you extol.

"So how come, after all those Preciaducho geniuses with the sultans and the feathers and the white horses, you and your father worked as laborers in a bakery from the time you were ten?" Jacob asked Father.

"Hard times," grunted Father impatiently. "To support the children and give bread to the hungry. And my Father, may he rest in peace, was a learned man, and we children didn't have enough to eat."

"Your father wasn't a learned man." Jacob straightened up. "He sold *sahleb* and *Hamle-m'laneh* in the street and ironed tarbooshes and finally died of hunger and left you nothing but debts. Until Mother opened her dairy, you lived like bums, but your mother spent all day looking at herself in the mirror and thought she was the daughter of Valero."

"In the morning a tarboosh presser, and in the evening a learned man." Father blanched. "And anyway, who is Valero? What Valero? The ones who came a hundred years ago, and we've been in Jerusalem for fifteen generations." And he shouted abruptly, "Better ask her, your *pezgada* mother, about their Simhat Torah, how her father the *goy* and her Russkie brothers would drink in the synagogue of their village, and get so drunk they forgot they converted, would go out to the street with sticks and holler 'Beat the Jews!'"

Mother shook, and her face grew pale. Her fingers, groping on the table like the white canes of blind people, sought bread crumbs among the waves of the cloth. All her strength abandoned her when Father began mocking her and her origins.

"Not Russkies, not Russkies," she muttered.

"Those Russkies built you the bakery. Without them you'd be a miserable laborer today, a nothing," said Jacob calmly.

"*Nada de nada que disho Kohelet!*" shouted Father. "I could have inherited Ergas's bakery, he was childless, poor man, and today the bakery could be like Angel's, the biggest bakery in Jerusalem."

"So why did you go from Jerusalem to the Galilee on foot to marry that Russkie girl from the family of the uncircumcised?" Jacob went on.

"I didn't go," said Father, mealy-mouthed; "I happened to pass by there, saw her lying in the mud with the geese, I asked, Who's that? They said, Do that poor girl a favor."

"You went! You walked there on foot!" shouted Mother. "And you came to talk to mukhtar the Alhadef, that you deam about me all your deams, that the Alhadef should fix wedding with me for you."

"The Alhadef, the Alhadef," Father mimicked her with his stylized viper's fury. "Boors *habla* the Holy Tongue. Go ask your mother the *goya*, who deams deams and cleans widows, who doesn't know the shape of a letter, let her tell you how the *rabbin* with the beard made her father the circumcision without tying him up with ropes. We haven't heard that one in ages."

If anyone else had said such things, he would have been condemned to a horrible death, but as often happens to strong people, this insult turned Mother's muscles into flaccid tatters.

"The children I brought you, the flour sacks I dragged for you, the dough with these hands of mine I kneaded for you my whole life." Her large hands were raised in the air, in the mute entreaty of an animal, in the stunned plaint of a child, and from there they dropped to her mouth to block the wailing that burst out.

Today I think, and I'm not sure I'm right, that in those days Father was married to two women: to the fair girl who tormented his memories with her foreignness and her beauty, who kept ascending and descending the ladders of his dreams; and to her, our forlorn mother, stammering and mighty, "the cow *in forma de* human being," who shared his bed, kicked him in her sleep, crushed his chest with her scary, importunate hugs, and added a stupid definite article to every proper noun.

He pulled the small white kerchief out of his pocket, wiped the corners of his mouth foppishly, and stood up to leave the table. But this time something terrible and unexpected happened. Jacob got up and ran after him, caught him by the shoulders, and stopped him by force.

"You won't call her a *goya!*" he shouted.

"Wicked son of a righteous father," whispered Father. "Sense *de kulu.*"

"You won't call her a *goya*!" Jacob shouted again. "If she's a *goya*, then we're also *goys*! And you won't call anyone names here! Sense in your own ass, yourself. I'm fed up with you, understand? Fed up with you! We're all fed up with you!"

"Go, get away from me!" yelled Father in a thin, horrible voice. He raised his hand and smacked Jacob on the face.

In a wink Father was thrown to the floor and Jacob ran out.

Chapter 48

My brother absentmindedly took a piece of leavened dough, chewed and sucked it, rolled it between his tongue and his palate. "Believe me," he said, "it's lucky for me I'm a baker. That the dough leads me and I don't lead it. That I can work and not lie in bed all night without falling asleep. Those two poor parents you saw in the morning—what nights they spend. Like Ahasuerus. Open memorial books and insomnia. And it's lucky for me I work every night, and in the morning I'm tired and I've got Michael on my hands, and I don't need pills to fall asleep, or the sun and the moon and the birds to tell me that the world continues. Every night with the bread is like a full cycle for me. Yeast is born, lives and is consumed, and dies, like spring and summer and fall and winter, a full cycle in one night in the bakery. You remember the myth we learned in school about the Greek princess or goddess who died in the fall and rose in the spring? You wrote about it in your baking book, didn't you? Or was that about the ancient Egyptians and their Tammuz and all that? He wasn't theirs? Never mind.

"Those two parents, I'll show you the graves of their sons. Bandboxes. Every morning with bottles of water in a shopping bag to water the plants, and rags to polish, and a whiskbroom to clean the pine needles and the bird droppings. It's horrible how the graves are still new and gleaming. Like that fly of Brinker's, as if only yesterday the stones were cut, the inscription carved just this minute, and the bodies inside are surely still warm, and time for them has stood still. For when a son dies before his father, it's against the laws of nature.

"Stood still?!" he shouted. "They think time has stood still. When the day ends, doesn't the sun set? And when the night ends, doesn't it rise? And in the winter doesn't it rain? And at four in the afternoon did the wind stop coming from the sea? And that's what's killing them, that everything goes on and all the laws still hold, that nothing, in fact, has happened. Because if the sun shines, and the moon at night, and the rain falls and the dough rises and the whole world works according to all the laws—then at best it's a sign that their sons are also rotting there in the grave according to all the laws, and at worst it says that their little deaths were only part of something much worse and much bigger, a big plot everybody tries to understand and nobody can."

That whole night, Jacob didn't return home, and every few minutes Mother went out of the bakery to look, and in the morning she was so worried she took Brinker and went to search for Jacob in the fields. "You stay here," she told Simon and me. In the afternoon they returned empty-handed, and Jacob came back a few hours later—scratched, miserable, dead tired. He told a fragmentary and confused tale about wandering on the mountain and jackals wailing nearby, and he was so worn out he let Mother support him up the stairs and sit him down at the kitchen table.

"You want eat?"

"No."

"Drink?"

"No."

"Make up your couch?"

"I don't want anything, Mother," whispered Jacob, the stalk of his neck vibrating. "Just to wash up. Not to talk, not to drink, not to eat. To wash in hot water."

"Hurry the fire," Mother said to Simon.

She got up, grabbed Jacob under his arms, stood him on his feet with a manly gesture, led him to the shower, and the lock banged loud and clear. Father and I huddled against the door and peeked in through the cracks, pretending not to notice one another, like the two slaves who peeked into the bedroom of Hector and Andromache.

Mother sat Jacob on a chair, knelt down in front of him, unbuttoned his shirt, and took off his shoes. The weave of his socks was engraved on the pads of his heels. Then she stood up, leaned his forehead against her stomach, and took off his shirt. Half naked, my brother's thin body shone in the gloom. Mother unbuckled his belt, bent down, wound his arms around her neck, and said, "Hold on tight." When she straightened up, he was hanging on her body with his head drooping on her chest. Her hands moved over his shoulders, down to his waist, hips, thighs, taking off his trousers and his gray work underpants.

Now she sat down on the chair, and Jacob, naked and soft, dropped into her lap, his head and hands lax, his eyes closed. Mother examined him from head to toe, searching for scratches and wounds, and the whole time, she wept softly, for his love, for her love, for her days gone by, and for his days to come.

With her teeth, like a sheepdog, she extracted thorns and splinters from the palms of his hands. "Where did you go run around?" she groaned. "Where did you go?" With her fingernails she picked out the burrs trapped in the hairs of his stomach and thighs.

"Shame, shame," Father bleated behind me.

Scared and quiet, the antennae of her hands moved over his body, stroked the skin, felt around, searched for a reply and traces.

Finally she put him on his feet again, put him in the shower, and stood there with him in her clothes under the stream of hot water, soaping him, scrubbing him, not overlooking any fold of skin or crevice of flesh.

"Close your eyes," she said, and with a big towel, she wiped him until his body turned red, and the whole time she wept, and now and then, she kissed his forehead and the bridge of his nose and murmured into the hollow of his neck. The water pasted her dress to her skin, and Jacob, as in sleep, smiled with pleasure and put his hands on her shoulders and his head on her chest.

"Don't do that!" Father suddenly yelled over my shoulder, and assaulted the door. "He's a grown man!"

The small metal bolt was ripped out of its socket, and a hot vapor burst out. Father's small fists pounded on Mother's shoulders and Jacob's head. His feet kicked, his mouth screamed, his clothes and his face got wet in the stream of water.

"You mad dog," said my brother tranquilly.

"Don't do that!" Father's teeth were bared, his eyes were narrowed, his forehead trembled like a gruel of hatred.

That stylized and withered rage made me nauseous. I went to the bakery and started fermenting the yeast and scraping the bowl with a spatula.

Then I poured in the measuring tins of flour and water, turned on the kneading machine, and returned to them and announced through the door in a loud voice, "The dough is rising!"

Father joined me, glancing at me sideways as if he wanted me to begin a conversation or express an opinion. When Itsik and Joshua Edelman came, they immediately noticed that something wasn't right, and that whole night we baked in silence.

The next day, when Mother called us to breakfast, Jacob also came to the table and started eating with gusto.

"You'll go a little to my home," said Mother after a few minutes.

"Go, go to the Russkies, stubborn and rebellious son, he that smiteth his father and his mother!" said Father so Jacob wouldn't think this was Mother's idea, but his punishment.

"Shut up, Abraham!" said Mother, and turned to him with the slow rotation of her shoulders. "Yes?! Enough you did!"

We were surprised, because she never talked to Father in a threatening tone, but this time, her face was flooded with that familiar violent flush that rose from the gorge in her chest and heralded evil.

"Get done and we'll fix you up the suitcase," she said.

Father pecked at his food and looked like an old, routed checkers player who wagered on a dinner he couldn't afford. Afterward he hid in the bakery and raised noises of work there. Mother packed clothes for Jacob, and then she closed herself in a room with him and dictated a letter for her brothers.

Before we left the yard she said to him, "Go tell him goodbye."

"I won't."

"Go tell him goodbye." She pushed him.

Jacob went into the bakery and came out a moment later.

"He doesn't answer me," he said.

"Why should he answer you?" said Mother. "Come on, let's us go."

Only she, the donkey, and I accompanied Jacob to the railroad station. Simon wanted to come along too, but Mother told him to say goodbye to Jacob at home. His face twisted with grief. He hugged Jacob, and when we left the house, he limped behind the cart until Mother shouted at him to stay.

An autumn day it was, during the week of Sukkot. The first rain was about to fall. I knew that Leah was sitting in her room watching from the window, cursing the clouds and waiting for the train whistle. We boarded the train with Jacob because Mother insisted on making sure they didn't seat her son next to a "Haifooite." When she was eight years old, a merchant from Haifa had cheated Dyedushka Mikhail, and ever since then, as far as she was concerned, everybody from Haifa was a scoundrel and a thief. She reminded Jacob again of where he was to get off; for the third time she described to him the lane between the fields, a shortcut that would bring him straight to her brothers' house, and again she made sure the note she had dictated to him, with the names of all the Tartars, their sons and daughters, grandsons and granddaughters, was in his pocket.

"You won't eat there for nothing!" she warned him. "You'll work in field, that's good for you."

Then we hugged each other, and Mother said, "And go to grave of the grandfather Mikhail," and when we got off the train and were back on the platform, we saw Yehiel Abramson run to the station and buy a ticket.

"Where are you going, Yehiel?" I asked him.

"To Tel Aviv," answered the librarian, sad and very solemn, "to the funeral of Shaul Tshernikhovski."

Chapter 49

Every morning I hear work boots climbing up to the porch. And with them comes the sour smell of Father, now wafting from the chunks of dough stuck to my brother. Jacob sits down on the top step, sighs, throws his floury shoes aside, wiggles his toes, and goes to wash. Father learned this morning wash, with a loofah and soap, from Ergas the baker, and I too, through the years and the distance, still keep it up in America. Sweat, flour dust, and steam block the pores of the skin, and bakers are liable to be afflicted by "baker's rash" if they aren't strict about scrubbing their chest and arms every day.

Two days ago Romi snuck behind her father. She silently opened the door of the shower, with one hand she pushed back the curtain, and with the other hand she photographed him. Blinded and surprised, Jacob tore the curtain from its hooks, covered his groin with it, and ran after her, shouting, "Don't do that! Don't!"

Hearing shouts, I came out of my room into the corridor. My brother's naked body looked thin and pale under the dripping nylon shroud. Romi, a laughing, light-footed huntress, ran away, shouting, "Caught you, Daddy, caught you, I've got you," and leaving behind quick traces of wings of strong thighs, a reddish flash of hair, and sharp childish breasts that split the air.

Jacob was so angry and humiliated he started crying. "What does she want from me?" he asked me over and over. "How will it end?"

Two days later we found the picture on the kitchen table, enlarged and framed, propped up on Arthur Spinney's old sugar bowl.

"Look how beautiful you are, Dad," said Romi. "*Chez nous à Paris* we would have made you a movie star."

When the picture was taken, Jacob's eyes were shut because of the soap. But rage, the hairy brother of desire and envy, spread over his whole body and was already drawn on his face even before he noticed his daughter and her camera. The water poured gray and white stripes on his head, over-flowed onto his surprised chest with singed hair, onto his belly, down to his thighs, and his thin shapeless shins.

"Really *kipazelik*!" I remarked, and Jacob glared at me.

"I told you, I'll make an exhibit of you, and I'll call it My Father," Romi announced, and pirouetted.

Suddenly Jacob smashed the glass on the picture and grabbed his daughter's neck with one bleeding hand. "You won't make fun of me," he growled. But he was scared of his rage, and let go of her immediately.

"And under every picture, you'll write a few words about yourself," Romi expounded, "in your own handwriting. Tell him, Uncle!" She turned to me, her face aflame, her eyes gleaming.

My heart stopped. She was about fifteen the first time I saw her, and to this day it's easy for me to feel again the amazement and embarrassment that struck me then. In my heart I compared her to our mother Sarah when she was first revealed to the eyes of Abraham. Like an almond branch blos-soming over a pond and its image reflected underneath—that's how the two of them seemed to me. With her long, bony, adolescent limbs, and without the flock of geese, Romi looked more boyish and harder than her grandmother, but she was still the tall, light-footed girl who galloped in the rainy valley of my imagination, with thick straw-colored eyebrows and splendid eyes set so far apart that neither noticed the beauty of its twin. It was then that I also noticed for the first time her pansy-colored irises, blue-yellow, so different from the gray of Mother's eyes.

When she was two or three, Jacob sent me a picture of her running around naked in the yard with white panties wrapped around her head like a turban. One eye was laughing, and a coppery curl of hair peeped out of the crotch of the panties, which were stretched obliquely over her face. Even then she had that strong, straight back and those broad shoulders. "Believe me," he wrote on the back of the picture in a rare attempt at humor, "I don't know how to take this child. I have the feeling she should have been yours."

From time to time I would send her picture postcards from America, and when she started first grade and learned to write, she began answering them. Incidentally, I sent gifts and postcards to Benjamin too, but he answered only once a year—heavy words of thanks that seemed to be written with the soles of his shoes. Romi's letters were short and joyful; they always began with the words "Hi, Uncle," ended with "See you, Uncle," and even then reminded me of a verse of Shaul Tshernikhovski that Yehiel loved to sing at the top of his voice as he stitched together worn-out bindings.

Before the shadows of evening fall,
As long as life does breathe and ring—
Let us rejoice in love and exalt,
Let us shout, uncle, let us sing!

Romi attached a picture to every one of her letters. At first she drew pictures and wrote on them "house" next to the house, "tree" next to the tree, and "cat" next to the cat, as if she had doubts about the intelligence of the recipient and the power of his memory. Only later did another possibility occur to me: that naming was her way of establishing ownership. After all, that's what Adam did. At any rate, when she grew up, she perfected her system, and on every photograph she wrote a few words about what was happening in it. "Grandfather sitting on the bench," "Dad in the rain, collecting water in buckets," "Benjamin climbing the tree."

She used a Kodak Retina I had sent Benjamin a few years before, when he was seven. "This is a gift from your uncle in America," I wrote him, "on condition that you send me a lot of pictures. Of you, your little sister, your father and mother, Grandfather, Brinker, Simon, Tia Duduch, your grandmother's grave, the house, and the bakery." But Benjamin didn't use the camera, and Romi found it tossed in a drawer; she resurrected it, and the two became my strongest link with my home and my family, and from a few perspectives, you will soon understand, with my life in general.

Her first photograph reached me when she was nine. "That's me," she wrote on the sand under her feet. "I did it all by myself. Simon just pushed the button for me." She is standing in the yard, a sheet wrapped around her waist, her face painted with stripes of white plaster and red mud, her feet bare. A strong sun emphasized shadows between her ribs and erased her fair nipples. Two chicken drumsticks were stuck in the snakes of her rolled up hair. "Hi, Uncle. I dressed up as a cannibal. The shadow on the ground is Simon's. My feet are awful hot in the sand. I ate Daddy, I ate Mommy, and when I come to America, I'll eat you too. Your poor orphan niece Romi."

Even then she was very careful to dot the "i" of her name, and not with a point but with a little circle. "So you'll be able to read my name right," she explained to me later on.

A few years later, when I saw that she had persisted and improved, and that Jacob, like Father in his day, wasn't disposed to spend money on her expensive hobby, I offered her the deal I've already mentioned. For her bat-mitzvah I sent her a Leica and a tripod, and when necessary I supplied her with filters and spools, photography paper, instructional manuals, and lenses. In those days, I became very friendly with the photographer who took the pictures for my bread book. She was about thirty and had no sense of humor, but she did have a sense of composition and an original concept of time, and she urged me to foster Romi's talent. It was she who told me you have to photograph people with especially fast and sensitive film, because the photograph, she claimed, shortens the life of the person pho-tographed by the length of the opening of the shutter. According to her, liv-ing creatures compete for a limited quantity of time in the world, as they compete for food. "Someone who dies young leaves us unused time," she said, "and someone who lives long shortens the lives of those who are left." A few years after we parted she was killed in a dreadful automobile acci-dent. A month later a lawyer phoned me from Baltimore and told me she had left me a picture of herself naked and all the years she hadn't had time to use.

Romi answered me with pictures and captions that proved both her ripening talent and the wicked charm of her youth.

"Mom and Dad fight all the time, and I don't know about what."

"I look at a picture of Grandmother that our nice retarded neighbor once took, and I think, Too bad you didn't wait for me, Gramma, we could have been good friends, and now you don't even know I exist."

"When they came to tell us about Benjamin, Dad fell on the ground, screamed, and went nuts. Too bad I didn't photograph that for you."

"I want to photograph you together," she demanded now. "The two brothers."

"Stop bothering us!" Jacob got angry.

"I'll photograph you whether you want me to or not," she said.

"Go photograph your friends in Tel Aviv!" shouted my brother. "You won't make a career from me! A disgrace, that picture, a shame!"

And when he saw me standing there listening, he shook his finger at me too, and said, "Like you, just like you. Two rats! To eat without sweating, to enjoy without suffering, to see without glasses. You and your books, her and her camera. If you weren't related, I would have matched you up by now."

I was silent, but Romi was incensed. "You'll thank me for these photographs someday!"

Like a big golden hornet, she circled her father, and when he turned to her, his whole body was shaking and his hands were groping in the air; she pushed him back, and was surprised, and so were we, at how easily he fell on the chair. Then she walked around him, came to him from behind and leaned her chest on his shoulders. She wrapped her arms around his neck and buried her mouth in the nape of his neck and whispered there until my whole body bristled with desire and pain.

"No one ever loved you or will love you like I do," she sobbed. "More than you loved Mom, and certainly more than she loved you, and more than you punish yourself for Benjamin, and more than you love Michael. I'm the only one who knows what's happening to you. It's yourself you put into the oven every night. Yourself and us."

"Who is us?" snarled Jacob. "Who is us?!" His voice, a hoarse roar, choked in its own rage, and even before the words struck the walls of the room, the screen door slammed, wooden clogs banged on the stairs, the sobbing grew distant, and gravel sprayed under the spinning tires. Then Father came out of his room and asked, "What happened?" And Jacob said through clenched teeth, "What happened. On top of everything he asks what happened," and he got up in disgust and went off to the bakery.

Chapter 50

How much can you still miss the Jacob," said Mother at dinner.

For a whole year my brother was in the Galilee. Once Mother went to visit him, and every month he sent us a letter. The mailman's shout was heard in the distance—"Hold the goose"—because the goose, hissing and pecking, would attack any stranger who came into the yard. Our mailman was a short, thin man who strode very fast, and demanded at every house, "Quick, a glass of water, or else no letter." His upraised little finger shook with thirst. His Adam's apple bobbed like a buoy in stormy water. His gulps were so loud it was hard to believe they were produced by such a tiny body.

"Why do you drink so much?" I asked him.

"Liquid is important for the body." He waved his index finger. "You have to drink a lot and not waste. Watch out for the heat, sad movies, and women."

Our mailman bred canaries and goldfinches, and their hybrids won medals. Male canaries, he disclosed to me, love *umbuz*, as he called the grains of hashish he fed his warblers, "and it's no wonder they sing so nice." A vision burned in him: to turn the future state of the Jews into a songbird superpower. "Every family will get a pair of rollers from the government, and we'll export the chicks." Once he brought along a cage with a bird in it and told me, "You're a lad with a soul, right? Hold him in your hand a minute. Carefully. You feel the little heart, how fast it beats? The way he trembles now, that's how he'll sing later."

I would read Jacob's letter to Mother, write down her answer, add a few words of my own, and leave room for Simon. Jacob asked us not to come visit him; he said they were nice to him, that he worked in the field and didn't eat the bread of charity.

"He's coming back," Mother repeated; "he's coming back and he'll take the Leah too."

"Now listen, Mother, listen and remember!" I finally told her with a firmness I had never dared use with her. "I don't want the Leah, and I don't want the bakery, and stop telling me that all the time!"

Father saw me storming out into the yard, and a few minutes later he came out too. He circled around me a few minutes and finally said, "Now he's hers, and it's you and me against them."

"I'm not against anybody, Father," I said.

"You're young yet, stupid. A little fish doesn't understand anything about the sea," said Father. "You think the whole world is just stories from your Yehiel's books? Soon we have to think who will get the bakery. You want the inheritance, or you want to stay hungry, like the cat who lived in the widow's garbage can?"

Simon heard the rustle of the envelope opening wherever he happened to be, and in a wink he would appear and stare at us imploringly. He listened intently to the reading of the letter, and ripples of pleasure spread over his face even before I got to his paragraph, which always started with "Hello, Simon, what's new?" and ended with "Your big cousin Jacob." After I finished reading, Simon would get the letter and dash off to one of his corners, where he read the lines back and forth again, sucking the words one by one. And it wasn't till much later that he came back and returned the letter to Mother to keep, contented, as if Jacob's good words had infiltrated the grief of his flesh and consoled him. Only later did we learn that his childhood nightmare of black dots came back to him that year.

An adolescent he was then, and would collect stinking cigarette butts, and I told Yehiel that Sholem Aleichem and John Steinbeck were right: smoking does make a beard grow faster. Sometimes Simon would disappear from the house for a few hours, and Father was sure he was off raping women and careless British soldiers, and he already imagined the worst thing of all: a trial in which he, Abraham Levy, great-grandson and descendant of sages, proofreaders, doctors, and poets, was accused of improper supervision of his ward.

I was sent to track Simon down, and thus I discovered that he wasn't raping but robbing. In those days electrical cables were covered with lead, and the boy tore them off, and stole them from abandoned warehouses and chicken coops under construction. Returning with his booty, he made a small bonfire in the yard, bit through the soft wire with his teeth, and put the strips in a skillet he heated over the fire.

"Look-look," he said to everyone who passed by, belching smoke from his nostrils, and pointing excitedly at the skillet. The molten lead had lost its gloomy gray heaviness and had turned into a light-headed, impulsive, flickering metal. Simon rocked the skillet from side to side, made the white liquid run here and there, followed its glow, and finally cast it into a bucket of cold water, which fizzed and hissed in pain. The startled lead hardened into small, sad-looking idols that scared Father to death with the sorcery spread over their contorted limbs. Those statuettes took on a thousand shapes in the agonized leap from one state of matter to another. Simon hid them in one of his hiding places and it wasn't till many years later that he took them out to give them to the daughters of Joshua Edelman, who were to be born and also to participate in the chronicles of my family.

Father would also appear in the kitchen, pretend he was making coffee for himself, listen to the reading of the letter, and not say a word. Even in those days, he had begun sending out his secret letters, and looked to me like a survivor on a desert island, tossing bottles with entreating messages. Only later did I understand that that was the start of his senile mania of searching for relatives, those who now show up at our house with his letters in their hands. I think I already told you about them. Some of them are childless people who want a home, others are scoundrels looking for an inheritance, still others are afflicted with boredom and bereft of love. Father treats them skeptically and harshly: as they stand on the other side of the fence, he poses riddles to them, examines them with mysterious codes to be completed and unexpected family passwords that make the pupils of the impostors contract. Then he dismisses them. The genuine relative, the one probably riding on a white raven, hasn't yet arrived.

Now I delivered the bread all by myself. I planned the delivery route so I came to the Levitov house last.

"She's waiting for you to braid her hair." Zivia smiled and took the loaf of bread.

Every morning I braided Leah's hair. I did it the way you braid a challah: with four plaits, not three. In the village we were already considered a couple. I was a youth of eighteen, serious and romantic and strong; I loved her with devotion, concern, and gratitude. With the enthusiasm of youth I expounded on the slippery concept of "the most beautiful woman in the world," explaining why Orpheus looked back and proving why he was not to be compared with Lot's wife but with Cyrano de Bergerac.

"Why?" asked Leah.

"Because neither of them," I informed her importantly, "wanted to realize his love."

She smiled. "Too bad you weren't there to tell them that." And she took the roll I had baked for her and went to school with me in the cart. From there the donkey would return home by himself. Jacob, from his exile, didn't ask how she was and didn't want me to tell her anything. From her I learned that she didn't get a single letter.

That summer was sad and sweet. Longing for my brother and love for his beloved filled my body, and in an unexpectedly pleasant way I also grew close to Mother, who told me stories and answered my queries. "'Cause I liked the him," she smiled when I asked her one day why she had married Father. We were sitting on the front porch shucking ears of young corn Brinker had brought her. Our eyes filled with tears from the irritation that doesn't have to be explained to someone who is experienced in it, and is a waste to describe to someone who isn't. Mother said that "when I was a girl," they would heat not only the water heater with the stripped ears but also the baking oven. She smiled at me again, and I suddenly bent over and put my head on her thigh. For one moment of favor her hand played in my hair, and then she pushed me away with a laugh. "You're not baby no more."

Jamila brought her a proven love stimulant: the green oil that saturates the berries of the arbutus. I stood next to them holding the towel while Jamila massaged Mother's arms and legs with it. Then Mother told me to leave them alone, and Jamila laughed with her enormous camel's teeth.

But when Mother went to consult Chenou Apari, she let me accompany her and listen to their women's conversation.

"I wanted to live like two doves," she whispered.

Chenou Apari laughed. "Madame de Pompadour said that if a couple lives like a pair of doves, it's a sign that one of them is suffering."

The women in the beauty parlor nodded and smiled wearily. Chenou Apari knew the smallest and truest secrets.

"Show me your ring, Sarah," she said.

Mother took off her wedding ring and gave it to her.

"No!" said Chenou. "You don't give a wedding ring from one hand to another. You put it on the table, and I take it from there." And to me she said, "She doesn't understand anything. *Rien.*"

"Doves or not doves," she added skeptically, "a woman always has to be careful. On the one hand, to do very good to her husband so he won't look for anything outside, and on the other hand, always to go with all the *bijoux*, the bracelets and rings and earrings on her. Not to take them off in the shower or in bed or washing the floor or doing the laundry. If he suddenly throws her out, if he just says to her, 'Get out of the house,' then fine, she gets up and goes right away, as she is, with all the gold and silver on her."

I also got closer to Brinker then. Professor Fritzi sometimes came to visit him, but the neighbors stayed away from him, and his wife and son had practically disappeared. Dead Livy finally got a whiff of her own odor, and was so panicky she started sending letters and preparations to Jewish doctors in Boston and London. Noah delved into stupid issues of *Screen Life*, stank of Players cigarettes, and perfected the art of playing the songs of the Herman Brothers on saws and combs. Brinker often complained to me about his son's behavior. "Noah also and if no Tel Aviv every day very five-five," he grumbled. And I said, "It's not so terrible, Brinker, it'll pass."

I was the only person who was able to understand his opaque sentences, and we could talk like that for hours. We told each other secrets, plans, and hopes. "Also that you here mother and if one two went and so on and so on," he said with surprising confidence, and his hand sketched ellipses of entreaty on my thigh. I promised not to give away his secret to anyone. I now know that Brinker was the only friend I treated with complete candor. I loved him and knew he would never betray me, for even if the Germans conquered the country and Brinker was tortured and broke down, no one would understand a word he said.

Our continuous conversations imparted a new ability to me: I began understanding languages I had never studied. A twitch of the corners of the mouth, the play of wrinkles on the face, the dilation and contraction of the pupils, wagtails' flight of the voice—all allowed me to decipher what was said. Brinker's oral hieroglyphics helped me translate Edelman's Yiddish, Mr. Cocosin's Russian, Jamila's Arabic, Duduch's stifled weeping. Suddenly I even understood the Hindi spoken by the soldiers at the nearby base.

Chapter 51

efore Benjamin was killed, whenever I closed my eyes, I would see one picture. Leah coming into the bakery, coming with the smell of the rain from her wet braid and her warm feet. That was the moment you always remember and that was how I wanted it to remain. Even when we stopped getting along, I wanted that to be the picture my closed eyes saw. But now when I shut them, I see only him."

Suddenly the bread truck went off the side of the road, shuddered, and stopped in a cloud of dust, and Jacob took the fog of his glasses off his nose and wiped them on his shirttail. Grains of flour and sand were blended with his tears as they were mixed up in the sweat of our youth when we unloaded the flour sacks, sticking to the thick lenses and scratching them.

We were on our way to Tel Aviv. I had asked Romi to invite us to a dinner of reconciliation between her and her father.

"Don't worry," he said. "This doesn't happen to me often. Only since you came. I've become a bit weepy. All of a sudden I've got an audience." And he asked if I wanted to drive instead of him.

"No," I said. "Even in America I don't like to drive, and I sure as hell don't want to here. Let's wait a little, and then we'll go on."

Not long after I came to America I bought a blue DeSoto. That was twenty-five years ago, and I haven't put more than five thousand miles on it. And most of them were driven by Romi when she visited me after she got out of the army.

"You know those pictures? The ones you see only with your eyes closed? Do you have pictures like that too?"

I didn't answer him. What should I answer? Jacob is candid with me and doesn't hide anything from me. Not now, and not when we were young either. That's how he was when he fell in love with Leah and consulted me, that's how he was in the letters he sent me in America, and that's how he is now.

"They told me, Time heals all wounds. They said, Time will take care of it. That's what they said. You know what? Maybe time does take care of it, but it doesn't take care of us. Nothing is wiped out and nothing calms down, and he's the only thing I see. Every day, just him." Bewilderment and pain were mixed up in my brother's voice, and some measure of grievance not directed at anything specific, and his hunger to be close to me bothers me because I can't answer him in the same coin. Ever since those conversations I had with Brinker, candor is something I allow myself only with strangers. To them I tell my innermost lies. To passengers on the night trains when I travel on lecture tours, to guests in the hotels I stay in, to readers of the recipes I write. And to you too, sometimes.

"I loved him the way you should love a son, no more and no less," said my brother. From our father he inherited an obstinate fondness for the correct thing, for habit and custom, even though he won't admit it.

"Of course I loved him, and brought him up, and did everything a father should do for a son, fed him and dressed him, watched him and took care of him. But why should I lie? I can tell you. You are my brother, even if you didn't want to see, even if you didn't want to know. Even if you ran away."

Romi made us pasta, gave us wine, hovered over us, caressed us, photographed us.

"It's unbelievable what stupid things people make from dough," grumbled Jacob at his fork loaded with spaghetti, and Romi burst out laughing.

"Why don't you stay here tonight?"

"No, no," said Jacob.

"I already made for you a couch," she announced. Our mother died a few years before she was born, and when Romi imitates her, she imitates the stories she's heard about her. But the imitation is always exact: the voice is Mother's voice, and the words are her words.

Jacob couldn't help smiling, and Romi begged, "Edelman can work one night with his son he can. Call them, Dad. Let's have a good time, the three of us."

But Jacob persisted in his refusal, and at midnight the two of us got up and went home, and for the first time since I came here, I spent a whole night working with him. The body, I discovered, remembers better than the brain. Forgotten movements unfroze in my flesh. Series of actions fell into place once again. Slumbering muscles awoke, threw off their fibers.

"Someone who remembers never forgets." Joshua Edelman watched me as I removed the bowl of the kneading machine from the sockets of its wheels and brought it to the worktable. Jacob smiled. A full kneading machine weighs about a quarter of a ton. A man in the prime of life can't move it, but an old and experienced baker does it easily.

"That used to drive Benjamin crazy," said Jacob. "When he was seventeen, he was already such a hulk, a wild bull, and he'd take flour sacks off the truck two by two. But he just couldn't move the kneading machine, until Father came, weak and old and burned out, and showed him how."

"And what difference does all that make now?" he said in the morning, as if he had consulted all night with the maw of the oven. Itsik and Joshua Edelman were gone, and he closed the oven door and climbed heavily out of the pit; and still on his knees, he lifted his floury head to me. "I loved him, but Romi was my favorite, and now, with Michael, everything seems different. Look at him. Who could have guessed I would have such a child? Did you ever see such a child? Come to your daddy, come to me."

Michael came into the bakery as he did every morning, to get dressed near the oven. He went down into the pit, looked up from there and smiled at me as people smile at nice strangers, and Jacob's hands were already moving around his neck and delicately massaging his shoulders.

"And I can't forget how Leah and I, the only time in our life we travelled abroad, to Cyprus it was, I bought Benjamin some black fisherman's hat, a sort of silly Greek cap they sell to tourists. Something for a few pennies. But for Romi I bought a transistor radio. I think it was the first transistor in the village. It cost a lot. At that time, transistors cost a fortune. Leah saw the gifts and didn't say a thing. She said she was cold and tired, and she went to sleep."

His hands strum the shoulders, read the vertebrae of the thin spine, memorize the ribs. "Get dressed, Michael, and go carefully and tell Tia Duduch to give you breakfast, and tell Simon to take you to school."

When Michael leaves, Jacob rushes to the window and watches him until he enters the house.

"Why did I do that? Believe me, I don't know," Jacob takes up where he left off. "We came back home, and the children came to the port with Father to meet us. Benjamin was thirteen then, and Romi was eight, and the two of them were so excited and happy they couldn't wait to open their presents, and I remember Benjamin looked at Romi's new transistor and at his rag of a hat, and he didn't say a thing. And you know kids, they compare

242

everything—why did he get more than me, that kind of thing. But not Benjamin. He accepted the verdict: that that's the way it was between him and his father. For a few days I thought about it, and then I stopped, because Benjamin didn't wear the hat, and one day went by and another day, and things happened, and finally I forgot the whole story, and it wasn't until a few years later, when Benjamin wasn't alive anymore, that Romi showed up one day with that hat on her head, and it all came back to me.

"Who knows how memory works. What preserves it, what finishes it off, and what stirs it. Maybe if he wasn't dead, it wouldn't bother me today. But now, the way it turned out, it kills me. That look of his there, and that he didn't say a thing. That he accepted it. And I didn't say a thing to Leah. I didn't say a thing to anybody. Not to Mother and not to Romi and certainly not to Father. This is the first time I've talked about it with anybody. About that, and that I didn't protect my son."

"What do you blame yourself for? For not going to the army with him and watching over him there? Stop it, Jacob."

"In words you'll always defeat me, but we both know the truth: every cat protects its kittens, and I didn't protect him. And I do know how to protect a child. There isn't a child in the world whose father protects him like I protect Michael. If he fell from the sky, anyplace I am, I'll get there on time and catch him in the air, and if anybody ever touches him, if anybody hurts him, I'll murder him with my bare hands. I'll hold on to him like an *etrog* in cotton. The way Mother held on to the *levadura* she brought from Jerusalem. From the day that poor child was born I've carried him. All the time. Even before I knew about his disease. That's a son of old age, my last one, you saw yourself how much he looks like me. The spit and image of me."

"He doesn't look like you at all," I said. "He doesn't look like anybody in our family."

"He does too!" Jacob raised his voice. "He does. You just don't see anything. Blind as you are! Even Father says he's just like me when I was little."

"All of a sudden you accept what Father says?"

"What does it matter?" shouted Jacob, and a tone of entreaty and threat was twined in his voice. "And why are you talking like that anyway?"

"Father says Michael looks like Uncle Elijah," I said cruelly.

"What Elijah?" Jacob jumped up. "Where did Elijah come from all of a sudden? What's my child got to do looking like some Elijah. This is me myself. I look at him and see myself. You don't understand that?! This child came from my loins, my flank, like the shoot of a tree. I gave birth to him like yeast. I split in two. Leah had nothing to do with it. Nothing. You hear?! She was an incubator, that's all. I used her womb because I don't have one."

Nausea rose in my gorge at that last sentence. "I don't like that style," I said to him.

"Oh . . . sorry," cried Jacob. "Somebody here doesn't like the style. The gentleman who writes books doesn't feel good. How could we have forgotten? Everything else is fine. Leah lies in her room like a mummy, Benjamin and Mother are lying in their graves, Michael has to be watched all the time, Romi is killing me, Father is crazy, but our uncle from America has a problem with the style."

I remained silent.

"You don't like it when I say 'womb?' Especially 'Leah's womb,' eh? And that I was there for the Caesarean and saw everything, you surely don't like that. And don't look at me like that. I can be a shit too. I saw the inside of her, me! Not you! Muscles and fat and intestines and womb and everything. Like the chickens Dead Livy used to slit open, with bunches of undeveloped eggs."

"I'm sorry," I said. "I didn't think you'd respond like that."

"Never mind," said Jacob after a long silence. "At our age nobody's going to change anymore, and at our age you don't make experiments anymore, and you don't find new friends. So I'll talk to you because I'm used to you and because I don't have anybody else, and you'll make do with my style, because you don't have a choice. Just as I make do with your life, you'll make do with mine. Anyway, I wanted to say that I do protect Michael and I didn't protect Benjamin. I only fought with him and pestered him, but I didn't avenge his blood. After all, I know exactly who's to blame there. It's his officer who got the directions wrong and the officer who led the second group and didn't ask for the password and started shooting right away. It's the battalion commander who gave instructions like an imbecile, and it's all those geniuses, the fat officers at headquarters who screw the women soldiers. You think Romi didn't tell me about those shits and how they're always getting fresh? If I know them, they planned the whole operation with some chick sitting on their lap putting on lipstick. So is it any wonder they didn't take care of getting them out the way they should have? And is it any wonder they left him lying there? Yelling in the dark among the reeds until he died? And is it any wonder they all got out of it with minor reprimands in their files, and that's it? Or that they didn't tell me what happened and I had to find out by myself? I went to the hospital and found a guy who was wounded there, and he told me the whole thing, how it happened and how Benjamin got hit by a bullet and fell and hollered and hollered and nobody found him. Only when he stopped, somebody came on his body, half lying in the water of the Jordan. But who am I blaming? After all, I lost him even before they killed him. And I lost her too. A long time before. Now I deserve to see only him, no matter where or when, whenever I close my eyes, I see only him, and not the picture of my Leah coming into the bakery, drying her feet and wringing the water out of her braid."

A few hours later, on the way to the pain clinic, Father questioned me about what I thought of Romi's apartment. He had never been there and wanted to know "what she cooked" and "if it was clean in her house."

"A woman without a man is like a ship without a captain," he said; and then he whispered so the cab driver wouldn't hear. "A boy comes, sees one like that *satanika*, and doesn't sit still for a minute. Right away he gets up and runs off. Why should he stay?"

Near the entrance to the hospital, he started moaning. I knew he was practicing and I didn't interrupt him. The pain doctor greeted him with a smile, and poked and prodded until Father began groaning and whimpering in strange tones. He looked like a big organ, and the doctor was a virtuoso player.

"Have I got bad pains, Doctor?" he asked hopefully.

The doctor laughed. "You're asking me, Mr. Levy? They're your pains."

When he saw that Father was offended, he said, "But I've prepared something for you that can help both of us."

"With God's help," said Father.

"Instead of you describing the pains to me in your own words, I'll suggest words to you from our questionnaire," said the doctor, spreading a sheet of printed paper in front of Father. "You see?" He leaned over to him. "Come on, let's go over these words. This new pain of yours, for example, what word suits it best? Throbbing? Beating? Lashing? Burning?"

Bewilderment and suspicion crept over Father's face.

"Stabbing? Piercing? Splitting? Drilling? Poking?"

"Your Honor will forgive me ... After all, we've already talked about that, pains aren't a cup or a cat or an oven. It's not one word. Pain has to be a little story. It has rules. A little story that starts with 'like.' Pain like the leather-knife of a shoemaker who cuts the *gildas* on Passover, pain like a mirror shattered into a thousand pieces in your body, like the ice that will form from the winter wind, like the sharp little stones that pierced your body when you were a child and ran in the street and fell on your knees. Do you have things like that in your questionnaire?"

"There isn't a person in the world whose pains fit the description of another person's," the doctor told me helplessly. He gave Father drawings of the human body, front and back views. "Mark it for me here in the drawing, Mr. Levy, where the pain is. If the pain is external, write the letter E, and if it's internal, write the letter I."

"There is no external pain," declared Father, for he knew he was gaining the edge. "If it's pain, it's inside; if it's outside, it's not yet pain."

"I mean deep pain, inside the body, or pain on the skin, outside," said the doctor.

"If Your Honor says so." Father yielded.

On our way home I told the cab driver to let us off at the end of the street, because I wanted Father to walk a bit and move his limbs. He got out of the cab absentmindedly, and when he noticed my fraud, he was furious. "Why not at the house? We haven't walked around enough today?"

Slowly we went up the street, my hand supporting his arm, and when we passed by the nursery school, we saw Brinker standing at the fence. He was listening avidly to the voices of the children playing behind it, his lips moving. New leaders have come to power in the village, and they don't let the old strawberry grower come to nursery school anymore. During the day he stands behind the fence, and at night he seeks an open window with words flowing out of it.

"He's been standing like that for years, poor soul," said Father; "looking like an old cadi going into water that's too hot."

"Brinker doesn't work anymore," Jacob told me. "By now his fields are so disciplined and experienced he just tells them what to do."

"Hello, Isaac," I called to him, as I had done a few times since I came. But years and cataracts had been added to his aphasia, and Brinker looked at me with a dull effort and said, "Hello hello well here two afterward," and resumed his listening.

"You can't believe how much he loved your mother." Father surprised me with a mocking sweetness. "At her funeral he cried like a child of the Mugrabis who got lost in the *souk*. Even more than me he cried."

I was stunned, and Father laughed. "You know what it is for a *yekke* to cry at somebody else's wife's funeral? Hee-hee-hee . . . "

Chapter 52

eah knelt on the floor. A carpet, strange and soft to the eye, glowing with a thousand hues, was spread around her thighs.

"Don't close the windows," she said when I came in; "I want air."

A warm, lovely morning it was. I remember the date because it was May first, and we weren't going to school. I put on my glasses and my breath stopped even before I understood what my eyes beheld. Thousands of small, colored, square stones were scattered around her.

I grew weak. "What's that?" I choked, even though in my flesh I already knew the answer.

"The mosaic," said Leah calmly; "you don't remember the mosaic Brinker found in the vineyard?"

"You stole it?" My voice trembled.

"Dummy," laughed Leah; "your brother stole it and brought it to me in a bag."

"How did he know about it?"

"You're so blind. Brinker came to your place at night, when the dough began rising, and your father was in the bakery; and he took your mother to the vineyard to show her the mosaic, and Jacob followed them, and that's it."

That quick salvo, a stoning by truth, knocked me down. The sharp little stones hurt my knees.

"And all these years, you've hidden it?" I asked at last.

"I should have told somebody?"

"Yehiel and Brinker should have known about it," I said.

"No," answered Leah harshly. "They shouldn't. This mosaic is mine. Not Yehiel's and not Brinker's, not anybody's."

"And you've succeeded in putting her together?" I asked after a long silence.

"Who?"

"The woman, the woman in the mosaic."

"So it's a woman . . . ," cried Leah. "He didn't tell me. I didn't really know what to put together." Suddenly she laughed. "He came, poured all the stones on the floor and said, 'I brought you the hardest and most beautiful puzzle in the world, do what you want with it'—and he left."

Later, she told me, she divided the stones into groups according to color, and had already constructed a great many mosaics from them. "I've already had flowers and birds and a wonderful man."

"You want to put it together?" I asked.

"Yes," said Leah; "yes." And her voice became deep and trembled, and I galloped to the library.

Yehiel was busy pasting a picture of Albert Einstein in one of his albums, leaving an empty space underneath to be filled with words.

"You already killed him?" I asked. But Yehiel wasn't in a mood to joke, because outside the rhymes he found so disgusting were echoing:

On mountain, on vale,
From here to Bombay,
All cheer and all hail
The first day of May.
Down with oppression,
Down sla-ver-ry,
Down with aggression—
Mankind be free!

The children's thin voices rose in the air, and Yehiel hurried to open the windows of the library so everyone would see he wasn't observing the holiday. One of the teachers shouted "Scandal and disgrace!" The red flags passed, and I went back to what I had come for.

"Yehiel," I said, "you remember the mosaic Brinker once found in his vineyard?"

"Yes."

"You photographed it then, right?"

"No."

"Come on, Yehiel, I need the picture," I said.

"What for?"

"I need it," I said. "What do you care what for?"

"I won't give the picture. Not to you, not to anybody."

"I won't take it away from you, I'll just make a copy of it."

"No."

"So, you make me a copy, if you don't trust me."

"No."

For a few minutes I strolled among the shelves and the books, and then, hidden behind the blue wall of the volumes of *Tarbut* and *Miklat*, I said, "And if I give you some last words you don't yet have in your collection, will you give it to me?"

A silence fell in the library. I emerged from the shelter of books, and saw the signs of internal struggle in the librarian's expression.

"What, for example, do you propose?" His dry tongue rustled in his mouth.

"For example," I said very very slowly, "Farewell, my friends! I am glad to have seen you again! Pray for me."

"I want real last words," Yehiel folded his arms on his chest; "not from books."

He immediately took the picture out of his desk drawer to stimulate me, and I gave him the real last words of Uncle Rafael Haim Levy, who dropped dead at the end of Yom Kippur, right after he poured three liters of over-fermented *pepitada* into his parched intestines: "Give me a plume, I want to write."

"Very interesting," gasped Yehiel; "Heinrich Heine himself said something similar." And he leafed rapidly through his albums, and showed me Heine's last words, "To write . . . Paper . . . Pencil . . ."

"My father has a lot more uncles like that," I said.

"Here, take it, and bring more words," he said and gave me the picture of the girl. "I've got other copies."

Leah and I began putting the mosaic together, and Father turned out to be an inexhaustible source. His garrulous relatives excited Yehiel Abramson both with their polished style and with the strange circumstances of their deaths. They all behaved like literary heroes. None of them managed to overcome the temptation to die without saying something important.

"Issachar Fijoto may he rest in peace, who was found floating in ripe old age in the bathhouse of Livorno with two salamanders on his belly, said, 'I want to put my pants on now.' But when they brought him his pants, he had already vomited worms and died."

"The physician Dr. Reuven Yakir Preciaducho died at the end of summer, when the poor soul strained himself blowing a Shofar. Blood spurted from his ears, and his last words weren't found until they took the Shofar and banged it on the table."

The writer Grazia Aguilar, "a sickly woman who died in the prime of life," quoted in her last breath a verse from the Book of Job: "Though he slay me, yet will I trust in him." I was also surprised when Father informed me that she was a "relative," and I was even more surprised to discover that he spoke the truth, for her last words were documented in the book *Women of Valor Among the Daughters of Our Nation.*

But one day, when Father was quoting the last words of an ancient uncle named Elijah Shaltiel—"Ministering angels, ministering angels . . ."— I remarked to him that two weeks earlier, he had attributed those very same words to one of his great-grandfathers, Simon Uziel of Saloniki.

Father, who was usually fanatic about his stories of the illustrious members of our family, smiled with surprising sincerity and declared, "What difference does it make who said and what he said? They're all dead anyway."

Yehiel wasn't upset at all when I confessed my father's sin to him. "So what?" he said. "He's not the first and he won't be the last. Every person can invent last words, and sometimes they invent correct last words." And he gave me *Heart of Darkness* to read, to see that Marlow—who told Kurtz's beloved, "The last word he pronounced was your name"—was the cruelest liar of us all.

And from here to other inventions, as you can see, was a short step.

Chapter 53

Silence. I photograph: Michael and Simon are playing outside. Simon is lying on his belly and Michael is walking on his back, massaging Simon's painful flesh with his heels. Simon moans with pleasure, and afterward, as much as his age and his limp permits, he jumps in the yard, and Michael tries to tread on his shadow. Whenever he succeeds, Simon bleats in torment and Michael shouts with laughter. Finally Simon picks him up with a sweep of his arm and carries him into the house. "That's it for today, come to your father."

There was a terrible heat wave the night Michael was conceived. My brother told me the air was so rarefied and inflamed it was hard to breathe. Birds fainted in their sleep and dropped off the branches of the mulberry tree. Bars of pink and gold took shape prematurely in the east, and looked like incandescent metal. For the first time in his life Jacob felt that the heat outside was greater than the heat inside the bakery, and in the morning, when he finished his work and the sun rose, it was even heavier. As usual, he took off his floury shoes on the porch, ate, shaved, and washed. And then, naked and firm, he snuck through the corridor to Leah's room and quietly opened the door.

Duduch, with her sharp senses of a wet nurse, immediately understood that Leah had conceived. Father was too engrossed in himself to pick up signs outside his skin. And Romi, who had never gone into Benjamin's room, didn't know a thing until her mother was in her sixth month and suddenly emerged naked in the corridor with her belly rounded like Mount Tabor, and her nipples enlarged and darkened by pregnancy, looking like the eyes of an owl.

"What happened to her?" The girl was stunned, and when her father told her, she was alarmed.

"I beg your pardon, my dear sir, but such things aren't done!" she flashed at him, and then asked what the child would be called.

"Michael," said Jacob; "after Grandfather."

"And if it's a girl?"

"I don't have girls," said Jacob.

"Sometimes you're really terrific, Dad," said Romi.

Every day at dusk Jacob lay on the floor next to his wife's bed. He would stretch out on his back and run his eyes over the room. The sun declined, its last rays penetrated through the slits in the shutter and played delusions of gold on Leah's hair. Outside, the sharp shrieks of jerboas in quest of love and prey were heard. Jacob's hand enjoyed the coolness of floor tiles in a closed room. Sometimes, he'd raise the sheet, look and touch. A great yearning awoke in him, he wrote me, to see her internal organs. I smiled to myself. Vladimir Nabokov and Thomas Ute and Thomas Mann had already written those things: "My only grudge against nature was that I could not turn my Lolita inside out and apply voracious lips to her young matrix, her unknown heart, her nacreous liver, the sea-grapes of her lungs, her comely twin kidneys." And even if men don't admit it, they were right. And Jacob put his ear to the slopes of her belly as if he were listening to a big conch. A smile rose on his face. Breakers of distant water were heard, the fizz of waves. The tiny prisoner was toiling to sever his bonds, wanting to break out.

In those days I had a gigantic Pravoslav lover from the Ukrainian community of Pennsylvania. I suspected her of using me to test the vigilance of her husband and her god. Mutual relations of supervision, surveillance, and jealousy arose between the three of them, and she forced me to cover up with thick blankets even in summer. The Western Union man knocked on my door just as my lover was closing the shutters, turning out the light, grabbing my hands, and asking them, "Who wants to take a walk in the dark?"

I wrapped a towel around my body and went to the door. My friendly savior handed me the telegram and I went into the kitchen.

"I had a son," it said in Latin letters and Hebrew words. "NOLAD LI BEN."

I didn't go to Michael's circumcision, just as I hadn't gone to Mother's funeral. I went to the boardwalk of Cape May, sat on my regular bench facing the ocean, and followed what was going on. "Meditation and water are wedded forever," said Melville; and from my distant crow's nest, my look vaulting over ten thousand kilometers, I saw Simon raking the yard for the guests and Jacob setting up tables. My brother scrubbed the worktables with boiling water, scoured them with the baker's ancient mixtures of ash, lemon, and myrtle, put them on wooden trestles, and spread white cloths on them. Enormous copper bowls were brought up from the cellar and rubbed with Orassa copper polish. Arthur Spinney's old set of dishes was taken out of the closet, and Tia Duduch plunged into the kitchen. Three days later I saw her emerging with a procession of covered trays, bearing dozens of varieties of tiny dishes, marvelous and wicked, for they can be neither described nor re-created, and as soon as they are eaten, as I know, their taste has already turned into a tormenting and yearned-for memory that will never return.

Melville was right, "meditation and water are wedded forever." From Jerusalem the bus chartered for the Levy family came early, with rejoicing and singing, like an enormous cage of canaries. The trip lasted a whole day since the driver had to stop twenty times to allow the old folks to stretch their bones, urinate and pray; to let the children throw up; and to enable candidates waiting along the road holding letters from Father to join. They got on the bus and the aunts' section in the back seats immediately bubbled over with gales of identification and conjecture.

The bus approached the village and stopped first at the cemetery. Here the musicians put down their violins and jolly little *Pandiras* drums. The old men and women adjusted the caps and veils on their heads, and went to Benjamin's grave to weep and take pride, and to Sarah's grave to make sure the black basalt tombstone was still in place. Most of them knew her only from the stories. They knew she had stolen Abraham from his mother's house, that she had a dozen brothers, and every one of them was like a *legnio de banio*—clumsy and stupid as that log to heat the hot water tank; that she beat the infants' rubbi so bad he went deaf in his right ear. They also knew she had a white raven who spoke a human language; that a Greek priest used to serenade her under her window and weep loudly; that she didn't eat meat "neverever"; that she disgraced the family, "and died young of cancer poor thing." Now they came to her tombstone, on hesitant tiptoe, huddled together and pushed one another like sheep, looked at the grave with relief and trepidation, but bent over politely and put stones on it according to custom.

Their women, small and beautiful, held lace hankies in their left hands. Their children, swarthy and disciplined, all parted their hair on the right side and all wore white shoes purchased in honor of the occasion. They brought Michael embroidered *kemizikas*, an elderly Yemenite circumciser, and big bundles of *tispishti* and honey cakes, which made Father so happy he immediately called Romi and whispered an order to hide it all under his bed, "so the Russkies won't eat the *Dolcuras*."

The Tartars came from the Galilee in a caravan of cattle trucks groaning under the load of their bodies. Embarrassed and pleasant they were. Their square teeth showed white when they smiled. Their eyebrows moved in the wind like husks of ripe stalks of wheat. They too had time to pass by the cemetery, to murmur over the tombstones, and to kick off their sister's grave the stones placed by the Levys, for they discerned at once that those weren't local stones, but amulets from the Pool of Shiloh, and even though they were tiny, they were heavy as blocks of lead. They brought along cool jars of horse milk and kefir, pieces of sourish cheese, and a gorgeous wooden cradle. One after another, they came to Jacob, hugged him vigorously, planted noisy trios of kisses on his cheeks, and nodded their big heads at all those assembled. With the studied caution of strong men, they shook the hands held out to them and patted frightened shoulders.

Fondly and curiously they surrounded old Duduch, who sat on a bench nursing Michael. But when they started whispering among themselves and pointing, Simon's face grew dark. Short and stocky, morose and heavy, he turned to the Tartars with a courteous sentence, especially formulated, "Stop that, this here isn't a show!"—and he nudged his mother to get up, and led her into the house.

Suddenly, in the middle of the circumciser's blessings, a silence fell among the guests, for Jacob put a box at the wall of the house, climbed up on it, and opened the wooden shutters of Leah's window. No one asked what it meant, but a whisper passed through the audience and a few of the women dabbed at their reddened eyelids. Everyone understood my brother's despair and hope—that the circumcised baby's shout would rise and go in through the open windows, wake the mother from her sleep, and bring her back to the living. After all, everybody knows that the sound of an infant weeping in pain is the most penetrating and rousing sound in the world. But the blessings were recited, the diaper was removed, the foreskin was cut, and an awful thing happened: the child's shout wasn't heard.

The ears that wanted to hear the cry of pain heard only the thin whistle of silence. The eyes that gaped to see the waking mother appear at the window closed and poured tears. All the faces became gloomy. Michael's refusal to raise his voice in weeping struck them a more mortal wound than they had thought. This was a mocking of tradition and a violation of custom, as if the child were announcing, "My lot will not be with you," as if he fled the common lot of torments.

Duduch was the only one who was happy. She didn't care whether the child wept or not. She took him back in her arms and nursed him until he was sated, drummed her fingers between his shoulders until he belched, and sang him her soft, wordless murmuring. She had nursed many children by now, but not one of them filled her with the soft sweet heaviness this child gave her. A magnet was concealed in his flesh, attracting and extracting from every person the good stored up in them—love and milk, a tear and a smile. In the evening, melting with pleasure, she brought him to Jacob's bedroom, laid him in the new crib, kissed his cheek, and left the room. Michael lay with his eyes wide open, didn't fall asleep and didn't cry. Finally, Jacob couldn't help picking up his son and putting him in his own bed, placing his ear on his belly, listening to the pitch of the pain that wasn't felt, and the two of them fell asleep together.

Chapter 54

Thus, like one of the routed deer in my father's desert stories, I was driven to my fate. Declining to look in front of me, refusing to learn a lesson, a Pharaoh of love, stupid and hardhearted. I am one of those people who identify the prophecy only after it has come to pass; and, like Elijah Salomo and Duke Anton, I couldn't interpret the warning signs. I remember telling Leah that the day we finished putting together the mosaic, Jacob would come back and take her away from me. But Leah told me, correctly, that I was an idiot, and anyway, she added, we would never get the mosaic together properly. And indeed, every time we thought we were done and we called Yehiel, he came and walked around the girl, that Alice Vrebohm of his love, and said she hadn't yet recovered her squint.

But one Saturday it happened—or perhaps better, "it fell out," soon you'll see why—and I was forced to understand.

That morning I gave Brinker a lesson, and afterward, as I walked on the road from his house to Leah's, a soft humming was heard beyond the horizon and a tiny plane appeared hovering in the skies over the village. Those were the final days of the war, and the Italian bombardment of Tel Aviv was still clearly remembered, but this plane spelled innocence and affection, and everybody came out to look at it and smile. It hovered a few minutes, vibrated gently, like a butterfly borne on the warm air, and finally dropped a black dot out of its belly which fell in one of the farms with a loud explosion, raised an enormous heap of clods, leaves, shards, and pears, and hollowed out a deep crater in the ground. The plane went off tranquilly, made a big circle, and this time changed its mind and plunged toward the center of the village like a deliberate, precisely aimed arrow.

People fled in all directions, protecting their heads with their hands, smitten and lying on the ground, but the plane, with the well-known indifference of aviators, twisted serenely, and slowly dropped to the field where it crashed and caught fire with a barely audible crack. By the time we got there, it was all devoured by fire; and shouts were coming from the cabin, "Antonella, Antonella, Antonella, Antonella."

The unfortunate pilot was burned and dying. A silk scarf on his neck became webs of ash, his leather cap was melted onto the bones of his skull, and his flying jacket was scorched like paper. People pulled him out of his cabin, and Yehiel Abramson rushed in, sat down next to him, took out his notebook and pencil, and filled four pages with the name "Antonella," which grew weaker, paler. At first the *T* grew blurred, then the *N*s melted, and a long *A* of pain was heard until the pilot gave up the ghost on the *L* of his beloved, a long, choked-off *L*, which would have filled Leah with endless pleasure if it were written on her back.

The fire died out, the sooty head fell silent. "He had the dreadful death," said Mother sadly, "of man angels."

English army people came, took the remains of the pilot and the plane, photographed, measured, asked questions, and went away. For a few more weeks the village people talked about the strange accident. Like the RAF experts, they didn't know Italian either. But I, the expert in languages, did. As he plunged into the village, the pilot said, he was blinded by the pain of longing for his beloved and lost control of the throttle and steering wheel of the plane. It was Jacob's old mirror that stirred to life and shot its bold light at him. I didn't tell anyone, certainly not Leah; and meanwhile the war ended, new pears were planted, and the pilot was forgotten. But sometimes I heard Mother whispering Antonella, over and over, with different emphases, as if she wanted to plumb the secret hidden in the consonants of that name bound up with so much love.

Joyous, pleasant days came. The librarian was afflicted with such a plague of collecting his ardor confounded the proficiency of his judgment, and Leah and I filled his albums with last words that had never been said by famous dead people who had never lived. Like the fisherman's greedy wife, Yehiel demanded to meet with Father and get his favors without intermediaries, but I told him that Father considered the last words as family heirlooms, that he bequeathed them only to me, and that Yehiel mustn't confess to Father that I was turning them over to strangers.

Wailing with laughter, falling into each other's arms, and rolling on the prickings of the mosaic, we made up the Argentinian poet born in Alexandria, Jose Ismail Niente, who said, "The road was so long and I strayed on it by myself"; Tshitra Griva, head of the pigeon breeders of Calcutta, who uttered the words: "Real death is preferable to death in life"; and the Swedish military commander Gustav Brison of Falun. On his blood spotted bed ("in the tuberculosis sanitorium," added Leah), the ("gray haired") general smiled, withdrew his ("hand") from under the ("starched") dress of the ("redheaded") nurse, and said ("in a feeble but clear") voice, "This is the easiest war of them all!" ("Before he closed his one eye forever.")

"Did he mean the war against the Poles, the war against death, or the war against love?" asked Yehiel.

"Aren't all wars the many faces of one war?" I answered solemnly, for by then I already knew the influence such nonsense had over him.

But time was a harder opponent than the librarian, and the inevitable day did come, and it was planned and carried out with an artist's hand. A sudden ("and splendid") spring day besieged the village with the brilliance of its temptations. Bees hummed ("diligently at their") flowers, gray old people, pale ("and scaly, sallied") forth from their winter shelters and stood warming themselves in the sun. Bedclothes lost their ("shame, and were") spread out on porches for all to behold.

"What a great sun," said Leah, pulled me by the hand out of the library, led me to the hills, and knocked me down on the lawn. "Come on, let's bring Yehiel some last words of an electrician," she laughed in my neck, "who wet the floor." But I told her it was a waste to bother. Yehiel had no use for the last sentences of simple people.

No one was there. Only the vacuous eyes of Skull Rock looked at us. Leah untied the laces on the low neckline of her embroidered blouse, took it off, and lay down on her belly.

"Write on my back," she asked.

The elastic of her sleeves left red marks on her arms. Thin shudders of pleasure passed from her skin to my finger.

"You think I'm pretty?" she asked, her mouth buried in the grass.

"Yes," I wrote.

"Write 'No,'" she laughed; "the N is nicer."

We lay in the shadow of the rock. Leah took a little mirror out of her purse, leaned her chin on her clasped hands and examined her reflection. Not with an expression of coquettishness, but of melancholy and suspicion.

"You really think I'm pretty?"

That day was green and blue. Anemones, ranunculae, and poppies mottled it with red dots, chrysanthemums and mustard plants with yellow ones.

"Yes," I said.

"Really pretty?"

"You're pretty," I told her; "the very most prettiest one in the world. The prettiest one I know."

"How many girls do you know?" smiled Leah. "How many girls have you seen, especially with that stubbornness of yours, of walking around without glasses."

She trembled and turned over onto her back.

"You see the dot I've got on my chin?"

"Yes."

"You see I've got two teeny little hairs growing out of it?"

"I see," I said.

"Will you pluck them for me? I'm scared to do it myself."

She rummaged around in her bag, gave me a tweezers and leaned the back of her neck on my thigh. Her eyes closed in complete trust, her lips were open a bit, her nipples shrank in the light wind. Her breath, sweet and warm, flickered in front of my mouth as I put my face close to hers to see better. A ladybug walked on the slope of her neck without understanding the bliss that had fallen to its lot.

The two hairs were thin and fair, almost invisible, but their roots were very deep, and Leah moaned as I pulled them out, and pressed her fingers on my wrist.

"O, splendid and sterile Dolores, our lady of pain," I murmured in her ear.

"Stop that!"

I couldn't resist then, and I certainly can't resist now: "By necessity, by proclivity and by delight—we all quote," I quoted.

The sun was going down and a chill permeated the air. Only Chenou Apari and I knew how much the sun ruled all of Leah's behavior. Cold rainy days dulled her senses, washed out her skin, depressed her spirit. "Come on, let's play," she shook, "that I'm straying in the forest and you show me where the strawberries grow under the snow."

Her cheek slid on my shoulder, her hair concealed her face and filled the hollow of my neck, her chest breathed on my arm.

"Come on, let's go back," she said.

She leaned on me as she put on her shoes, and put her hand in my back pocket, "to get warmed up," she said.

Slowly and surely, with eyes closed, I put together the puzzle of the memory of that day. Slowly, we came back to the village. Chrysanthemums spread their bad smell. Black dots of storks glided in the air. A bee-eater caught a wasp on the fly. His beak struck. That night Jacob returned home and took Leah away from me.

Chapter 55

The burner roared. Father and Itsik Edelman were braiding dough. Mother, leaning over into the bowl of the kneading machine, was cleaning the partitions with long, powerful movements of the spatula. It was a Thursday night, the hardest night of the week. Simon was tossing sacks to the sieve; Joshua Edelman, who was cutting dough into pieces, looked proudly at his son and said, "He who works fast is the first one to finish, he is."

And suddenly, like a big blade, the smell burst inside—the wild incense of trampled ragweed, the bitter-brittle reek of nocturnal animals, tragacanth calyxes of flowers that open in the dark. Smells we knew from the fields of the village, but that had never broken through the denseness of the bakery.

Father's fingers stopped their quick motion and became visible again, Edelman's scraper and Mother's spatula froze in midair. I clasped the measuring can of flour until a metallic crack was heard and its square shape acquired a waist.

"He's coming," said Mother, and only then did she grasp the meaning of her words and screamed, "The Jacob comes."

The bakery door opened and my brother came in. He looked like one of the peasants we always wanted to resemble. The hair on his arms, which was burned in the fire of the oven, had grown back again. New cracks embellished the palms of his hands. The sun, something the baker doesn't see much of, had turned his skin brown.

The damp vapor of the bakery steamed up his glasses, and he took them off and exposed different, clear eyes. Mother leaped on him and shook him. He buried his face in her neck, then broke loose, came and hugged me too; and I felt new muscles bulging in him and strong heavy bones surging up under his skin. He stroked Simon's bowed head and told him, "Hello, how are you?" Then he went to Father, hugged him in his arms and said, "Hello, Father, I'm back."

"You all saw: he came to me last," my father wrote me a few years later in one of his peskier letters; but that night he said, "There's no time now, we have to work," and he turned to the table.

"All of you go to bed," said Jacob, and looked at me. "The two of us will bake."

"You won't get done," said Father. "It's Thursday."

"We'll get done," said Jacob. "Simon will help us."

Father groaned, doffed his baker's hat, took the dirty apron off his waist, and hung it on the nail on the wall. His movements were slow. His expression was downcast. Mother held his elbow, either to support him or to lead him, and the two of them left.

"You too, pals," said Jacob to Itsik and his father. "Take the night off, on me."

Edelman said, "Come on, Itsik, we've got a new boss, we have," and they left, too.

Jacob sat down on the worktable, pinched off a strip of dough, chewed and sucked it absentmindedly, and then he got up and started braiding challahs at an increasingly rapid pace.

"So," he said, "you won't tell me anything?"

"Did you find what you were looking for?" I asked.

"What?"

"The woman who would smell the bread."

"I didn't," smiled Jacob. "But I did meet all the Tartar relatives, I worked in the fields, I slept with a woman."

"Who?" I was scared.

"One of our cousins who looked like your twin sister."

And after a full minute, when I was shocked, and didn't ask anything, he added teasingly, "And that isn't like anything else."

Outside, the air suddenly fell silent, stopped moving, and a faint thunder was heard in the distance—one of those spring storms that clears its throat before it begins speaking. The late spring rain beat a few impatient knocks on the tin awning of the entrance, struck with a thousand wet clappers on the solar tank, and continued with a soft dripping on the tiles. But this time I didn't need signs from outside. All I had to do was glance just once at Jacob to know that all of Mother's prophecies would be fulfilled.

I went outside. The rain fizzed and whispered when it struck the blazing cover of the chimney. A dress of silvery capering drops was hanging from the street lamp, and beyond it a nimble figure was seen, fleeing from the downpour and covering its head with its hands. I heard the rapid rush of the wings of its steps on the flooded road. All it once it turned toward the gate, crossed the yard, passed by me, and burst into the bakery.

I followed it in. My brother was standing in the pit in front of the oven door, his hands holding the pole of the baker's shovel, his face turned up, and Leah was standing above him. She moved restlessly, trembled from the rain and the cold. I felt Jacob's breathing become shallow and rapid; I sensed the song of his knees, the Adam's apple stuck in his throat. Then I learned that, after all is said and done, lovers have to search only under the lamp post, not in dark places where they lost whatever they lost.

"Get out of there." She held her hand out to him.

Only now, when I saw her through his eyes, did I realize how much Leah had changed, how beautiful she had grown in that year.

Jacob gave her his right hand. And she grabbed it and pulled him out of the pit, turned her back to him and said, "Take out my hairpin, Jacob, I'm all wet."

He had bought her the big mother-of-pearl pin three years before from Chenou Apari, and tossed it with a note onto her porch, and she hadn't worn it once until then. Now she undid her soaked braid, and it spread out in a slow fall with no beginning and no end, as if crawling with a thousand warm, wet lizards. Raindrops gleamed on her eyebrows and nose and lashes, and the heat of the oven steamed the pure smell of rain from her head.

She bowed her head, squeezed her abundant tresses and the water streamed out of them like a river. Leah had never cut her hair. When she was a baby, she was afraid of the banging sound of the scissors; when she was a child, she was afraid of the groping hands of the hairdresser; when she was an adolescent, she was afraid of the change; and by the time she was grown, her hair was longer than all the braids in the village, and cutting it seemed to her like lopping a limb off her body. She once told me that if she cut her hair, she would feel pain, and blood would flow from her cut hair.

With a bit of melodrama that seems quite ridiculous to me now, I thought it would be this picture we'd both see from now on whenever we closed our eyes. I still believed then that wounds of love never heal. I didn't yet know how fast and completely they're cured.

"You want tea with your bread?" Jacob asked her.

He set the big kettle on the Primus stove, put the little teapot on it, and gazed at Leah, who sat down and took off her shoes. Her socks had been white when she left home, but now the rain and mud had made brown spots flourish on them. I looked at her round heels, whose traces had once enchanted my brother, where the rainwater now traced pale and melancholy wrinkles of resignation.

Outside, it was raining harder. A mighty thunder crossed the sky, and my brother picked up the teapot and put it to Leah's nose to intoxicate her with the smell of the leaves. The corners of her mouth trembled. The gray chill, the metallic drizzle, the nether world of a winter that refuses to end—were the terror of her body and soul. Once again she spread the plenitude of her hair, shook it, ran her fingers through it, and then combed it slowly. Jacob leaned over and put a hand on the soles of her feet.

"You're freezing, Lalka." He straightened up. "I'll give you dry clothes."

He went to the tin locker, took out a bundle of laundered work clothes, and turned to me; and, with complete ease, so confident, so obvious, he said, "Leave now. She wants to get dressed."

I left.

Chapter 56

A few years later, on a pilgrimage to New Bedford, Walden Pond, and a few other holy sites, I took a ferry to Martha's Vineyard. On the deck I made friends with a tall, beautiful Irishwoman of about forty, and we had the conversation of redheaded Americans when they meet by chance on a trip. She was in charge of acquisitions in the Judaica Library of Harvard University and, she told me, knew perfect Hebrew. I was an expert in raising strawberries, a native of Prague, a young widower (a drunken locomotive engineer had gone off the tracks and crushed my wife against the wall), and the father of one-year-old twins.

"Hebrew," I said with an excitement designed to find out if there was more than one liar in the vicinity. "Isn't that a language written from right to left? Say something to me in Hebrew."

"What shall I say?" She was embarrassed.

"Whatever comes into your mind," I answered; "just so I can hear the sound of that language."

She stared at me with her bright eyes, and without batting an eyelash she described from right to left a picture in which we both appeared in an old armchair to be found, I understood, in the underground stacks of the library. The description was so direct and detailed I could barely maintain the tranquil Czech countenance widowed strawberry growers are blessed with. When we got off the ferry, I asked her if she would agree to share a room with me at Peter Coffin's Inn. She laughed, asked if I wasn't afraid to sleep with a man-eater, which sounded very promising in English, and my heart leaped. The next night, she smuggled me into the enormous stacks of the Lendner Library at Harvard. The smell of the old books and the proximity of their wisdom, she said, inflamed her flesh. I was familiar with many of them. A painful drawing of a bespectacled chicken sparkled on *The Complete Book of the Solution of Dreams* by Rafael Haim Levy.

"Say something else in Hebrew," I maintained a serene countenance.

The beautiful acquisitions librarian took down her hair, pushed me gently into the old armchair in the office of the stacks, and when she leaned over me, I suddenly imagined I understood why I had left the bakery, and I started telling her, until she got scared and asked me to stop shouting.

Later my wounds healed, my flesh subsided, time put a new skin on my heart. About ten years ago, when I turned forty-five, my editor's wife invited me to celebrate my birthday in New York. Her husband had gone off to some conference on the West Coast, and she didn't stop laughing. She was an amusing and very smart woman, and her thighs had a wonderful, inexplicable odor of saffron. I remember she said one sentence that seemed to have been stolen from Chenou Apari: "Egotists are the best lovers in the world."

"That's because we masturbate so much," I said to her.

She clasped my hand in her gloved one and suddenly brought it to her lips. We went to the big church on Fifth Avenue because I wanted to show her where the guards shot Thomas Tracy's tiger that escaped, "the tiger which is love." Then we had lunch at the Oyster Bar. I have a strange weakness for live oysters. I find their taste repulsive, but they have a hidden element that invigorates my body. We drank pear brandy, and, somewhat giddy, we climbed up from the catacombs of Grand Central Station, crossed Forty-Second Street, and ascended between the two stone lions of the Public Library to see the exhibit of "Travel Books of the Nineteenth

Century." From there we went to her house and, on the way, pressed between hundreds of small, square, hard Japanese tourists, I saw an old woman skating on the ice rink. Her eyes were shut and teeny bronze bells were tied to her fingertips. She twirled around, and right at that moment, that forgotten question was reborn in me, and with it, holding onto its heel, also the clear answer. I understood then why I left the bakery. I laughed aloud, and said "nothing special" to my companion, and again today I don't intend to say a single word of explanation about that old renunciation which, in any case, has nothing to do with the stories of the Duke, the Albanian servant, the breasts, and the jealous man. There is no need to explain every single thing. We shall give the reader "an opportunity of employing that wonderful sagacity, of which he is master, by filling up these vacant spaces of time with his own conjectures." And he has already had to answer harder questions on his own. Why did Orpheus look back? Why did Jacob weep? What was Chichikov plotting? Why didn't Cyrano reveal the secret of the love letters to his Roxanne? Why didn't I accompany my Mother on her final journey? Why did you refuse to meet me when I called you from the railroad station in your city?

I left the bakery, I went to the window and put on my glasses, but the pane was covered with drops outside and vapor inside, and Leah undressing and dressing looked like a pale fog that would never come into focus.

I walked around the bakery, and peeped inside through cracks in the boards that blocked the window, the one where Mother used to sell bread.

"What are you peeping at?" I heard behind me.

Blood flooded my head in a hot wave of wrath. Without saying a word, I turned around and kicked Simon hard. He was about fifteen then, broad-shouldered, stocky, and very strong. But I was taller, older, and angrier than him, and shock, insult, and disgust summoned all the strength of my muscles. He was knocked on his behind, his lame foot hit a rock and folded. Not a single groan escaped from his mouth when he got up and assaulted me. I kicked him again, and again he was repelled and fell. When he pounced on me the second time and tried to bite me, I grabbed his neck with both hands and dragged him to the mulberry tree. I banged his head on the tree until his body grew slack as a rag, and then I tied him to the trunk.

I went back to the window and peeped through the crack in the frame. Leah had already dressed. Lost in the wrinkled work clothes, she sat on the work boards of the rolling machine, and Jacob sliced a challah for her.

"Butter?" he asked.

"Yes," she said.

"Want a pickle?"

"No. I don't like pickles."

"Olives?"

"Yes. Please."

"You like strong tea, Lalka?"

I was nauseous.

"How much sugar?"

"One."

Her voice was tired and monotonous. As if her mouth and tongue understood her future before her brain and heart did.

My brother bent down and put the cup next to her, took two steps back, wiped his hands on his pants, and looked at her with tense expectation.

She immediately accepted his offering. And I, who had made her laugh all that year with a thousand nonsensical stories, who had described to her the empires of the sun and the lands of the moon, who had plucked out two painful hairs from her flesh, who had put together the stolen mosaic and false sentences with her, who had quoted lies to her that did exist and truths that didn't—I understood Jacob's superiority. I saw him smile to himself, then he immediately assumed a grave expression again, and went back to his work, because another batch of dough had risen, and when the dough rises, the whole world rises with it.

"Where are you?" he shouted. "Where did you disappear? Come and help."

Leah sat at the long table, plaited her hair in a braid as long as a leg and as thick as an arm, and wrapped it in two heavy twists around her skull. Then, with her finger, she started gathering the challah crumbs that had dropped from her lips. My father and mother also used to collect bread crumbs from the table. Father would take the crumb in two fingers and put it on the tip of his tongue, looking like a spoiled bird feeding itself. Mother would sweep them from the table in one palm to the other, and the last one shot the booty into her gaping mouth. But Leah absentmindedly pressed her fingertip to the crumb until it stuck there, mute and numb, then she put her finger into her mouth and sucked her plunder off it with rounded lips that made her look surprised, as if she didn't understand how such a small crumb could give her so much pleasure. Years later, when I wrote my second bread book, I devoted a whole, very amusing chapter to people who play with bread, like Doctor Thomas in William Auden, who molds his bread into little balls; Doctor B, Stefan Zweig's chess player, who shapes chess pieces of bread in his small cell; or Till Eulenspiegel's dough puppies and kittens. But mainly I wrote about collectors of bread crumbs from the table, each with his own style. I wrote about them with nostalgia, for I knew every one of them, and finally that nostalgia too, like all the rest of my yearnings, turned into a collection of fictions.

Jacob put the steaming basin of water on the bottom of the *gareh*, and I imagined Leah's finger pressing on my body. I imagined I was stuck to it and lifted with it wherever it went. I imagined an awful weakness attacked my knees, and I turned and left the bakery. I untied Simon from the tree, sent him to help Jacob, and spent the rest of that night on the toilet seat in the bathroom of the library, sitting and leafing through books.

"*Honi soit qui mal y pense,*" I read what was written on the margins of the drawing, "Shame to him who thinks ill of it." I was sure that Gauguin was mocking those who thought ill of the truth of the tale of Leda and Zeus, like Rilke in his poem. Not until a few years later, in New York, did attorney Edward Abramson, Yehiel's uncle, explain the boring truth to me: Gauguin's Leda was supposed to decorate a set of plates ordered by the royal court or some order of knights who used that as their device, but, he added, even though Gauguin was a banker, he was "graced with artistic integrity," and he found evidence for that: only in his painting does the swan take Leda as swans do, from behind.

At dawn I returned home. Jacob and Leah were no longer in the bakery; and Simon, morose and mute, was loading loaves of bread onto the carriage. I went to the Levitov home where Zivia was waiting for me on the porch.

"Lalka went out in the middle of the night and hasn't come back yet," she said anxiously. "I thought she was with you."

"She's all right," I said; and added, "I want to talk to you."

"About what?" she asked.

"About me," I said. "I want to go to America."

"America?" Zivia was amazed. "America, of all places?"

"I'm a big boy now," I told her; "Jacob came back. He'll take the bakery and Leah, and I don't have anything here anymore. I don't want to be like Simon in the house."

"Your parents know?"

"Not yet."

"And you need money to travel."

"I need money for the ship, and a little more for the first days, and I'll pay it all back to you."

266

"Your mother will kill you," said Zivia. "And me too."

"She'll just thank you."

"Wait here," said Zivia.

She went up to the second floor, came back a few minutes later, and counted the bills into my hand.

"Here," she said, and her voice was choked and tearful as on the day I came to their house for the first time. "It's not a loan and it's not a gift either. It's payment for work. There's something I want you to do there for me and then I can die in peace. Now, wait here a few minutes."

She sat down at her Singer and sewed me a money belt, and before I left she grabbed my hands and said, "I feel bad for you and Lalka."

I never saw Zivia again. After I came to America, I wrote to her from time to time about my searches and about attorney Abramson's help, and when I finally did find Leah's father, Zivia got up, sold her house, and went to join him. I talked to her on the phone a few times. She had a new voice, the sort women use to announce that they don't want to look back; and we never met again.

Thus, and for that reason, I went, and I don't want to go on with that. After all, you've already grasped my ability to be prolix, and if I refrain from this pleasure, you will surely understand that I have a good reason for it. I will tell you only that Mother didn't accompany me to the port, and Father said goodbye to me at home. I remember his hands trembling on my back and his voice in my neck. "You're leaving me alone with them." Simon's black look, Tia Duduch's weeping, fluttering like a fledgling on my breast bone, Mother's "Traitor!" swooping at me from the window—those were my escorts.

"Not for that did the grandfather Mikhail make the circumcision without the ropes or without the anesthesia," Mother kept grumbling; "and sold everything with flour mill and water and work horses, and apple trees, and go suffer and die in the Land of Israel. So after two short generations, his grandson go into Exile. And for what? For the Jacob's Leah."

Chapter 57

A few days before I sailed, I did something terrible. That morning, I went to Chenou Apari's beauty parlor with Mother. She went in and I went off to buy a notebook and pen because I was toying with the idea—which, ultimately, wasn't realized, of course—of keeping a travel journal. As I entered the beauty parlor, Chenou Apari shut her mouth, but her words were still hovering in the air.

"A human being sometimes waits twenty years for his love," I heard her saying, and I knew she was talking about me. "Love never dies. *Jamais! Chez nous à Paris* the love it has patience, like wine. You wait and wait and in the end its turn comes."

Chenou stretched her hand toward the sea, in the imagined direction of Paris. Thin salt lines of sweat were outlined under her sleeve. The women all sighed and turned one single, yearning, excited look to the west. Their eyes crossed the Mediterranean Sea in a rapid and imaginary flight, passed like pining spirits over the Greek islands, shuddered the calm of the shallow Adriatic bays, drilled tunnels in the Alps, and overflowed onto the plains of Champagne beyond them. Fare thee well, toil and labor. Get out of the flaming, aging, scorching East. Get thee gone, rags, dustpan, iron! There, beyond marvelous names—Dijon, Chablis, Fontainebleau—cloaked in the perfumed mists of the Seine, lay Paris—"capital of enchantment, Holy of Holies of its beloved mistresses." The Paris of Chenou Apari, whose trees drop their leaves even in spring so her poets won't find themselves at a loss for images. Whose women tap out music on the paving stones with their heels. Whose men leap over fragrant silk handkerchiefs strewn to guide them in the paths of love.

When we came back, Mother asked me to go with her to Brinker to bring him the pot of food; and he, beaming with happiness at her knock, opened the door and took her hand.

"Stars, stars, now there were also such . . . Four what and if you will and there stones and nothing 'cause so," he told her.

"What is he saying?" Mother asked me.

Brinker's eyes shone. His brow gleamed with a light I couldn't mistake.

"No bird and the girl also in five everything in grapes in five because of," he smiled with her hand in his.

"What is he saying?" Mother asked me again with clenched jaws.

And then it happened.

"He says he loves you, Mother," I said.

My voice was so feeble and choked that I heard myself through the space inside my mouth and the bones of my skull. "He says he has loved you from the day you came to the village. That before you came, his wife smelled good, and since then she has simply died for him. That he should have told you all this back then. He says that all those years his love hasn't calmed down for a minute, that that's what keeps him alive and that's also what will kill him; and every time he sees you, his mouth goes dry and his chest presses him right under his lungs like a child who sees a woman undressing."

Brinker's words gave me courage and strength.

"He says very simple things, Mother, that you think love is something complicated, but it's not. He's got a few things to tell you, together they are love: that he dreams of you when you're not here, that he loves everything you do and everything you say, that he thinks you're the most beautiful woman in the world, that he will never stop feeling these things, and that it's still not too late. And if there is something else he hasn't thought of, tell him now."

I inadvertently grabbed her other hand. "And he says that even though he suffers with that illness, he's not a fool. He works in the field, he understands everything you say, and you'll learn to understand what he says, like me, and anyway, you don't have to know a lot of words for this kind of love.

"And he pleads with you, Mother, neither one of you deserves the life you got. You've made enough mistakes in life and the time has come to fix it. Before, he didn't dare talk like this, but now he's not afraid anymore, because nobody understands him anyway. And he says you shouldn't listen to Chenou Apari, that she's a dummy, that you don't need to explain to anyone what love is. Everybody knows what love is until you ask them."

A big transparent tear collected in my Mother's left eye, rose, over-flowed, crept down until it disappeared in the opening of her collar. She looked at me, at Brinker, and back at me.

"Villain," she said to me; "and liar. You're such an evil! That you got from him, from your lying father the Abraham."

Her eyes narrowed, her voice deepened, her face flushed. She drew her hand out of Brinker's clasp and put it on my head. Heavy as a beam it was, and I shut my eyes underneath it and waited for what was to come.

"You won't have family of your own. You won't have wife of your own. You won't have child of your own. You won't have land of your own," I heard her saying.

She turned and went home, and I followed, stunned and bearing the train of her weeping.

"That was terrible," I told Leah. "She simply cursed me."

"Let her curse. Superstitions," said Leah; "and you're even worse than her. Isn't the man a complete fool. He talks like a fool and looks like a fool and goes to play with the children in the nursery school every morning. What do you want from your poor mother? You found somebody to play those games with?"

"They're not games," I said; "that's exactly what he said to her."

Leah grew furious. "Stop it! You forgot who you're talking to?"

"To Lalka," I said.

"Smart ass," she was angry. "What's got into you lately? What do you want from me?"

"I don't want anything from anybody anymore," I said.

The stevedores untied the ropes of the anchor and the *vaporetto* started shuddering, shook the boards of the deck, the railing, and the body of the passenger leaning on it. The heavy, dark body of the ship moved slowly. The strip of filthy water between it and the pier widened. Another complicated maneuver and the ship turned to the open sea. Only Jacob stood on the pier, and the red woolen thread Mother had tied to our wrists was stretched and quivering.

"Move, cow," in my heart, I urged on the ship; "move."

A long time after all the passengers withdrew to their cabins and the sun's glow was gone, I was still leaning on the railing of the deck in the gloom, for I still saw my brother standing on the pier, waving to me. Only when the air grew cool, and it became too dark and wet to bear, did I turn to go back to my cabin, and immediately bumped into one of the pipes, tripped, and hit the steel railing; I lost my way and stumbled onto the deck, and finally rolled down a frozen, echoing, metal staircase. I understood then that this time, too, I had forgotten to take my glasses.

Thus, blinded and cursed, dread choking the laughter that wanted to ascend from my belly, I sailed off and left my country, my love, and my family beyond the fog. Aside from a few errors, some more and some less amusing, it wasn't so awful. No gigantic stoker led me in the labyrinths of the ship, no woman was happy to see me in the cabin I entered by mistake. The experience of my nearsighted childhood came to my aid. The burned smell of crude oil of the engine room, the smell of cooking from the kitchen, the smell of the sea from the deck, the aftershave lotion and morning farts from the passengers' cabins—all easily directed me. I learned the way from my cabin to the dining room and the deck, and that was enough for me. After all, you don't see anything on the sea anyway. The wonderful words I knew—the blue immensity of the sea, the immensity of infinity—turned into monotonous, tedious waves, repeating themselves ad nauseam; and the line of the horizon, an object of yearning and infinity, was closer than the horizon on dry land. Sometimes I looked straight through a small hole I created between my fingertips—a game every myopic knows, a tiny optical miracle that sharpens vision but reduces the world to a pinhead and is merely the continuation of the ancient debate between the expert and the Renaissance man, between the reducers and the magnifiers, between Cyrano the goose and Casanova the cock. But most of the time I walked around in the bubble of my blindness. The water and the sky blended at a distance of a few handsbreadths from the end of my nose, and I was exempt from the well-known need of ship passengers to be moved by every shrieking seagull or the stupid capers of the dolphins.

We quickly left the Mediterranean Sea, that reeking internal courtyard, and anchored in Lisbon to load and unload cargo. Defended by the armor of prejudices, I didn't go ashore. I'm not ashamed of my prejudices because I have amassed them through reading and not through experience, and therefore I take pains not to test them in reality. From *The Assyrian*, I already knew all there is to know about Lisbon, about the melody of the *fado*, and about the girls called *Obrigado*. And in any event, I was worried I wouldn't be able to find my way back to the port; or that I would make a mistake and board another ship and find myself pursuing whales and gold. I pondered the ships whose decks I frequented by dint of my nearsightedness: the *Snark*, the *Nellie*, the *Lady Victoria*, the *Pequod*. The ships that sailed on paper seas, "all the ships whose names are like jewels flashing in the night of time": Tartarin's *Zouave*, the *Hispaniola* of *Treasure Island*, the *Forward* of Hatteras, or Hook's *Jolly Roger*. And Gargantua's *Swallow*? And the ship of the dead? And real ships? Magellan's *Trinidad*, the *Santa Maria*? Scott's *Terra Nova*? Darwin's *Beagle*? And which of the two *Endeavors*? Captain Cook's real one or the fictional picture in *Mystery Island*?

271

Impressed enough? Sometimes I overflow my banks, a trash can filled to the brim with superfluous facts.

For three days we were in Lisbon, and we "blindly plunged like fate into the lone Atlantic." One month and eight thousand kilometers later we cast anchor in the enormous, hot port of New Orleans.

I groped my way down the gangplank, was borne by the stream of people, and trod on the solid, singing ground of America. Foreseeing what was to come, my heart was pounding. I didn't yet know that a good and monotonous life awaited me here, bereft of victories and defeats, barren of excitement and anticipation. After all, you can see for yourself how much better I describe the first twenty years of my life than the thirty-five years that followed. "When any extraordinary scene presents itself, (as we trust will often be the case) we shall spare no pains nor paper to open it at large to our reader; but if whole years should pass without producing anything worthy his notice, we shall not be afraid of a chasm in our history." Once again Fielding, who else? I always loved his addressing "the reader," and now that I've got my own "reader," I won't miss the chance.

For hours, I wandered around the foreign, damp streets of the city, among the twisting smells of coffee and Persian lilac, breezes of gardenias and rum, among tempting voices of parrots and trombones, tambourines, and foghorns, until I took heart and asked one of the passersby where I would find an optician.

I went in. A sharp smell of tobacco hit my nose. A tiny metal bell betrayed my arrival. A man whose head was like a blurred fleecy cloud in the sky of the room. He sat me down on that chair, facing that white chart, fastened those metal frames on my nose, and asked me if I knew the English alphabet. I was about to pass out, and I only nodded weakly. He peered into my eyes, changed lenses, wrote down his results, and asked my name.

"Come back here tomorrow, Mr. Levy," he told me. White spots of eyes and teeth glittered in the black of his face. But I was afraid that if I left there, I wouldn't be able to find the place again the next day. In despair, I went out and sat on my suitcase in the doorway of his shop. When he saw me like that, he took pity on me and invited me back inside. Two hours later, he emerged from the room at the back, came to me and said, "Here are your glasses, young man."

I got up and stood facing him obediently. He put the glasses on my eyes with that marvelous movement of all opticians everywhere, and I saw before me an old Negro, bespectacled and balding, with white eyebrows and whiskers and a big graying moustache, blinking at me affectionately.

Strength was restored to my heart, life and hope to my flesh. I returned his smile.

"Never forget them again," he said to me sternly, as if we had known each other for many years. "Don't forget them and don't lose them. You're not a child anymore. I don't know where you came from, but this country won't stand that kind of indulgence."

A few years later, when I stood among a group of immigrants in a hall where we all recited the pledge of allegiance to the American flag, I remembered that sharp and painful moment when the old black optician granted me my new citizenship by putting his glasses on my eyes.

He examined the bridge of the glasses, heated and bent the temples until he was satisfied, and then he tied a black thin braid string, so I could hang them on my chest when I felt like taking them off.

"Will you have a friendly cup of coffee with me?" he asked, reversed the sign hanging on the door of his shop, and invited me to the small room at the back. To my great surprise, he made real coffee like Father's, in a little pot, boiled it, and took it off the fire, again and again.

He asked me where I came from, and when I told him I was born in Jerusalem, he got very excited. "A marvelous work and a wonder," he cried; "that a beautiful girl will subdue me . . . "

"And eat me grape by grape," I completed the sentence, and the two of us burst into the laughter of lost brothers finding each other after forty years. I told him that Rudyard Kipling's old sea-lion preceded Saroyan's educated shopkeeper with such sentences, and he tapped me on the shoulder. "You've smashed one of the idols in my collection," he smiled; "you deserve a free dinner." He sat me at the table, heated and served a strange and marvelously tasty concoction of rice, meat, and fish, spiced with a thick green vegetable he called okra, but in my opinion it was merely leek. Afterward, we drank very strong liqueur. I sneezed, the optician lit a cigar, and inhaling deeply, told me his forefathers were captured by slave traders in Mauritania; some of them were sent to the cotton plantations of Louisiana, and some were forced to convert to Islam and were sent to the Holy Land to guard the Dome of the Rock.

"And you," I asked, "are a Moslem?"

"No," laughed the man.

"Christian?"

"Neither Christian nor Jew am I," he answered me with absolute seriousness. "I am a pagan, like my fathers before me. Monotheism and optics don't live in peace with each other."

He laughed to himself again, and I looked at him attentively. I already knew Kashvala, Queequog and Bumpo, but I had never yet encountered a flesh-and-blood idol worshiper.

"When wrestling and when making love," he said suddenly.

"What?" I said in amazement.

The old optician smiled sadly. "A naïve and wonderful lad, you are," he sighed. "When wrestling and when making love, you take off your glasses. Then and only then. Understand? War and love go better when sight is short."

For a long time I listened to his words. An old man he was. His age, his isolation, his faith, and his occupation made him understand the world in his own way.

He told me about his wife who had been run over many years before right at the entrance to the New Orleans zoo. "All the parrots in the zoo screamed at the same moment, a truck driver panicked and turned his face, and my wife was crushed to the wall of the zoo."

He sighed. "How can you believe in one god when things like that happen? Only a big group of them could be responsible for such a commotion."

Afterward, his face beamed as he told me about his two sons, whom he had raised by himself. One was a teacher in a school for chefs, and his brother, a marine sergeant, had come back from Tarawa in the Pacific a few months before, healthy, hearty, and decorated. From the drawer, he pulled out four tiny infants' shoes. "These are the chef's, and these are the marine's."

And he went back to the issue of love and war, strode around the little room like a lion enclosed in the cage of his thoughts, declaring that taking off glasses is merely a declaration of intent. I had spent enough time with Yehiel Abramson and Isaac Brinker to identify the type. There was no doubt in my heart that the old optician devoted long hours to his teaching. His words were clear and orderly, and he recited them fluently.

Later he said simply, "Your turn to talk."

I told him about the one pair of glasses for me and Jacob and he clapped his hands in grief and amazement. I told him about the older sister we had had, and her terrible death in the earthquake in Jerusalem, and he rubbed his eyes. But when I took out of my suitcase the women I had torn out of Yehiel's albums the night before my trip—he got scared. He again pulled out the sharp small flashlight, and shone it in my eyes.

"Why didn't you tell me you've never slept with a woman?" he asked after a brief examination.

His breath smelled of nutmeg and mown grass. His fingers were gentle and soft as they spread my eyelids wide apart.

"Because it's the truth," I answered.

"One day, my lad," he whispered in a low, cracked voice, "you'll meet a woman who'll be able to talk with you about everything that interests you, and the first martini she makes you will be just as you like it, and she'll put rum and sugar in the coffee just as you like it, and you won't have to exchange the records she buys you. She'll know how to make you laugh, she'll write poems to you with a wet finger on your back; and inside her flesh, if you hold your breath at the right moment, you'll feel the handshake of the three angels. But, watch out! One day, the woman will smile, reach out, and take off your glasses, take them off and put them on the night table."

Now he raised his voice to a shout. "And at that moment, get up and run away! Don't turn back, don't stop to explain, and don't answer any questions. Get up and run away!"

Superbly equipped, I left his shop and went to the railroad station, boarded a second-class car of the Crescent, and rode to New York. Zivia Levitov's money belt rustled on my belly. In my coat pocket was Yehiel's letter to his uncle, the New York attorney Edward Abramson. On my nose were the eyeglasses of my new friend from New Orleans, and another pair he gave me as a gift were in my bag. His tasty food lined my intestines and his good lesson lined my heart. He was my first benefactor in America, and I will never forget his kindness. America passed before my eyes, greeting me warmly. This was a new country, tasty to the palate and clear to the eye, free of fog, of the sharp shards of memory, of all the screens of pain.

Chapter 58

I apparently closed my eyes, and perhaps also sank into a brief doze of the aging because when Romi leaned over me from behind and puffed on the back of my neck her "spunky hunky unky," I panicked for a moment.

"I won't do anything to you," she said. "Come on, I want to show you something."

She led me in the dark corridor to the kitchen door, hushed my mouth with two fragrant fingers, and whispered, "You think you know him? Well, take a look now and see."

My brother was sitting on a chair, bent forward. Michael, his eyes closed, half naked, his thin body gleaming in the gloom, stood between his father's knees. Only a wall lamp was lit, casting shadows from the two of them.

Jacob's hands moved over his son's shoulders, the curve of his hips, his belly and thighs; he took off the rest of Michael's clothes, and I was filled with the teasing embarrassment of peeping Toms. My brother put a small box on the table, and took out two doctor's flashlights. One of them, the one with the blinding mirror, he put on his brow, where it twinkled like a Cyclopean eye; and the other one, the small hand-held flashlight with a system of concentrating and magnifying lenses I had sent him a few years earlier not knowing what he wanted it for, he put on the table.

"This is his ceremony, every day," murmured Romi. "Ever since Michael didn't cry at his circumcision."

To see better, Jacob took off his glasses and put his head close to his son until his nose and lips were almost touching him. His nose moved like a plow over the boy's smooth skin to see if Michael was burned or pricked or cut. He combed the hair on the child's head with his fingertips, groped around on the little scalp, and examined the cover of its bones, stroked the vault of the forehead, lit the tiny flashlight and peered into his ears and behind them, strummed his fingertips on the child's chin, and turned it up to examine the whites of his eyes.

"Maybe Grandfather's right," Romi whispered behind me. "Maybe Michael really is like that Elijah of yours." She said that, and I saw the journey of immortal protein molecules that sprayed into Duduch's body, infiltrated her flesh with love, and rose in the splendor of her breasts, poured out in her milk, and flowed into Michael's mouth and intestines; the feeling was very strong and the pain seemed like that secret writing whose splinters are deciphered in my flesh.

"Don't you dare!" My niece's hand and breath bound me to the spot, because my body was beginning to quiver as if it wanted to get up and burst inside.

Jacob held his son's lips between his finger and thumb, and rolled them back gently to reveal their insides. Michael opened his jaws wide and stuck out his tongue like someone who is accustomed to that, and Jacob stuck a little dentists' mirror inside, lit the depth of his mouth with his flashlight, looked for swelling in the gums, white in the throat, a hole in the molars, a bite in the tongue. Then he took hold of the little hands, turned them over and searched for scratches and pricks.

"Tell me again how you got that finger cut off," Michael caressed Jacob's hand.

"You fell down," Jacob stated; "your hand is skinned."

"I was running," answered Michael.

"Somebody was chasing you?"

"No, I was just running."

"And where was Simon?"

"Behind me, and he picked me up right away."

"Be careful when you run."

My brother's two weak eyes and nine and a half fingers, whose skin had been refined to silk by years of kneading, combed the fair, delicate body, fluttered down its slopes, sought a wound, a bruise, a redness, a burn. He discovered a wooden sliver in the pad of the index finger, extracted it with his teeth and his tongue, and Michael laughed. "You're like a dog, Daddy." On the tiny wound, Jacob dabbed a bit of blue iodine, and Michael raised his hands to expose his armpits so his father could palpate the glands.

"Does that hurt?"

Jacob twirled him around and put his ear to Michael's back.

"What hurt?"

"When you cut off your finger, did that hurt?"

"Take a deep breath," said Jacob, and "cough" and "wait a minute," and he gathered his son in his arms, puffed on his neck until the two of them burst out laughing, and picked him up and put him on the kitchen table.

"It hurt a lot," he said; "the very most worst hurt in the world."

Carefully and quietly he caressed the skin, gently pressed the flesh, felt its texture and resonance, tapped the bones and limbs.

"Sometimes I can feel his pains, here, in my fingertips," he told me a few days later, when I could no longer contain my curiosity, and asked him to explain what he was doing. "When it all started, I learned only to observe and look for signs, but by now I feel the pain itself."

"Only Father's pains you don't feel," I told him.

"Do me a favor. Just stop driving me nuts with your theories."

Like most human beings, my brother Jacob also believes that all pain has to have a reason. Father's X-rays show that there is no defect in his vertebrae to cause such torments, that his intestines are sound, that his knees are old but healthy; and Jacob, who hangs onto old grudges, whose soul was disgusted with Father's complaints and tales, suspected that Father's pains were merely a direct continuation of the *shakikira de raki* of our childhood.

"It's not so simple," I told him; "not everyone has the strength for those things."

"Listen," the frost rose in Jacob's voice, "what are we talking about anyway? What strength? What pains? You haven't been here for thirty years, you didn't have to bear him, you didn't have to bear anything that happened to us here. So now you take care of your father, and I'll take care of my son, and leave me alone."

Hard and awful words, and we said them so calmly.

"She fell asleep even before Benjamin was killed," I told him. "You think I don't know all those things? Everything you did to her after you got married?"

"I don't have the strength for old accounts," he told me. "What do you want? To get the bakery now? To take Leah? You can take both of them. You can take everything. All of you can take it all. You and Romi and Father and Leah. Photograph me, pester me, leave me, sleep for me. I don't need anything more from you. Just leave me that child. He's mine."

I saw him bend over his son, examine his toes one by one, stroke the shins, concentrate anxiously on the ankle and the knee, which are liable to give trouble. Afterward, he drummed gently, with his fingertips, on the inside of the thigh, and Michael, familiar by now with his father's signals, spread his legs a bit, and Jacob gently moved aside the little testicles and peeped under them, then turned Michael over onto his belly and scanned his shoulders and back and between his buttocks and down his legs, to the delicate ligaments of his calves and the pads of his heels.

"Once he used to take his temperature every day," said Romi behind me, her voice thin rivulets at the back of my neck; "and I threatened to photograph that and send you the picture."

Michael was then about three years old. Stretched out on my brother's lap, his head down, his hands limp, and the little thermometer sticking out of the nakedness of his body, shining in the soft light that will never go out. I looked at that picture often because it had a magic that captured my heart, a magic whose source is not the grief on my brother's face, or the tranquility on Michael's face, but in the dull gleam of the mercury shaft.

"You don't have a temperature," Jacob picked up his son and stood him between his legs. "You're just fine," and he kissed Michael on the forehead and on the bridge of his nose and in the hollow of his neck, and the naked boy smiled with pleasure, put his hands on his father's shoulders, his head on his chest, and closed his eyes. They stayed like that a few minutes, and then Jacob put on his glasses and dressed his son.

"As you told me in the America," Romi said beyond my shoulder, adding a definite article to America and chuckling; "remember? When you explained to me when you take off your glasses?"

For a moment, weary and yearning, I heard my mother speaking, and exhausted, I leaned my head back. But Mother was dead now, and the grace of Romi's chest alarmed my neck, and I turned pale, recoiled, and got up.

Chapter 59

Jacob inherited the bakery, won Leah, stayed home. In the evening, he fell asleep in the arms of his wife, and when he got up at midnight to go to work he loved to see how she rolled over to his warm place and smiled in her sleep. In the bakery the bricks flamed with a deep even heat; the yeast fermented, swelled, and died; the dough rose; the loaves were shot into the oven. To this day he bakes his bread the way our father did, and in the very same oven, he only changed the steam boiler for an electric bellows. He refused to put the electrical carousel ovens into the bakery, and except for the old Kemper kneading machine, the only machines he used were the Fortuna, which cut big masses of dough into pieces, and the rolling machine whose big drums shaped the snakes for braiding challahs.

Jacob and Leah's married life filled Mother with admiration. She told Chenou Apari how he combed her hair, how he coaxed Duduch to make her masapan, how he smiled when she smiled, and moved his lips when she spoke. "Now there's the love in house," she said; "the Jacob rocks the Leah in his arms like baby."

"You don't do that," hollered Chenou. "A woman is not God. One never gives her all there is, one does not show her everything that is inside. One must keep a small savings on the side."

Mother was stunned and offended. In her eyes, Chenou Apari was not only a connoisseur, but also a guide, and sober talk of that sort seemed like treason to her.

"Ooh . . . *Ma chérie*," Chenou noticed Mother's blush, and laughed. "Love she can be even worse than money. It flows between the fingers, it runs away, there is always a hole in the pocket of lovers, you always have to keep something for a rainy day. Not to give everything, all of it. To be *comme-çi comme-ça* selfish."

Her hand stroked Mother's shoulder. "You thought all the time that love is something of the heart? The heart it is only the beginning. Love needs sense, and that is something nobody finds in the heart and doesn't learn at the Sorbonne. *Chez nous à Paris*, we say, 'Everyone who loves gets a chance to return to Paradise.' So? Everybody tries, is there somebody who succeeded? For three thousand years now the very most wisest men are writing about love. So? Is there any progress to a solution?"

The first rain after his marriage filled Jacob with excitement. He set a big bowl under the gutter and collected rainwater to shampoo Leah's hair.

"Your son is a fool," Chenou Apari cooled Mother's emotion. "That's no good. You mustn't look back. Only criminals and cretins go back to the beginning."

Leah laughed when Jacob asked her to shampoo her hair in the rainwater, and went with him to the bakery. It was evening, and work hadn't yet started. The flour dust hovered in the air and the belly of the oven still hoarded the heat of the night. Jacob set the basin of water on the Primus stove, and when it heated, he said, "Bend over, Lalka," and he dipped her hair and washed it with laundry soap. The soft water foamed, and Jacob rinsed and soaped, and rinsed again, and as that smell rose, his excited movements of a lover became the experienced movements of a baker, and then the priestly gestures of the burnt offering, until Leah said, "Stop it, Jacob, I'm getting cold." They lay in the flour storeroom and the coarse weave of the sacks rubbed her shoulders and behind red, and then the two of them fell silent and embraced each other, and Leah, who felt Jacob's choppy breathing on her neck and was alarmed at the new chimneys he was to climb and the additional fingers he was to lose, trembled and smiled. "I love you, Jacob, you don't have to do all those things, just be with me. I'm glad we're together."

A few months later she got pregnant, and Jacob wrote me that he was the happiest man. "When I'm with her, I feel good on all sides," he wrote, and I laughed, because my brother was a clumsy and amusing writer. "I love Leah, I love the bakery, I love the child growing in her belly."

I asked Edward Abramson for a day off, I got up early and took a ferry to Sandy Hook to look eastward from there, because out of yearning, I lived Jacob's life; and out of jealousy I thought his thoughts; and out of love I contemplated his son who was to be born. Even back then I could understand how withered, thin, and blasted were the years to come for me in America.

My eyes crossed the ocean, whistled over the Rock of Gibraltar, traversed the Mediterranean, and landed with the precision of a stork returning to its chimney. I heard the roar of the burner, poor Brinker's operas played on the old hand-cranked gramophone, and above all that, the clapper of Benjamin's body, the humming of his mother's bell.

The bliss that spread over Jacob, blew in his throat, filled his body. Back then, no one yet knew, not even him, certainly not me, that Mother was ill with her first and last illness, the sickness whereof she died.

Chapter 60

At that time, I was living on Twenty-Third Street in Manhattan, in a tiny, very comfortable apartment, allocated to me by Attorney Edward Abramson in a building he owned, which also housed his office. My window looked out onto the chiseled side of a building that looked like a gigantic iron. I ate breakfast in a nearby Hispanic café. I loved the onion omelets they served there, the strange spices I had previously smelled among the red bindings of *Bug-Jargal*, the aromatic coffee, product of the commercial firm of Otto Seyfang of Wren Street. I was happy with the comforts of my new country, with the pleasure of working for Abramson, who read the letter I brought him from Yehiel, burst out laughing, but to this day I don't know why, and asked me what is "Wellerism."

"Why do you ask?" I inquired suspiciously.

"To determine your salary," he told me.

"Quite enough to get, sir, as the soldier said ven they ordered him three hundred and fifty lashes."

Edward Abramson's second laugh was an exact replica of the first. "Dickens," he declared solemnly, "is the alpha and the omega of writing." And he informed me that I had passed the test, and appointed me his personal secretary.

"What does a personal secretary do?" I asked.

"I can't tell you, sir, as Eve said to God when he asked her where she bought her clothes," answered the old man; "you're my first personal secretary."

He authorized me to "pour substance into the job," and warned me that, even though he was a "soft and patient" man, he also had limits of anger which were not to be crossed. He wouldn't hesitate to fire me, he declared, if I ever dared take a bookmark out of a book.

I coordinated the appointments of his medical check-ups, competed with him in contests of general knowledge, made his appointments at the Harvard Club, telephoned the chef of the Silver Palace where he dined once a week in a private room (Abramson loved Chinese food but abhorred ginger). I cut out newspaper items for him ("Cut out mainly acts of folly," he instructed me; "that's how I keep my youth"). I conversed with him (he determined the subjects three days in advance of the conversation so I could prepare). In a special notebook, I documented the course of his checkers, which he played on a board of ten by ten squares with an old Hasid who was brought from Brooklyn and returned there in my boss's polished old Duesenberg. I read him the letters he received, most of which were personal, detailed, and quite perplexing, written by women with "an imagination of silk and a memory of rock." I made bets with him and, when need be, telephoned his bookie, whom I privately called Mr. Jingle because of his abrupt, panting speech.

Now and then I was called to his home to bake bread for him because Abramson detested American bread. "Make me savoury meat such as I love," he said. And sometimes, his wife also participated in these feasts of fresh bread, butter, raw tuna chopped and peppered, black tea, and pickles. The pickles were also brought by the Duesenberg from Brooklyn, but weren't returned there.

Mrs. Abramson assessed me with her eyes. She lived in a separate house, on the other side of the park, and once every two weeks I called her to make their appointment, which was always held in the same suite in the Westbury on Madison Avenue, not far from my benefactor's house. "That's how you preserve love," he explained to me, even though I hadn't asked anything, and the two exchanged a smile. A tall young woman she was, with a broad grin and broad shoulders, and she dearly loved her man. On the inside of her left thigh, she had an infantile, fragrant, wonderful fold, with a little purple tattoo inside it of the Cyrillic letter ш, which I privately called the "S of lust." When I told her that the Cyrillus twins of Saloniki took it from the Hebrew, she laughed and told me that if I weren't a strange fellow, she would have been offended. She showed me her collection of dedications, called me Sylvester Bonnard, and sent me as a living gift among her lady friends, who were all married and brazen and possessed a common stock of preferences and witticisms. From the way they behaved with me, I soon discovered that they reported to one another on my progress. I was an oversized carrier pigeon for them, transmitting their notes in my flesh; but I wasn't fastidious. Generous and laughing they were, and they made me forget my sorrow, diluted my longings, taught me to see with my fingertips, to hear with my tailbone, and to taste with the hollow of my neck.

A year later, the War of Independence broke out in Israel. Yehiel joined the army and his old uncle almost went mad with anxiety. "He's too old!" he shouted. "Why do stupid things?" He ordered me to hang big maps of the Land of Israel on the wall of the reading room, and the two of us moved flags and arrows on them. And when Yehiel was killed, I held the spiral library ladder as the old uncle toiled up and marked a tiny black square on the map of Jerusalem around the monastery of San Simon.

Yehiel's death grieved me very much. I didn't weep, but my whole body suffered torments, and for a few weeks I found myself muttering a line from a poem Brinker loved to recite: "I am like a banner surrounded by distances," and every time I whispered it to myself, I felt a strange pain in my gullet, as if the words struck a hidden chord in my throat. I knew that Yehiel died immediately, and I wondered if he had succeeded in saying or thinking some last words. (Incidentally, about two years before, simpleton that I was, I sent him Gertrude Stein's last words. "What is the answer?" asked the author on her deathbed, and after a short laugh, she dismissed it with "In that case, what is the question?" I forgot that the last laugh was one of Yehiel's ideas, and Gertrude Stein, as he hastened to inform me in a letter which was all wrath poured out, anticipated him with "the wretched act of plagiarism of a dying writer.")

Abramson's wife, who clearly discerned my mourning, introduced me to a widow of about fifty. A simple calculation will tell you that she is now over eighty; but in my memory she is preserved in the amber of lust and yearning.

"You're such a good boy," she would say to me again and again; "you're the last gift life has given me."

I still recall her charming conversation, her lenient flesh, her acquiescent breasts. One day she told me that if I wanted to know the nature of my new country, I was obliged to memorize the sayings of Poor Richard. But I preferred Benjamin Franklin under his real name over the Edelmanesque peskiness which allows itself the refuge of pseudonyms, and his autobiography was the aperture through which I learned to know America. To this day, I know how to watch out for that kind of Philadelphia thought that hasn't yet disappeared from this country, that thought that wants to put in one basket musings on morality and science, calculations of military quartermasters, maxims about love, and analyses of the best way to clear horse manure off the city streets. To the credit of Benjamin Franklin and my lady friend, let it be said that they proved the justice of the praise women her age merit. He in his essay "Advice to a Young Man on Choosing a Mistress," and she in her own way. If you will allow me to quote myself, she charmed me with the flavor of Adam's fig tree, she stayed me with the flagons of Shulamith, and gave me pleasures that even Bathsheba didn't grant David. It was only the death of my mother that plucked me out of the dreary and comfortable Paradise arising around me.

Chapter 61

I f that had happened to her today, we might have been able to save her."
Romi and I were standing at the tombstone, a warm black basalt stone the Tartars excavated from the valley, cast molten copper letters in it, and transported it to the village cemetery. No, sorry to destroy your hopes, not in a cart drawn by women.

"An evil child is growing in my stomach," Mother said to Chenou Apari.

Impending death restored to her belly the forgotten heaviness of pregnancy, but no one paid attention to it. Father was blind with hatred. Jacob with love. Leah with youth. I was far away. Tia Duduch, I assume you have already noticed this yourself, is a dear woman deserving of pity, but let's admit the truth: she had never been anything but a fool, a quality she bequeathed to her son in abundance.

Only Chenou Apari understood, and Brinker too saw and knew and feared. But ever since I left, he had no translator or interpreter for his love. Over and over again he held Mother's hands, and talked and emitted his fragments of words; but to touch her body, to ask, to point—that he didn't dare do.

"Nothing would have saved her, Romi," I said. "If it had been cholera or a snake bite or a train accident, nothing would have happened to her, but what was built from her own body, from her own flesh, even she couldn't have overcome it."

"She and I and you, that's something else. Don't you think?"

"No," I said. "Maybe once, but not anymore."

"I love you, Uncle, even when you lie," said my niece and nudged my shoulder. "Let's play that I'm a lie-detector and you're a miserable criminal."

"Let's play that you're a table lamp and I'm laundry powder," I answered, and for one blind moment I pressed her hand in mine, and didn't say anything more to her about my mother's death. Not to her or to any other person. Even with Jacob I never talked about our mother's last days, even though a highly combustible mixture—a mixture of curiosity and guilt, with the terrible touch of relief—burned in my guts. So I won't even tell you more than what I told here. Not because the "Reader" can guess that by himself, but because the issue is separate and doesn't have anything to do with the love of Duke Anton or the habits of Doctor Burton or the stratagems of Shaltiel the matchmaker. It's enough for me to tell you that in the year between my trip and her death, I didn't get a single letter from her. It was Jacob, who wrote to me faithfully, who described to me how she collapsed in the yard. "I heard the noise and I thought the mulberry tree fell," he wrote. He didn't imagine either that anything could kill our mother, and certainly not so fast. A week went by and the telegram came. IMA META. BO HABAYTA—it said in Hebrew with freezing English letters which only augmented the dread: MOTHER DIED. COME HOME.

I'm writing all this to you on the porch, which is now in lieu of my regular bench on the boardwalk at the beach of Cape May. Jacob and Michael are in the kitchen, Father is lying down in his room, Mother is in her grave,

Tia Duduch is weeding her irrigation bowls in the yard, and Simon is tossing sacks of flour in the storeroom. I stretch my legs and and stretch the time, and see the old pickup truck arrive. It's Romi, returning from work in the city, taking the four steps that lead to me two at a time, saying, "Hi, Uncle," and going to drink "something cold in the kitchen."

"Let me go, for the day breaketh," this moment says to me. It wants me to write so it can pass.

"In our family," my father said to the doctor the day before yesterday, "there were people who knew all the secrets of time and the good way to old age." And he immediately listed for him heroes who practiced holding their breath, who specialized in honor-thy-father-and-mother and in decelerating their pulse, righteous men who "scattered bread crumbs for the winged creatures each month at the celebration of the new moon" and practiced great parsimony in ejecting their seed, "since every spermatozoon takes maybe a quarter of a second of life from its owner."

Jacob burst out in a big laugh when I told him of that last diagnosis. "According to that, you've got a big minus," he said to me; "and I'll live to be two hundred."

My father taught me the baker's clocks of rising, fermenting, and burning. His skies were the black night skies where the sundial doesn't move. His time is so soft and wild, cruel, and demanding obedience. "When the dough begins to rise, it's impossible to leave it," he kept repeating, and explained to us that time isn't a stream or an avalanche or a space, but a merciless succession of lost opportunities.

"All moments are right," he declared; "you just have to know for what." Then he fell again from the heights of his meditations to his pathetic everyday maxims. "He who asks you the time in the middle of life, don't give him your daughter for a wife." And when an idea rose in his heart, he immediately changed it into the detestable pennies of "the wisdom of Solomon," of "an important moral," or "the good way." Edelman, who also preferred the Solomon of Proverbs to the Solomon of Ecclesiastes, nodded happily and said, "He who asks you what time it is does not have money to buy a watch, does not."

Do we sit on the banks of time or are we borne on its flow? Is it in us or are we in it? Father's pain doctor grimaced when I asked him such questions about the nature of pain. "Forget it," he told me; "a human being in pain doesn't ask such questions. That's a luxury. A philosopher with a toothache stops asking 'how?' He only asks 'why?'"

And Father, who was an expert in both pain and offense, summed it up. "Pain offends everyone in a different way."

Few people came to Mother's funeral. Her brothers from the Galilee. A couple of people from the village. The women of the beauty parlor. A representative of the Bakers' Union who delivered a eulogy: "It is written: in the sweat of thy face shalt thou eat bread, and you, Mrs. Sarah Levy, thus you were. In the sweat of thy face you were an example to us all." Brinker didn't say a word, but his weeping was loud and eloquent and understood by everyone.

Tia Duduch made the *Chorbaika* of mourning. Chenou Apari wound a black velvet ribbon around her arm and Father didn't utter a sound. "He was surely thinking of all the bad things he still planned to do to her, and how she fixed him once again, the Russkie, and kicked the bucket on him early," Jacob wrote me, and added, "And I hope that, a few minutes before she died, she broke her habit of loving him."

The edges of the envelope were torn and pasted again, and on the back of the letter, two neat and numbered remarks were added:

"P.S. 1: Now everything will crumble. Everything will fall. Like dough that has been hurried with too much sugar. She held it all together. Tia Duduch can't do that, and Leah is still too young, and I'm not a woman.

"P.S. 2: And one more thing. I won't forgive you for not coming home for her funeral. You bastard. Only in body and face are you like her. In your soul you're just like him. You bastard. May you rot in hell."

Chapter 62

"I n the middle of the night I woke up with a stomach ache I didn't understand," Romi wrote me.

Like an embroidered cloth, the words covered a table, where my niece herself sat at one end, looking straight at me. I returned her gaze and put the photograph back in my shirt pocket. A summer storm hung in the air, gathered humidity and force. The seagulls soared over the shore. A hawk on a low murderous flight skimmed the surface of the water.

Shouts of the quartermasters and drivers penetrated from the open window. A bad smell of eucalyptus stood all around. Romi lay in bed a few minutes, her eyes open, angry. The pain wasn't like anything she had ever known, and therefore she couldn't describe it in words or compare it with other pains. She imagined hot, dull lead that flows by whispering, stumbles, recoils, and pierces its way through. For a moment she thought they were menstrual pains, wanting to prove to her that, despite her efforts, she was still a woman; but this was neither the day for them nor the regular intensity. She put both hands on her stomach and pressed, and the pain, a rat with its back to the wall, flashed its teeth, wriggled around and slipped away. All night long she groped, guessed, and raged, because she couldn't explain pain as a warning or ultimatum, but rather as a simple and base treason. She did without breakfast—"three bruised olives, one blob of cheese, and an exploded hardboiled egg"—got out of her bed and went to headquarters.

"I need a day off," she said, turned around immediately, ran outside, and threw up on the concrete path leading from the commander's office to the parade grounds. Only then, after her insides were cleaned out, did she understand what had happened to her. She went back to her room, set the cocked camera on one end of the table, leaned her head on the other end, looked straight at the flickering well of the lens, and photographed herself.

"This is me, Uncle," the words filled the table, rose and overflowed it. "See what I look like. Last night I was nineteen years, five months, and twenty-two days old. That was Benjamin's age the night he was killed, and I have no other explanation."

"I feel like I've crossed a border," she continued on the back of the photograph. "I passed him. As of today, I'm the big sister."

"Well, yes," my brother said to me when I remembered and told him about it; "there are things like that. There are worse things, too. All kinds of things happen."

He stopped the kneading machine, assaulted the dough and started kneading it with his hands. People don't know how difficult kneading is. The dough is as pliant and mocking as a girl, heavy and opaque as lead. Jacob kneaded it with the movements of other ancient professions—taming, potting, and massaging—put chunks on the table, folded the corners inside, punched, fastened, flushed, and flattened, and his face was contorted with the effort. His sweat, the snot from his nose, "his repressed tears, the warmth of his blood, the dream of his seed that he loved"—it was all blended in the dough. At Benjamin's funeral he didn't shed a single tear. A strange expression was spread over his forehead, and his hands groped at the walls of air at the sides of his body as if they wanted someone to support and be supported by him, and didn't find anyone. Leah had already fallen asleep in her son's room, and Father was standing near Duduch, and I was observing Romi, who was standing next to me and trembling, and the two lionesses of my own age who were hugging one another and crying and returning my glance, and after the *shiva*, in their big apartment in Tel Aviv, with the infinite longing of the flute of "The Dance of the Good Spirits" borne in the space of the room, they told me how they once returned from a weekend in Safed, and near Haifa, they picked up a blond sergeant who was hitchhiking; and when they asked him where he wanted to go, he answered, "To your place, girls," and fell asleep on the back seat.

"And that was your Benjamin," smiled one of them.

"And we took him home with us," said her companion.

"And he was such a good boy," sighed the first; "like he was sent to us, the last gift life gave us."

"Where did you know him?" asked the first.

"I didn't know him," I said; "I'm a friend of his father's. Many years ago I was with him in the Brigade."

Benjamin was born on a hot summer day, and so, said Jacob, he was "Leah's child." My brother held his son in his arms and wept as men do when their first child is born, tears I shall never weep, and only Mother could define it properly: the weeping that brings the tears out of the bones. The baby was big and beautiful, with good-nature and complacence reflected on his brow; and when he looked around and yawned his infant's yawn, it seemed to Jacob that he uttered a roar outside the range of the human ear.

The quarrels with Tia Duduch began right after the birth. One of the nurses in the maternity ward heard a chorus of screams from the nursery. She hurried there and discovered an old woman suckling Benjamin, and all the other infants were weeping in envy and supplication. Duduch was thrown out immediately, but later, when Benjamin was brought home, she began walking around, whimpering at the bedroom door, like a stray dog at a butcher shop. At midnight, when Jacob went to the bakery, Leah was left alone with the child, and the incessant rustle of the old aunt's feet filled her with dread. A smell of milk wafted in the air, and Benjamin held his hands out to the door, and turned his gaze there. "Get away, go to sleep!" Leah shouted from the room and, to be on the safe side, she took her son into her own bed.

Father was very glad to intervene in the commotion. He immediately mentioned a widow who lived in the courtyard of the Hazakiro Efraim Sa'adon, "the one who had a drop of boiling tin jump into his eye and poison his whole brain until the poor guy died." And that widow too, he warned Jacob and Leah, used to sleep with her little son in the same bed "and she'd dream dreams of widowhood that went into the baby like the cesspool of the Ismaelites would go into our water pits, and they made him grow a yellow beard on top and a black beard down below, and at night, he would kiss his mother like a grownup and stir her desires."

Leah was sure Jacob would keep his father and his aunt away from her, but her hope was disappointed. Jacob didn't say anything, and everybody went on doing what they did: Duduch continued to lay in wait for an opportunity, Father continued to impart his moral, and the widow abandoned her infant at the door of Rabbi Salvendi's library, "where Elijah of blessed memory used to sit and study," and she herself ran away to Beirut where hunger led her to livelihoods so indecent they earned her the nickname "*putana de tres puertas.*"

"Hee, hee, hee," Father laughed his Sholem-Aleichem laugh, and Leah clenched her eyelids and lips, and didn't answer.

"And the orphan," Father added, "grew up and became a great merchant, and once, when he went down by ship to the island of Malta on business, who did he see? His old mother dressed in rags, scavenging for food in the garbage at the port."

He waited a moment and then, a bit disappointed, asked himself the question that should have been asked by the "Listener," if he had been as aware and intelligent as the "Reader":

"How did he know that was his mother?"

Leah trembled and kept silent.

"Because she had six fingers on each hand, which is a bad sign," Father triumphantly shouted the answer to his question; "and it came to her because when she was in her mother's womb, her father went into the women's section of the Ashkenazi synagogue in the middle of Kol Nidre."

"Keep them both away from me, you hear?" Leah said to Jacob. "That aunt of yours and that father of yours."

"What's gotten into you?" asked Jacob. "Here's a woman bursting with a lot of milk, and our child is drinking from a bottle. What difference does it make if you give him to her?"

"It's because of her I dried up!" Leah shouted at him.

Benjamin grew and was weaned, but hostility was hoarded in Leah's body, and when she'd comb her hair, her comb sprayed blue sparks. Jacob looked at her and his knees felt like folding and kneeling. "That was a big mistake," he told me; "Chenou Apari was right, I didn't love her in the good way."

Her fingers dug strongly into her hair. "Come here, Benjamin," said her eyes beyond the screen of hair. But Jacob hugged his son with the soft ropes of his arms and said, "We men will just sit here and look."

"I want to Mother," Benjamin protested, at first with playful grumbling, then with resentment, and finally with the wrath of children, which increased until all at once it turned into the angry weeping of humiliation and helplessness, like the weeping of kidnapped bakers.

But Jacob didn't let go. "Shh . . . Shhh . . . Benjamiko," he said; "look how Mother combs her hair."

"I'm here, Benjamin, I'm here," said Leah. "What do you want from him, Jacob? Why are you holding him like that? Why do you call him that?"

"How?" said Jacob, and didn't open the clasp of his hands.

In the fields the squills bloomed, obstinately outlining estates whose owners were already dead; swallows screamed the tidings of autumn; and my brother's heart expanded and was apprehensive. In that season, he would go to the field and wait. He kicked the balls of dried thorns, which were easily uprooted from the earth and pushed in every wind; he crumbled clots of soil between his fingers, something farmers do, something he had acquired the year he spent in the Galilee. Like a Babylonian stargazer, he shaded his eyes with his hand, examined the soaring of the crows, analyzed the colors of the leaves, and waited for the first rain clouds. When he finally saw them, he was gripped by the restlessness that ferments in the flesh of other men only in the spring.

A few days later, the sky was thick with clouds. In a squall of activity, Jacob took buckets and bowls into the yard, and put them under the gutters. When they were filled with rainwater, he moved them into the house. Benjamin immediately ran to his mother and clung to her legs, overcome by a vague dread.

Groans of effort and the rustle of hair, the child's crying, and downpours of rain arose from the letter Leah sent me. One was heard next to the other, and they didn't blend with one another. The Primus turned blue and red under the big basin, Jacob spread large towels on the floor of the bakery and, with the tyranny of supplicants, he said, "Come, Lalka, come."

The tremor in his voice and in his amputated finger betrayed his excitement, and subjugated Leah's heart. He removed Benjamin from her, and forced her to kneel, until she bowed down on all fours over the bowl.

Leaning over her back, her hips between his spread calves, his knees stuck like spurs in her ribs, he shampooed her Ishtar braids in the soft, fragrant water. He didn't yet know then that rainwater would poison her body, that her flesh would grow chill, that the flash of her hair would be dimmed by the ashes of mourning. As winter grew deeper and Tammuz died—so her mood declined, too. Autumn birds screamed mockingly at her, the clouds wrapped her in their sadness, the bulbs of the squills implored her from the earth with the venomous hands of corpses. She was a woman of sun and summer. Right after the shampoo, winter struck her with blue lips, white throat, and red chilblains that shone on her palms. "Let's play," she wrote me then, "that I'm the princess in the tower and you decide who you are."

Benjamin stood on the side and whimpered as his father struggled with his mother, dipped her head in the water, and shampooed her hair. "But what happened? What happened?" I heard the shout. I went out of my room to the corridor, walked along the white line and saw him banging bitterly on her closed door. "Why? What did I do to you to deserve this?"

Chapter 63

Y ou don't believe me. You don't believe me either. "Why didn't you go to your mother's funeral?" A boring, stupid question, constantly repeated. And the rest of the questions, have I answered them? A reason for Duduch's bitter fate, have I given that? And did Father really poison the goose, as Jacob thinks? And have I formulated what is common to Castorp and Humbert, Nadia and Marfa? And who are the black Tartars? And how did Tshernikhovski sin against Miriam? And we don't even know who she is. Strange. People demand from a text what does not exist in the real world. They demand more logic and consistency from books than they do from life itself. See, about six months after Mother's death, an old green pickup truck appeared in the village, unloaded a big shipping crate next to the highway, and took off. The village children ran to the shipping crate, heard voices coming from it, and ran away. Afterward, they grew bold, approached it, and threw stones until one of the boards was shifted and a hand peeped out, tested the air, and pulled an arm out behind it, then a shoulder, then a woman. The children were terrified, fell silent, and looked at her from a distance as she sat down on the ground, sneezed, and warmed herself in the sun. Then the woman went back into the shipping crate, and came to the bakery at night.

You, you small and obstinate soul, Hans Brinker of ideas, will hasten to state that this event, whether fiction or fact, doesn't fit into the chronicle. And I reply that "for a little reptile of a critic to presume to find fault with any of its parts, without knowing the manner in which the whole is connected, and before he comes to the final catastrophe, is a most presumptuous absurdity." Jacob, who was standing in the pit in front of the maw of the oven, didn't see the guest, because he had his back to the door; but the sucking of the air in the chimney brought to him the sharp smell of her unknown body, which was drawn in and passed by him like the bitter breath of chrysanthemums. He turned around slowly, leaned on the walls of the pit, and saw a woman about his own age, looking downcast and weak, but very handsome, gazing at him. He was about to ask her what she wanted, but the woman's eyes left him, for they didn't find any use for him, passed over Itsik, Simon, and Father, and landed on Joshua Edelman, standing in his ridiculous underpants and cutting dough. The woman went to him, grabbed his hands with a gesture that was both possessive and imploring, and said something to him in Yiddish, in a tone that made you think they might have known each other all their lives. Then she spread out a strip of sparkling white cloth she had brought with her, and Edelman put a loaf of bread on it. The woman swathed the loaf in it and left, carrying it in both hands, pressed to her withered breast.

"What did she say to you?" asked Jacob.

"That's a woman from the Holocaust," said Edelman and adjusted his drooping testicles. "She said she smelled the bread she did and had to come."

"Next time ask permission when you give away our bread," said Jacob.

The name of the woman from the Holocaust was Hadassah Tedesco. Every night she came to the bakery, and Joshua, who started wearing work pants that week, gave her a loaf of bread, deducting the cost from his salary. Hadassah didn't eat the bread in the bakery, but wrapped it up in the white diaper, and carried it to the shipping crate. "I agree," she said to Joshua when he gave her the hundred seventy-second loaf of bread and asked for her hand; "but know that I'll give you only daughters."

Chapter 64

Slowly, the house adjusts to the death of love,
As the tree to the grief of falling leaves,
As the field to the corpses of dried out bushes.
A cloud will ride on the bitter wind
And the autumn on the shrieks of swallows.

(The original says "whistles of swallows," but I took that small liberty of liars and translators. Incidentally, my dear, just so you won't think I've stopped writing, I now amuse myself composing tales about the white line I drew for Father on the floor and its possible results; and two weeks ago, I finished a story about my brother and his little son. I started it on the porch and finished it in Romi's apartment in Tel Aviv, because Jacob, my suspicious and curious brother, would sneak in and peep over my shoulder.)

The wars of shampooing and suckling sapped Leah's strength and extinguished her eyes. The following years saw her obedient and despondent, dragging her feet to the basin of rainwater and dunking her head in it. Once she didn't take it out again until Jacob grew terrified and pulled her out to breathe. He dropped her on the floor furiously and went out to the yard. Benjamin rushed to her, dried her hair with towels, combed it with his fingers, tried to stand her up and drag her to the house, until the sound of his groans and sobs woke her and she crawled to the bedroom.

In the early hours of the night, when my brother lay behind his wife, hugged her wooden body, breathed entreaties into the rind of her neck, and listened to her recalcitrant breathing, he would hear his son's quiet footsteps sneaking up to the door of the room, stopping, lingering, going off, and coming back. And later on, when the noise of the burner was heard rising from the bakery, and the sour smell rose and came and said Jacob wouldn't leave the dough now, Benjamin came, climbed on the bed, crawled in, and lay behind his mother, clung to her, and fell asleep.

Light and wandering, time piled up for him, cursed the earth with the touch of its seeds. Leah got pregnant again, and when she gave birth to Roni, a big, gray-eyed baby, all covered with a thin down of red hair, Mother was no longer there to recall and to weep. Benjamin mangled his sister's name and called her "Romi," and Jacob got mad. "If you call Roni Romi, I'll call you Benjamim."

"You found somebody to fight with, a five-year-old child?" said Leah.

"It comes out Romi," claimed the five-year-old boy; "what can I do?" And within a month, everybody was calling her that.

Meanwhile, Tia Duduch reverted to her lurking to suckle. Her one eye, filled with hope and hunger, twinkled through the keyhole. Her feet shuffled again on the other side of the door. Big wet spots appeared again on the bodice of her black dress, and the smell of milk wafted again in the air.

The blood drained from Leah's face and the milk from her breasts. "I don't want her to look at the baby like that," she said to Jacob; "I don't want her to come near her. She wants to take her too as she took Benjamin."

"She didn't take Benjamin away from you; she doesn't want anything from you," said Jacob. "It's the smell of infants that does that to her, poor soul."

Leah did a lot of reading, thinking, sleeping; and sometimes she took a walk in the fields or went to the city. She didn't work in the bakery, and no one dared imagine her great revenge. Neither its force nor its suddenness. One morning, when Jacob had taken off his work shoes on the porch, he noticed the blurry figure of Benjamin sitting in a corner of the porch outside the frame of his glasses, playing with something that looked like a tremendous snake cadaver. Jacob panicked and jumped up, turned his glance and saw that the snake was Leah's braid. Even before his knees melted from the shock, he managed to get to his son and snatch the braid away from him so fast and hard the boy screamed in fear and pain, fell down, and rolled on the floor.

Leah heard him and ran to the porch. "Don't you dare touch him!"

Jacob approached her, terrified by the awful hatred that blossomed between them, by her challenging, shorn head; and Leah shifted her weight to one leg, put her left hand on her hip, and ran the fingers of her right hand through the spikes of her hair.

My brother's strength deserted him. He dropped the braid, descended from the porch, and stumbled to the bakery.

"Take it!" shouted Leah, swinging the braid over her head like a sling-shot. "Take my baby to suckle, take my hair to shampoo."

The braid flew in the air, slowly twisted and fell silently on the ground of the yard.

From now on things went on in a quiet, orderly, and terrifying fashion. Leah closed herself in her room, Jacob and Benjamin passed by one another with the dexterity of enraged tenants whose bodies don't touch, Tia Duduch ran the house and suckled to her heart's content. The day after the first suckling, the infant down fell off Romi's body, and when she was a year and a half old and was weaned, the gray of her eyes split, and turned yellow and blue.

That whole time, Father barricaded himself in his room, where he wrote letters. To me and to disappeared members of his family. Among the ornate American envelopes that regularly came to Abramson's office, my father's occasional letter looked like a pauper at a party of rich people. He didn't believe that the paste the government authorities put on the back of stamps would endure the hardships of the journey, and chose to use his own tasty, coarse baker's paste—flour mixed with water, molasses, and egg whites used to stick bakery labels on loaves of bread. "From the ants climb-ing up to the mailbox, I know that a letter came from Father," I wrote to Jacob. For good measure, my father pressed the stamp with the pad of his thumb for a few minutes so it would hold firmly to the envelope, leaving a clear fingerprint, a personal postmark more touching than the contents of his letter. Mother's death didn't diminish his hatred, and I quickly skipped most of the long paragraphs he devoted to her.

Rhythmic and measured, time paced. After Purim, the strides of spring began to be heard. The songs of the finches and the robins came on the tail of the retreating winter, the cracking of buds and earth were heard and "the Passover man" came. During the seven days of Passover, when the bakery shut down, and the bricks cooled, you could go into the oven, adjust and repair it.

Nobody knew the name and age of the Passover man. For the sixteen years I lived in the village, I had seen him every single year and nothing about him ever changed. In my opinion, he was seventy-five years old at birth, and never let go of a single minute of the time stored up in his body. He was a socialist with a beard and sidelocks, who used to introduce him-self with the words, "The first Yemenite who doesn't believe in God."

"So why do you have sidelocks?" asked Father.

"For beauty," laughed the Passover man.

The rabbinical supervisors also came for the holiday, conducted cere-monies of purification and bread burning, and every year they told us that stupid Midrash about the modesty of *matza*, which is thin and flat, as opposed to the arrogance of bread, "which puffs up and becomes haughty." Afterward, with threats and intimidation, they demanded holiday gifts, and when they finally took off, the Passover man climbed the mulberry tree, shouted the benediction on the journey after them with guttural, mocking felicitations, and took from the branches the bag of pitas he had brought with him, to sustain him during the week of Passover.

"You know why the Ashkenazim make holes in their *matzas*?" he asked. We all smiled. "Why?"

"Because their *matza* makes such a constipation with the holes, just imagine what would happen without them."

His laughter was almost inaudible, he just shook his whole body, like the laughter of Hasids from Brooklyn when they win at checkers.

Then he put on his work clothes—baggy Arab trousers, bare feet, and white shirt—sprayed the inside of the oven with water, and only after the whispering of the furious bricks fell silent did he open the flues of the chimney, hold in his teeth a small bucket with the tools and material he needed for his work, and crawl into the depths. There he sang and gathered up the drippings of bread that remained in the oven, filled cracks, tight-ened bricks that had come loose, and smoothed the bumps in the floor that damaged the baker's shovels.

For seven days he lay there, wrapped up and singing like a gigantic fetus. No one understood the words of his songs, but it was clear to every-one that they were love songs. Plaintive, yearning, and lucid, they were heard throughout the village, because the oven became an echo chamber for them, and since the worker didn't close the flues of the chimney, the songs rose up in it and Jacob's old mirror beamed them all around. Then Leah woke up, hugged Benjamin, and said, "Let's go for a walk."

Benjamin loved the Passover man. He thought it was his loud song of spring that restored his mother's joy and gaiety; and when the worker appeared at the gate of the yard, the boy immediately ran to greet him. But Leah was set in motion by the force of the hidden mechanism that puffed up and opened the eyes of the trees, put sap into the stems of the thistles, brought butterflies out of their cocoons, and delivered the irises and the anemones from the cold embrace of the ground.

Then Jacob packed a small basket of provisions and took his wife and son to the valleys between the mountains, where they rolled around in the meadows, and Leah laughed, chewed flowers, absorbed sun, and drank her fill of warmth. Romi didn't come along on these journeys, just as she never entered her mother's room in winter, and just as she doesn't enter there now either. She stayed at home with Tia Duduch, playing with a sliver of blue glass her aunt had given her.

Chapter 65

I could picture Leah walking, lying, running, eating, dressed, and naked. I saw her laughing, angry, smiling, and crying. I could write again on her flesh with my fingertips if I only had something to write. But in vain did I endeavor to imagine her with short hair. From the morning we first met to the day I left, she was always crowned with the tiara of her braid. After she cut her hair, I asked Jacob to send me a picture of her, but he didn't respond. "It's important to me," I begged, and Jacob ignored my letter. But a year later, he sent me a negative of a family picture, and I ran to give it to the nearby photography lab and to buy newspapers for my boss.

"Go out to the field and hunt me some venison," laughed Abramson whenever he saw me going down to the street.

The photography lab was in the next block, and its owner was a short, mustached Irishman, whose precise, efficient gestures stirred memories and affection in me. My attention was drawn to a wonderful picture of a white-haired man with a dark cloak and a mustache hanging on the wall of the shop. "This is the photographer Alfred Stieglitz, you've certainly heard of him," the shop owner said. "Ansel Adams photographed him."

His tone of voice wasn't foreign to me. With the same expression with which Yehiel would open albums of last words, he opened a photograph album and showed me granite cliffs, wooded valleys, and gleaming forests of poplars.

"The mountains lined up in a row before Ansel Adams's Hasselblad," he announced solemnly. "The forests combed their treetops, the smiles of the rivers glittered, the sea licked his feet and implored—take my picture."

I think that the quality that endears me to married women causes opticians, librarians, and photographers to invite me to their workrooms. The man asked me if I had ever watched the development of a photograph, and suggested I come to the lab with him.

"You might find it interesting," he said.

Awestruck and hypnotized, I stood above the tiny pool of chemicals, and to the great amazement of the photographer, I took off my glasses and bent over until my nose touched the developing fluid. Ever since I came home, Romi has invited me several times to her photography lab at the university to see her most recent successes in the hunt for her father. Her darkroom is too small to hold both of us and, when I lean over and peep as if enchanted into the developing tray, she stands very close behind me. Her breath caresses the back of my neck like warm teeth, her chest makes the flesh of my back tingle.

"Let's play," she gurgles, "that I'm an unfortunate Greek virgin, and you're a terrific old minotaur."

"Let's play," I answer, "that you're the Little Match Girl and I'm the spare tire of a bus."

"Shame on you, Uncle!? You dirty old man."

But back then, in the photography lab in New York, the blurry spots were added to the distant dots, and the shadows of fog touched one another, joined together, and created the enigma of the face of my family. An awful pain rolled into my eyes, a pain that was merely the memorial to its forgotten brothers, those that had attacked me when I saw Mother's hair floating in the camomile water, the maiden of the mosaic in Brinker's vineyard, Leah undressing through the fogged window of the bakery, Mother washing Jacob, all those sharp splinters of time that slice their way through my flesh.

My faraway, drowned family quivered in its tiny pool, was slowly formed and exposed, so different from the memory, at any rate, from my own memory, which always rises from the dead all at once, shot like a Leviathan from the depths, and is never afflicted with fogginess or gradualness or lack of focus; but, as we both know, only with unreliability.

"That's my father," I said to the owner of the lab.

The picture was taken in honor of the pouring of the new cement floor in the bakery. The seat of the carriage, whose ancient velvet was newly covered, was taken out of the house, and Father was seated on it. He insisted on putting a representative loaf of bread on his lap, and was the first to take shape on the photographic paper. Jacob and Leah were sitting on an empty bread box. By now her hair covered the back of her neck, but it was the first time I had seen her without her braid, and a sigh emerged from my mouth. Benjamin stood behind her. A sturdy serious boy, and there's nothing in his look that foretells his death. His forehead was broad and low, his hands were strong on his mother's shoulders, and his smooth, wheat-colored hair hid one of his eyes. His prominent cheekbones gleamed in the sun and two asymmetrical furrows descended from the sides of his nose to the corners of his mouth, giving him a wolfish and grownup mien, misleading in its ferociousness, which didn't suit his good nature and his eight years. Romi, who was then three, lay in her father's arms. Thin flour dropped from his clothes, turned her face white, and made her look like a clown.

Tia Duduch looked at me with her opaque eye. Simon's gaze couldn't free itself from the force of gravity of his eyes, which looked like two black holes in the paper. After Mother's death, Jacob was struck by a need to immortalize her, and stood the Patriarch's old carriage on the side. The loaf of bread our mother had painted on it was faded by now, and the silver molecules on the film easily captured the traces of their counterparts in the ancient crucifixes gleaming underneath it. Next to the carriage was the gray, immortal Fargo which, today—yellow, joyous, and repaired—is Romi's pickup truck, "my sweetie, the talk of Tel Aviv."

An enlarged picture of Mother, on a black mat in a glass frame, in half profile, smiling and with surprised neck muscles, stood between Father and Jacob. I remember when it was taken. Two years after we came to the village, Professor Fritzi brought a camera on one of his visits, and his brother took it and lay in wait for Mother behind the fence. When she passed by he called out her name, and when she turned around he pressed the button, and the two of them smiled. "Now I've got a copy of you," he told her in a low, steady voice when he brought us the picture. Her eyes turned to the side stare at me, wide apart, demanding, cursing, following me wherever I go.

It was Brinker who also took the new picture, but now it was a sick and different Brinker. He shouted, "One one two blue wool two skies!" and pressed, and everyone sighed, and shed their smiles, and moved with relief as if the cords that imprisoned them in one frame were cut. Then Jacob led Benjamin to the new floor, made him kneel down, pressed the palm of his hand hard into the wet concrete. A childish palm that already had a manly breadth, but still showed the mounds of baby fat. Next to his son's hand print, Jacob sank his own palm, a strong soft palm; years of stroking and kneading had imparted to its four and a half fingers the might of a vise, whitened the grooves of its fingernails, and smoothed its skin.

"Put the good hand in the cement," Benjamin told his father; "not that ugly one without the finger."

"That's a very good hand," said Jacob; "it can even braid challahs."

Beneath the hand prints in the cement, my brother scratched with a nail, "Jacob Levy and son Benjamin, Bakers, April 1955."

"Now, Benjamiko, that's your bakery too," he said; "you'll grow up and work here, like Father and Grandfather."

Mighty and indolent, time slipped by and we, dear fools, launched our boats on it. Here and there, wherever it encountered an obstacle, it created small swamps that authors call "memory" and "longing" and "hope," but the wise reader knows there's really nothing in them, and it's a waste to linger over them and describe them. In the years that passed, Benjamin's hand grew powerful until it was bigger and stronger than his father's hand. On the shelf of his room were the blue *General Encyclopedia* of Masada Publishers, *Above the Ruins* by Zvi Lieberman, *Yermi of the Paratroopers*, and a brochure on the battle of Mitla Pass with a picture of a soldier named Judah Kan-Dror; and when he was seventeen he had already begun to run in the fields, preparing to go into the army. Father grew old, took to making frequent visits to old-age homes "to get used to the smell of old people," and adapted himself to the proximity of the Angel of Death by going to strangers' funerals. Jacob was singed at the maw of the oven. Romi gave the blue glass back to Tia Duduch because she had found her brother's abandoned Kodak Retina and peeped at the world through it; and Leah went deeper into the gloom of her Hades, training for the death of her son.

When Benjamin was nineteen years, five months, and twenty-two days old, and was killed in the Jordan Valley, he didn't leave a thing behind. Only the promise of that hand was left there, imprinted in the floor. Every morning, Jacob puffs away the flour and dust that have collected in it, and Michael also approaches it sometimes, puts his own hand in it, his tender right wing, and smiles in wonder.

The owner of the lab drew my family out of the developing solution, and transferred it to the basin of fixative.

"Nice picture," he said; "nice family."

He wanted to hang it up to dry, but I pulled the dripping picture out of the basin, and buried my face in it.

"What are you doing? Let it dry!" cried the man.

"Make me two more copies," I said; "the same size. And send me the bill."

I took the wet, wrinkled picture, clasped it to my chest, pushed the door open, and left. At the corner of the street, I swept the newspapers from the stand, and didn't wait for change. I went up to my room and after looking my fill at the picture, I picked up the paper and saw the main headline, "The World Mourns. Albert Einstein Dies in Princeton Hospital."

Then I burst into tears. Albert Einstein did to me what neither my mother's curse and death, nor the distance, nor the ruins of longing, nor the heaps of repentance could do. With dripping, resisting eyes, I read that Einstein did indeed say some last words as he gave up the ghost, but the nurse on duty at his bed, one Alberta Roszel—I'll never forget her name, to her eternal disgrace—didn't understand his German.

Thus, in honor of the death of Albert Einstein and in memory of his lost last words, I wept for Leah's shorn hair, for the grief on my brother's face, for my mother, for the loaf of bread on my father's lap, for Yehiel who was spared a great heartbreak, and for the last words of Yehiel himself, who had prepared them for so long and in the end, they weren't only stolen from him, they weren't even spoken, and certainly not laughed, because the bullet that hit him shattered his jaw, ripped his tongue, and choked his throat with blood.

Chapter 66

The woman from the Holocaust filled herself with bread, absorbed sun, healed, blossomed into a beauty. Edelman and Itsik looked content and cared-for. Their clothes were clean and ironed, and their faces were happy and smiling.

Hadassah was younger than her husband by twenty-seven years and older than him from every other point of view. Father said Itsik wouldn't let a stepmother come between him and his father "because only a French mouse agrees to share love." But Father was wrong. Hadassah granted her only dowry, the shipping crate she had come in, to Itsik. "A young man needs a corner to be alone in," she said, and won her stepson's heart. She baked and sold pastry, and added income to her growing family.

Within four years, she gave birth to four daughters and then stopped having babies. "She closed the oven, she did," said Joshua. Her labor pains always began in the morning, and by the time Itsik ran to call for the pickup truck, the new baby was already washed and wrapped and given to Duduch, and at night Edelman brought cake and wine to the bakery and announced proudly, "The *shpritza* had another baby she did."

"How do you do that every year on the dot, Joshua?" asked Jacob.

"Look here, please," Joshua explained; "nine months is the pregnancy? Three months is rest for the belly? Together that's twelve months. Exactly enough for the old balls to fill up it is. What don't you understand?"

Hadassah's fertility made him the happiest of men. "She's got yeast in the *manoush*, she has," he said, and when Father asked him if he didn't also want a boy baby, he said, "He who has daughters, afterward come sons-in-law. But he who has sons, afterward come daughters-in-law."

Hadassah didn't nurse her daughters, because she wanted to get pregnant again immediately, so they were turned over to Tia Duduch. She nursed them in their house, in our house, in the yard, on the bench in the street, and in Chenou Apari's beauty parlor. Her missing eye contorted her expression, her black dress, and wrinkles of years and wonder made her look old before her time, but the breast illuminated the hairdresser's shop with its beauty, and some women told Chenou Apari they would leave the beauty parlor if Tia Duduch continued to nurse the babies there. "It's disgusting," one of them was enraged, "to see that old woman pushing a tit at the month-old baby, the one-year-old, and the two-year-old, one after the other."

Chenou went to the door, opened it wide, and said, "*S'il vous plaît*, Madame, yes, yes, you with your big mouth and your big ass, get out! You're disgusting yourself. *Chez nous à Paris*, you know who would do your *friseur? Comte Guillotine. C'est tout*. And now, *merci bye-bye avec au revoir*." And when the woman left, she exulted after her. "Better one tit like Duduch has than two rags like you've got."

As they emerged into the world, the Edelman daughters were ugly as rats. And only after they were a year old did they acquire that infantile sexuality, which was indeed coarse and surprising, but very appealing. They were four wonderful, healthy little girls, laughing and noisy, and in their own way, even handsome, despite their puffy lips and the blackish fluff that sprouted on their arms and on the slope of their cheeks.

As they grew, they visited our yard a lot. The littlest one was then two years old, and the biggest was five. When they knocked on the door, Simon shouted, "Who's there?" even though he knew; and the little girls shouted together, "Us, the dolls." And they said the word "dolls" with a lilt, like their brother Itsik. They would undress and spray each other with the garden hose, screaming and crawling in the irrigation bowls around the trees. They especially loved to climb our mulberry tree, and they never fell because they were gifted with great strength, a marvelous sense of balance, and prehensile toes they had preserved from infancy.

Simon, a man of thirty by the time the oldest one was born, treated them to "*Chinga*," as he continued to call chewing gum; and he even excavated the lead dolls he had made and buried years before, and gave the girls the tiny, heavy household idols as gifts. But when the girls wanted to hug him, he recoiled. From time to time, as he sat on his cot, silent, puffing on his cheap, stinking cigarettes, one of them would approach him, try to climb up his leg, and sit on his lap. Then Simon would get up and go off to another corner of the yard.

"Either he hates babies or he's afraid he'll infect them with something," Jacob wrote me; "maybe with his pains. He still tells me sometimes about those black dots that come into his body."

A dry odor wafted from Jacob's writing paper—a page torn out of a notebook that Benjamin hadn't filled, with thin staple holes in its spine. A few grains of flour dust that dropped off my brother's writing hand rose from his letter, irritated my eyes and made them tear. Once in an envelope I found a few crumbs of bread crust that dropped from his mouth. I gathered them up and put them in my mouth, and a terrible shock jolted my intestines. How, in truth, do pains move from person to person? By touch? Memory? Breath? Thought? And how did Doctor Reuven Yakir Preciaducho decant the blood of Zoga into the veins of the duke? And why did the English judge acquit Elijah Salomo of spying? And why did I give up? And is the love of black Tartars really different from the love of other human beings? Your questions make me laugh. And why a black panther? A blue flower? A white whale? Red hair? Sky-blue ass? I have always admired Saroyan for not bothering to explain the surprising kiss Thomas Tracy gave the mother of his beloved Laura. We give the Reader "an opportunity of employing that wonderful sagacity, of which he is master, by filling up these vacant spaces of time with his own conjectures."

A few months later, I got the first hint of how the rest of my life would turn out. Abramson pointed out to me that I had overlooked an interesting announcement in the *New York Times*, a piece on builders digging foundations not far from Battery Park who had discovered a few old glass bottles. These, it turned out, were two-hundred-fifty-year-old Dutch beer bottles.

"Just think about that story," Abramson said to me with a forced smile; "it has to interest you at least as much as it interests me, as the mouse who ate the strychnine said to the cat who was about to swallow him." A deep cough burst from his throat. He was very sick, and the two of us already sensed his end.

In the following days, I learned that archaeologists had rushed to the construction site and came up with cracked Delft soup bowls, rusty hoops of fishermen's buckets, a greenish copper door hinge. I remember chuckling to myself as I read. Why, Tia Duduch's laundry basin had wandered with the family for four hundred years and was still in use; and the lace work spread on Romi's bed, which Mother stole from Bulisa Levy the night she escaped from Jerusalem, was older than the Liberty Bell. But the Americans brandished their forefathers' old kitchen utensils as if they had discovered the lost vessels of the Temple.

Abramson laughed the dry laugh of old Ashkenazim competing in numerology in the bath house, and said, "My young friend, you and I don't need that, we've got enough. But what Americans long for most isn't money or power, but history. Sell them history, and you'll be a great success. Understand?"

I loved my old boss a lot. I knew he was about to die and that I would soon have to find myself a new house and new work. I understood that his advice wasn't just idle words, but a last will and testament. "What history to sell them?" he repeated my question in amazement. "Bread, you fool. What's more historical than bread? What's more ancient than bread?"

So I wrote about fleshy, rising dough, about the trap of the spreading smell at night, about the "good soft" hands of bakers who don't exist. Of course, I didn't forget the cliché about the baker who modeled women of dough for himself; nor did I overlook the well-known charms of the miller's daughter, whom I had never seen in my life except in writings. I didn't tell about the baker's lungs sick with flour dust, his broken back, his burned chest hair, or the cells of his body that go crazy night after night from loss of fluid. Nor did I tell about Edelman's enormous filthy work underpants or his hanging testicles. I concocted recipes, invented facts, made up the legend of bread—the most historic, comforting, romantic, and human of all foods.

I brought the first copy of my book to my benefactor's bed at Mount Sinai Hospital, but by then the doctors had connected Abramson to machines that puffed morphine and sugar and air into him, and drew urine, intelligence, and all his strength and evil out of him.

Three weeks later he died. I organized his funeral, consoled his wife, wrote a eulogy for him that was published in several Jewish newspapers; I took the money, the Parker Vacumatic, and the books he had left me, and once again set out on my way.

For a few weeks I headed south in New Jersey until I came to the town of Miriam on Cape May. The first time I walked on its famous boardwalk, which was destroyed in a tornado about twenty years later, a murderous bird plunged above me, with clear eyes and a clear belly. For a moment, it flew over a strip of water, and then pulled out its prey of fish. I identified it immediately. The osprey, the American fish hawk from Yehiel Abramson's picture album. Fascinated, I watched it rip the fish and eat it on the pillar of the jetty. Then the hawk soared, and its claws dipped and plowed the water, like a murderer washing his hands.

I rented a house there, put up book shelves, hung my beautiful women on the wall, and went on writing. "Memory is responsible for nearly all the three-volume novels," said Cecily to Miss Prism. Did Oscar Wilde know he was preceded by the Greeks in this diagnosis? Don't worry, my Mnemosyne, I won't bother you that much.

Chapter 67

I remember every detail of that morning. I had just cleaned and oiled the chain on the oven door, and the birds in the mulberry tree were screaming like lunatics."

"That morning"—that was how my brother called the morning he and Leah were informed of Benjamin's death. The chirping and shrieking burst from the mulberry tree and penetrated the bakery, and he assumed a jay or a snake had risen among the branches to rob eggs and nestlings. The distress in the birds' voices haunted him. And finally he grew enraged, grabbed a baker's shovel, and went outside.

Dozens of bulbuls, sparrows, and blackbirds hovered like an agitated cloud over the tree, were swallowed among the branches and ejected from them as if they were shot out. Jacob poked the baker's shovel into the foliage, rummaging around until Brinker's cat jumped down and fled from the yard. As he turned, wiped his forehead, and was about to go back to the bakery, he saw the officer, the doctor, and the clerk of the reconnaissance unit coming into the yard, and a terrible quiet reigned. In this country, this is a familiar ceremony. Its rules are firm, its words are known, its stage is prepared. Only its actors are chosen at random, from the audience.

Leah saw them through the window of the bakery. She was sitting at the little table doing accounts. Hadassah Edelman taught her to use an abacus with wooden beads, and her fingers could shift the black and brown balls with tremendous speed. Ready and practiced she was, and didn't need any more explanations. But Jacob, who had never rehearsed like her and Father, began walking backward, and even before he understood, he shouted "Benjamin!" fell down, crawled, clasped the legs of the startled officer, wailed and barked as if he were stricken with rabies.

Leah put down the abacus, and as if, at that moment, she accepted some decision or confirmation she had been waiting for all those years, she remembered to stick her pencil behind her ear before she shut her eyes. Ripples of pain spread in expanding circles and smoothed the tiny wrinkles in her face, shook her skin, and dissolved under the opening of her shirt and beyond her hairline. Her skull struck the table leg and banged like a pitcher on the concrete floor. There was no blood, but her forehead grew soft with the calm of fainting. The doctor sprinkled water, slapped, even pulled out a syringe. But Leah opened opaque, soft eyes, put a restraining hand on his arm, and said, "Leave me alone, I want to sleep."

She stood up, left the bakery, followed the path across the yard, climbed the four steps, and on the porch a new heaviness forced her down on all fours. Thus she crawled in the hall to Benjamin's room, went in, and got into his bed.

Outside, Simon shouted, "Get up, Jacob, get up from the ground!" His voice was childish and terrified. Father came out of his room, and clung to the wall of the bakery as if he was "it" in a game of hide-and-seek; and Tia Duduch was already on duty in the kitchen, rolling her sleeves up over her elbow, and washing the big pot to soak the beans for the *Chorbaika* of mourning.

"I saw it all. I didn't believe it. I was paralyzed." Romi got up from the sofa and went to the window, presented the straight strong back of a boy, the pure nape of a little girl, and the sturdy thighs of Diana. Monkey screams rose from the nearby Tel Aviv zoo and a motorcycle woke all the dozing residents of Ibn-Gabirol Street. "If I smoked, I would have a cigarette now," she said, turned around, and stared at me with her blue-yellow eyes. She put her hands on her hips with a familiar gesture. I knew she would imitate Mother now.

"He's not anymore," she recited; "he had the dreadful death."

At that time, I had a lover, an exhausting, tall married woman, who was toiling on her thesis: "Annals of Debate. Is symmetry a natural characteristic of the world or a value we attribute to it?" Her identification with the subject of her work turned our copulation into an indifferent, humorless, extremely exhausting issue. I remember that in my efforts at self-defense I once uttered a saying of Chenou Apari: "If a couple comes together, it's a sign that one of them had a bad orgasm," and she didn't laugh. A high forehead she had, and pale, sharp nipples which were sensitive to light and look and couldn't bear the touch of a hand; and her great advantage was that she gave me the feeling I was sleeping with myself; so I became as eager as an adolescent boy, angry, and ridiculous. I felt then like a concrete example of one of my father's more amazing similes: "Like a Turkish woman whose key to her pants fell into the sea."

She constantly amused me with the way she fell asleep. She would bump and grind with her behind toward my belly and thighs, as if she were mining herself a pit to spend the night in. She leaned her head back until the nape of her neck touched my nose, and then, in the space between waking and slumber, she emitted a few brief, jolly stupidities, a confused Brinkerish flux I easily understood. "Tomorrow we'll go on a trip, and even if he then says and the girls and they also grabbed him two days ago and me too," and she fell asleep.

I loved to feel how her sleeping flesh let go of my drooping flesh.

"Like a goldfish expiring in an abandoned net," I said to myself in Hebrew.

"What?" she murmured suddenly. "We were too and they didn't tell me."

"Nothing. It's a poem. Never mind, you don't know it, sleep now."

I put my hands under her ribs so the weight of her body would put my arm to sleep. "Mrs. Abramson's alarm clock," I called that system of waking up, because I learned it from her. The prickles of blood would wake me up right on time to send my married women to their homes and their husbands returning from their daily work.

The Western Union man rang the doorbell just as my adherent of symmetry lay supine on her back and spread her white arms back. "You kissed that one more than this one," she said in a tone of self-indulgence incomparably repulsive in the ears of one who has just ejaculated.

I got up, wound a big towel around my body, and went to the door. My friendly savior handed me the telegram. "Benjamin was killed," it said. As always the words are Hebrew words but the letters are English letters.

BINYAMIN NEHERAG.

I parted from her with a cruel kiss, in opposition to the basic assumptions of her thesis, only on the right breast; I bought Romi the printing machine she had asked for, I packed my suitcase, and I flew to Israel.

For a month I was at home, and Romi didn't say more than three consecutive sentences to me. About fifteen she was then, and I told Jacob that her shyness seemed strange to me, after nine years of correspondence.

"It's the age," Jacob told me; "and let me remind you that her brother has just been killed."

My amazement increased when I returned to America. Letters and pictures she had written and photographed when I was with them in Israel were waiting for me in the mailbox. Her father and I walking hand in hand in the yard, two terrible pictures of me, in one I'm bending over and peeping in the keyhole of Leah's room, and in the other it's hard to figure out if I'm asking forgiveness or doing Swedish exercises at Mother's grave. A picture of me and Father, drinking arak with ice in transparent tea glasses, eating cucumbers and playing dominoes on the porch.

"I want more pictures," I wrote her after I overcame my perplexity. "And here's a nice poem for you, to show you I'm not mad." And I attached the ancient lines Yehiel would recite and that kept rising from their drawer inside me ever since I saw her:

And a wildflower was Amnon,
The eye of his leaf dark blue;
And his sister Tamar—on his chest
Was an eye of yellow hue.

In the distance, the murmur of the ocean and the roar of the highway were heard, and I got up and closed the window. Cape May is a tongue of the continent and isn't named after the month, but after a person; and the town of Miriam is a sleepy, polished beach town, where some president once spent a short vacation, thus awarding it a position in history and on the local tourist map. I'm fond of it for its peaceful aspect and its serenity, its overgrown trees, its Victorian houses, the practical pleasantness of its inhabitants, and its name, which isn't one of those obscure, menacing, ancient names I left behind: Ashdod, Sodom, Eshtaol, Kishon, Tabor, Haifa. What is the interpretation of those crumbling mounds of consonants no one understands? Where did their meaning get lost? Are they remnants of ancient languages? Similes of a pain that will never evaporate?

My neighbors, to my great good luck and pleasure, aren't too pesky. I spend my time reading, in Hebrew and English; writing my column, which is published in several dozen gourmet magazines; enjoying rendezvous with women which aren't as frequent as you might think; watching the sea and the ospreys; and doing this writing, some of which gets to you and some of which I hide in my private journal, which I have already mentioned. Sometimes I allow myself a small private sin: I go to Baltimore to eat the best oysters on the East Coast, and then I go to the big Pratt Library to peep at the manuscripts and think about Yehiel.

In summer, the area fills up with vacationers. From time to time, warm rain falls, distant lightning is thrust into the ground. Then I go on a lecture tour my agent carefully organizes during the year. She's a young, vigorous woman, and one day, when I came to her office in Ocean City, she played with me the game of "This Little Piggie Went to Market," but in the Hungarian version, beginning with the sole of the foot and not the palm of the hand.

I lecture to gastronomic clubs, which flourish here like squills in the autumn; to students, who get academic credits for every subject in the world in this spoiled country; and mainly to groups of women in towns like my own. I have time, and since I don't like to fly, I do most of my travelling, even the longest trips, by train. At the beginning of the season, I get an envelope from the agent containing all the tickets, schedules, lines, stations, and telephone numbers I need. And at every station, always beyond the small red brick building, a woman is waiting for me in a blue station wagon under a big green maple tree. She drives me to my modest hotel, where I delve deeply into a Bible someone has bothered to leave for the benefit of the bored sinner, and stand naked at the door memorizing the instructions for escape in case of fire, until she comes in the evening to take me to the hall where I lecture. Some of them write me letters afterward and I answer them all. I assume that my nearsighted eyes, the eyes of a cub yearning for a nipple, and that ancient voluptuousness attributed for some reason to kneading and baking, are what endear me to those good women.

A few train conductors know me by now. The headwaiter in the dining car asks me how I am. In the bar car which rumbles along, I'm at my best. I start a shallow conversation about the ineffable romanticism of the train, including the inevitable story by Gabriele D'Annunzio about the slap on the face in a tunnel, successfully read the passengers' palms, politely ask about the book my neighbor, a drunken, affectionate old woman, is reading. "Did you know, Madame, that it was written in serial form, under the fictional name of 'Boz?'" I am a lodestone for passengers who want to pour their soul into a listening ear. I also tell them stories and open my heart to them. I haven't enjoyed anything so much since my conversations with Brinker. To them too I can reveal the truth, without any embellishments, for I will never meet them again. Did you know that, as a youth, I impregnated a girl in my homeland and was sent to my uncle, the American senator? I tell of my dead sister Laura, my grandfather, the coffee taster, my mother who was very short, almost a dwarf, and had a pastry shop, about my father a self-taught philosopher who devoted his whole life to researching the infinite and died when I was seven in a sanitorium for consumptives. He left behind 149 psalms he wrote on an ostrich egg, and a big redhead orphan boy (me, my dear lady, me).

Chapter 68

"This is where I read your letters."

"And Dad's?"

"Here," and I moved a little to the right on the bench.

Romi laughed.

I usually come here on foot, a half-hour walk from the house. But this time Romi drove me in my car. Her compassion was stirred. "My poor baby, nobody takes you out," she cried when I opened the garage door the day after she came. The old DeSoto, gleaming and well-kept, looked back at her and smiled with big chrome teeth.

"I'm mad about this car, you know it's as old as I am?" She parked it expertly, ran on the boardwalk, came back to me, jumped over the bench. Under her feet, the boards groaned. It's an old wooden boardwalk, set on pillars along the waterline, and the local authorities had bolted benches facing the sea to its boards. In a straight line they are arranged, anchored at intervals in the floor and the law, so that a person isn't disturbed and can ponder in the vicinity of other ponderers. You can look at the waves and close yourself in, or smile at your neighbor and get acquainted. Nobody knows the correct distance between one solitary soul and another better than the Americans.

We sat. One of Romi's legs was stretched out in front of her, the other was hugged to her chest. Dolores? Lalka? Our Lady of Pain? Or was it Claudia who sat like that?

When she was discharged from the army, I invited her to come visit me. I was then approaching my fiftieth birthday, contented, somewhat weary, steeped in that comfortable age prior to loss of rights and already exempt from obligations. Most of my failures and transgressions fell under the statute of limitations, and I had already succeeded in adopting the tolerance not many men are blessed with. Like Franklin's older mistress—smiling, experienced, generous—I left my own flesh alone, and even forgave it.

We pulled rock-hard, salty pretzels out of a rustling cellophane bag and looked straight at the ocean.

"Did you see me when you looked from here?"

"A dark, illimitable ocean, without bounds, without dimensions," I hummed to her with pleasure. How beautiful is that sentence that Yehiel would read to me in Doctor James Burton's tone as he recited in the bathtub, or perhaps after all, that was John Burton the governor?

I planned to come to New York the night before her arrival to buy both of us gifts in Argosy and Book Basket and to pick her up at the airport; but Romi asked me not to bother. She would spend the night with a girlfriend in Brooklyn and call me from there.

I spent a whole night of anxiety, a strange, irritating mixture of the dread of infants and the nightmares of fathers, until she called. She's here, with the sister of some guy who was with her in the army, somebody you don't know, Uncle. Everything's fine. Yes. First you go touring and then you come to uncles. Don't worry. I'm a big girl now.

"Those were the last words of plenty of girls in this country," I announced.

A motherly-childish authority in her voice kept me from ordering or pleading. "I've already got one father," she laughed; "and he worries enough for both of you."

And she disappeared. And I, old orphan that I am, walked around like a lunatic. "They don't tell me a thing," I mimicked old Forsyte on the phone, and the sister of some-guy-from-the-army said, "I don't need to tell you who Romi is, do I? Don't worry about her, she's gone travelling."

Eager, fast, and excited, my niece galloped over the continent, sending me COD arrows from all corners, time, and distance.

In the street in Oxford, she was amazed, "A Negro played the trombone just for me, and his cheeks were puffed out like two transparent balloons until you saw all the very most thinnest veins under his skin."

I found Oxford in Kansas, Maine, Connecticut, Ohio, Mississippi, Nebraska, New York, Wisconsin, and even New Jersey, and I left the atlas next to the telephone.

"I don't know what they call this place, but very ugly people live here. I sent you a picture of them 'cause I knew you wouldn't believe me."

Warm rain, "with drops this big," fell on her in Florida, where she worked as a skinner on a crocodile farm.

"Why don't you stop all that already, and come here?" I scolded her. "For thirty years I've been living in America, and I've never heard of people working in such disgusting things."

"What did you think, Uncle? That the crocodile skins himself? I'm big and strong and nothing disgusts me."

"The workers?" She laughed. "What about the workers? Really, Uncle, I stink so much from the carcasses that Dead Livy is a narcissus compared to me. Nobody even looks at me."

Conversation from Pottsville: "I'll be here a few days. A wonderful old man drove me in his pickup and invited me to his house."

"And you agreed?"

"Why not?"

"Why not?! I have to explain to you why you tell such people no? And in a place called Pottsville to boot. Where is it anyway? Dammit!"

"Why are you cursing, Uncle? After all, a wonderful old man. He's got radishes in the garden. Did you ever taste beer with radishes and butter? You should try it."

"How old, what do you mean by old?"

"Old, do I know? Forty, fifty, sixty, well, like you and Dad. He even told me I could be his own daughter."

"Yes?!" I screamed. "And you mean to tell me that that stupid, banal line, as worn out as a monk's prick, worked on you?"

"How do you talk, Unk?" she laughed. "You cesspool mouth, you know what a marvelous breakfast he made me?"

Unk doesn't answer.

"You want to talk to him? Here he is, looking at me and not under-standing a single word I say."

I slammed down the receiver.

Chapter 69

How do you get from place to place?"

"All kinds of ways."

"What does that mean, all kinds of ways?"

"Bus, train. . . . Ooh, now I've got a ride with a German tourist. A silly old fool on a motorcycle. He's terribly funny and it's cheaper to travel in twos."

"What do you mean, cheap? You sleep in the same room with him?"

"What's got into you lately? I don't think screwing interests him in the least. He's a little screwed up about that."

"Could you be more specific, Romi, my dear?"

She laughed. "Screwed up, you know . . . I mean, strange. *Von* some-body. From a family of dukes and barons and things."

"That's just what I needed to hear. A strange German with a motorcy-cle. How is he strange?"

"Do I know?. . . He says strange sentences. Sometimes he looks at me and asks, *Wollen Sie mit mir sterben, Romilein?* I hope I said that right."

"Have you gone absolutely crazy? What am I going to tell your father? That you're riding on a motorcycle with a German who asks you if you want to die with him?"

"Everything's fine, Uncle. I'm big and strong and I've got insurance. Don't worry."

Her voice grew weak, her laugh disappeared.

Like a late summer tempest, she whirled over the land, moved, tram-pled, and called at any hour and from anyplace. At five in the morning and two in the afternoon. From a railroad station or a gas station, from motels and cafés. Sometimes a strange laugh, other times a terrible shout—"Uncle, Uncle, Uncle!"—and a click, and afterward I didn't sleep for two days and three nights, until she got in touch again. "I shouted? When did I shout? Oh, that . . . Nothing happened." Somebody "tickled" her terribly and she couldn't talk.

"I'm getting along, don't worry. Yes, I'm eating. Even breakfast. Yes, all the nutrients."

"What are you living on?"

"Now? I'm working for a photographer."

"What side of the lens are you on?"

"It's not what you think," she laughed. "We photograph old couples, their first meeting."

"What?"

"They come, tell us the story, how they met and all that, and show us old pictures, and I write down all the details, and organize the same place for them, with the same clothes, and Philip photographs them as they sit there and cry. *Chez nous à Paris*, we love very most of all to recall love."

Philip. The nausea rose in my throat. In his high waisted, bell bottom pants, his little testicles well bundled up, and a string of beads around his neck.

"Where are you now?"

"Hey, how is this place called?" I heard her shouting in her Israeli English.

"I'm in a phone booth."

Her words swayed on the waves of the nearby laughter of a man. An uninvited Humbert awoke in me. Ah, ah, ah, said the little door.

"Who's with you, Romi? What's going on there?!"

Am I pleading? Threatening? No, I'm just an old fool.

She hung up on my shout. She had already adopted the disgusting American custom of cutting off a conversation without saying goodbye.

A week later, in the middle of the night, she shouted from the garden, "Open the door for me, Uncle! It's me," and she burst in, her braids filthy under an old Greek cap. "Could you pay the taxi? I haven't got any more money."

My heart stopped. Her long, strong arms around me. She brought a fellow with her who had *kibbutz* written all over his face. He limped a little, wore glasses, was three or four years older than her and two or three centimeters shorter. The two of them were clumsy as calves, hungry and smiling as dingoes. I made them a midnight snack of eggs and salad, I sat with them as they dredged up memories of their travels, I looked at them with my weary grandfather eyes as they chuckled with dripping mouth, nudged each other, exchanged slogans in the secret language of youth.

"And the one who took us in the old Studebaker?!"

"And the woman lawyer who wanted us to drive her car and tried to start with you?"

"Me? She tried to start with you."

"And that nut who tried to convert us to Islam in the street?"

"No, he was an Assyrian."

"There are only seventy thousand Assyrians left in the world," I tried to contribute; "and ten black Tartars."

"And that idiot policeman who believed us?"

"Listen, you guys," I said finally; "forgive me for interrupting the party for a moment, but at this hour, I'm usually sleeping. Come with me for a minute, Romi."

We went into my study. All at once the air grew thick.

"You sleep together, you and this fellow?"

"Why that tone? Uncle, Dad knows him. He's the one who told him about Benjamin." And a few seconds later, she added, "What happened? Why are you like this?"

"Romi," I said to her; "I'm a bachelor, I'm old, I'm tired, and I'm not used to real people. Where and how do you want to sleep?"

"Whatever and wherever suits you."

"What suits?" I suddenly started. "What am I? The Widow Douglas? Mrs. March? What do I care? From what you've already managed to do on this trip, you're a big girl now. Just tell me so I'll know how many sheets and blankets to take out, and I'll make up a couch."

"Together," she said. And then, "You're mad at me? Uncle?"

"We'll talk tomorrow," I told her; "I want to sleep."

I turned to leave the room and she, from behind, wound her arms around me, and put her neck on my shoulder. Shame to him who thinks ill of it. A remembered, marvelous force was amassed in her hands. "And stop bombarding me with names from books. They don't impress me a bit, and I know you're making them up."

"I didn't make them up."

"You haven't even said hello to me," her words grazed the nape of my neck.

"Hello," I grumbled.

"And I didn't say thank you for the ticket yet."

"I'm glad you're enjoying yourself, Romilein," I said, and went to the closet.

Chapter 70

"What finally happened to her goose?"

"He was old by then, and the neighbor's dog tore him to pieces, and my mother almost went mad with grief."

"Dad told me he flew away after she died, and didn't come back."

"Your dad's a romantic, Romi."

"I think so too." Then, "It's awfully beautiful here."

An enormous ocean, rolling, stretching. Once every few months it bursts onto the shore with a declaration of intent, and the rest of the days it's lazy and tranquil. So different from the Mediterranean Sea, that rustling yard of nations, where everybody knows everybody else, everybody bears a grudge against everybody else, everybody slanders everybody else. Neighbors' shouts, lines of laundry and memory are stretched from shore to shore there, old painted mermaids sink to the bottom exhausted. And here—an ocean, wide, spacious, coolness. The confident silence of giants.

There, a sea of gossipers, escaped prophets, lovers returning after a long separation. And here latent mighty arbitrariness, hinted in the movement of the water. "Nor does this—its amazing strength, at all tend to cripple the graceful flexion of its motions." Years ago, when I chose the regular bench I sit on, I came here at night, armed with a knife and a compass, and I scratched an arrow in the banister of the boardwalk. On a clear day, when the sun is at the right angle, when I take off my glasses and look in the exact direction, I can make out the flickering on the chimney of the bakery which no longer blinds anybody but me.

The sea is a leaden sea, gray and slumbering. Its smell brings tears. Its water is cold. Only once a year, on the afternoon of June twenty-first, the longest day of the year, I take a swim in it, a kind of ritual, and even that is only to compare the sensation with the memory of my last swim. Usually, I'm satisfied to sit idly on the bench, reading and observing my old obedient friend, the horizon, and I can send it far away or bring it close, at will. I delude it and it deludes me, and the sun, as it sets, warms the nape of my neck. Even after thirty years on the east coast, I'm still amazed that the sun doesn't set in the sea but rises from it. It is big, far away, red, and dripping.

"Let's play something," said Romi suddenly.

"Play?" I shook myself. "What?"

"Let's play that I'm Simon and you're a piece of candy."

That was the first time I heard her talk like that.

"Don't start with that," I told her.

"I'm a big girl now," she said; "I can, I want to, and I know."

"My dear Gwendolyn," I said to her; "you aren't big. When you are big, your father and I will let you know it."

"Let's play that I'm the kangaroo and you're the dingo."

"Who did you learn that from?" I was troubled. "Your mother?"

"Benjamin used to say things like that to his girlfriends, and I would peep and listen," she said. "Let's play that I'm a sea lion and you're a stubborn oyster."

This time I laughed. "Somebody started reading books? You bring the vinegar and I'll bring the pepper?"

Not far from here, the continent sticks a big tongue out into the ocean. Its length is a few kilometers of sand, an ornithology station, and ancient cannon emplacements at its end. We walked along it. A brother and his brother's daughter. A son and the memory of his mother. A father and his daughter who won't be born.

"Lying on the sea is the misshapen North Wind, he babbles into the water, telling many a wild story, tales of giants and droll derring-do." Crab shells are scattered on the beach, evidence of life that rotted inside them. The shore plants collect small knolls of sand against their bodies. Some fight the sand and the wind with the dance of a submissive, supple body; others are low, branching out on the ground, and grabbing it with their teeth. Some are stretched out, fleshy and hairy; others are tall and the blades of their leaves cut into your flesh. Gigantic albatrosses are also seen here. They glide in the air most of the days of their lives, and when they land they pace back and forth, looking anxious and disturbed about the firmness of the ground, which for them is deceitful and misleading.

"The ancient Egyptians invented both beer and bread," I told the ornithologists of the bird sanctuary who invited me for a drink. Surprise! On

318

the wall of their office I discovered a familiar face: the ornithologist Alexander Wilson, whose unexpected leaps from Yehiel's notebooks to the barns of my brain and from there to the office wall of the sanctuary jolted my whole body.

"Bury me where the birds sing," I told them his famous last words.

Simon Nathan and the Edelman Girls

(An Imaginary Story About Real People)

eople coming home late, night workers, and insomniacs know the bend in the coast road, where the smell of bread suddenly knocks on the car windows. Like a sleeping child, it embraces your neck, nestles against your heart, fills your stomach with longing. For a moment, your soul is stirred, but your fingers immediately clamp the steering wheel, your foot prods the accelerator, and the good smell of bread goes off and evaporates behind you. Few are the human beings who submit to the cry of their heart. Which of us hasn't forsaken the landscapes of his childhood like that, at the side of the road? His one love? His dreams and his destiny?

If the traveler gives in, gets out of his car, and follows the smell, he would enter the nearby village, go up the street, come to the yard with a small bakery, where he would see Jacob Levy, a diligent, sullen baker, standing downcast in the baker's pit, his hands grasping the baker's shovel.

Jacob's face is furrowed with lines, his eyes are narrowed, and his forehead is like parchment. *The Book of Bread* by Herbert Frank says that thirty years of baking bread is the equivalent of forty-three years of other work because of the enormous heat, the disturbance of sleeping schedules, and the balance of liquids. But Jacob Levy, a taciturn and singed man, doesn't need books to understand why he looks older than his age. Fifty-five years old he was, and already knew the loneliness that climbs into the windows of his body and grows in his heart, a loneliness that has both the normal seclusion of all bakers and the special withdrawal of his own life.

This story, beginning in Jacob's solitude, will end in a more horrible Jacob's solitude, and between the two ends, only a few more details will be presented. These, like all details, are likely to bring a smile or a yawn or a tear, but neither do they add nor do they detract. And it has already been said that a chisel and a tombstone are enough for the truly important details of life: one name and two dates. Time and person. His beginning and his end. The Italian archaeologist Ermette Pierotti, poet and architect, who explored the graves of Jerusalem, added, "And the bores will set up a memorial to them, with words of praise, apology, or explanation."

Jacob's father and mother had already gone to their reward, his first born son was killed in the army, and his wife lay in the bed of her dead son, lay in it and slept. Jacob would come to her, ask her to get up, shake her, caress her, pry her eyelids open by force, scold, and plead—in vain. Hypnos and Thanatos, the twins of sleep and death, rocked her in their arms, slowed her heart, blocked her eyes.

In the room the air stood still. The dust, which is wont to hover, settled. Gnats, which are wont to fly, were congealed where they stood. The light, which is always insolent and shameless—grew soft and recoiled.

Every evening, Jacob set the alarm clock and put it at the head of his wife's bed, but it ticked heavily as if someone took hold on his ankle, and when the moment came to ring—it didn't have the strength, and was choked and silent.

What? When he looked at his wife, Jacob wondered whether time is a river everything is swept up in. A swamp we sink in? Perhaps it is the stick of a relay race, passed in great haste from hand to hand? Or maybe it is the ancient chaos from which the world was created and to which we return?

A baker was Jacob, and knew well the ways of time and its processes, the cycles of birth, begetting, and death. There were days when he looked at his sleeping wife and saw her as in the days of her youth. There were days when he said to himself, How good it would be to find her dead. And most days he thought how he could beget a new child.

For a long time now he hadn't slept with her and sometimes he masturbated. After all, that too is a way—awkward, but surprising in its precision—of measuring time. Jacob was ashamed of the painful pleasure the masturbation of middle age gives those who transgress, and sometimes he wept, for the joy of youth and its potency had dissipated from the act, leaving only expertise, and when the spurts of his seed stopped throbbing, he felt like a woman after a miscarriage. When he was an adolescent, he recalled, his member had sung in his hand, twitched like a canary held in the palm; and now it seemed like an old family friend, forgiving and discreet.

One evening, with an awful shout, Jacob spilled his seed on his wife's blanket, and then went out and sat on the porch in the dark until the time came to go to the bakery, thinking again of how much he wanted a new son. Here let us say that this phenomenon of men yearning for offspring with all their might has been researched among the Black Chest Indians of the mountains of Mexico. They believe the child sprouts in the body of the man, and that the womb of the woman is merely a flower bed to grow it; and when the time comes to give birth, they eject the female friends of the woman, and three old male midwives release the baby from her body. The men also take charge of educating the sons, since women, as they learned, lose the lust for play as they mature. One way or another, when maternalism is roused in the heart of a man—Black Chest or not—there is nothing stronger. Anyone who has experienced it knows that's how things are, and anyone who hasn't is simply dull of ear. In any case, there is no need to expatiate on it here.

Once Jacob was filled with anger and courage, took off his clothes, and lay in his wife's bed. He placed his stomach up against her back, crept his left arm under her neck, and put his right over her loins. Years before, he would embrace her like that, kiss and pant over her shoulders, and the breath of his nose would caress the nape of her neck; and Leah, that's the name of Jacob's wife, smiled to herself then, purred and pushed her behind to him in pleasing increments of desire. A body of wells and tempests she had then, imbued with love. The reader knows very well, even if he isn't willing to admit it, that the ways of love of human beings are oppressingly similar; but Jacob and Leah had their own custom: with his fingertips, Jacob would drum light, secret signals on the inside of her thigh until Leah would laugh and spread her legs in a responsive, lazy sweetness, not known by any woman but her. But when he did it once again that day, and stroked and kneaded her flesh, and he was pained and embarrassed by accrued potency—Leah turned her head and said in the weak, clear voice bereaved women speak in their sleep, "You want another child to die? That's what you want?" The words that came out of her mouth had a bad smell, and Jacob fled from the room.

Thus five years passed. Every night Jacob baked one thousand five hundred loaves of bread, Leah lay in her son's bed, and no other events took place, except for the stubborn passing of time, and that happens whether we tell about it or not.

Five years passed and the yearning for a child swelled in Jacob's insides, and finally his body began shaking because it was filled to bursting. Now he knew that his will and his fate were bearing him toward a deed he had never done, and he was only waiting for a sign to tell him the day had arrived.

His wish was not disappointed. One night a heat wave rose from the south. It was so strong and terrible it confounded the ways of the world. Blackbirds went on singing even after darkness fell, the moon turned red, a wet, salty wind came from the desert. Jacob, facing his oven, had trouble breathing, and every movement of the baker's shovel seemed like digging in a blazing swamp. A baker he was, and such signs weren't alien to him. In the morning, after he sent off the bread, his body was beating inside him so much he did without his breakfast and went to refresh himself in the shower. For a long time he stood under the stream of water, washed and purified himself, shampooed his hair, shaved very very close, quietly passed through the corridor, and went into Leah's room.

The dense air of a lair prevailed here. Grief is wont to extract bodily sediments that give off their odor: a transparent gauze of sweat, teardrops, webs of saliva. Jacob lay behind his wife's back, didn't caress, didn't knead, didn't kiss. He pulled up her nightgown, clasped and rubbed himself in the slumber of her buttocks until his flesh remembered and tensed against her nakedness. Leah neither felt him nor changed the rhythm of her breathing, and Jacob—whose life had taught him that time doesn't turn around, and he didn't believe in other miracles either—thrust his hand between her thighs and forced them apart.

Her vagina, forgotten and drowsy, was warm but dry and frail as a mound of sand. Jacob filled his mouth with saliva, poured it in the hollow of his fingers, and moistened her thoroughly. Leah didn't budge, but her flesh returned to life, sprouted little leaves, responded with its heavy, good smell.

Bitter and firm was Jacob. He dug into her only four or five times, and emptied his seed into the gloom of her abysses. Not with the usual throbs, but with a measured and alien oozing. He didn't give pleasure, he didn't take pleasure, and the one and only enjoyment he felt was the joy of the thick abundance accumulated in him, of a kind he never experienced before.

A few hours later, when the flow of his seed reached her womb, Jacob woke from his sleep because Leah suddenly moaned as if she had received a great blow, and her whole body struggled like a shot bird. A hard, vigorous contraction passed through her lower belly, and pushed his soft flesh out. Jacob got up, wrapped himself in a sheet, and left the room.

Jacob's old aunt, named Duduch Nathan, and her son Simon also lived in Jacob's house. Simon, an old bachelor, limping because of his crushed thigh, worked with Jacob in the bakery, and Duduch took care of the household.

A hired man also worked in the bakery, a veteran laborer named Joshua Edelman. At an advanced age, Edelman married a woman, and she gave him four daughters who all looked as alike as four wooden Matryoshkas, who are born from inside each other and are distinguished only by their size. Simon, who was very fond of them, would give them presents and let them ride on his shoulders, two by two.

Once, Duduch had been like a wet nurse because her milk hadn't dried up after Simon was weaned, and she didn't have another child. Now, when she heard the quiet trickle rising in the house, she thought she was hearing memories, or, even worse, hopes. But the rustle was real and the old aunt followed its traces, passed through the corridor, opened the door, bent over Leah, and listened. It is hard to picture in words the smile that rose on her face, and so let it be said simply that it really looked like the smile of an old wet nurse when she learns that her expectation of a new infant is about to be fulfilled. When Jacob saw his aunt's face, he understood immediately that his wish was to be granted: his seed was absorbed, his wife was pregnant, and a child would be born to him.

From that day on, the two of them waited together. Jacob for an heir and his aunt for a suckling. Every morning they left peeled almonds and dried apples for Leah, next to her bed. Together they turned her from side to side, and together they picked up her blanket to examine the swelling of her belly.

Sometimes Leah would get up to tend to her needs—with her eyes closed, her hands stretched out like antennae, her feet sliding over the floor like apprehensive bloodhounds. "I'm so fat," Jacob heard her murmur in wonder before she disappeared back into her cave. But even when the child began kicking, she didn't wake up, her eyelashes would just flutter suddenly, like the wings of a pinned butterfly. By now she was very heavy and it was hard to dress her, and when she came out of the room naked, her stomach high and her eyes closed, it seemed to Jacob that she was observing him and the world with the nipples of her breasts.

None of the neighbors knew of her pregnancy, but everybody said that Jacob was beginning to bake bread like no one had ever baked before. No wonder since, while kneading, rising, firing, and removing, Jacob dreamed of the child. Strangers began coming to the bakery at night, snatched and tore loaves, ate as if they were ravenously hungry, and watched him work. "Put the money in that box," Jacob said, and didn't add a thing.

In the seventh month of her pregnancy, the doctor decided that Leah would have a cesarean birth. He set a date and arranged for Jacob to be present in the operating room because of the "special circumstances."

324

On the appointed day, Jacob ordered the village ambulance and went with Leah to give birth to his son. In the hospital, they dressed him in a surgeon's gown, and put a cap on his head, that could have been a baker's cap if it weren't green. They laid Leah on a metal table and thrust a syringe in her back. She was so big and puffing she looked like a beached whale he had once seen in the newspaper, washed up on the shore by waves and despair.

The surgeons quickly sliced open her lower belly; their brief words came in fragments. Their sweat and their knives glistened. Over their face masks, their eyes blinked. They separated the segments of skin and attached them to the side, sponged the blood, and parted the yellowish, docile rolls of fat. The nurse placed a cloth screen over Leah's neck as if she were liable to look at her tormentors and their work, and it seemed to Jacob that her head was also separated from her body by an executioner or a magician. The surgeons cut the stomach muscles which had already despaired and grown flaccid, rolled back membranes and coverings, dug and revealed the womb. Jacob moaned. The hidden longing, what all men know but only German and Russian immigrants admit—to see the internal organs of the beloved—was realized before his eyes.

Suddenly Leah's eyes opened wide, and stared at him relentlessly. "Turn out the light, Jacob, I want to sleep," she said in an amazed, weak voice.

The baker dropped his head and trembled. Blood and flesh swirled before his eyes. A purple womb gleamed, a mighty eggplant on a bed of intestines. He wanted to fall down on his knees, to put his head there, to touch and kiss, but the surgeon cut and thrust his hand between the pieces, and with the joy of magicians, drew out a fair, tender child.

Jacob's eyes filled with tears. Unlike those who are doomed to a normal birth, who come into the world crowned with a diadem of blood and feces, ugly, angry, ready for battle—this child was angelic and luminous. A fertilization without pleasure, a slumbering pregnancy, and a birth without struggle granted him a good temperament and a pure, smooth face. He didn't utter the first cry even after the doctor smacked him on the behind, but his breathing was even and good, and the surgeons smiled with joy.

Tears of bliss were Jacob's tears, blended with grief. With one look, he saw that this wasn't the child he had prayed for, but love melted his pain and filled him with force. The pediatrician completed his examination and gave him the child, and before they could stop him, Jacob turned, pushed the doors open and went out of the operating room into the anteroom and from there to the corridor, ignoring the shouts of the doctors and the outstretched hands of the nurses. His old aunt Duduch, who could hear the silent trickling of fertilization and the indistinct song of embryos, was already pacing up and down the corridor, quietly groaning and waiting.

"Here, Aunt," said Jacob; "I brought you another child."

On the tree in the yard of the bakery, the mulberries ripened, swelled, and turned dark. The four daughters of Edelman the laborer came to pick the fruit and make it into jam. Simon hopped to the mulberry tree and stood underneath it.

"Be very very careful, little girls!" he cried in terror.

The people of the village said this worry was simply an excuse to peep under their dresses, but the truth was that Simon hoped for only one mulberry, ripe and gleaming, that would drop on him from their fingers and stain his skin. Edelman, who knew that, didn't rebuke him, and that night the two of them baked alone, because Jacob stayed at the hospital, peering at his son through the big glass window of the nursery, and as parents are wont to do, making experiments. Thus he realized he couldn't evoke the child's face when he closed his eyes. Jacob thought it was weariness that worked against him, but later, when he fell asleep on a chair in the corridor, he discovered that he couldn't dream about his son either. Thus he understood that the child was born with a strange defect: he didn't have the ability to be inscribed in memory.

A week passed, Jacob named his son Michael, and a new and awful enigma was added. When he was brought into the covenant of Our Father Abraham, Michael didn't cry. Jacob was terrified. It's one thing to be erased from the closed eyes of another person, and quite another not to feel pain, for a person who is not tormented or punished cannot grasp the nature of the world and watch out for its attacks. Along with the anxiety also came grief: for a person who does not feel pain cannot bake bread. But love and worry filled Jacob's whole body, leaving no room for regret.

The months passed. Michael smiled, turned over, and sat up. Sometimes Jacob saw him lying on his back, stroking his breast and stomach, or pinching his fingertips hard, one after another, and pulling the skin of his lips, and he didn't disturb him; for he knew the child wanted to waken and bring his mute flesh to life. When Michael cut his teeth, his father was afraid that, because of his illness, he would split his tongue with them, but nothing happened. Michael sucked Duduch's milk, stood up and walked and cheered the heart of all who saw him; and Jacob knew that all that bliss was simply a semblance, the pretense of an infant who, in his love for his father, wants to prove to him that he is only a child like all other children. And indeed, more than once, Michael fell down and hurt himself, and even though he didn't feel the pain, he would run crying to his father, and say, "It hurts me, it hurts me." Jacob would ask, "Where does it hurt?" and hug him and spoil him and kiss him and do all he should do, but he didn't allow himself the tranquility of the deceived. In his heart, he knew his son was imitating other children, doing what they do when they fall down and hurt themselves, just as men imitate the manners of courtship and the words of love. Which one of us doesn't want to be like the cruel Orpheus, the naïve Albinus, the sinner Gregorius—all those great lovers, who surpass all their readers, and absolutely for sure the writers who invented them? And which one of us wouldn't go on the routes marked out by the ancient teachers of love? Either we are obtuse as the suitors of Penelope, make the mistakes of Solomon, are easily tempted like Enkidu, or in time of desire also copulate in the manner favored by Hector and Andromache. The poet Rilke already said that two inventions turned men into sluggards and made the human race degenerate: the first was that of some idle Neanderthal who showed off by bringing his mistress a bouquet of flowers instead of a slaughtered lion. The second, of course, was the invention of the wheel, father of all laziness and sin, but that doesn't have anything to do with our issue.

Thus the child grew, and when he was two and a half years old, he was weaned from Duduch's milk, and began eating his father's bread. In the evening, the two lay down to sleep together, and at midnight, when Jacob got up and went to the bakery, Michael also woke up and went strolling through the rooms. He was graced with an insatiable curiosity and perfect night vision, and by dint of these, he cruised in the darkness of the house. He generally completed his night journeys in the bakery, where he sat down and fell asleep on the old kneading crate, but sometimes, sleep pounced on him from ambush and overpowered him in one of the corners. His slumber was so sound, and his metabolism so delicate he would slowly freeze, and Jacob, who knew his son's habits and was filled with terror by the angelic ways of his body, would rush to look for him. Sometimes he found him wrapped up behind one of the doors; once in the shower, with a foamy brush still stuck in his mouth; once the child dropped in the yard and fell asleep under the big mulberry tree, and by the time he was found, he was covered with the dark spots of fruit and the dust of the wings of hawk-moths. Jacob was frightened, crouched over the cold, delicate little body, rubbed and kneaded the flesh between the palms of his hands, puffed the warm air of his lungs on the frost of the naked stomach, on the fish bone of the thin ribs, breathed into the paradise of the waking, kissing, wondering mouth.

One night, just when he turned three, Michael opened the door of his dead brother's room and went inside, and in the morning he asked his father what the room was and who was the woman sleeping in it.

"That's the woman's room and the woman sleeps in it," Jacob answered him.

Michael didn't ask anything else, but from then on, he would visit the woman every night, hover around her in his bright nightshirt, stroke her face with the wings of his fingers, and sometimes climb onto her bed, cling to her back, and listen to the familiar rustling of her body, infusing sleep.

Simon Nathan, Duduch's son, was five years younger than Jacob, and in the village they used to compare him to a beast. It was his low forehead and short stature, his limp, his broad shoulders and neck that earned him this slanderous name of violence and stupidity. Once farmers had lived in the village who could appreciate Simon's strength and diligence; and more than once they had called on him to bridle a runaway calf or to undo a recalcitrant bolt; but as the years went by, the plots of land were sold to citizens of the nearby city, clumsy white villas sprouted on them; and now the children of the wealthy gather at the fence of the Levy house, hurl clods of dirt at Simon as he sleeps in the yard, and run for their lives when he opens his eyes.

Jacob, usually an impatient man, loved his cousin, took pity on him, and knew he had to keep him busy constantly. When Simon completed his work in the bakery, Jacob ordered him to shake out and fold the flour sacks; when he finished that, he sent him to clean the yard and rake the fallen leaves off the roof; and when that was done, he told him to change the tires of the pickup truck, and to air out the flour sacks he had folded before. Good souls, who are found in abundance in every village, said that Jacob was taking advantage of his cousin; but Jacob ignored the gossip because he knew that work and responsibility were the foundations of Simon's life, and loyalty was his *raison d'être*.

Simon mainly loved to watch over Michael, and since Jacob never stopped worrying, he became the child's guard and nurse. First in the yard and the house, then he went with him to kindergarten, and from there the two advanced to first grade. Every morning, Simon hung Michael's school bag on his shoulder and limped along behind him, looking to the sides and leaving in the red sand the holes and furrows of a stick thrust and a leg dragged, along with the trace of his healthy leg, deep as a pit with heaviness and strength. In the crush at the entrance of the school, he sheltered

Michael from the coarse boys, and then he went back home to eat his breakfast. At recess, he returned to the school to watch Michael at play; and in the afternoon he brought him back home. Jacob, who was pacing around on the porch by then and looking in the street, hugged his son, listened to his birdlike heart galloping in his chest, led him to the bedroom, took off all his clothes to see if he was wounded, if he was pricked, if he was cut or burned. Outside the room, Simon waited in great terror until Jacob came out, tapped him on the shoulder and said, "He's all right."

Like the Nile, time rolled between its banks, and when an empty pit chanced to occur on the side of its path—it hurried to fill it. Thus, wrote Democritus in his derisive missive, empty brains are also filled with knowledge, hearts with love, and scrolls with words. Time showed its signs especially in the four identical daughters of Edelman the laborer. They began growing up, and if they passed by an observer at the right pace, he saw before his eyes a kind of short, quick movie of swelling, flowering, and maturity. But he who is trained on books and not on movies will perhaps prefer another metaphor, to wit: the little one was the trace of the big one, and the big one was the prophecy of the little one. One way or another, everyone who cast a glance at them felt that their flesh was soft and fragrant, and a thin and a sweet rot, the kind that molds certain wine grapes, was waiting under their skin. The joy of research and experiment that awakens in every man at the sight of identical twin girls was doubled at the sight of them; and the knowledge that they weren't twins only increased the perplexity of the flesh and the longing of the heart.

At that time, the youngest had turned seventeen and the oldest was twenty, and they already roused uneasiness wherever they turned. Annoyed women and scared men gossiped about them. They said that when the oldest one reached puberty, she invited her sisters to get acquainted by touch and sight with the innovations that would happen to them, too. They said that each one felt what was happening to her sister, they breathed and dreamed at the same pace, and got their period all together. They said they would go into the bathroom together where they made dirty pictures, for while one soaped the second one, the third knelt on the toilet, and the fourth smeared her thighs with wax. And eight mouths laughed, sighed, and screamed when the sisters were multiplied in the big, embarrassed mirror on the wall.

Many men wanted to be their companion. But in the evening, when a suitor came, he found all four of them waiting for him on the porch, wearing the same dress and smiling with the same lips.

"We do everything together," they told him, and there were fellows who dropped their bouquets of flowers and fled right then and there, because the man hasn't yet been born who is willing to close his eyes and kiss a woman knowing that at the same time, she is also behind him, and her two identical reflections are looking at him from the side, feeling, comparing, and giggling.

Simon didn't pay any mind to any of them. Even if two or three of them came, he didn't pay attention to them. Only the appearance of the four, their eight identical, dark eyes, their forty nimble fingers, their million and a half blue-black strands of hair, their four mouths emitting the very same vapors—only that captured and tormented his soul. Sometimes, they would come before dawn to help their father paste the labels on the bread, and when they entered the bakery, with their kid-like smiles and their loud sounds of giggling and bleating, and planted their eight legs around the bakers' pit where he stood—Simon missed the distant loaves of bread, sweated like a mule, and spilled pans on the floor.

In the room of her dead son lay the woman. The waves of time lapped the edge of her bed, her body breathed and shed tears and hoarded and relaxed. At night a little child would hug her neck and put his ear to her back. Since she didn't answer his questions, he would write on her skin with a wet finger the new words he learned in school, the events that happened, and the names of the stars his father taught him. Jacob saw that Michael observed the night sky a lot, and he would go up to the roof of the bakery with him to count stars and name them in the heavens; and Simon taught him to whistle with a blade of grass, to hunt lizards and poke them to stick out their tongue. But even those nice things didn't wake the woman from her sleep.

At school, Simon was a regular guest by now. At recess, the little children would play with him, try to open his clenched fist. Uncle Simon's hand, Michael wrote on the woman's back, is big and strong, but when the bell rings after recess, it gets soft all of a sudden and opens and there's always some squeezed and very sweet chewing gum in it.

"He who works hard deserves it," said Simon. "Go to class now, very slow, don't run, Michael." And he went back down the street, poking his stick in the sand, his head heavy and drooping. But when he saw a pit left there the day before by the stick, he smiled to himself and poked his stick right in the very same place.

Summer reigned over the village. Strange cars glistened at the neighbors' houses, young boys and girls burst out of them, and sharp, joyous shouts soon rose from the lawns. Through the holes of light in the hedges, Simon saw young and gleaming skin, shining bathing suits, slivers of sprayed water in all colors of the rainbow. Dark girls were hurled to the water with pleas of fear. At night, a thin smell of beer, shaving lotion, and inflamed flesh rose and climbed to the sky. Music came from wide-open windows, and clappers of ice rang in glasses. Edelman's daughters, who had a talent for cooking, enticing, and commerce, supplied refreshments for the parties. No longer were they seen in the yard and the bakery. Sometimes Simon saw them in the street and they came to him pleasantly and asked how he was; then he smiled in embarrassment and managed to get out of his mouth only, "Wazznew, wazznew," and once he even amazed himself for, with enormous ease, he replied, "What's cooking?" And then he was the most blissful man until he understood why they laughed.

"Autumn is coming, I saw a wagtail," Michael wrote on the woman's back.

The nights became cloudy and chilly, her face also seemed to become morose, and she slept more soundly. He was about seven then, and already helping Simon change her sheets. Simon was so strong he could pick the woman up in his arms despite the dead weight of her body. Then Michael would pull the old sheet from under her, and quickly spread a new one. In the afternoon, they would play "Flying." Simon would pick him up, stand him on one of the branches of the mulberry tree, and wait for him with open arms. Michael would close his eyes and jump, and Simon would always catch him in the air. In the evening they ate Aunt Duduch's treats, and Michael went to sleep with his father; and in the dark of night, when the smell of yeast spread in the air and raindrops drummed on the oil tank of the bakery, he wrote on the woman, "Now I'm going to my father," and he ran in the dark to the bakery, to sleep in the old, warm wooden box, where, back when his father was a child, the grandmother Michael didn't know he had kneaded the dough.

The sun rose higher, the fields were turning green, the winter was melting. All night long, the spring rain fell, and at dawn came a cheerful wind from the east and stirred the blanket of clouds. Spring shone on the village with the beauty of its temptations. Flowers opened and bees wallowed in them. Surprised old people and grateful lizards came out to warm themselves in the sun. Male doves danced on the roofs and cooed in their deep rutting voices, oafish with love.

Spring wound clocks of light and warmth in human beings. Children leaped like lambs, women and men looked shyly at one another, and when they passed by a mirror or a puddle, they stopped to identify their new reflection in it. All winter they were pent up in their cold body, and now it turned into a joyous and warm cocoon of flesh, obeying the clock hands of sunrise and sunset. Leah also moaned suddenly from the Hades of her bed, smiled, turned over, and stretched, but didn't get up.

Simon was filled with a dull, tormenting restlessness. After he took Michael to school, he returned, opened his cot in the shadow of the mulberry tree, and stretched out on his back. At the ten o'clock recess he went back to school, watched, returned home, arranged sacks in the bakery storeroom, took off his shoes, went back to his bed, and stared between the branches. The majestic mulberry tree bloomed, sang with the joy of blackbirds, uttered soft cracks of sprouting, and gleamed with its new little leaves. Simon remembered Joshua Edelman's daughters climbing on it like black and white cats, laughing, chattering, dropping leaves, and picking the fruit. It had been a long time since he had seen them, except by accident or by slow rummaging around in his memory that hurt like picking a scab.

In the afternoon, he slowly walked up the street to the school, in his regular path on the side of the road, nodding to passers-by and seeking the pits his stick had left in the sand that morning. And here came the four daughters toward him, rubbing against each other as they walked, laughing and chattering. He was embarrassed, and was about to hide between the fig trees when the girls saw him and came toward him, waving to him. Their mother made them identical blue and white striped dresses, and walking so close together, in their billowy, uniform cotton dresses, they looked like a gigantic, splendid kite.

"Hello, Simon," they winked to each another, and laughed.

"Hello," answered Simon ponderously.

"Where are you going?" They surrounded him with a circle of clasped hands and identical smiles.

"To bring Michael from school," said Simon. His flesh shrivelled and tightened. He wanted to break out of the ring of hands and go on his way, but he didn't find the strength he needed in his muscles.

"We went to order cheese and butter and olives for our business," the oldest one, the twenty-year-old, announced.

"And then, we thought, why not go see what's happening in our old village," smiled the second one, the nineteen-year-old.

And the third simpered, "And with our friend Simon, who once gave us dolls and has surely forgotten us by now."

Simon, inexperienced and unaware of the great danger latent in women who drawl "dolls" in two syllables, smiled for a moment at the sweetness stirred in him by the memory of those innocent days.

And the seventeen-year-old said, "And now we met him," and came so close to him that the good smell of her mouth rose up to his nose, and when he recoiled, the breasts of the nineteen-year-old pushed into his back, filling him with a soft, supple panic.

"Ooh . . . " cried the girls. "He fell down . . . Simon fell . . . Come, let's pick him up."

They bent over, grabbed him, and shouted, "One, two, three, oops!" They put him up on his feet, shook him out, and beat the dust off him; and the oldest one took out a white kerchief and wiped the sweat and dirt and blood off his face; and when Simon turned to go back to the school, they went with him, still surrounding him with a blooming, ringing circle that never stopped.

"What's this, Simon?" they asked. "Michael doesn't know the way home?"

"I bring him every day. You don't know?"

"Why?"

"'Cause Jacob wants."

"You do whatever he wants?"

"Sure," Simon was encouraged; "everything. Yesterday, I even cleaned the chimney."

"And if he wanted you to go into the oven when it's hot?"

"And if he wanted you to get undressed in the middle of the street?

"And if he wanted a French kiss from you?"

Simon was very embarrassed by the speed of the bundle of questions, and his inability to answer them, and the dizziness that attacked him; and as he was seeking his wits, the circle stopped moving and talking, and Simon managed to grasp the wrist of the eighteen-year-old, and tried to get her out of his way.

"You're hurting me!" the twenty-year-old shouted from behind his back, and Simon was terrified and let go and once again didn't know what to do; and the four girls all pressed to him as one, and were so close and exhausting to him that he was forced to recline right on their bodies, and he leaned and recoiled, recoiled and leaned as if he were surrounded by a big wreath of thorns.

"You don't want to come work for us, and bake us rolls?" the youngest one asked.

"No!" Simon panicked. "What do you mean? I work for Jacob."

"You're like a brother to us, Simon; we all sucked from your mother," said the nineteen-year-old, and she and her sisters went back to circling around him; their limbs moved in their dresses, and the spring light illuminated the bright bells of the fabric, limned in turn the contours of their eight legs, and intimated the four swollen knolls of their groins. His pains vanished. The moist words—"sweets," "sucked," and "brother"—wound around his body like cords. Bubbles frothed in his flesh. His strength and heaviness left him. He was swept off in the whirlpool of the girls, tottered, and was borne like the dust spun in the fields by autumn winds.

At the edge of the village, the paved road ends and turns into a dirt path leading to the hills, the islands of grass, the tiny meadows where porcupines, jackals, human beings, and martens copulated, leaving behind crushed beds of weeds. Drunken nymph butterflies strayed in the air, ants opened the straw plugs of their nests. A big rock stood in the field, looking like a skull, and at its feet a tiny valley, humid and soft, which the girls knew from their Saturday outings. By the time they got there, Simon was so weak that all it took was a light puff the eighteen-year-old blew into the hollow of his neck, and he immediately fell into the trap of the arms of the other three standing behind him; they laid him down, and stretched his hands and feet on the ground.

The children had already gone home and Michael was still waiting in the classroom. His father's command not to go home alone kept him there. He wandered in the forest of upturned chair legs, drew stars on the blackboard, and peeped out the window to see if Simon was coming to get him. At last, he decided to wait downstairs.

He paced back and forth, and when he turned around the third time, he saw three men standing by him. They were old, with bright eyes, and Michael looked at them in amazement, for they appeared so suddenly, they seemed to come from the sky.

"We got a letter," said the first.

"And we came," said the second.

And the third said, "Let's go home now," and he knelt down close to Michael, put hands light as feathers on the boy's shoulder, and looked at him with eyes of light. Then he straightened up, and Michael put his hands in theirs, and went with them down the lane, a wall being on this side and a wall on that side. His feet, like theirs, left no traces in the dirt. His steps, like theirs were so broad and soft that he understood they were hovering in the air.

"One, two, three, oops," they said to each other, and swung him hard, and he laughed with pleasure and immediately shouted because the ligaments in his shoulder blades were pulled, and the feeling was surprisingly strange.

"What're your names?" he asked.

But the men looked at him with their dazzling eyes, and didn't say.

Beneath him, Michael saw big, unfamiliar fields of spring, and sweet vapors of mignonette rose in the air, and a distant and surprising smell of cyclamen dying belatedly. He wanted to roll around and tumble in the meadows, to shout and caress his face with the soft petals of buttercups. But he couldn't flee the silky grasp of the man angels.

"One, two, three, oops," they said, and swung him harder, more painfully, grabbed him and made him fly; "one, two, three, oops."

The sun began to go down. Shadows gushed to the little valley and filled it. The coolness woke Simon. He saw dozens of black dots gliding in circles above him—eagles and bustards from the mountains and the distant deserts. Four damp and identical handkerchiefs were left in the trodden grass next to him, striped with blue and white. Simon lay on his back and counted the black spots in the sky until they circled, came down, and landed on his skin, and once again penetrated his body.

His heart stopped. Suddenly he remembered he was supposed to bring Michael from school. The eyes of the holes in the rock looked at him. Twisted beaks bisected his flesh. A horror of great darkness fell upon him.

Far above six wings were rowing, and their beating grew distant; and after the noise of the wings, a thin sound of silence, and then, clear and sharp, the child's shout of pain. It was so sharp and slicing it was unmistakable, for the sound of an infant weeping in pain is the most penetrating and rousing sound in the world.

Flashing, the shout turned over in the air, down-down it blazed and fell, broke on the chimney of the bakery, shattered into a myriad of tiny pieces, so fast and shining it is hard to describe them in words; but they were much like a downpour of gold that poured and penetrated his mother's sleeping body.

The Italian archaeologist Ermette Pierotti, poet, historian, architect, and orphan, wrote in his book *Ancient Graves North of Jerusalem* that one night, on February 27, 1856, a vehement east wind came from the desert and covered the roofs of Jerusalem with a thin blend of salt and sand. Panic reigned. Neither the city elders nor its dead could remember such a strange storm. That night, no one fell asleep, and the next day, in the area between the Tomb of the Kings and the mosaic of Orpheus, Pierotti's workers exposed a small grave with only one word carved on it: "Mother."

Pierotti was all atremble. A strange desire gripped him: to fall down and put his head on the grave. But he was a man of science, and tried to control himself. He had never heard of such an inscription. He was accustomed to ornamented, glorious tombstones carved with poetry and praises, and here was a tomb without even a name, or birth and death dates. If not for the word "Mother," you might think it was the tomb of a child, for the people of Jerusalem don't write names on the tombs of their children. He was still standing and puzzling when the sickle of pain struck both his legs, and forced him to the ground. His head struck a stone, and he almost fainted. With an unnatural force, he brought his lips to the carved inscription, and blew away the grains of dirt; and when he had done that, his eyes filled with the salty dust and with tears, and a great tremor went through the air with a sound of taut ropes before a tempest.

A few minutes passed. Pierotti collected his forces and got up, looked around, and saw that people were beginning to gather on all sides. There were a few excavation workers, two donkey drovers, five passersby; a dozen shop owners closed their shutters and came, followed by three Franciscan monks in thick sandals and brown cloaks, and seven porters from the cotton market; the hashish roaster of Karaite Street covered his coals, the blacksmiths of the Mugrabi Forge wiped their eyes with black hands; the Sudanese cattle drovers, the *flaneurs* from the cafés, Moslem teachers from the *madrasas*, and students from the yeshivas all came, and Pierotti looked at them and knew that all of them, like him, had lost their mother, and their pain was heard in Ramah, lamentation and bitter weeping.

Naked, white, her eyes shut, Leah reached the body lying among the bushes and knelt down to it. She took off her son's shirt, licked the blood from his skin, stroked his face. It seemed to her tongue and fingers that the child was sound asleep and steeped in blissful dreams. She tried to pick him up from the ground and take him home, but Michael was softer and heavier than he had ever been, and she lay next to him, like a gigantic dog, warmed his body with hers, and didn't pay any mind to the people who had come from the houses and yards, and gathered around, looking on in embarrassment. Finally, the ambulance driver also came, the same one who had taken her to the delivery room seven years before, covered her with a big blanket, and took the child to the emergency room.

One person broke out of the crowd and approached, and then another person and another, and a big heap of small orphan stones quickly rose on the mother, and Pierotti put his own stone, too, and withdrew, and never came back to expose and excavate that tomb, even though a thieving instinct urged him to break into the body of the woman, touch her bones, curl up and strum his toes on her ribs, put his painful temples on the calm of her loins. For which of us didn't love his mother and who didn't leave her behind, fleeting, forlorn, lying, and dying? And who didn't sin against her? Against the landscape of his childhood? His destiny? The one truth in his heart?

Chapter 71

Big rhomboids of concrete, like the checkered path on the back of a viper, led from the back door of the emergency room to the morgue. The lawn grew wild in the spaces between them and covered their edges.

The morgue attendant, a tall lean man with black hair and blue eyes, accompanied my brother and opened the locked door for him. Cold air burst out, touched Jacob's ever-warm face, struck his stomach, and slipped out as if it were hurrying to spread the news.

The corpse was laid on a high, gleaming metal bed, covered with a striped sheet, fastened at the neck and ankles. My brother untied the laces and exposed the head, and then his fingers were twisted. With one tug, he yanked the sheet off the whole body, and only then did he see that the morgue attendant was still standing next to him. He was about to ask him to leave him alone, but the man suddenly began talking:

"Your boy?"

"Yes."

The body was completely naked, and as bodies are, was smaller than it was in life. Someone had already cleaned the crusted crumbs of blood off the skin, the childish lines had been wiped off the face, and the open eyes imparted a seriousness and maturity to it.

"It's not good what you're doing," the morgue attendant declared; "to see him like that."

"Mind your own business," said Jacob.

The man didn't recoil or drop his eyes. He smelled strongly of tobacco. "You shouldn't remember him like that, laying dead," he said. "A boy, you should remember him standing, playing, laughing."

"No," said Jacob with a composure that surprised even him. "This is how I want to remember him. So that I'll know he's dead, and won't come back anymore."

He grabbed the cold hand, already stiffened by death, and pulled it away from the body a bit. Under the armpit, tiny and precise, the entry wound of the bullet was exposed. About twenty centimeters underneath was the exit hole—a withering flower of flesh that had already turned blue and yellow and gray, ugly and awful in its magnitude. Benjamin was hit by one bullet from an Uzi, soft and heavy, that pierced and tore his lungs, struck the shoulder blade, ricocheted, and came back through the abdomen, sliced and burst out above the pelvis.

"A soldier?" asked the morgue attendant.

"Yes, a soldier," answered Jacob. "And now leave us, please. I'll call you later on to close up."

The man withdrew to the wall, but didn't leave the room.

Benjamin's death was visible only in the slight contortion in the corner of his lips, in the tiny bristles of beard that continued to grow, in the blue-gray of his fingertips. Jacob lowered his eyes to the dark brown triangle of the military tan at the base of his neck, the flat, strong, surprisingly white stomach. Benjamin was fair of skin and hair, but like his mother, he was never sunburned. All he needed was five minutes exposure to its rays and his skin turned dark, and took on a deep and pleasant tone.

Jacob saw that, in contrast to the light hair on his son's head, the curls of his groin were black as soot.

"I hadn't seen him naked since he was little," he told me. "We weren't the kind of father and son who took showers together after a football game or washed together on an outing."

"My father did the same thing when my brother was killed," the morgue attendant said behind his back. "He wanted to be sure that it was him inside the coffin, and since then he doesn't sleep anymore."

"Your brother was killed in the army," Jacob turned around.

"Seven years now. He was a scout. One bullet from a fedayeen right in the forehead. Here," he pointed between his eyes. "Papa went crazy, put the coffin down when they passed by the mosque, broke the boards with his bare hands like eggshells, saw him laying there dead, and then he didn't sleep anymore. It's been seven years since then, and my father doesn't sleep, and he doesn't go to the mosque anymore either."

"I'm going now," he added after a long silence. "I'll wait for you outside, to lock up after you."

"Wait a minute," said Jacob.

He took the old Kodak Retina out of his bag and gave it to the man.

"Take a picture of us," Jacob repeated.

"You mustn't!" groaned the man. "Don't do that."

"Take a picture of us," Jacob repeated.

The man took the camera, retreated a few steps, waited until my brother folded his arms on his chest and looked straight ahead, and then he pressed the button.

"God help you, my brother, may you not be sorrier," he said.

"One more," said Jacob; "to be sure."

The man hastily closed both eyes, pressed the button again, put down the camera, and went out.

And Jacob was left alone.

Chapter 72

I'm coming to the end. So say the things I won't begin, so the sadness pounding in my chest tells me, the stories I haven't told, the uninvited guests gathering on my body.

I haven't told the end of Chenou Apari, I haven't revealed where the mosaic is today, I haven't confessed to my meeting with Leah's father ten years ago, and I haven't answered the question of questions—where is Leah's shorn braid.

I've got a few more stories in my hands; if you want to read them, I'll be glad to give them to you; and if you ask more questions I'll answer them too. I've got a Parker Vacumatic, I've got writing paper, and I've got time. I've got plenty of time, as the man condemned to death said to the hangman who apologized for being late. I wrote a story about an old man who looked for relatives, I wrote about a man who broke the neck of his wife's cat, about a boy who had sparrows building their nest in his hair. I've also got a story about an educated sensitive man who took a widow as a wife because he desired her twelve-year-old daughter, but I won't send you that one, because it's the absolute truth. It happened in the village next to ours. It began with love, continued with wandering and treason, and ended with murder, and "the Reader" won't find in it the logic, structure, or good sense of a good novella. But I will send you the tale of the Karaite canary breeder. Did you know that, in 1927, there were only twenty-one Karaites left in Jerusalem, and every time they had a baby, one of them died on the very same day?

It's twilight now, and I'm still surprised that the sun doesn't set in the sea, but rises from it. Light and soft am I, despite my size and my strength. Like Prince Paris, I am dragged, pulled in the dust behind time. My skin is flayed, my flesh plucked, my bones scattered, and behold this wonder—I feel no pain.

"So, when I discovered the picture of Dad and Benjamin in the morgue, I decided to go on photographing him," Romi told me.

"And you thought he told you everything," she said when she showed me the picture and observed the shock that spread over my face. "A good picture, right? Interesting who took it. An amateur who got lucky. So now you tell me, if he was photographed like that, what does he care if I photograph him at home?"

Now she's in the garden of my house. In my work pants and a big T-shirt, she's crawling on all fours, pulling up weeds. "You know your grass is salty?" she calls to me. A pretty young woman she is, confident in herself and her strength. The twilight refines gold from the ore of her hair. The muscles move in her arms, long and clear. After Father's death she came back to me in America, and had a great success here. Two pictures of my brother have already appeared in a New York photography magazine. In a few days she'll go back to Tel Aviv, and I imagine I won't see her again for a few years. Not that there's any reason for us to part like that, but I have already learned to guess the face of things to come. My days are like one another, my stories are like one another. And my women, too, I admit, are like one another. He who knows what is good no longer needs experiments.

And once a month I dream of my mother. Always the same dream, for he who knows what is bad, also no longer needs experiments. In my dream the telephone rings. I pick up the receiver, and she calls me by my name twice, half questioning, with thin wonder, as if she wants to make sure her curse is still working. Well, I promised not to say anything more about my mother's death, but I didn't succeed.

The exhibit "My Father" was presented in a café in Tel Aviv. I helped Romi hang the pictures: My Father Making Breakfast. My Father Taking Bread out of the Oven. My Father in the Shower. My Father Sitting at His Son's Grave.

Jacob is very photogenic. Photography doesn't improve him, but it does refine his grief and makes him look contemplative. At night, when he sat down to put on his boots on the porch, my brother grabbed his chest with both hands, as if he were connecting the strips of his heart together. Here is the dark wall of his back, his clenched fist at Leah's bed, "My Father and His Wife." Here is the shadow of his hands on the walls of the bakery. Here am I, with him on the porch, "My Father and His Twin Brother Talking." Coming back from the bakery in the morning, Romi caught him leaning on the trunk of the mulberry tree. In the evening, she lay in wait for him and Michael in the kitchen. One salty drop landed on the child's shoulder, crept down his bare chest, draws the eye of the viewer, leaves a wet, shining path, like the tracks of snails on the tiles of the porch. Not sensational revelations, but so very painful.

Only "My Father Shouting," where my brother is standing in the bakers' pit, the palms of his hands on the wall of the oven and his head stuck in its maw—she didn't show. "I deserve one request," I told her; "don't hang that one."

Her hand on my arm, her shoulder touching mine, she guided me and introduced me to her friends who had come to the opening.

"This is my uncle, you see, don't you?"

"You've got a great uncle," said some girl.

"You can make a date with him, but not tonight," said Romi; "tonight he's busy."

After midnight, the guests dwindled.

"We can go now, too," said Romi.

"Will you take me home?"

"My place?"

"Home," I said; "I want to sleep."

"Sleep at my place."

"Let's play that you're drunk and I'm deaf, Romi."

"Just to sleep with you, uncle, nothing more."

"No," I told her; "I'll take a cab."

She drove me to the village. The old pickup truck was very squeaky, the high-beam headlights of the cars illuminated tears on her right cheek.

"Six years since I got out of the army, I've been photographing him, arguing with him, cutting his life into rectangles, crying and learning and fighting and working—and that's it, in one night it's all over, and all you think is that I'm looking for a screw. You've got no idea what I'm talking about, do you?"

"I do."

Afterward, from my bed, I heard the roar of the burner in the bakery, the rustle of the thin rain, the pickup truck going off. A little while later, the sourish smell spread in the air. I closed my eyes and Romi was standing over me. "The dough is rising," she said.

Her shoulders were white in the darkness, the bed groaned under the weight of her body, the down on the back of her neck touched my lips. At four in the morning, I woke up with a horrible dread, and groped hastily for my glasses. Michael was standing near the bed staring at me. By the time I understood I had been dreaming and calmed down, I also saw Romi, trembling at the wall.

"What do you want, Michael?"

"To see the two of you hug like that again," he said.

She grabbed his hand and led him out. "I'll take you to Mother," she told him. "She's cold all alone. Come, sleep with her. Come on."

But Michael got out of her grip and flew out of the room.

"You think he'll tell something?" I asked.

She sat down on the bed. "I wanted it to be like in America," she said at last. She quickly stuck her legs in her pants, stood up, tucked in her shirttails, and closed the fly.

"I'm going," she said; "I'm all right. And don't worry, he won't tell anything, and even if he does, nobody will believe him. They know his tales. He already said that Dad climbs on the chimney at night, that man-angels teach him to fly, that Simon caught Itsik stealing from the storeroom and choked him until he fainted. He's got a very strange imagination, my little brother."

She kissed me on the chin and left.

Michael didn't tell anything. Ten days later, my father died. Thirty-one days later I shaved the bristles of my beard and went back to my own house.

Chapter 73

I'm coming to the end. So say the cells of my body, dead crab shells on the sand, the air that turns dark as the storm comes on. I conclude because one way or another I have answered most of your questions. Incidentally, these stories aren't as complicated as they sound. You don't like the great resemblance ("too symbolic," you said) between Mother and Romi. Good God, is it my fault that they're so much alike? *Chez nous à Paris*, a grandmother sometimes bequeaths her likeness to her granddaughter. And the affinity you contrived to find between Duke Anton and myself? And your "three stages of proximity to reality"? You want me to send you back to Munthe and Fielding?

That day, at four in the afternoon, Simon came to Tel Aviv and told me to come home with him. Tia Duduch grabbed my hand and led me to Father's room. Jacob was already standing there, his hand over his mouth, his shoulders shaking.

"He's been like that since morning," he said. "Why didn't you answer the phone?"

Father was barely breathing, the ligaments of his thin, dry joints, the purple spots of liver and spleen were dim on his body. Exhausted, he lay and looked at us. When he heard the word "doctor," he shook his head from side to side. Then he started talking.

"What, Father?" I leaned over him. "What?"

The seams in his skull looked like underwater mountain ridges. "*El nono vino . . . El nono vino . . . ,*" he said, in the language of the forefathers he had forsaken; "here's Grandfather coming." Again and again he vomited the soft words, threw them out with a slow twist of his neck, until they were pressed heavily, lined up in a row, gathered strength, added speed and took off, heavy and dripping like geese over a lake.

He didn't talk anymore, and I knelt down by the bed and put my head on his stomach. His hand fluttered in my hair. The air squeaked in his lungs. I thought of Yehiel Abramson, who had missed an opportunity to hear last words; and even if they weren't the words of a famous person, they were last words after all, that couldn't be contradicted, and didn't have other versions.

Then Jacob burst into great weeping, took off his glasses, and left the room, and I remained there alone with Father. After all, that's what I had been called for. To help, to tend, to atone.

The hours passed. Bubbles began rising on Abraham's lips and burst without a sound. Few and small they were, for he didn't have much time left, and every one of them consumed only a minute or two. His hands turned gray, his breathing declined, and the pains began to desert his limbs. I knew them all. The sonovabitch villain from the knee, the *diablo* of the back, and worst of all—the wicked Turkish *Dolor de Istomago*. Pale and big, they leaped out of the shell of his body, hopped all around with their long white necks, groping for my feet in the blindness of their wrath.

A terrible, deep gurgle rose and shook Abraham's chest. For the first time in his life he closed his eyes, and I, with the face of a child, my tongue stuck out, tried to open the parchment eyelids with my fingers. An ungraspable moment is the moment of death, even the *punto de masapan* can't compare to it for delicacy. Therefore, human beings cover the face of the dead and remember the act of covering, and don't torment themselves, like me, capturing and preserving the moment of the end. For it slips away like the reflection of memory, and thinner it is than the shadow of a ripple, shorter than a thought about taking off in the air.

Thus I sat. Then a wonderful smell of bread rose and came to my nostrils. The smell of fresh bread baked so very close to me. I got up and went outside. The rain had stopped, the sky was clear, and the smell burst from the bakery of my brother Jacob.